THE ENEMY WITHIN

NOEL HYND

A TOM DOHERTY ASSOCIATES BOOK
NEW YORK

THE ENEMY WITHIN

Edited by Pat LoBrutto

A Forge Book
Published by Tom Doherty Associates, LLC
175 Fifth Avenue
New York, NY 10010

www.tor-forge.com

Forge® is a registered trademark of Tom Doherty Associates, LLC.

ISBN-13: 978-0-7653-4509-7
ISBN-10: 0-7653-4509-9

First Edition: March 2006
First Mass Market Edition: August 2008

Printed in the United States of America

0 9 8 7 6 5 4 3 2 1

*For
Patricia
with love*

ACKNOWLEDGMENTS

The author gratefully thanks his longtime friend Thomas Ochiltree for his invaluable assistance in the research of this manuscript.

The author welcomes communication from readers at NH1212f@yahoo.com.

Coming events cast their
shadows before them.

—WINSTON CHURCHILL

PART ONE

chapter 1

It is cold on December mornings when the wind howls in from the Potomac and cuts icily across the National Cemetery. It is colder still when a young woman is being buried.

The coffin was above an open, patient grave, draped with the fifty-star flag of the United States. A young military chaplain named Sullivan presided. He was already frozen.

It was twenty degrees. It felt colder.

Sullivan glanced at his watch.

Eight thirty A.M. He eyed the one man and one woman in attendance. There was also an honor guard of four soldiers, one from each branch of the armed forces. The woman in the coffin had paid a terrible price to have them there.

The chaplain gave a nod, not to the soldiers but to the civilian witnesses.

"Let us begin," he said softly.

As if on cue, a light snow began to fall.

Two ironies simultaneously. The deceased had hated the cold. And this was not a beginning. It was an ending.

Sullivan spoke softly, rapidly muttering a prayer that no one could hear because of the harsh wind. Words on the icy air, brief and appropriate, but impersonal. The snow thickened.

At a few minutes before nine, the casket descended into the earth. The honor guard fired final salutes, rifles crackling toward an iron gray sky.

The service was over. With a nod, the chaplain dismissed the soldiers.

The man and the woman who had been observers looked at each other, each silently connecting to a sadness that was difficult to describe. The man walked with a severe limp.

It was not that there was nothing to say. It was that it had all been said already.

Their thoughts, however, could have filled volumes, not the least of them being that cemeteries are filled with memories and spirits.

Neither was any stranger to these. The woman reflected on a quote from John F. Kennedy. "Life is unfair."

It was. And Kennedy, murdered while in office, was buried only a hundred yards away.

chapter 2

WASHINGTON, D.C.
YESTERDAY AND TODAY

The primary task of the U.S. Secret Service is the protection of the president of the United States, the vice president, their families, and other notables, including federal judges, candidates for the presidency, and visiting heads of state.

Every generation, there have been dramatic examples of agents doing their jobs: Special Agent Clint Hill crawling onto the body of Jackie Kennedy, protecting her when her husband had been shot. Special Agent Larry Buendorf, who wrestled a loaded pistol from Squeaky Fromme when she aimed it at President Gerald Ford. Special Agent Tim McCarthy, who charged—and took a bullet in the midsection from—the pistol of John Hinckley, who had already put one bullet within half an inch of President Ronald Reagan's heart.

Part of the skill of a good agent is the ability to blend into the background. Agents accompanied Chelsea Clinton to Stanford University while other agents accompanied her father—and Presidents Ford and Eisenhower before him—onto various fairways with machine guns stowed in golf bags.

In the early 1960s, there was the agent known as Father

St. Joseph, who, in the garb of a priest, chauffeured women in and out of the White House for John F. Kennedy.

United States Secret Service.

The name evokes images of men in dark glasses, earphones, and suits jogging beside the presidential limousine, or scanning the hands of people greeting the president. But the majority of agents are stationed in one hundred field offices around the country—and a few around the world—officially and unofficially. A typical workday is devoted to investigative tasks of varying difficulty, mostly checking out the more than twenty thousand reports received annually from citizens about a perceived threat to the president's life.

About two hundred serious threats are investigated every month. Annually, about five hundred of these cases are sufficiently serious to lead to an arrest. Since September 11, 2001, the number has increased dramatically.

Additionally, four or five individuals in an average week attempt to penetrate White House security. Half of these people are armed, an equal number are mentally ill. Some hit the Secret Service "daily double"—they are both armed *and* mentally ill. Most are dangerous and most have a grievance, usually imagined, against the government. Many have been egged on by talk radio windbags, some hear their own private voices. The most dangerously delusional are often the most normal in appearance.

So many individuals try to get at the president of the United States that the reality of stopping one hundred percent of them is a frightening concept. Some of them, unknown to the public, get dramatically close.

During the Clinton administration, one nut with an automatic weapon sprayed gunfire at the East Wing of the White House. Another crashed a light plane onto the White House lawn.

In 1995, to make the final line of protection more cohesive, the Secret Service established a security perimeter around the White House, closing off Pennsylvania Avenue to traffic, thus preventing a car or truck bomb from being set off in front of the White House.

It was there on July 24, 1998, that the security perimeter stopped a gunman named Russell Eugene Weston Jr., who had traveled from Montana to Washington to kill the president. Thwarted in his attempt to get near the White House, Weston turned his attention to the Capitol. There he murdered two policemen before being shot himself.

A young Secret Service agent named Laura Chapman arrived in Washington the same day as the Weston incident and worked her first full shift at the White House. She would stay on that assignment for approximately eleven years, including sick and injury leave. She would work primarily for Bill Clinton and George W. Bush—"Elvis" and "Pointy Ears" in Secret Service jargon—over the course of her career. She liked both men personally yet on occasion was appalled at the personal behavior or policies of both. Then she worked for a third man, Bush's successor, whom she never grew to know too well.

Over the years, she was usually one of a few female agents on duty at the White House.

Later she would remember thinking—in reference to the Weston incident as well as others—that when there is homicide within a man, it is often impossible to stop him right up until the moment he strikes.

Many things haunted Laura Chapman, but the accuracy and irony of that thought would be among the foremost for the duration of her life.

On her first day at the White House there was an assassination attempt.

And then, on her last official day on the same posting, there would be another.

Or so she believed.

chapter 3

The frightened Mexican known as Chico balked at the top of a steep sandy hill. It was dark and past midnight. He had led the two Americans this far and even though the night was hot, his feet were cold. An odd pair escorted him. A big blond *gringo* policeman and a *gringo* gangster. The two *gringos* confirmed Chico's lifelong feeling that there was not much difference between the cops and criminals north of the Rio Grande, or Río Bravo as the Mexicans called it.

"Down there, *señores*," the Mexican said, indicating. The moon was a bright half crescent, a big yellow tattoo on a black sky.

The two Americans glared at him.

"Show us," said one of the *gringos*.

The one who spoke was the *gringo federal*. He stood six two, he was a *güero*, a blond man, in his mid-thirties. He had a tough clean face. His hair was as short as his patience. His hand held a 9mm Glock. His bearing suggested that he had experience using it.

The Mexican trembled. No question who was in charge.

They stood at the summit of an unofficial burial ground two miles south of the Tex-Mex border at El Paso–Ciudad Juárez. A patch of moonlit hell on earth. The terrified people of the local village, Tiaczipia, called this area *el camposanto de los ángeles*: a dumping ground for murder victims, both local and sometimes from as far away as Mexico City. Just bury them properly and the local police, *los rurales,* would never ask embarrassing questions.

"Hey, why you no kill me now?" Chico snapped. "You

going to kill me no how, so *Madre de Jesús,* you kill me now and get it done!"

The Mexican's breath smelled like kerosene.

The American lawman angered. It was scary, a man with a cannon in his hand gradually losing his patience. He spoke softly. Velvet wrapped around steel. The blond man was methodical and patient, with sharp intelligent blue eyes. But he was cold as cobalt.

A genuine assassin.

"One more time, Chico," the American said. "You *don't* show us where the grave is, and I *do* blow your brains out. Then I leave you here so that you can bake in the Mexican sun tomorrow morning and the vultures can pick at your eyeballs. *¿Comprende?*"

The Glock pointed upward with its five-inch barrel. The American poked the Mexican in the chest with the gun. Hard. The Mexican winced.

"Bullets hurt worse, Chico," the blond man said. "So move."

The second American was a shorter, darker man known as Vincent, a muscle boy from South Florida, swarthy and unshaven. He was connected to a South Beach syndicate that laundered money; found, trained, and exploited high-priced whores; and did import-export of questionable pharmaceuticals.

Vincent was a Salvitalian. Italian father and Salvadorian mother. He spoke three languages, none of them well, all of them with a menacing brand of inarticulation.

The Salvitalian had murdered four men and one woman in three countries. He had maimed a few more, blowing out kneecaps and backbones as business dictated.

He was sweating like a pig, too. Still, no one moved. The Mexican knew damned well that when three people walked down this hill usually only two walked back up.

Sometimes only one.

"Hijos de puta gringos," the Mexican said. "Don't matter if you kill me."

"Okay," the blond man said softly. "We'll do it the

unpleasant way." The American reached into his jacket pocket and pulled out a silencer. He briskly screwed it onto the Glock.

The Mexican had an epiphany. "*Está bien, se lo muestro*— all right. I show you," he said. He cursed long and low.

The Mexican led the two Americans down the long sandy hillside. They faced north and could easily see the Rio Grande, the lights of El Paso and Ciudad Juárez, and the long straight highways of the South Texas badlands that led into the border cities.

The *federal* let his eyes wander. He saw the spotlight at the border crossing and could discern the U.S. flag that waved there.

The Mexican continued to curse in Spanish. Vincent shoved him in the center of the shoulders and told him to shut up. The blond American kept a ten-foot distance, the Glock pressed to his leg.

The terrain was soft, uneven, and marked with brush. The Mexican knew where to step. Vincent carried a hand lantern in one hand and a shovel in the other. Both Americans watched the Mexican's feet carefully, following his footsteps one by one.

They found a set of sagging steps anchored into the steepest part of the incline. They walked upon rotting slats that passed over trenches a dozen feet deep. The wood groaned.

The gunman was alert for Chico to make a run for his life. He was ready to fire across the Mexican's legs to bring him down if he had to, but he was not going back—not to Washington, not to Texas, not even back up these rickety steps— without finding what he was looking for.

The steps led to a dilapidated shack, a one-time checkpoint. The shack was wooden with a flimsy door. A padlock, just as flimsy, hung on a latch.

"Cut the fucking light," the blond man said, referring to the lantern. Vincent found the right button.

"Any reason to expect anyone here?" the blond man asked. The Mexican shook his head. The blond man raised the Glock, the silenced nose pointing upward. "Break open the door."

Chico put a shoulder to the door and shoved hard.

Once, twice.

Chunks of rotting splintered wood flew from the door at each impact. But the old copper hinges held. The Mexican hit the door a third time. Three times lucky.

The wood gave way with a crunching sound and burst from its bolts. The Mexican stepped back. Vincent held the Mexican's arm while all three waited.

Any hail of bullets would have come here. The *federal* stayed behind the Mexican. Let the spic take the first six shots, he figured, then he could empty his own artillery into the place.

Vincent pushed the Mexican through the door. The Americans kept the Mexican close to them, using him as a human shield. Vincent lit the lantern.

No one home.

Cobwebs.

A filthy floor strewn with shredded newspapers, dead tequila bottles, and bald tires.

Drug paraphernalia in one corner. A mattress littered with used condoms.

"You got a real stinkhole of a country here, Chico, you know that?" Vincent said. "What's this? The presidential palace?" Vincent had a voice like two large stones grinding together.

The Mexican gave a jerk to his arm. Vincent slapped him hard across the skull.

The cabin was the size of a one-car garage. There was a narrow, uneven doorway on the other side, open and leading out to the continuation of the wooden path another hundred feet down the hillside. Vincent waved his lantern again for a second and slashed the pathway with a quick yellow beam.

They continued downward. They passed a small wooden cross, jagged and crooked. Some brave kid had climbed the hillside and constructed the cross out of wire and a smashed orange crate—probably for a brother or father who was buried there. Maybe a sister.

Local religion or local superstition. The natives of Tiaczipia had lost their share of relatives to the hillside. Gang wars, drug feuds, badly timed moments of adultery, and crazy Saturday nights. Plus that particular Mexican attitude toward death.

They proceeded another fifty feet downward. The *gringos* were dumped on the west side of the path, Chico explained, and the Mexicans on the east.

After a few more moments, the Mexican stopped. He looked at a formation of rocks and trees. He pointed to a patch of clay and dirt fifteen paces west of the wooden path.

"There, *señor*," he said softly.

He indicated a mound of earth that was larger than the others. The body down there was fresher and perhaps bigger. "I buried him myself. Me and my brother. My brother's a priest."

The American looked at the spot and looked at the Mexican. "Nice," he said. He took the shovel out of Vincent's hand and pressed it to the Mexican.

"Now *show* me," the blond man demanded.

The Mexican was furious. "You say you only want to *see* the spot!"

"I lied," the American answered. "Dig."

Chico exhaled a long disgusted breath. "No."

The American readied the pistol.

Chico glared back, snatched the shovel, and pushed away a rock. A swarm of insects buzzed up. Chico cursed and waved the swarm away. The Americans retreated several feet.

Vincent remained standing, shuffling his large feet, always glancing around. The big man was riddled with apprehension. Meanwhile, the blond man settled down and sat on the skeleton of a discarded chair, holding his pistol across his knee.

"Don't keep us here all night, for Christ's sake," the

American said. "Get to work and we can all get out of here."

He lit a dark cigarette and smoked it, settling in for a dig that could take a while.

The Mexican hoisted the shovel and angrily set to his task.

chapter 4

CIUDAD JUÁREZ, MEXICO
JUNE 7, 2009; 1:45 A.M.

In the makeshift cemetery, the earth came up easily by the shovelful. The grave was fresh, which helped too. Vincent paced and kept the lantern partially muffled.

The blond American surveyed the little dunes that marked the rolling sandy plot while the vestiges of his cigar smoke drifted slowly like little ghosts. When the American looked very carefully into the Hispanic side of the dumping ground, he saw that the sand was littered with small pathetic offerings to the murdered.

Catholic statues. Plastic saints. Tiny bouquets, real and fake.

Rosary beads. Little wax disks that had once been candles.

Grieving wives, mothers, and children no doubt made quiet pilgrimages here. All the more reason to let the lantern be seen. It would keep the innocent bystanders away tonight. As for the police, the *rurales* knew better. In northern Mexico, nothing got a man's throat cut faster than wandering across the wrong activity in the moonlight.

The American's gaze slid through the shadows and settled ten feet away on the carcass of a dead cat. In pieces. Chopped up. *Santería* or a teen gang?

He finished a sixth cigarette. A solid nicotine kick coursed through him. Then he heard a distinctive crack from the shovel. The Mexican had hit bones. The blond man quickly stood.

Vincent moved forward, also, and went to the unmarked graveside. The *federal* took the lantern from Vincent. The Mexican stepped out of the hole. The American gazed down. So did Vincent. Vincent looked away fast and cursed.

"Keep going," the blond man said to the Mexican.

"But—?"

"Goddamn it! I need a good look! And you're going to give it to me!"

The Mexican's next lunge hit the skeleton even harder, but the third was not as loud because it hit dirt as well as flesh. As the American continued to stare down, dirt came away from a dead man's decomposing face. There was a maggots' nest around the nose, and worms. Big thick ones crawled out of the dead man's mouth.

The eyebrows were still on the corpse, though the skin was darkened. The teeth were in good shape, but the lips were gone. The lower part of the skull was contorted in a ghoulish grin.

"I want to see his clothes," the American said without emotion.

The Mexican cursed in Spanish, but cleared away the deep blue dress uniform of a United States Marine. The name plate was missing. So were any medals. But the merit ribbons were still present, and the dead man's arms were folded helter-skelter across his rotting chest.

That answered a question the blond man needed to know: There were discolored chevrons on the marine's arms. Faded yellow and red. The deceased had been a gunnery sergeant.

"That him?" asked Vincent.

"That's him," the other American said. He lowered his gun.

"Good job, Chico. *Gracias,*" he said.

The Mexican sighed in relief.

Several seconds passed. "If you want, *señor,*" the Mexican

said, "I come back tomorrow with a crucifix and I plant it here for your *amigo*."

"Yeah," the American answered. He looked lost in thought for a moment, then he came back to earth. "Crucifix. Great idea, Chico. There's a dead U.S. Marine down there. So some holy mumbo-jumbo statue of JFC is sure going to make him feel better, huh?"

The Mexican started to sweat again.

He was about to say something else when the blond man raised the pistol and pulled off two shots. He fired so fast that the Mexican, hit flush between the eyes with the first bullet, was still fully upright for the second one, which smashed into the center of his forehead.

Chico dropped like a puppet, strings amputated.

A groaning gurgle spasmed upward from his throat.

Then nothing else.

Vincent recoiled, faintly splattered. The murder was brutal even by underworld standards.

"Good God," the Salvitalian muttered.

The *federal* stared at the body. One of the Mexican's legs was quivering. So the gunman leaned forward and pumped a final bullet through Chico's heart. The leg spasmed a final time.

Vincent grimaced again.

The blond man looked at him and handed him back the lantern. "So what the hell's wrong with *you? You've* killed people."

Vincent thought about it, but did not answer.

"Get his money," the blond American ordered.

"What?"

"We killed him. We might as well rob him."

"Are you crazy? Let's get out of here."

"He had a thousand dollars in fifties on him two hours ago, birdbrain," the blond man said. "And he hasn't been out of our sight. What does that mean to you? Anything?"

Vincent wavered.

The Salvitalian looked at the hard Irish face and he looked at the dead Mexican. He did not want to think about the ghoul-headed military corpse three feet deep in the sand, though he could feel the dead man's eye holes staring up at him. This venue, and the world that surrounded it, was more alive with spirits than anyone could have feared.

Vincent knelt at the graveside. He set aside the lantern and ransacked the Mexican's pockets. Sure enough. The Mexican still had a thick wad of American money. A roll of fifties packed into a wide blue rubber band.

Vincent was rising again when the other American poked the nose of the Glock against Vincent's skull. For half an agonized second, Vincent knew what was coming.

He opened his mouth to yell but the words never escaped his throat.

The *federal* pulled the trigger twice quickly. Blood and bone erupted from Vincent's skull, so close to the gunman it sprayed him. Vincent tumbled across the body of the Mexican.

The field of death was now very still, very quiet. Even the tortured souls and spirits weren't immediately to be heard from.

The gunman took the rolled-up thousand dollars from the ground. He pocketed it, despite bloodstains on some of the outer bills. Then he pulled the empty magazine from his weapon and slapped a full clip back in. He pushed the weapon into his belt. He turned off the lantern. Using his feet, he pushed both bodies into the burial ditch.

He went to work with the shovel, enlarging the grave. His arms were strong and sure. It still took thirty minutes to create enough space so that the dead marine would have company.

No point leaving something conspicuous.

Plant a pair of stiffs two miles south of Texas and it would take a long time—if not forever—for anyone to ask questions. Leave a display, particularly *this* display, and there could be trouble.

It would take another half hour on a hot night to put the dirt back down and spread it out. It did not have to be perfect. Just complete. No one who knew any better tampered with a grave in *el camposanto de los ángeles*.

But by 3 A.M. he was walking back up the hill alone, secure in the knowledge that the current president of the United States would soon be as dead as the three men he had left behind.

chapter 5

WASHINGTON, D.C.
JUNE 19, 2009; 6:13 A.M. EDST

The car air conditioning emitted a low steady hum as United States Secret Service Agent Laura Chapman drove her ten-year-old Lexus to the White House. But as she drove, Laura studied her rearview mirror more intently than the average motorist.

The rearview: *Objects behind a woman may be larger than she thinks*.

The radio was set to an all-news station—WTOP AM in Washington. And there was plenty for her to latch on to, and not just that the record-breaking heat and the usual summer weather had turned the city into a ninety-plus steam bath, with no end in sight.

But what else was new?

New?

Well, there was much discussion about the recent direction of politics in Eastern Europe. Poland, Lithuania, and Slovenia had elected far-right governments in the last ten months, part of a political movement spreading its way westward. The shift in the political landscape was a popular response to the Islamic militancy that had spread across Europe in the last decade.

Some saw the trend as a resurgence of European nationalism; others called it fascism. Whatever it was, it was there. Islamic mosques were now being defaced with swastikas and many ethnic Europeans thought that was not a bad thing.

Best to keep the *hajis* in their place, the wisdom went. But it wasn't entirely a European problem. Since the ill-fated American venture in Iraq in 2003, the number of converts to Islam had increased dramatically in the United States, as well. Church attendance in America continued downward, while mosque attendance soared.

Half a planet away, China had annexed Taiwan and was "repatriating and re-educating" dissident Taiwanese—most of whom were never seen again—while the world stood by. Meanwhile, pesky bands of guerrillas—"pro-democracy Maoists"—had won a few firefights with government forces in Jiangxi province. The Chinese government was flooding army troops into the area to eradicate the problem of pesky "democratic Maoists" before their decadent philosophy caught hold elsewhere.

Domestically in the United States, the NDNAR—the National DNA Registry—now had a database of two hundred fifty million names of living persons believed to be in the United States, much to the horror of civil libertarians. Almost everyone, in other words.

The NDNAR had been founded by executive order in the waning days of the Bush 43 administration and had withstood all legal challenges so far.

Elsewhere, and mildly more amusing, Leonid Brezhnev's granddaughter Tatiana, who had emigrated to America with her parents in the 1990s, had been elected mayor of Burlington, Vermont. She had run as a conservative Republican.

New also was the full diplomatic exchange between the United States and post-Castro Cuba. And then there were plans for thirty-two teams in major league baseball next year, including new franchises in New Jersey and Las Vegas.

Laura normally listened for the baseball scores. She had inherited a passion for the Boston Red Sox from her father, who had also been in the service of the government. But her focus was not on sports this morning. It was on her rearview mirror.

"Damn," she said to herself, one nervous finger tapping on the steering wheel. "I mean, I know I'm sensing something."

Now, granted: Laura Chapman could be a major head case on occasion. Often she would see things, people, ideas, or patterns of behavior that maybe were not there. Or perhaps they were.

No one really knew because sometimes she saw important parallel things—a subtle but ominous connection or correlation of people and of otherwise unrelated events—that other people did not notice. Or care to notice. Or just plain *missed*.

And, granted again, she had recently enjoyed several months of "time off for personal reasons," meaning med/psych leave. But Laura had graduated from the care of Dr. Sam Feldman—one of the resident Secret Service shrinks—with as clean a bill of mental health as any veteran of the United States Secret Service could hope for. After all, most Secret Service employees who worked in the White House pressure cooker burned out after five or six years. Laura was the exception for having hung on for so long.

So she was normal. Or what passed for it in her line of work.

Hell. Perfection was only something that was aspired to, not something that was expected from individuals. Who in Washington did not have a few dents in his or her armor? Working for the United States Secret Service was a Catch-22 sort of thing: you had to be resolutely normal to be offered a position . . . and then a little bit "off" to accept it.

Thus, over the last six days, during the very hot early summer of 2009, Laura's festering imagination had caused her to look over her shoulder more than a few times in a few days and come to a conclusion:

She was under surveillance.

The most plausible explanation: The Secret Service had homed in on her and she was once again under the tight scrutiny of the people who employed her. She had mentioned her feelings to no one, but as she drove to work this morning, she was resentful.

But she had decided that she was going to let it play out

for a few more days to see where it led. Invariably, these things led to a resolution, though often a thoroughly unexpected one.

Thoroughly unexpected, and sometimes equally unpleasant.

chapter 6

ALEXANDRIA, VIRGINIA
SATURDAY JUNE 13, 2009

The surveillance notion had taken hold the previous Saturday at her home, a comfortable two-bedroom apartment in Alexandria, Virginia. She lived alone.

Laura's instincts kicked in. She had that *gut feeling:* the sense that eyes were upon her.

So she ran a test. She drove to a sporting goods store at a mall in Crystal City. She stood for twenty minutes in the tennis section, selecting a racket. Not far away had stood three middle-aged women. One carried an infant and another carried a yellow plastic purse. The third had a shopping bag: Bloomingdale's.

After purchasing a racket and moving on to a nearby Borders, a pair of college-aged men kept her in their peripheral view. They followed her from Film Criticism to Demonology to Women's Health. Now she was almost sure. The pattern didn't make sense in a random world.

Time for proof: She picked up a novel in French and sat in the store's cafe for half an hour, reading and sipping a green tea. Her watchers stopped for coffee at the same Starbucks.

This had all the crude handwriting of Service surveillance; quick profile changes, back-up cars with cell phones, and two or three teams standing by in case a forward party overran or was noticed. Long on money and manpower, short on finesse. The Secret Service had never understood the subtleties of streetwatching. They threw around people and cars until it was impossible to lose sight of their target.

It was a halfwitted way to go about business.

It was so lame-brained that Laura was insulted to think that no one thought she would pick up on it. It also made her angry on another level: She could have run a much better surveillance herself, but God forbid that the guys who ran the Service would ever put a woman in charge of something like a domestic surveillance operation.

At her third stop of the day, a supermarket, the watchers were still upon her.

Unskilled streetwatching teams frequently have neither time nor inclination to change their shoes. In the supermarket, Laura was joined at the produce aisle, this time by two women. Both watched her without directly looking.

Got 'em! From their footwear, she recognized both.

One woman in a navy dress wore battered Reeboks, blue and white with a slight tear on the inside below the left calf. The second woman, wearing shorts and a sweatshirt, had a pair of sandals, a silver buckle on the outside of each. The former belonged to the woman who had held the infant in the sport mart. The latter belonged to the lady with the plastic purse.

The watchers looked like policewomen borrowed from the District of Columbia Police Department. It was written all over them. They might as well have been wearing big flak vests that said POLICE.

Two nights later, Laura had risen from her bed an hour after settling in to sleep. It was a time when sleep was sporadic and troubled, riddled with nasty groggy dreams and creepy images. This instinct had roused her from the netherworld between rest and wakefulness: another feeling, this time somewhat spooky, a sense of not being alone, though no one else was visibly present.

She noted the time. Three sixteen A.M.

She picked up the Service-issue Sig Sauer automatic that slept on her night table. Then she walked to her bedroom window and edged back the shade.

She spotted a car across the street, down the block, its engine idling. With binoculars that she kept by her front window, she looked carefully. She saw the tiny orange glow of a cigarette.

Within the car: a lone man, unfamiliar, sitting, smoking. Virginia plates ending in 509 on a Ford Bronco, the front part of the plate obscured by a hydrant. She noted vehicle and time.

So, I mean, why is he there?

The car hadn't been there when she had returned home. Who sits in a car in Alexandria all night and smokes? Who, except some prick who watches for a living?

Damn them!

"I mean, what the hell do they want from me?" she muttered to herself.

NDC. No damned clue.

Okay, okay. That psychiatric counseling, those sessions with Dr. Feldman: Someone somewhere probably still held that against her. But who in the Service did not have at least a couple of screws loose after a few years? Stress was what this job was all about. They should have called it the United States Stressful Service. One good screw-up and a lifetime of loyal work goes down on the wrong side of history.

And, by the way, shouldn't her "difficulties" have been a dead issue by now?

Or was someone still trying to raise it? What were they fixated upon?

Her unsettled relationship with her father? That one should have been buried long ago.

Her sexual partners? She had slept around a lot less than most of the men in the Secret Service, so what was the big deal?

Or was this crude surveillance a sign of the opposition, whoever *that* was these days?

The intelligence landscape had been scrambled since September of 2001 and then again following the intelligence failures surrounding the Iraq war. Little amorphous cells of conspirators floated across the landscape, bound by no rules except their own. And with the incompetents in INS and Homeland Security stirring the mix, it was a wonder any operation could move forward smoothly.

She longed to have a conversation with her father about all of this. He would have had some interesting opinions.

The car with the smoker was still there at 4 A.M., but was gone by 5:30—Laura kept rising from her bed to check—replaced by a telephone van farther down the block. Maryland plates this time, which made no sense for a repair vehicle in Virginia.

She sighed dismally. *Gotta calm down. Gotta calm down.*

She had a substance for such occasions. At the lining in her mattress, she found the little area that she had cut away. She reached in until her arm was immersed to the elbow.

For a moment, she was alarmed. She couldn't find what she wanted. Then she found the foil packet and pulled it out. Her stash of marijuana was running low, but she only needed a puff or two to get high. She lit up, a little jingle of made-up doggerel dancing in the back of her mind.

> *Puff, the magic dragon,*
> *Lived near D.C.,*
> *And always kept two joints around,*
> *One for him and one for me.*

This was her way to settle down and her little joke on the Service at the same time.

If they only knew . . . if only they knew . . .

A quick smoke calmed her. Surely, she told herself as she drifted off, she was not the only closet pothead in the Service, nor the only agent perpetually on the brink of a second nervous breakdown.

Hell, as far as the weed was concerned, there probably hadn't been a presidential candidate since that tight-assed Dole who hadn't smoked the stuff at least once. And everyone in the Service knew the story about how Willie Nelson, the hillbilly Dalai Lama, went up to the roof after performing at the Carter White House and toked away.

The thoughts amused her; the notion that if the folks out there in Red State America knew how the capital really functioned, their jaws would drop. So now, for the sake of nerves and tranquility, a few more tokes. The smoke sent her back to a peaceful sleep.

So, when Laura started her drive to work on the morning of June 19, she watched her rearview mirror. Already, on the Virginia side of the river driving along the George Washington Parkway, she figured she was being followed by a committee of at least three vehicles and probably a fourth, judging by the subtle ballet danced by several vehicles to her rear.

She drew a breath and reassessed.

She studied her rearview mirror again as she crossed Constitution Avenue.

She scanned and spotted what she felt were two members of this morning's surveillance team. One a dark green Dodge and the other a white Chevrolet. They had been with her for two miles, never venturing up to pass, never dropping too far back. She had had a team every day this week, or so she perceived.

Instinctively, her right hand moved to the 9mm Sig Sauer automatic that rode at her belt. She fingered her weapon. Who the hell knew who was following whom these days?

One small part of her urged her to say to hell with everything, her job in particular, and throw a few shots into the pursuing cars just to sing *sayonara* to the current situation. But that would have landed her back in the shrink's office, if not worse.

So the Sig Sauer stayed holstered. And she remained on the edge of her sanity, just a short, friendly, cozy hop from a complete psychotic break: that mental hole-in-one that used to be known as a "nervous breakdown."

Her escort pulled away as she approached the White House. She felt like flipping them a finger, but her self-control held. After all, if they were doltish enough to let their mark pick up their surveillance, they probably weren't smart enough to know she was aware of them.

So why tell them something they did not know? Just because she could read their minds, didn't mean they needed to know what *she* was thinking.

So to hell with 'em.

She went through the checkpoint at the south gates to the White House, gave the guard a friendly smile plus her usual four inches of skirt above the knee, and reported to work.

To hell with 'em all!

chapter 7

WASHINGTON, D.C.
JUNE 19, 2009; 5:12 P.M.

Like most agents eventually chosen for the Presidential Protection Detail at the White House, Laura Chapman had previously worked regional offices of the Secret Service around the United States. Boston. Los Angeles. St. Louis and Chicago.

Currently the senior member of the PPD after more than a decade of White House duty, she had been, up until recently, the perimeter agent on the PPD, the agent who analyzed the overall safety of the president's whereabouts. It was a grueling, never-ending job, its factors changing hour to hour, its pressures incessant. But that duty had been reassigned to a younger male agent in March. Laura increasingly entertained the notion that her career was about to go in the same direction: reduced responsibility.

A lower profile assignment, maybe within the White House, maybe not.

When a woman passed her mid-thirties in security work, the bosses could not *wait* to slap a gold watch on her wrist and shove her out the door. Hell, if she did not go away, she would be bucking for promotion into the higher administrative ranks of the Service where a woman could not possibly have been less welcome. The Service hierarchy remained a boys-only operation.

Sometimes she thought that maybe she should leave her post honorably and quietly. No fuss, no protest, no angst. She still had many options in the private sector. But then again, she had always been a bit of a tomboy, gravitating toward what she referred to as the "ACE factor": Action, confrontation, and excitement. And security, personal protection, was where the ACE factor was. So she hung around, not always appreciated, but loyal to the Secret Service.

She remained physically fit in her mid-thirties, lean and athletic without being bulky or muscle-bound. She was five seven with light brown hair. She was pretty in a wholesome "American girl" sort of way, without having movie-star looks. She even had to dress down a bit for the job of guarding the president, in order to be less noticeable as a bodyguard.

She ran four or five miles three times a week and visited a gym twice weekly to do weights and pound a light punching bag. She kept trim and strong and looked eight to ten years younger than she was. She put in her proper time on the pistol range. She was certified for advanced scuba and looked sharp in a bathing suit. She could turn male heads. She knew how to seduce and knew how to be seduced. And she could be tough.

Once, during the summer of 2006, a mugger had accosted her in Georgetown when she had been winding down from a run. Standard D.C. yoke job: He grabbed her from behind with one arm, pressed a blade to her throat with the opposite hand, and started whispering something about money and a blow job.

In a sweatshirt and trim shorts, she must have looked like a GWU co-ed to her assailant.

Very bad idea, definitely a poor choice of female victim.

"Which do you want first?" she asked.

When he released her slightly to reply, she broke the man's jaw with a reverse smash of her elbow. Then, in indignation, she broke his nose, his left wrist, and ruined his sex life with her left instep. She had him tied to a mailbox with his own belt for twenty minutes before the D.C. police and the ambulance arrived.

But did any of her *skills* still matter?

So what that she had better instincts than dozens of younger agents? Who cared that she could read a street or an assassin's thoughts better than a legion of textbook-trained recent graduates of the FBI Academy at Quantico? Few in the Service were better at the *mental* game of presidential protection. That was why she had been assigned to the White House in the first place, and that was why she had lasted at the White House so long—that unique skill of seeing things that no one else saw.

But the protection game had recently become meaner, even brutish. *The Washington Post,* in a recent series on the FBI, the CIA, and the Secret Service, had described the first decade of the new century as the "new epoch of thuggery in American security work." As a result, certain enclaves of the Service remained steadfastly male, such as the White House.

This was the era that followed September 11, 2001. No one thought the *Post* was wrong on its "thuggery" comment.

Nonetheless, she could barely conceal her slowly smoldering anger when she spotted an official envelope sitting on her desk at the end of this workday, Friday, June 19.

Oh Jesus! I'm transferred! Or fired! Or something!

Chapman always checked back at her desk before starting home for the day. The crisp white envelope was waiting for her. Contents and conduit a mystery.

Treasury Department. Secret Service stationery.

Something official, hand delivered! With her name on it, properly spelled.

This was how agents were officially snuffed.

Sometimes an agent learned exactly what she had done wrong. More often she did not. She either accepted her new posting or she turned in her shield and her weapon within the hour. Otherwise, the discharge could swiftly change to "dishonorable."

She knew the procedure. The third Friday of every month

was the "Executioner's Day," the day the transfers and firings came down from Treasury/Personnel on M Street. It had been that way since the second term of Franklin Roosevelt, back when agents rode on the running boards of the presidential limousine. No reason to mess with tradition now.

Chapman stared at the envelope.

There was a surveillance camera in the room, like in most rooms in the White House. Who was on the other end of the camera these days, she wondered, and why had *she* been singled out?

Chapman cursed to herself. She finally picked up the envelope.

For a few seconds, her adult life flashed before her. Education at the University of Massachusetts, full academic scholarship, where she graduated summa cum laude with a BA in history and a minor in psychology. She had also starred in field hockey—four varsity letters and two bone-crunching, character-building years as women's varsity captain of an outstanding squad that the NCAA had ranked eighth in the nation—and crew. Summer jobs as a lifeguard on Cape Cod, another summer as a USAID worker in Honduras, where she gained a colloquial fluency in Spanish. An academic semester in France.

She drew a deep breath.

Gut feeling: *Nothing good arrives in a manner like this.*

"Whatever," she muttered.

She controlled her anger. Two fellow agents filed into the room, their own desks nearby.

Not her favorite duo: Stu Larsen and Kurt Reilley. Recent transfers-in; on duty at the White House for less than eighteen months apiece.

Younger by a decade. A couple of high-testosterone blockheads who hadn't yet grasped the concept of their own mortality. They did not like her personally; the feelings were mutual.

She nodded to them. Larsen gave half a nod in return. Reilley had nothing to say yet. Tweedle Dum and Tweedle Dumber. She wasn't alone in her estimation of them.

Larsen was a gorilla, a six-four guy who took a size fifty suit. Shoulders reminiscent of a snow plow. A brain to match: typical of what the Service currently hired. Larsen was now the "Belt Man," the agent who held the president's belt, ready to pull the president back in case of trouble, when Numero Uno leaned into adoring crowds for a fix of unqualified adulation.

The other agent, Reilley, was a professional twerp at five nine, but had the ego and abrasiveness particular to small aggressive men.

Sometimes Chapman wondered where the Service recruited these guys. She had this suspicion: Midwestern state colleges where two SAT scores often totaled below nine hundred.

There was nothing on their desks, either. Larsen and Reilley had no similar letter.

Chapman wondered which of them would take her job. *Bastards!*

"Having a senior moment, Laura?" Reilley asked, without looking up.

She had barely moved since they had entered the room. "Screw you, Kurt," she muttered.

"Glad you're in your usual good mood," Larsen added.

"Screw both of you," Laura said. "And fuck the entire world around you."

From the corner of her eye, she saw both men smirk.

"You take life too seriously, Laura," Larsen tried next.

"Everything in this whole office, I *have* to take seriously," she answered. "With the possible exception of you two."

Chapman brought her attention back to the envelope before her. Tightly sealed. The back was taped. For her eyes only. Revised gut feeling as she fingered the letter: *It was inherently neither good nor bad but it was going to change the course of her life.*

"What do you got there, Laura?" Larsen asked. "Your walking papers to Salt Lake City?"

"Real funny, Larsen," she answered.

"Might be Des Moines," Reilley added. "Got an active

office there, plus all the fat-farm guys in bib overalls you'd want."

"Stuff it, Kurt," Laura said.

"You could end up dating the next Timothy McVeigh, Laura," Larsen continued. "That could crank your career up a notch."

She tuned them out as they waited for her response. Then she tucked the envelope in her pocket. She would be damned if she were going to read the letter in front of schoolchildren.

chapter 8

WASHINGTON, D.C.
JUNE 19, 2009; 5:29 P.M.

Laura walked from the exit of the White House that led to the south parking lot. It was still sweltering, heat rising in waves from the asphalt. She stopped and tore open the envelope.

Then she went motionless. The key phrases jumped out at her:

. . . you have been relieved of your duties on the Presidential Protection Detail effective 1700, Friday, June 19, 2009. The Department of the Treasury of the United States of America expresses its deep gratitude for your loyal diligent work at the White House over these past eighty-two months. The Service commends you in particular for the length and quality of your employment here. Further . . .

She snarled to herself. But then she stopped, confused. Rather than giving her the heave-ho, the second half of the letter summoned her immediately to a specially arranged meeting.

The petitioner was a man she knew well, Mitchell Hamilton. Hamilton was a liaison officer between the Secret Service and the Central Intelligence Agency. The location was Room 566-E of the Capitol. A reading room belonging to the Office of Protective Intelligence.

What was this *all about? The OPI?*

The Office of Protective Intelligence—streamlined and reorganized in 2007—was the division of the Secret Service that interfaced with other American intelligence agencies: Notably, this included the FBI, the CIA, and the recently overhauled Immigration and Naturalization Service. The OPI was where Secret Service agents functioned as intelligence agents in the most traditional sense.

The OPI had no shortage of territory. The number of deranged, disturbed, and threatening individuals and groups in the United States had sadly expanded over the years to more than fifty thousand. Even dormant files were reviewed weekly by a case officer.

Also, at any given time, there were about five hundred ongoing investigations of EDIs—extremely dangerous individuals—from whom a threat might arise to the president or someone who had been assigned to the Secret Service as a "protectee." Each file was monitored by a specific agent each day, with a specific agent responsible for each investigation. In their main headquarters on G Street, NW, new entries were made 24/7. Secret Service agents assigned to OPI were also responsible for establishing a safe environment and physical safety for the president and his diplomatic visitors, which was why Laura had coordinated procedures with the OPI before.

It was also how she knew Mitch Hamilton.

Obviously something major was up.

But what?

Her right hand fingered the edge of the correspondence as she finished reading. Her left hand wandered under her jacket and fingered her Sig Sauer. And why shouldn't she be nervous?

She folded the letter back into its envelope and walked

to her car. Whoever was on her case would have to raise a flag pretty soon now. Maybe things were about to fall into place.

So how is your patriotism these days? Laura asked herself with irritation. *Your sense of pride as an American, the feelings that made you want to join the Secret Service to begin with?*

Laura sighed. Reality check. There wasn't much idealism left in this job. And if there had been any razzle dazzle, that was long gone, also.

Laura had a brother who lived in New York. He was a copyright attorney. One day on the phone recently, he had complained of the tedium of his job and the "glamour" of hers.

"Glamour?" she had answered. "Imagine getting up in the morning, showering, and dressing in your best suit. Then walking into your back yard and standing there motionless for the rest of the day."

That was why the burnout rates were so high, she explained, and why a White House shift for an agent rarely lasted more than two years, and why she was one extreme exception for having lasted nearly eleven.

Laura arrived at her car and unlocked it. She climbed in.

She hit rush hour traffic.

What the hell did they want from her, she wondered relentlessly in the car. She blasted some classic rock and idly wished she were on a beach far away. And—all things considered—she wondered, was it good or bad that she was officially leaving the White House? Maybe she'd be on a beach in a few days, anyway.

This could go either way. And so far, her gut feelings were not giving her a clue.

chapter 9

Laura walked through the entrance to Room 556-E. She paused between two doors while the retina scanner sent a red beam across her face. She passed. Bolts fell on the inside door. No knob. The door unlatched as if opened by a ghost.

She walked through the second door and found herself revisiting not just her own past, but that of several security agencies, too.

Room 556-E was a small chamber with two desks and green carpets. Dead room tone, the result of soundproofing. One window with triple glass overlooked the Mall. Leather chairs. Reading lamps. Paintings around the room. One artist, one theme: The fight for liberty, or at least the American perception thereof—heroic bloodied white guys, Bunker Hill to Baghdad.

There was also one big overstuffed red chair with a hammer and sickle on the headrest. The chair had been swiped in 1954 from the Soviet Mission to the United Nations on East Sixty-seventh Street in New York. It had been nicknamed Stalin's Throne by the men and women who had previously spent hours in it, reading. Stalin had once used it himself.

Once in this room during the Reagan years, William Casey had been toasting the assassination of a tribal leader in the Philippines when he received an updated report. The operation had actually failed. Six of his best agents had been decapitated, their heads placed on village poles. A seventh had been thrown to his death from a cliff.

Casey fumed. The room fell silent. Then the director of the CIA ripped a Roosevelt-era lamp from the wall and hurled it against the floor. Moments later, Casey was at the writing desk, planning a response, the veins at his throat pulsating.

Three days thereafter, the village chief received his receipt: Dow Chemical products delivered by two dozen unmarked U.S. Navy helicopters. It was the Reagan administration, after all, and the DCI, who had been the Great Communicator's campaign manager, always got what he wanted.

The most recent time Chapman had been in this study had been six months earlier. She had been coordinating security for a state visit by the new British prime minister, the second since Tony Blair. Not an Englishman in sight this evening, however. Instead, Laura shook hands with a thin, six-foot, fifty-nine-year-old man whom she had known for several years, Mitchell Hamilton.

Hamilton was a senior case officer from the Central Intelligence Agency's Directorate of Operations, better known as Clandestine Services. He had been a tight friend of the current director of the CIA for four decades, dating back to Princeton and Exeter. The director trusted Hamilton more than most of the men who outranked him.

Mitchell Hamilton and Laura Chapman had first met in Washington in the mid 1990s. Laura had been studying for her master's degree in criminology. Hamilton had been a guest lecturer at Georgetown, working simultaneously as a talent scout for the CIA.

He had spotted Laura as talent right away. She had earned the highest mark among the thirty-six students in his class, and a gentle mentor-protégée relationship began. But by the time Hamilton was ready to pitch Chapman to the CIA, and vice versa, the Massachusetts State Police had already recruited her. There she made detective in an unprecedented three years, much to the resentment of most of the men she passed on her speedy way up.

She fell in love with a Treasury guy in Boston. They had a long, bittersweet affair, nearly married, but did not. Through him, she heard that the United States Secret Service was under a court order to hire more females and minorities. In February of 1996, the Service hired her.

The Secret Service brought her to Washington in 1998, following short tedious tours in several other cities. There she ran into Mitchell Hamilton again. Over the next few years, they had worked a few joint projects together—the Secret Service with the CIA. Their superiors recognized the relationship and used it whenever an operation that needed joint bureau cooperation was too important for interoffice b.s. Once, following too many martinis, Mitch had come on to her at the bar of the Four Seasons in New York. She had gently rebuffed him. Neither had ever mentioned the incident again.

"Hello, Laura," Hamilton said quietly. "How have you been?"

Against all rules of all agencies, he physically embraced her. She did nothing to stop it.

"I'm all right," Chapman answered. "You?"

"I'm hanging in," he said.

"Your wife? Your family?"

"One boy, Jed, graduated from Vanderbilt and works for Citibank in New York. David is a senior at Dartmouth." He paused. "Millie has some health problems, but she's doing well."

"Tell her I said hello. Your sons, too." Jed was Laura's age. Almost.

Mitch appeared slightly more stooped than she remembered him, more white hair with the gray, and slower in physical movement.

"I am about to ruin your day and maybe your life, too," Hamilton began. "Forgive me?"

"Probably not. Why am I leaving the White House?"

"First reassure me on your state of mind."

"What's that mean?" she answered.

"I know you saw Dr. Feldman. The shrink. How are you feeling?"

"I'm fine. Tell me why I'm here, Mitch."

There was an awkward moment when she saw some hesitance in his eyes.

Hamilton finally continued. "We need a top female agent who will bring something extra into a highly sensitive investigation. And that agent," Hamilton said, "would be you."

"I'm honored," Laura answered. "Why female? Am I supposed to seduce someone?" She was only half kidding.

"Nothing that glamorous," he said. "And you'll have your answer in a moment."

It quickly occurred to Laura that Hamilton was stalling. Then the bolts fell a final time. The door opened again.

A trim but sturdy man entered the room; dark hair, wide shoulders, a face that acknowledged both Laura Chapman and Mitchell Hamilton, but which also meant business.

Laura blinked once in surprise. The man was William Vasquez Jr., director of the United States Secret Service, newly appointed within this current administration.

"Agent Chapman," he said as greeting. They had never met previously. His eyes scoped her out quickly, with a slightly surprised double take. She was used to that from men who weren't expecting a female Secret Service agent to appear in any way feminine.

"Good evening, sir," she said.

Vasquez nodded to Hamilton. "Mitch," he said. "No need to waste any time."

Vasquez handed a briefing book to Laura. She accepted it.

"Find a comfortable place to sit. Then read this," Vasquez said. "Then we'll chat."

Laura examined the book. From its blank cover, there was no telling what it contained. She sat down at a desk, broke the official seal, and scanned past the stiff pages that warned of dire legal sanctions for revealing what she was about to read. At the top was the usual flat paranoid my-way-or-else eagle with olive leaves in one claw and arrows in the other.

Then Laura began to read, and her heart began to race.

chapter 10

The content was as straightforward as a slap in the face.

According to a source that merited attention, a hostile foreign government had agreed to pay a lone professional assassin ten million dollars to murder the president of the United States.

The assassination was to take place in fifteen days, on the morning of July 4, three Saturdays hence, including tomorrow.

The FBI had uncovered the plot—if there really was one—when a source in Miami had walked into their local office with information to sell. It was a slow day and the feds were into the New Era of Paranoia, scared to death about missing something big.

They threw a few bucks on the table. The source sang like a lark.

The FBI moved the source to a CIA man named Richard McCarron, an Agency case officer in the same city. The source's code name was now Charley Boy.

Charley Boy told everything to McCarron. The source maintained that someone from a federal police agency from the United States had banked five million dollars in the Cayman Islands, the first of two payments, the money coming from outside the United States. What was nerve tingling was the implication. There was only one federal police force that could possibly get close enough to the president to complete such a mission.

Laura finished reading the document, a detailed ten-thousand-word report that ran sixty-one tight pages. She flipped back and reread certain sections.

She tried to create perspective: in concept, nothing new.

In 1991, Laura recalled, Saddam Hussein had dispatched three hit teams to murder President George Bush. Another team was sent—out of revenge for the Gulf War—after Bush had left office. Two teams had lost their nerve and disappeared before American agents could intercept them.

Then there had been the final team.

Everyone in the Secret Service knew the story, even if it had never reached the public. The document covered it with a sidebar.

Three members of a hit team—two Libyan males and one female traveling with Egyptian passports—had journeyed as far as Roanoke, Virginia, in October of 1993. Former President Bush had been slated to address the National Press Club in Washington the next day.

But the evening before a possible encounter with their target in Washington, the three-person team was met by agents of the Mossad, acting on intelligence provided by the CIA. All three were known to Israeli intelligence as also having taken part in anti-Israeli operations in Spain and Italy.

The Mossad murdered all three as they slept overnight in a motel. CIA housekeeping picked up the bodies and the personal effects and cremated everything. New mattresses replaced the old ones with the bloodstains. The bullet holes in the walls were spackled, the room cheerfully repainted the same peaceful blue and white hues as the Israeli flag: someone's cute sense of humor. An annual five thousand dollars from the CIA's "rodent fund" allowed the patriotic innkeeper to remain happy and keep quiet forever.

Finally, Laura raised her eyes. Hamilton's gaze awaited her.

"So. If this can be believed," Laura said, "someone *within the Secret Service* has been hired to kill the president? Is that it?"

"Yes," Hamilton answered. "And that's as far as I take you on this, other than coordinating any CIA assistance you might need. From here on, you work for Mr. Vasquez."

Laura considered the case for a moment that felt endless.

"What indicates that this could be legitimate?" Laura asked.

"We've managed some corroboration from Grand Cayman," Director Vasquez began. "A similar amount of money was been deposited in one of the financial laundries down there. A real account under a fictitious name. Fake U.S. passport used to open the account. A trace led nowhere, as your briefing book told you."

"And if we do have a traitor here somewhere," Laura said, "then we have one who is dangerous beyond imagination."

"Obviously. So the first part of your assignment will be to find out *if* this threat really exists," Vasquez continued. "I myself remain skeptical. I can't imagine that a foreign power could actually get to someone in the Service. Nor do I think our security at the White House could be penetrated electronically. But we're not in the business of guessing. We need to *know*."

"But *if* a foreign power infiltrated us?" Laura asked. "And if we *do* have a cyber lapse?"

"Then we have unique security problems," Vasquez answered, "as you've already grasped. Just for starters, you'll have to address this investigation by yourself, at least in the initial stages. I can give you some tech support. Computers and background. And maybe a few people who won't know what they're researching. I'm going to channel a few things to you through Mitch, so it looks like Agency, but you'll report to me directly and in private. We can't afford to risk alerting a man we need to apprehend."

"And since you know it's a male agent you're after . . . ?"

"We figure, you, as a female, are not him."

"Well, that part's brilliant, isn't it?" she said, lifting the grim mood for a moment.

"We like to think so," Hamilton said.

"Who else knows about this?" Laura asked.

"The field is very narrow beyond this room. The DCI knows and the head of the National Security Council knows."

"Does the president know?" Laura asked.

"Not yet," Vasquez said. "Before I speak to him, we have to ascertain that this threat is one hundred percent legitimate. Then, if the threat *is* real, as I hope to God it is not, you'll need to tear apart your own Service by yourself."

"How do we know Charley Boy is reliable?" Laura asked.

"The directorate of the CIA vetted the source," Vasquez answered. "Expert analysis. The vetting was done outside our agency due to its sensitivity. The story checks so far."

"Is the source in protective custody?" Laura asked.

Vasquez again, terse and sharp: "No."

"*No?* Why not?"

Hamilton answered. "The source has a job. As you'll see. Charley Boy accepted our money but otherwise has declined any immediate assistance."

"That's a little strange, isn't it?"

"Very," Vasquez said.

The Secret Service director then made reference to NASRO, the much disliked National Security Re-Organization Act of 2007, which allowed federal investigative agencies to coordinate efforts, share information, and make their own share-or-not-share calls on individual investigations. NASRO often created more problems than it solved, though it did allow marginally more flexibility for file sharing at those odd times when they acted competently.

The concept was called lateralism, and it allowed foreign snoop agencies like the CIA to work with domestic partners like the FBI and the Secret Service where the situation warranted. So far, the Bill of Rights was having a tough first decade of the twenty-first century.

"How old is the product?" Laura asked, indicating the report she had just read.

"Landed on my desk five days ago," Vasquez said. "With a loud thump."

"Miami received it a week ago," Hamilton added.

Laura asked, "A week? Why the time lag?"

"First tier vetting of information," Vasquez said. "It takes time."

"A week can be significant," Laura said. "The extra time would have been helpful."

"Maybe it sat in someone's car," Vasquez answered. "What I *do* know is that you're going to Miami Sunday. See what *you* think about the source. Much depends on your take."

Laura listened carefully.

"In Miami," he instructed, "have Charley Boy tell you the same story. Don't take notes, don't make recordings. Carry a weapon, but no Secret Service ID."

Hamilton reached into a briefcase. "We've already fixed you up," he said.

Out came a Virginia driver's license, a law enforcement pistol permit from the Virginia State Police, plus a federal permit to carry state-to-state. All bore Laura Chapman's picture; the Virginia permit also had a memory chip for a laser eye scan. The federal permit excluded Laura from airline security and would get her past pesky state weapons laws if a problem arose.

So now Laura Chapman was also Linda Cochrane, a detective with the Virginia State Police. The documents had her height just right but had trimmed five pounds off her actual weight. Not a bad thing.

The bogus IDs were top-notch CIA stuff, Laura recognized, and she was pleased to be reassured that they were practicing at least one of their black arts—forgery—with a laudable degree of finesse.

"And if anyone checks these?" Laura asked.

Hamilton answered. "You're in the Virginia computers as of this morning. Same as the rest of the IDs we'll give you. Everything will triple check."

Laura nodded. Linda Cochrane was now on the ledgers of the Virginia State Police as well as the DMV. Laura's picture had been filched from the Secret Service file and spruced up a trifle. Even someone within the FBI or the Secret Service would not be able to nail her new ID as a phony. Her new documents were issued on the exact forms used by the state of Virginia.

Laura examined the identification. She memorized her new DOB: 12/24/1976. Only the year had changed. She memorized her new home address.

"Nice job," Laura said. "And it's nice to be thirty-two again instead of thirty-five." She fingered the license carefully and with admiration. "Excellent product."

"I did it myself," Hamilton said, appreciative of the compliment. "Nice to be hands-on every once in a while. Like your photo?"

"Very much."

To Laura's uncompromising eye, the only tiny fault with the false IDs was that they looked too fresh. She made a mental note to scuff them. Rubbing diluted coffee on them would give them the necessary patina of age. She marveled how the CIA could miss the obvious.

"This will get you and your weapon on and off the plane in Washington and Miami," Hamilton continued. "Don't use your Secret Service weapon. You have a back-up piece?"

"I have a Colt thirty-eight. Stashed somewhere, as you so delicately put it."

The director gave her a grudging grimace. "Ever fired it?"

"Every morning out the window. It keeps squirrels out of the bird feeder," Laura said.

"Thought so," Vasquez said. "I like an agent with a sense of humor."

"Who's joking?" she asked.

"I have your plane tickets here, too, Laura," Hamilton said, "plus a work address for Charley Boy in South Beach. It's a private establishment. Your contact is a man named Robin. Robin is the gatekeeper where Charley Boy works. Big man. One of our local people. He'll also cover your back while you're there."

Laura nodded.

"How's your Spanish?" Vasquez asked.

"Good enough to get myself in trouble."

"She's fluent," said Hamilton. "French, too, if you want to know."

Intrigued, Vasquez turned directly toward Laura.

"Et où avez-vous appris votre français?" Vasquez asked.

Laura answered without missing a beat. *"Je l'ai étudié quatre ans au lycée, et un an à l'université, et après ça j'ai travaillé à Paris, tout en faisant un cours à l'Alliance Française le soir, juste après le boulot."*

"Où avez-vous travaillé à Paris?"

"Dans une boutique de vêtements pour femme, comme vendeuse. C'était Boulevard Raspail. Ce qui était très commode, parce que l'Alliance Française était à trois cent mètres."

Vasquez said in Spanish, *"Usted habla muy bien. ¿Y su español? ¿Lidiaba usted toros?"*

It was Laura's turn to smile. *"Eso no,"* she answered smoothly. *"En lo que se refiere al español, soy autodidacta, pero también estuve varios meses en Honduras, trabajando en la misión de USAID."*

Vasquez turned back to Hamilton. "I didn't know we hired people like this," he said with an edge and without a smile.

"Normally we don't," Hamilton answered.

Vasquez folded his arms and turned back to the attractive woman in front of him.

"Interesting. So you've had a lot of experience outside the country?" he pressed. "Exposure to foreign people and ideas? Influences that most of the people in our Service wouldn't have seen very much."

"You could say that," she answered. "And if you did, it would be accurate."

"There are those in this government who wouldn't care much for that sort of thing."

"I can't change what I've done with my life," Laura said. "It is what it is."

"In the future, some things have to change around here," the director said.

How he meant that wasn't clear. A strange stillness gripped the room before the director narrowed his eyes, looked back to Laura, and broke the silence.

chapter 11

"Our man Robin does not react well to deviations from plans," Vasquez said. "So be careful. Call on Charley Boy to inquire about a real estate matter. Between ten and twelve tomorrow night. Your name at the door is Mrs. Cochrane. Robin will try to blow you off," he explained. "Be insistent. That's part of the safety signal. And don't bring a weapon into the place. There's a frisk at the door and metal detectors on the stairs."

"No weapon?" She didn't like that part.

"Not in 'the establishment.' "

Laura spent a moment assimilating. Hamilton pulled a small package from his pocket. He unwrapped it. Two items.

The first was an extra cell phone. Four ounces, metallic blue. Secure line, latest thing. Assembled in America from parts manufactured in Sri Lanka. It was a near-perfect counterfeit of the popular Nokia Generation 21.

"I have a phone," Laura said.

"Now you have another, but only for a day. This one's for your contact in Miami. Charley Boy is to keep this for communication."

Laura nodded.

"A CIA job?" Laura said, turning the handsome little phone over in her hands.

"Correct. It's loaded."

"Nice."

The bells and whistles included a directional signal beam that was always on. The phone's location could be located via satellite to within fifty feet. Similarly, every message on it would be recorded and accessible only to operatives involved in this operation.

"There's a Mr. Charles Yee in Electronic Support in Langley," Hamilton said. "Telecommunications. Brilliant man. MIT. Any question on the phone and its functions, talk to him."

Hamilton gave her Yee's phone number. She entered it in her cell. Yee was her only Y.

"Don't take your own PID, either," Hamilton said. "Too identifiable. We have a fresh one made up to match your new IDs. Mr. Yee again was the presiding genius."

The PID—personal information device—was a handheld descendant of the old iPod and other first generation PDAs. The new one they handed Laura was an IBM knockoff, another example of CIA tax dollars at work.

She turned and put it away. Vasquez picked up the conversation again.

Langley saw Charley Boy as an ongoing asset, he continued, so force was not to be used and the asset's identity was not to be compromised. Charley Boy had already been taken care of with cash: low-range of five figures. There was going to be yet another payday for the source if things panned out all the way, and this payday, it was said, would scrape the lower range of six figures, plus a new passport. So there was no reason to think the source would get a case of situational laryngitis.

"Being a snitch is a highly lucrative profession," Hamilton interjected, "as long as some sorehead doesn't put a tire around you, soak you in gasoline, and flip you a match."

"Point taken," said Laura.

Vasquez gave Laura the details of her flight to Miami. She was to put all current business on hold and would be listed on emergency personal leave. A trumped-up family problem. No one within the Secret Service was to know exactly where she had gone or for how long.

"I'll have an office for you when you return. Plus an assistant named Vanessa. You'll need to at least file a report and do minimal follow-up. If you do major follow-up you'll need the same office."

Laura held Vasquez in her gaze for a few seconds. Then, "Questions?" Vasquez asked.

"One, in general: You theorize that there may be an assassin within the Secret Service. And you want a female agent to investigate because the suspect is male."

"Correct," the director answered.

"There are many other women in the Service, including several who work at the White House. I'll do what I can. But why me?"

Silence. Then Vasquez spoke.

"It's highly unscientific," he said, "but you have this reputation. You sometimes see things the rest of us don't."

"Okay. I'm flattered," she said. "I think."

The events of the most recent five days coalesced and painted a picture. The surveillance. They had put it on her to vet her, to prime her for this job. The dates of the surveillance matched the dates of the first reports out of Miami.

"That clumsy surveillance that's been on me? Your people, huh?"

Vasquez sat quietly and did not answer. A non-denial denial.

A leaden silence filled the room. "Never mind," Laura said.

"On the vetting of government employees, do you have access to the Ralph Edwards Room?" Hamilton asked.

"I do."

"Do some heavy vetting tomorrow before traveling on Sunday."

The Ralph Edwards Room housed the files containing the background vetting—surreptitious and official—of every Secret Service employee who had ever drawn breath.

Vasquez stood. "You know Sam Deal in Miami, right?" he asked.

"Worked with him once three years ago," Laura said. A surge of distaste rumbled through her. "Medium-time source, big time lecher."

"Treasury assignment?" Hamilton asked, staying with the original point.

"It involved some kind of back channel currency transaction in Panama. Not sure what we were buying that day or for whom."

"Sam's people are very good at that," Vasquez said.

"But not flawless," she said. "Plus, Sam's a snake."

"Call on Sam personally when you're in Miami. He has contacts everywhere. You can't tell him exactly what you're looking for, obviously, but Sam's our best single source in Miami."

Laura dreaded the meeting already.

"Uh huh," she said. Sam had never seen a skirt he wouldn't chase.

"We'll also need Sam to establish some twenty-four/seven security around the source. Tricky stuff here because the source doesn't want the security."

"I understand," Laura answered. "Who else? I hope it gets a little classier."

"It does. Richard McCarron. He's your Agency contact in Miami as well as the 'control' for Charley Boy. After you've seen Sam, McCarron will find you."

McCarron was a new name to Laura. Up until that evening she had never heard of him. And she thought by now she knew all the important names.

"Where will he find me?"

"The hotel bar the first full morning you're there. That would be Monday. Ten A.M. We'll set a reservation for you at the Park Central in Miami."

"I've been there before. I know the place. That's fine."

Hamilton held her steadily in his gaze for several seconds. Laura had the impression that Hamilton was proposing to add to what he had already offered.

"What?" Laura asked.

"When I was a kid, my dad was an AP bureau chief in Dallas," Hamilton said. "He was there November twenty-two of 'sixty-three." A small silence, then, "He told me that at the end of the day in Dallas a lot of folks flew rebel flags upright even while the state flag was flying low. Some of the rednecks were even bragging that 'Martin Lucifer Coon' would be next."

From the periphery of her view, Laura caught a nuance to Vasquez's expression. The director of the Secret Service shared Hamilton's concern, only more so. It was not a look that lifted her spirits, but it was one that she took with her.

"And your point is?" she asked.

Vasquez seemed to be studying her.

"This is a great idealistic nation that once gave ten million votes to George Wallace for president. There have always been some sick undercurrents in American society," he said. "And some of them change with each generation."

"I know," she said.

"I know you know," he answered. "But I thought the reminder was worth the time. Be very careful." He paused. "That's another way of saying, 'Don't get killed.'"

"I'll try not to," she answered. "But plant me in Arlington if I do."

"Not funny, Laura," Mitch said. "Not funny at all."

Two minutes later, Laura was the first to leave the room, alone.

chapter 12

WASHINGTON, D.C.
JUNE 19, 2009; 9:22 P.M.

Laura kept to her Friday evening schedule. She left the Capitol Building and on her way home stopped at the gym on Eighteenth and M streets used by most agents. She changed into snug navy shorts and a white polo shirt with a small U.S. Secret Service coat of arms on the left breast. From a gym bag, she pulled a pair of fresh white socks and a two-month-old pair of sneakers. From her locker, she also took a pair of light boxing gloves.

She warmed up with stretching exercises in the main gym. She then went to the second floor and worked fifteen minutes on the light punching bag and worked up a solid sweat. When she was pleased with her quickness and the impact of her punches, she eased off and grabbed a towel from a nearby stack.

She nodded to the man who took her place at the bag. He had been watching her. He, too, was in the Service, but not stationed at the White House.

She sat down in an adjoining area and toweled off. Across from her was a full-length mirror. Laura's gaze settled upon herself.

The woman who looked back at her, she admitted, was a woman in transition, physically and emotionally. Laura was alone at this moment, so she cast the towel aside for a moment, stood, and assessed herself.

Her shoulders were square, her breasts firm, her legs strong and nicely toned. Her figure remained sharp, but she also knew that workouts got the blood flowing and everyone looked better after some exercise. But in her face, she could see a few faint lines as well as the worry, tension, and concern brought about by her responsibilities, even if no one else could see them. What was it a friend in college had once said?

Age creeps in on little crows' feet.

She went back to her locker, switched into running shoes, and went out the door of the gym. Heat and humidity be damned. She ran up Pennsylvania Avenue and back down Connecticut, a route she had measured out by car as three miles exactly. Thirty-three minutes. She was not happy with the time. She was slipping. She used to be able to do it in under thirty. Hell, when she was in college, running varsity track, she could do three miles in twenty-two minutes and leave some pretty fair male runners in the dust.

She toweled off but did not shower.

She grabbed her gym bag from her locker and walked next door to the firing range.

She checked in with her Secret Service ID, cooled down further, and waited for her turn on the range. Ten minutes later, she donned a pair of safety lenses and took her place on a firing line.

The targets were those of assailants at twenty-five yards, bull's-eye-style circles over the hearts of would-be human targets. She fired seven rounds quickly.

She brought the target forward.

Terrible.

Four shots completely off the mark. One on the fringe of the circles, two nearby. The volley would have inflicted injury in a real life situation, but in real life, a typical shootout was three shots in a closed room, all from within fifteen feet. To miss with a first shot was to send death an engraved invitation.

From down the corridor, more firing. Nine millimeters. Forty-fives. Twenty-twos. Funny what a keen ear she had after all these years. She could tell a caliber by hearing it.

From somewhere in the past came a bit of Secret Service mythology: Women would shoot better if they laid their index finger aside the barrel and squeezed the trigger with the number two finger.

She tried it, just to loosen up. It felt ridiculous. It was another piece of department BS.

She went back to a regular grip.

She repeated on the range for another quarter hour. Her skills were just *off*. She felt disgusted. God forbid she would have to pull a trigger for real anytime soon.

Dunno, she said to herself as she was leaving. *Maybe at the end of this year I should take the hint and get out of this business, anyway. After a while, one can't get out, and I'm stuck here for the rest of my life. Is that what I want?*

Speaking of wanting, what was the vibe she had detected from Director Vasquez?

Damned if there weren't a whole plethora of questions unanswered. The karma she received from Vasquez was strange.

She walked to her car, feeling the busy bustle of a Friday night all around her, one of which she was not a part. Most people were done with work for the week.

She knew hers was just beginning.

chapter 13

As she drove home, Laura's thoughts drifted.

She might not necessarily have described herself as an old-fashioned flag-waver but she knew others would have described her so. And she would not have objected. After all, the sight of Washington at night sometimes still gave her a corny thrill.

Sure, she knew the faults of Washington.

The bureaucracies, the corruption, the lobbyists, the scheming senators, the halfwit congressmen who would trade a vote for sex in the office, the mistresses, the drunken unfaithful wives, and the presidents who were barely qualified for the job of commander in chief.

But she also was proud of the America whose technology soared to the moon in peace for all mankind. She loved the America where personal freedoms were both an ideal and a reality.

She loved the America that had rebuilt Europe and Asia after World War II, and the America that had stood up to Communism and kept half the world free in the process. What other nation in the history of the world could have— *would* have—done all that?

Frankly, she was still a woman who got a thrill when she saw the spotlight on the flag at night, who felt goose bumps when she watched Olympic athletes receive a gold medal for their country and heard "The Star Spangled Banner" played as the flag was raised.

She sighed. Those principles of patriotism were so simple and unwavering. The task before her was more complicated, just as the reality of America—and the times when the nation compromised its ideals—was so much more complicated.

Her thoughts shifted as she drove across the brightly lit Key Bridge into Virginia.

They moved onward to Miami. To Sam Deal. Laura had only dealt with Sam once before, but any episode with Sam was memorable. If she had to make a list of the ten most disreputable people she had ever met in her life, Sam would have been near the top.

Sam was the presumed head of an unofficial posse known as the Nightingales who worked out of Miami. The Nightingales' official name was Southern Security. They were a dozen men—give or take—focused on ventures mostly in Latin America. Guys with Spanish names and bad haircuts. They smoked too much, drank too much, and whored too much, for Laura's tastes. But they had their uses.

Sam's Nightingales also handled the domestic hit-and-run jobs that were too dirty for the CIA to touch directly. In his time, Deal had been one of the CIA's best "black bag" guys ever, elevating the domestic break-in to an art form. Sam's small flock was so successful in Central America that—if anyone had known what the *Ruiseñores* looked like—several small hot right-wing countries should have put them on their postage stamps.

Well, no matter. She did not have to take a shower with Sam; much as Sam might have liked that. She would just need his cooperation. She had dealt with worse in her career and used all the tricks in her arsenal to convince some pretty sleazy men to do things the way she wanted. Most likely, she would deal with worse again.

She flicked her car radio off and connected her PID to the car's sound system. She felt like some classic rock and, glancing down, found Queen's *Greatest Hits.*

Perfect. She fussed with the tracks.

Laura had a strange sense of herself sometimes; here she was in about as straight-arrow a job as a woman could have and she would shut the car windows and pump the music of her early teens. U2 and Queen. Well, a woman deserved a few guilty pleasures, did she not? And that Bono knew a thing or two about life and so did the late Freddie Mercury.

Radio Ga Ga.

Everything I'd need to know; I learned it on the radio. Right, Freddie?

Instinctively, she scanned her rearview mirror, sweeping her line of vision across the road behind her. She was surprised to conclude that she had no followers this evening.

Or did she?

A strange notion came upon her, followed by something almost audible above the music, something faintly resembling a ghostly whispering in her ear.

Wise words from somewhere:

Just when you finally would have appreciated the surveillance, you are alone.

She answered aloud. "What?" She took her eyes off the road.

Then it happened! A truck that had been many yards behind her to her right abruptly switched lanes. It moved directly in back of her, almost as if it were trying to rear-end her.

She gave herself some gas, feeling the car surge. But then in front of her, a D.C. cab swerved into her lane. It made loud contact with a passenger sedan.

"Hell! No!" she would later remember yelling.

She slammed on her brakes, foot to the floor!

The truck behind her flashed its lights and blasted twin air horns. It came up on her rear and she cringed, expecting impact. The lights from behind were blinding her and the cars before her tried to weave to a wobbly stop.

Freddie Mercury did not miss a note, and neither did Roger Taylor, the stickman. Laura jerked her wheel to the left and then she was at an angle, nearly a right angle, on the highway. She cranked the wheel back to her right and pulled out of a skid. More lights than she could account for were in her eyes. There was another sound of metal ripping into metal on the bridge and—

God above! Holy Jesus!

—she thought she saw the figure of a man in the back seat of her own car!

Right behind her!

It was just a flash of an image, but it was familiar and the man was smiling and he had a head much like a skull and he was opening his mouth to speak and—

She swerved again and avoided the two impacting vehicles in front of her. She kept her eyes on the road and pulled straight away from the collision, and from what she could see in the rearview mirror, there was two-car contact with the truck, too.

All this, within about five seconds!

Even above the music, sounds of metal impacting hard and—

Her heart was pounding, her palms were soaked. Her pulse raced so fast that she could feel the throbbing vein in her neck. She looked expectantly to the back seat of her own car and—

Empty. No one.

"Yeah. Right," she said to herself, her heart kicking.

She kept scanning the rearview mirror. No one had stopped.

What the hell?

She had seen impact, hadn't she? She had heard it.

Hadn't she?

Her hands were soaked. So was her blouse. Her heart refused to stop pounding.

Nothing behind her. And where had that image of a man in her car come from? What strange permutations of light and shadow had made her think she had seen someone?

She cranked the music. With difficulty, she gathered herself. She exited the Key Bridge into Virginia and drove past a sign that led the way to the cemetery at Arlington.

Was there, or was there not, an accident?

She shook her head. She didn't know.

She arrived home twenty minutes later. She poured herself a generous gin and tonic to go with dinner. Then she skipped half of dinner and doubled the gin and tonic.

Gin as a health food. *Well, why not?* It helped.

She settled down further. She gathered herself emotionally.

She convinced herself that this day had really happened, surreal elements and all, and that on Sunday she would go to Florida.

Toward midnight, another idea was upon her. It was a feeling again, something in the gut. She turned off all her lights and went to her living room window. She drew back the blinds.

"Damn!"

Sure enough, the space occupied by the telephone truck the previous night was now occupied by a cable TV van, one that hadn't been there when she had arrived home half an hour earlier. She knew for sure because she had made a point of checking the spot as she drove past.

She let the blinds slide back into place and stepped away from the window.

She wasn't just under surveillance, she told herself, she was under a microscope. She looked around her dark living room. Sometimes this room bothered her, too, sometimes she picked up strange vibrations in it, a funny karma, that almost told her that there was a presence there, a spirit, an entity, which she could not see but which was maybe conscious of her.

She had mentioned this to Dr. Feldman, who had helped her dismiss the possibility. Well, she told herself, the time was fast approaching when she might need the doctor's help again.

She sat in the living room, finishing her drink, her weapon not far away.

"Damn it!" she muttered aloud to herself. "*Why* are they doing this to me?"

What in hell is going on?

There was no immediate answer other than the silence of four walls, which she distantly thought she could hear laughing.

chapter 14

Laura turned uneasily in her bed, shot up to a sitting position, then settled back down. She could not throw off the dream.

The dream about the man in the water.

She is at a familiar beach. The waves pound like heavy machinery. The sun burns down. She watches a man in the water go repeatedly under the surf and there is nothing she can do.

"Call the lifeguard," someone shouts. "Call the lifeguard!"

In the dream, she turns to the someone. "I am the lifeguard," she says.

She turns toward the water. The man in the waves is a corpse, floating white and fetid, pointing at her, hollowed-out skull for eyes, skin disintegrating in the salt and foam. From a vantage point above, she sees herself, young and very fit in an orange bathing suit. Then her body wilts; she has the body of a crone, she's sagging everywhere and she's naked for the world to see.

She turned and thrashed, throwing sheets off her. Her eyes came open.

The bedroom was dark and still. Nothing to fear. Only a dream.

Oh?

Strange shadows took shape. There *was* a man in the room. He was near the door, facing her. Laura lay motionless and watched for several minutes. She could see the form, the arms.

No surprise after what had been going down recently.

Now the surveillance—the intruder—was right there in the room with her.

Her hand edged to the night table. Her Sig Sauer was under some clothing, loaded and ready. *Seven rounds in the weapon, pump off three, save four. Who knows who's in the room?*

Her hand went slowly to it. She found it.

Wet palm against cool steel grip. The profile of the intruder did not move.

Or did it? Just a little.

Then slowly, from somewhere unknown, reality unfurled.

The image of the man before her peeled away. Her eyes adjusted to the dim light.

She focused on the shirt she had left on the chair near the door.

The sleeves, the trunk . . .

She had almost shot her best blouse and her favorite swivel chair.

Laura sat up and drew a breath. She turned on the light.

God! she demanded of herself. *How crazy am I sometimes?*

She glanced at the clock. Four fifty-one A.M.

A hell of an awful time for that same old nightmare to recur. It came back maybe three times a month. Same damned dream all the time.

Same dead guy in the surf, often followed by some hallucination at home.

Unsettled business with the past?

Exactly. Twenty years ago when Laura had had a summer job as a lifeguard at the National Seashore a man had died on her shift.

Race Point. Provincetown, Massachusetts.

Not on my shift. Oh, dear God, do not let a catastrophe happen on my shift.

Never mind "Honor and Duty." The Secret Service motto should be "Not on my shift!"

A local man named Walter McKiernan, a veteran swimmer, fifty-six, had been swimming a hundred yards out. McKiernan had had a heart attack in the water and drowned. It had not been Laura's fault, it hadn't even been within the area she was supposed to be watching. But she had spotted the body, brought the man in, fiercely tried mouth-to-mouth, hooked up the electric shock system with the paramedics, and begged the man to come back to life.

But McKiernan was already dead.

She had heard the mutterings:

"What do you expect? The girl was probably daydreaming."

Never mind that she was the fastest swimmer among the guards, or that she was most adept at CPR, or that McKiernan had a blood-alcohol level of .11 percent. The locals explained the tragedy in terms of what happened when a "girl" was assigned to a man's job.

Well, screw them. It's not fair and it's not true.

Worse, the tragedy on the beach had incubated a deadly psychological cancer within her. It had been her first serious confrontation with suicidal depression.

The black dog, as she called it, having long ago borrowed the term used by fellow sufferer Winston Churchill.

A beast that pursued her psychologically.

There were times when Laura suffered several such downward mood swings, until she felt that a dark beast was after her.

The black dog.

Whenever the dog came around, he pushed her downward into a sense of worthlessness. Mentally, she would beat herself up, relentlessly criticizing herself for being in her mid-thirties, unmarried, with a pair of failed long-term relationships behind her and nothing to show for it but a job toward which she was militantly ambivalent.

The specter of thirty-five, with her career in the Service perhaps winding down, made the dog even more ferocious.

Sudden death never seemed farther away than a sudden unexpected knock on the door.

Her down moods never lasted that long. But her great fear was that the dog would drag her into suicidal despondency before she could pull herself out.

Somehow, somewhere, the killer beast always seemed to be loitering. This was the animal that had driven her to see the Service shrink two years earlier. Dr. Feldman had helped her dispel the most terrifying thoughts, including suicidal fantasies—not plans, to be sure, but unmistakable fantasies about place and means.

Mr. Black Dog meet Herr Sig Sauer.

Arf!

Bang!

Laura rose from bed, her weapon in her hand. She wore a deep red Georgetown T-shirt and guys' blue boxers, a leftover from her last relationship, which was now many months in the past. She wondered whether her incipient craziness had driven her last man away.

Probably.

She checked the window again and this time did a double take.

The surveillance van—*yes, of course that's what that is!*—was nowhere to be seen. The streets were empty, aside from neighbors' cars that she recognized.

She went back to bed.

She pulled her sheet and single blanket back to her, struggled to reenter the land of sleep, and was not entirely successful.

There was just too damned much going on in her head.

Her head rolled to her right, and in the darkness, she eyed her weapon again and she sensed the black dog not very far away. In the middle of the night, she could hear him barking and smell his foul breath.

She moved her hand again, but not quite far enough to grip the gun.

chapter 15

Major Gerald Straighthorn of the United States Air Force had long ago mastered the science of keeping his eyes simultaneously upon the horizon between sea and sky *and* upon his altimeter.

Today, he piloted his usual kick-ass ride-in-the-sky, an F-115 Warhawk, one of the wilier fighting aircraft that the United States had put in the heavens. The fastest ever in its class, up-teched in 2007 in speed and performance, and tarted up with the newest anti-radar technology. Yet today, the only things that Gerry Straighthorn and the co-pilot seated behind him, Captain Jack Kendall, were fighting were monotony and boredom.

The aircraft roared low ninety miles north of Tripoli.

Elevation a thousand feet, scaring the living bejesus out of any commercial craft below it, not to mention the private yachts: funny foreign flags on their sterns, with rich fat guys on deck getting cozy with naked women.

There was not much in the Gulf of Sidra these days. The waters off Libya had been trouble for thirty years. Most maritime activity stayed clear. The few yachts were floating whorehouses: wealthy Arabs taking time out from fundamentalist Islamic beliefs to get their rocks off with their hired Russian and Serb blondes.

Straighthorn liked to think that if he swooshed low enough, he could show the wealthy towel-heads some big American balls. Plus he'd do them a backhanded favor by blowing all those temporarily discarded bikini tops and bottoms right off the aft decks. It was not like they were going to file a complaint.

Land speed of the aircraft: nine hundred miles an hour. The Warhawks were snappy little bastards. They could race south-southeast from Tripoli to Benghazi in twenty-nine minutes if they clotheslined it, or thirty when they were screwing around, alternately dipping and rising to befuddle and out-tech the dumb-assed Libyan radar.

· This Warhawk was doing Lone Ranger reconnaissance.

Flying solo.

Its flight logistics were at the discretion of Major Straighthorn. Straighthorn had been in the Mediterranean for ten months and took a cynical pleasure out of making imbeciles of the Libyans, a task that he never found to be much of a challenge.

He liked to come up high enough to see that their radar had picked him up. Then he liked to drop down all the way to three hundred feet sometimes. Then he would cut sharply aft, roll the plane back twenty miles in the direction it had just come, reverse directions again and let out his throttles, tying an imaginary knot in the sky and pushing the air speed up to the big Mach 2.

Eventually, he would reverse yet again, and maybe one final time for good measure, popping into and out of Libyan radar, all the while emitting gamma beams that put traditional radar through a virtual food processor.

Straighthorn had reinvented the game that he was now playing.

He had done it so many times and had created such confusion that Omar Mesdoua's air defense command still did not know—when Straighthorn flew by—whether there was one American jet or thirty-two. Straighthorn dreamed of the day when his commanders would give him a big fat black Stealth II for just a few hours and he could fly through Mesdoua's backyard and spit in the chicken-assed strongman's eye.

But today Straighthorn was stuck with the game that he had already perfected. "Tying the Warhawk's tail," he called it: a maneuver of 95 percent brilliance and simplicity and another nickel's worth of sheer lunacy.

Back east in the Pentagon they did not know he was doing it. But USAF Command in Sardinia did and were having a laugh.

"Pulling Mesdoua's pork," they called it. And there was nothing the flyboys at Club Med liked more than to pull an Islamic strongman's pork.

Straighthorn had also sensed something that command back in Sardinia did not know. Over the last few weeks Mesdoua's camel jockeys had installed a new radar commander at the midpoint of their desert air defenses. This new little bastard was a coy little fox.

In reaction to Straighthorn, the new twerp switched the radar on and off. He played a jittery counter game with Straighthorn, hoping to lure him into flying too high or ducking too low, as he tried to deduce just how the USAF was playing their game.

As Gerry Straighthorn flew, as he rolled and reversed his plane and cut backwards and up and down, the major wondered what country had trained the little creep.

He wondered if he was a Russian. Or maybe from one of the former Soviet republics. Those poor aging toothless alcoholic bastards were all over the place these days.

Suspiciously, this guy in the Libyan desert had more intellect than Straighthorn had seen from any of the Libyan pilots. And yet the new guy was also missing the obvious. He was creating grievous gaps in his own radar by shutting down all of his country's air defenses for even five minutes.

If Straighthorn went through his aerial contortions, for example, lured the little bugger in the radar command post to shut down his transmitter, then flew close enough to the coastline, then caught the radar bastard in a blackout, Straighthorn could turn his aircraft due south without being detected. If he stayed at five hundred feet, he could be on top of Tripoli before any of them knew he was coming. Straighthorn would just have to watch for AAC guns when he got there.

Yet all this was IS, as the pilots called it.

Idle speculation.

Or idiotic shit.

Idle spec: Something that cropped up on an uneventful recon mission, when one should have been eagle-eyeing the controls or the horizon.

Then there was also the IC from captain to co-pilot.

Idle chatter.

"Hey, Jack. What's the difference between Mesdoua's air force and a flock of ducks?"

This one was for the boys back at the desks in Sardinia too, who monitored everything. And maybe for the adversary down in Tripoli, if they could translate fast enough.

"Dunno, Major. Tell me, and all of Europe and North Africa will know."

"A flock of ducks knows how to fly," Straighthorn said.

The two aviators laughed. What made it funnier was that it drew a response from the command colonel in Sardinia.

"Come on, you bastards, pay attention!" Colonel Ferris Small growled into the radio.

"How 'bout if I put my head under the radar again, Colonel, and take it to Benghazi? I could drop off Tampax for Mesdoua's daughters before the Libyans even get their sirens going."

In the rear seat, Jack Kendall was splitting up.

Colonel Small again: "Tail Tyer One, if it's not exciting enough, fly unarmed next time!"

"Yes, sir," Major Straighthorn answered.

"Yes, sir," Captain Kendall echoed.

Both men smirked. Not exciting enough?

That was part of the problem.

The United States Air Force had been flying this exercise three times a day without an incident since 1999, even back in the first years of the new century when Qaddafi was trying to kiss and make up with the West. That's why the Defense Department—congressional budgets again—had reduced this to a Lone Ranger run. Up until four years ago, there had always been two aircraft, in case someone's blind side had to be covered. No longer. No Tonto craft.

The new president, however, was sympathetic and was

about to restore back-up flights. Meanwhile, they could buzz closer to Libya and they had greater latitude to react.

A thousand feet above the water, Gerry Straighthorn moved his hand from the Warhawk's steering control bar to give a thumbs-up to Kendall. Then he flipped an upraised middle finger toward Libya. Again, Kendall suppressed laughter. As an entertainer among air aces, Gerry Straighthorn had no peer.

The major hunkered back to business. He tied the fourth knot in the sky for the day, over the course of one hundred thirty miles. The sky was azure blue and so was the water. Twenty-two minutes later, the F-115 was a hundred miles north-northeast of Benghazi.

Today's ride, another cream puff.

It was 10:58:23 A.M. local time, 9:58:23 GMT.

Straighthorn pulled his Warhawk into a steep ascent and turned northwest toward Crete, which he could see three hundred miles to his port side.

"We going back home to the Sardine Can?" Captain Kendall asked.

"Jesus, Jack," Straighthorn answered. "Scared me! Didn't know you were still awake."

"I better be. I know you're not watching where you're going."

"As they say in Quaker, screw thyself, Captain Jack," said Straighthorn.

The "Sardine Can" was Mediterranean flyboy for Sardinia. There were nasty air currents south of the big island that swept through from Africa to the Tyrrhenian Sea east of Italy—hot air from the Algerian Sahara thundering across the Atlas Mountains in Africa and then colliding with cold air sweeping from the Alps and the Juras in Europe. ˑ

Air pockets. Big ones.

Bang, bang, bang if an aviator hit one just right with a Warhawk. Bring a fighter through at low altitudes and a crew might just as well be dragging a surfboard on a dirt highway in Texas.

More airjock-speak back and forth, much of it for the ears

back in Sardinia. Straighthorn perused the horizons and his instrument panel as he jibed.

Kendall kept his eyes on the Libyan coast.

"Hey, I give you a smoother, better ride than any of those Italian girls I seen you dating, Captain Jack," Straighthorn answered. "Don't you forget it."

"Get us home in an hour and Captain Jack will get you high tonight," Kendall promised.

"Whoa! Sounds like a plan. Let's blow out of here."

The Warhawk ascended rapidly, Superman style, as if it might have been flying up the side of an imaginary skyscraper. The pilots saw nothing other than blue directly above them as they shot up into it, ready to roll, bank a final time, and return.

Then, "Gerry?" Captain Kendall said. "Shit! What the hell's this?"

"What's what?"

Simultaneously to Straighthorn's question, the Warhawk's alarm system went berserk and the radar howled.

chapter 16

ABOVE THE GULF OF SIDRA
JUNE 20, 2009; 10:01 A.M.

Something nasty and unexpected was coming out of nowhere. The pilot read concern in his co-pilot's voice. "What have you got?" he snapped.

Their aircraft had already turned toward Europe.

"Bogey at ten o'clock!" Kendall said.

"What the . . . ?" Straighthorn answered. He leveled off. Then, *"Can't be! Holy Jesus!"*

Straighthorn's eyes fastened to his radar screen. Far off to the northeast of him, commercial aircraft, mostly out of

Israel, Greece, or Egypt. Yet now inexplicably from the south: a rude little blip moving directly toward him, behaving like a fighter.

"Son of a bitch! We got company," the major said.

"His radar's locked on us!" Captain Kendall said. "Hey! Libyan radar fully back up, too! Jesus Christ, Gerry! What are they doing?"

"Holy crap!" said Straighthorn. His eyes danced from his HUD to the horizon to the distant speck that was the enemy. "Son of a bitch!" he said again.

The F-115 dipped its port wing and slid into a split-S, dropping from five thousand feet to eight hundred within seven seconds. The two aviators felt as if they had left their livers behind. On the radar screen, the blip kept coming, though now the second aircraft knew that the American plane had spotted it. It was already into evasive—but possibly attack—positioning.

"What's going on out there?" the radio crackled. Colonel Small again, much more serious.

"Contact and potential engagement," Straighthorn answered.

"Got a marking?" Sardinia asked.

"Still fifty knots away," Straighthorn said.

"Gerry! He's moving at five hundred knots!" Kendall said. "Dead at us! Altitude four thousand feet and descending." A pause and, "Missile site orientation locked on us!"

"Jesus Christ!" Straighthorn snapped. "He wants to fight!"

The blip on the screen was behaving like one of those irritating old Soviet S-22s, but it was now maneuvering into an overt attack position. What the hell was all this about?

"Preparing to evade and engage!" Straighthorn said.

"Tail Tyer, please repeat!" the radio barked.

"Preparing to evade and engage!" Straighthorn snapped back.

"Roger! Proceed!" Colonel Small shot back.

Kendall sent a wall of jamming back to the S-22.

"Permission to fire granted!" Colonel Small shouted. "Take out the bastard!"

"Roger, *sir!*"

Kendall again. "He's launching! One! *Two* valid missiles! Jesus Christ, Gerry!"

Air-to-airs! The S-22 had fired one high and one low. He had led the American aircraft with both projectiles, presumably in the hope that the Americans would pull right into one or the other in an evasive tactic, or remain frozen in a centered position to get knocked out by a third.

Already, Straighthorn had factored that into his equation. Libyan attack pilots could be pesky and aggressive, but— *thank Christ,* he thought to himself—they were also erratic and poorly trained. Since the mid-1990s most of them had been Syrian mercenaries.

Straighthorn had six seconds to save his aircraft.

He ducked to a low altitude and was practically surfing, no more than two hundred feet above the waves. He lurked at five hundred miles an hour for fifteen seconds and watched on his radar screen. The two air-to-air missiles went cuckoo, homed on each other, and sailed in tandem a thousand feet over his head, as if connected by a wire.

It was a beautiful sight.

Straighthorn knew his enemy. Third World pilots loved to bushwhack and run. Straighthorn turned his aircraft toward the coast of North Africa and saw that his assailant was already fleeing.

"Gutless asshole," he mumbled to himself.

"What have we got?" Sardinia demanded.

"Two air-to-airs. Evasion successful," Straighthorn reported. "Request permission to *pursue.*"

The new procedures from the new president.

No diplomatic horse crap. Take the gloves off.

They shoot at us, we make fish food out of them.

Time for fun!

"Granted, Tail Tyer One. What's your attacker?"

"Looks like an S-22."

Sardinia again: "What's your overtake/kill range?"

"Thirty miles. Seventy-five seconds."

Colonel Small, getting into the mood: "Kill him but stay away from the shore batteries."

"Roger, *sir!*"

It shaped up like a turkey shoot. A Warhawk could outrun, outdistance, and outduel a twenty-five-year-old Soviet fighter any day. The Libyan was driving the airborne equivalent of a patched-up '76 Yugo and the Americans had a zippy new '09 Corvette.

"Locked on," Straighthorn said to Kendall.

"Weapons ready!" Captain Kendall answered.

Jesus Christ, Straighthorn found himself thinking again. *This is one to remember.*

The ride had been smooth every day for months. Now he was within seconds of an embarrassingly easy kill.

Front pages of every newspaper in the world the next day.

Well, so be it.

He quickly gained two miles. The other pilot was not evading. He was racing him back to the terra firma of North Africa. *Hey, no contest,* Straighthorn thought. *Stupid, stupider, and most stupid!*

The Libyans must have reckoned that the Americans were under orders not to attack. And equally they must have thought that the USAF would not come close to the northern shore of Africa.

Wrong twice.

The other guy had fired first. A pilot mustn't engage if he's not ready to fight.

The S-22 was twenty miles in front of the Warhawk, making a beeline for the military airfield southwest of Benghazi. It was almost too cheap a shot for a veteran like Straighthorn.

But there it was. So he took it.

The Warhawk fired once, then a second time.

Radar from the desert was still on him, so after firing his own air-to-airs, Straighthorn ducked his craft back down low and threw on his gamma gun to rattle Libyan radar. The

towel-heads might scramble another few planes, and a numbers game was always a crap shoot. No point to let the enemy
know where he was.

He watched his missiles on his radar screen.

The first blip scored. His second missile caught some of
the S-22 fuselage as it broke up over the Gulf of Sidra. With
the naked eye, as his Warhawk banked low, he saw both
flashes of the kill.

A moment of sobriety.

A kill was a paradox: exhilarating, yet nothing joyous
about it.

The men they had blown to smithereens had been profes-
sionals, just as they were. Wives, children, parents, brothers,
and sisters would be left with holes in their lives.

The Americans stayed low for another dozen miles, then
throttled up again to just below Mach 1. No point wasting
time getting home. He wondered if the newspapers would
spell his name right the next morning.

Then his heart leaped. Anti-aircraft fire.

A tidal wave of old-fashioned flak filled the sky in every
direction.

Instantly he knew there was too much of it. He wouldn't
be able to fly through it. It was all over; above, below, port
side and starboard. It was coming out of nowhere and everywhere.

Several heavy hits of AA flak peppered his aircraft. His
Warhawk shook violently and spasmed.

"Gerry!" Kendall yelled.

Part of the tail rudder was gone. Then the tip of a wing.

"Yeah! I know! *I know!*"

The Warhawk could take severe punishment and still
spin home. But now the American aircraft veered wildly.
Straighthorn urged the aircraft to climb at seventy degrees.
It refused.

For a moment he leveled out at four thousand feet and
thought he was away from danger. And then all of a sudden, he
realized that he had flown straight into a trap. The Libyans—in

their warped logic—had traded aircraft one-for-one. They had *wanted* an incident. Their own pilot had been a pawn, as had been the clunky old S-22.

Straighthorn looked down into the sea. It took a few seconds but he found the battery that was aimed at him. He knew that the anti-aircraft defenses were somewhere under the water.

"Damn!" Straighthorn cursed. "They don't *have* those weapons!"

"Gerry!" Kendall shouted again. "Oh, Gerry! *Gerry!*"

Their aircraft was in a roll! There was another missile coming. Two of them. And they could not pull out!

A shattering impact from AA flak, followed instantly by the wailing of every alarm. In the space of a heartbeat, both men knew that their Warhawk was within thirty seconds of destruction. The missiles would finish them.

Another AA barrage battered them.

A brief scream came from behind Straighthorn's head.

"Jackie! You there?" Straighthorn howled.

No answer. The radio came alive from Sardinia.

"Sardine Can to Tail-Tyer One! *What's going on?*"

"Mayday!" Straighthorn shouted back above the sirens. "*We're hit!* We're going in!"

Already, he was thinking ahead of rescue parties. But he also realized that even if he survived the roll-yaw that now gripped the Warhawk, Mesdoua's people would have a two-hour head start picking him—or the pieces of him—out of the sea.

He read the radar on the lead missile. Fifteen seconds, maybe less.

"Let's go, Jackie!" Straighthorn yelled.

No response.

Straighthorn turned slightly, as far as he could.

Twelve seconds . . . eleven . . .

Straighthorn yanked the controls that would eject both of them. His last vision within the doomed plane was the neck of the man who had flown all these missions with him.

A chunk of metal had slashed below Jack's helmet and sideways through his throat. The co-pilot's head, half torn off, hung backwards. The front of his suit was flooded with blood.

"Oh, Jackie, no!" Straighthorn yelled.

Captain Jack would not be answering.

Then his scream took on the eeriest quality of all. His seat ejected high up into the once-friendly now-hostile sky. The impact of wind made him feel as though he'd been kicked in the guts.

All around him flak exploded, as he tried to catch his breath, recover, and get his bearings. Big red and yellow bursts, shock waves from them relentlessly punching him like the fists of a ghost heavyweight.

Then the next thing he knew he was upside down, then right side up, sideways, then steady again and he free fell. His chute was partially tangled, and the disintegrating Warhawk was headed toward a crash-down break-up into the gulf.

Straighthorn looked everywhere in a spinning fiery universe and he could not find his co-pilot. And just when he needed Him most—he thought he had no more than a few more seconds to live—he could not find God, either.

And, oh, was the president going to be pissed!

They had gotten their butts kicked and they had lost an airplane.

Yet, how?

They had been shot down with a weapon that the Libyans did not have. And as Straighthorn and the debris of his Warhawk came to earth, he knew someone somewhere had betrayed them.

chapter 17

Laura kicked away the sheet and single blanket. She swung her legs to the side of the bed and, tired, wobbly, stood up. She walked through her tidy apartment in the dark. She knew the way well. Nothing on the floors. Nothing to *physically* trip over, even if there was plenty to mentally trip her.

She arrived in her kitchen.

The first light was the one from the refrigerator. She pulled out a Diet Coke and opened it. She sidled into a chair at her kitchen table. She sat down and sipped. Christ, life was complicated these days!

Her thoughts, still rebounding from dreamland, pinballed in all dangerous directions: the image of a man in her back seat. Voices that seemed too clear to be only her own thoughts.

Vans that came and went.

Accidents that did and didn't happen.

Surveillance that was definitely there unless it definitely wasn't.

And then there was an assassin, maybe in Florida, maybe not, who was or wasn't there.

Sheesh.

She eyed the telephone in her kitchen.

All right, then. She would make the call, the one that she now knew she wanted to make to Dr. Sam Feldman, her psychiatrist. The job tensions were getting the best of her again. She needed medicine again. She needed to get a grip on her own mind.

She needed peace. Truth be known, she thought to herself, she still missed her last lover. She could have used a good man in her life. And a good solid understanding relationship to go with it, neither of which she felt she would ever find in this thankless job.

Sheesh, again.

Thirty-five years old and counting. Tick, tick. She sipped some Diet Coke.

Hello? Dr. Feldman? I need you.

She started to punch in the doctor's number. She knew it by heart. She would do it now, leave a message with the answering service and—

Her fingers froze. She was coming abruptly awake.

What *was* she thinking?

She was on a case. An important one. United States Secret Service. She was on her way to Florida the next day.

She set down the phone.

God Almighty. No time for mental breakdowns or psychiatric lapses. It was time to be bold. Straighten out the mess inside her own head without the shrink and without the medication.

"I mean, get your head together, woman," she muttered aloud.

Damn! What choice was there, other than marching forward? Enough of all this!

She finished only a third of the Diet Coke. She put the open can in the fridge. It would be just dandy at breakfast. She ran a hand through her hair and felt one of those surges of loneliness cut through her.

Emotions: She had to keep them all bottled inside herself. God knew, if she mentioned them to *anyone* in the Service, they'd use psych-disability to heave her into retirement.

A conversation with her father would have definitely helped. But where was *he* hanging out spiritually these days? She wandered back through her living room and slid back into bed.

She lay very still for a dozen minutes, focusing on the assignment before her. She took the first few wobbly steps of trying to put herself inside the mindset of a male United States Secret Service agent who had been hired to murder the president.

Then she dozed off.

Outside, half an hour later, a gray SUV with government license plates parked up the block from the van that had departed an hour earlier; same distance from Laura's front door, different direction.

Dawn broke half an hour later, and with it returned the brutal temperatures of the summer of 2009.

chapter 18

GULF OF SIDRA
JUNE 20, 2009; 10:11 A.M. GMT

The crippled F-115 hit the surface of the water at four hundred eighty miles an hour. The sound of the explosion could be heard all the way to the North African shore.

Jack Kendall, torn apart by metal fragments from his jet, was dead before he hit the water. Straighthorn was alive and riding his parachute downward when the Warhawk exploded.

He splashed down. But his left wrist was pulsating as if someone had worked it over with a sledgehammer. He used his right hand to inflate a life raft that was part of his seat mechanism, then jettisoned the seat into the sea. He climbed aboard the raft, making sure he still had his Smith & Wesson semiautomatic.

He knew he was going to need it.

Straighthorn's wrist was swollen to the size and color of an eggplant. No doubt about it.

Broken.

He tried to flex some fingers. The pain spread and the fingers would not respond. Everything had happened so quickly. He thought he recalled a sharp pain as his seat ejected. Most likely, the seat hadn't flown completely free. That, or a chunk of the aircraft had flown up and hit him as his seat had lifted out. If so, he was lucky. He could have been decapitated.

And now he was in a hostile sea forty miles north of Benghazi, on his own raft, bobbing up and down amidst six-foot waves in the choppy waters. Swell. He tried the emergency communications unit sewn into his flight suit. Dead. Sardinia could not hear him.

"Shit!" he shouted aloud.

No one anywhere near him. He scanned the gulf and could not find Captain Jack.

He called out. No answer. The pain in his left wrist was relentless.

Straighthorn used his good hand to fish a pair of synthetic morphine tablets out of an emergency pouch on his belt. He downed two, just in case the wrong navy picked him up.

He noted the position of the sun. That told him the direction and the time. Then, from the south, there were three noisy specks on the horizon.

Libyan Air Force. *Oh, hell!*

Choppers. They were coming straight toward him.

He clutched his pistol. If they wanted a fight to the death, he would damned well give it to them. He worked out a strategy to take at least one helicopter down with him.

It took longer than he expected for the whirlybirds to peg him. Then they all moved in his direction as a unit. The bravest one did a fly-by from a distance of fifty yards. The downed airman welcomed them with a calling card shot from his sidearm.

Not bad! He heard the shot clunk off the chopper's armor.

"That's right, you bastard!" Straighthorn yelled. "I'm *exactly* who you're looking for."

He felt like lobbing a few more shots at them just to show the Stars and Stripes a little. But he figured it would be suicide. And after all, he was still alive.

So he lowered his pistol. He waited to see if they would return his fire.

He kept the spare clip in front of him for a quick reload. He cursed the Libyan aircraft again. A trio of thirty-year-old

Laryanov-16s. Big clumsy Red Bloc dodo birds of the military aviation world. Straighthorn would have been embarrassed to fly in one.

They were relics of the final days of the Soviet era when Moscow was run by a succession—Brezhnev, Andropov, and Chernenko—of dim half-dead Red-party men who ruled from half-lit hospital rooms. Sometimes the Laryanov-16s dropped out of the sky on their own, taking a screaming crew of five with them. *Only an Arab nation,* Straighthorn mused, *would be dumb enough to still be flying these suckers.*

The helicopters dropped back into a disorderly, over-anxious pattern. They circled him for several minutes. A tiny air-sea ballet and standoff. Straighthorn almost had to laugh at them. A wounded guy in a raft was holding off an air force by firing a single bullet.

"Towel-headed chickenshits!" he muttered.

Major Straighthorn sat on the raft trying to guess whether they were planning to pick him up or use him for target practice. He reasoned that they did not want him dead. Alive was of a higher value, but Third World logic was often a contradiction in terms. Meanwhile he prayed that somehow some other U.S. flyboys would get there in time to prevent his capture.

But he knew better. Unless there were a submarine from the U.S. Sixth Fleet right under him, he was too far away from his own support to harbor any realistic chance of being rescued.

Damn the U.S. Congress and their military budget cutbacks, he cursed to himself. If there had been one extra U.S. fighter in this area the Laryanovs would not have dared venture out.

The southern horizon: a couple of maritime specks appeared. They pulled closer and when they were within a nautical mile, Straighthorn knew exactly what they were.

Mesdoua's halfwit navy.

Libyan patrol boats. Russian-made, also, like their pals in the sky.

Probably about fifty officers and men on each tub. Three

aircraft, two patrol boats, more than a hundred Libyans to pick up two Americans. Were they sure they had sent enough people?

Straighthorn hefted his .45. The choppers circled and shouted orders from a hundred feet. Pidgin English. He didn't understand it. They circled him like a pack of cowardly dogs, each afraid to move closer. If his wrist hadn't been hurting, he would have been bolder.

Straighthorn kept his pistol firmly in his right hand. As long as he was still in his raft, he was not yet a prisoner. And as long as he was not yet a prisoner, help could still arrive. He wondered if the bastard in the desert radar base had had something to do with this.

He prayed to see some flyboy pals appear on the other horizon. The Libyan helicopters would vanish at the first hint of American air power. But this was the delusional quality of the morphine speaking to him now. There was zero chance of a rescue.

Straighthorn watched the choppers circle, watched the patrol boats inch closer, and thought about emptying his .45 toward one of the choppers. If he could get the pilot or the Jesus nut—the nut that connected the rotors to the fuselage of the craft, the one that American crews yell, *Oh, Jesus!* if it gets hit—he could bring one chopper down before machine gun fire from the other two blew him to bits.

He thought of his wife and family back home. It took the death wish out of him.

He would let them capture him. His government would get him back. He knew the procedure. It would take some time and he would tough his way through captivity, but the United States government normally returned their captured soldiers home.

The patrol boats circled.

They, too, blared something over their low-tech speaker system. *A carnival of incompetence,* Gerry Straighthorn mused to himself. A pair of aircraft, a couple of ships, and no one could come right in for the capture.

The first patrol boat pulled alongside him.

On the deck: six Libyan sailors with rifles trained upon him. Again, Straighthorn was not sure whether he should start firing. If they were going to kill him, he would be damned if he were going to go quietly.

But then some batshit commander appeared, a guy who was about five feet nothing tall, but with a shrieking voice, a red beret, and a funny Mideast-dictator-style mustache.

The commander had a scratchy megaphone. He barked into it. Fractured English, right out of the "Wishful Thinking" page from the Libyan navy manual.

"Throw out gun! Surrender!"

All Straighthorn could think of was the pain in his wrist. That, and how the commander, in a red beret and khaki uniform—*khaki on a naval vessel, for Christ's sake!*—looked like something out of a Marx Brothers movie.

Straighthorn tossed his pistol into the water. It was a hell of a waste of a good American firearm, but he was damned if he was going to let some two-bit lieutenant keep it as a trophy.

Six sailors came down and took him into custody. He screamed when they grabbed his left wrist; they were too stupid to see that it was broken. He struggled as they punched him upside the head. All he could think of as he was taken onto the Libyan craft was that he had grown up in the peace and serenity of rural Oregon, and now here he was being taken prisoner in the middle of a strange gulf half a world away.

Life was strange.

More of the morphine kicked in.

The six Libyans overpowered him and he surrendered.

chapter 19

Despite a public perception to the contrary, the president of the United States was ornery, unpredictable, and volatile in private. He was given to meanness and fits of temper that sometimes left those around him speechless. Increasingly, there was even an irrational act or two. But who cared? Six months into the new administration and the opinion polls were still lofty.

Today, the new administration had its first major foreign policy crisis. Seated at his desk in the Oval Office, his reading glasses poised on the lower part of his nose, the new president seethed over the hastily prepared briefing booklet in front of him.

So some hotheads in North Africa had attacked a U.S. aircraft?

Well, they would damned well get their receipt for this, and so would any other moron who wanted to test *this* commander in chief. He would wait to see what was known of the two U.S. aviators aboard. Then he would let the enemy have it with both barrels. He was a tall, fit, and handsome West Pointer who believed in the West Point way of doing things—thoroughly, completely, and efficiently.

The new man felt no limits to his own ego. The country had turned to him after the Bush 43 administration, he reasoned, because there was no one else who was big enough to fill the executive office. And yet, he occasionally wondered why he had ever accepted his party's nomination for president. He marveled anew that he had won the election in 2008. And he was more convinced than ever that he should serve only one term—if he had the good fortune to keep his personality in check and survive this one.

Okay, so history would see him as a "caretaker" president. God knew, he reasoned, one term was enough. Why would any sane man even *want* this job? He had suffered from massive mood swings for years. The emotional rollercoaster had worsened since he had taken office. Fortunately, those pests on the press corps hadn't picked up on it. Not yet, anyway.

But all that was immaterial this morning.

Well, so be it, the chief executive figured. His inner toughness had been tested many times. Never once had he been found lacking. Not in Vietnam, not in Bosnia, and not in the Gulf. Damned if some punk dictator in North Africa would get the best of him.

He redirected his attention to his desk.

Libya. He seethed.

The Middle East was the Balkans with burnooses and camels. But this incident in the Gulf of Sidra was just what the new president had wanted.

I'm waiting for some little third world dickhead who wants to see whose balls are bigger

the president had written recently in a note to his National Security advisor.

The third world dickhead is going to get a nuke shoved up his ass.

The comment had been widely photocopied. It was proudly framed in several offices at the Pentagon.

The president was a Northerner. He was sixty-nine years old, a former general and a hero of various American military escapades in the 1990s and early 2000s. He had been on the National Security Council and head of the Joint Chiefs of Staff.

The door to the Oval Office opened. The chief executive was expecting the rolls and fresh fruit that he normally received for breakfast. They arrived every morning, on his instructions, in an antique bowl that had been—according to an archivist who had bent his ear the previous day—acquired for the White House by Dolley Madison when she redecorated in 1818.

The president glanced up and was startled when he recognized the visitor.

U.S. Secret Service Agent Andy LoRusso.

LoRusso, forty-one, dark-haired, handsome, was a veteran agent. The president held him in his gaze for a moment, then spoke.

"Morning, Andy. How they hangin'?"

"Very well, sir, thank you. More material from the Pentagon, sir," LoRusso said.

It was not unusual for an agent familiar with the White House to walk in unannounced. Agents became "part of the furniture" in the White House, vigilant but unobtrusive.

The agent laid a second briefing book on the desk, this one two minutes old.

"Thank you," the president said with a terse smile.

Then there was a double knock on the door. Agent LoRusso permitted the waiter from the White House kitchen to enter. No one spoke. The waiter set down breakfast and departed.

The president had an emergency meeting with the National Security Council in less than two hours, then needed to put himself on public display again thereafter.

The president turned to the second briefing book. He paused long enough to pick up a cup of coffee, served in that damnable White House porcelain—a delicate little cup with a thin handle. The White House could sometimes be a formal place to the point of being candy-assed.

Agent LoRusso departed. The corridor outside the office was empty. The entire White House was quiet. Silence bothered the president. Eerie silences always preceded the bloodiest battles. He wondered if he sensed something similar here.

The former general calmly focused on the second briefing

pamphlet. His rage grew as he thought of the two American airmen who had crashed down into the Gulf of Sidra. The president's gaze settled on the phrase, "condition and whereabouts unknown."

Then the president's mood swung again.

He picked up the bowl of fruit and hurled it against the door. It smashed deafeningly against the oak. Fruit flew through the office, as did shards of antique porcelain from 1808.

"Up yours, Dolley Madison!" the president snorted.

Less than five seconds later, the Secret Service agents posted on the opposite side of the door burst in, weapons drawn. Agent LoRusso was first, followed by Agent Michael Shaw.

They stared at the debris scattered around the office.

"Gentlemen," the president said evenly, "I'm highly pissed off."

"Yes, sir," Agent LoRusso said. Shaw said nothing but his eyes searched the room. Increasingly, they witnessed strange stuff from this president.

"Call housekeeping and get out," the president said.

The agents withheld any glance from one to another until they were back out in the hall.

chapter 20

THE GULF OF SIDRA AND EL-SAHYI FAYEZ
CIVIL DEFENSE BASE, TRIPOLI
JUNE 20, 2009; 12:26 P.M. GMT

Out on the gulf, a full search was underway: air and sea, and, for that matter, under the sea. The nuclear sub USS *Madison* was also streaking toward the crash area.

After the Libyans had whacked the Warhawk, rescue planes had scrambled immediately from Sardinia and Sicily.

But all the rescuers found was Lockheed debris. The Libyans had plucked Gerry Straighthorn from the water. They had also recovered the body of Jack Kendall. For Mesdoua's normally incompetent air-sea power rangers, a big day.

The crew aboard the Libyan navy cruiser had strapped the injured pilot to a gurney, then stood around as he cursed at them. Good thing that Major Straighthorn had taken something for pain, because they were not going to give him anything.

They took Straighthorn to Tripoli. Several sailors came for him, bastards in different uniforms. Straighthorn knew they were part of the "elite" Republican Guard of the president.

Elite. What a dastardly joke!

Straighthorn had never had any respect for these troops. Historically they were among the first to retreat whenever they had faced serious firepower. The elites often left their grunts and downtrodden conscripts chained to positions to be overrun by the enemy. When it came to the Libyans, Straighthorn had more respect for the guys who cleaned the latrines than for the officers.

Six of the elites removed him from the ship. They gagged him and blindfolded him. They took him to a truck and drove him somewhere for half an hour. Then they wheeled him into a cinderblock installation—he hoped it was a hospital—and then down a corridor. He was shackled by both ankles to his gurney.

His blindfold slipped enough so that he had about 10 percent of his vision back. All around him were excited voices in Arabic. Every once in a while, he caught some other language—French, German, Italian—and he hoped it was medical personnel. After a while, that was all he could think about.

The gurney came to rest in a small dark room away from everyone else.

Straighthorn's wrist screamed with pain. He knew the break was probably complete. He asked for a doctor. He heard footsteps come close to him, then he felt a hand on his head.

A clumsy pair of hands removed his blindfold.

Straighthorn's eyes took a moment to focus. In his face: a high-ranking Libyan officer.

The man had a toothbrush mustache, one of those Hitler-is-my-hero jobs, and a green beret. Regular army. The beret was crooked. He also had a cigarette. The stench was nauseating. Third World tobacco smelled like an industrial fire.

Straighthorn read the bars on the officer's lapels and made him for a colonel. The colonel looked at Straighthorn with approval. Then he fingered the right sleeve of Straighthorn's uniform.

"Who? What?" the Libyan said in English.

"Major Gerald Richard Straighthorn. United States Air Force," Straighthorn said. "Now I want to go home. Got that?"

The Libyan grunted. Straighthorn felt as if he were talking to the jerk caterpillar in *Alice in Wonderland*. The colonel placed his hands on the American's uniform again. Much of Straighthorn's sleeve was shredded. The Libyan soldier pulled the cloth where the American flag was attached. With a quick yank, the colonel tore the flag off and dropped it to the floor.

"United States. Your country," the officer said. He placed his pristine combat boot on it and rubbed it into the floor with his toe. The orderlies smiled, safely behind him.

Straighthorn looked the man in the eye. "Libya," he said. "Your shithole of a country." Straighthorn spat at the man and used his good hand to smash him flush in the face.

An incensed look crossed the officer's mug. One of hurt. One of shock. One of not comprehending the American's improbable strength and tenacity. The audience waited. Blood trickled from the Libyan colonel's nose.

The Libyan officer ordered three of his underlings to hold Straighthorn down. They did. He walloped the injured airman to the right side of the head, four, five, six times. Then he left the room, nursing his snout.

Several minutes passed, also slowly.

The American again demanded medical attention from

the orderlies. They stared at him. When he cursed them, they grew scared and fled the room.

More time went by. Minutes, then hours.

Unattended, Straighthorn lay back. He tried to gather his thoughts. Not easy. He felt as if he were mentally trying to pick up spilt marbles that were still rolling, and the pain in his wrist and head made them roll in kaleidoscopic patterns.

It hurt so bad he saw stars.

Eventually, he passed out.

Straighthorn was never sure how long he was unconscious.

An hour? Five hours? A day?

He awakened again, aware of a crowd of people around him. Then he felt something sharp hit his arm. He looked to his left. One of the soldiers—*not even a doctor, damn them!*—had plunged a syringe into his arm. One of the goons in khaki. Another red beret. He had a nutty look in his eye and another one of those toothbrush mustaches.

Straighthorn's first impression was that they were giving him something for the pain, which would have been the decent, civilized thing to do. But then, in another heartbeat or two, he realized that this was no damned anesthetic.

Straighthorn could not move. The madman in khaki was grinning as he pumped the syringe into Straighthorn's veins.

Straighthorn cursed at him.

The quack smiled, stepped back, and repeated the words.

The rest of the soldiers in the room laughed.

"Oh, Lord. Oh, Lord," Captain Gerry Straighthorn said. After his oath, he said a prayer.

He could have been in the O Club by now back at the Sardine Can, knocking back some brews. Instead, "You're killing me," he said.

"Yes, yes," the mustached bastard said. "Killing you. Necessary."

The man with the needle laughed. So did his khaki buffoon chorus.

Suddenly, the American airman guessed that the man probably meant it.

Killing him.

Oh, Lord! Oh, Lord, oh, Lord, NO!

Straighthorn felt something hot radiating out from his arm. Whatever junk they had pumped into him, it was pulsating out from his left arm, spreading a tingling warmth all over his body. It felt like a hot cobra wrapping itself around him. Then he felt as if he were losing the ability to breathe, choking to death.

That's what it was, he realized in one of his last gasps of lucidity. Something to induce paralysis. Something to make him look as if he'd stopped breathing and gone into cardiac arrest.

Murder by science, death by rogue chemistry.

"You can burn in hell!" Straighthorn muttered. "All of you!"

Many of those around him laughed.

The horse's ass with the needle nodded. Straighthorn wished he'd had a bayonet. He would have sliced the man's eyes out, then put the blade in his throat.

"Lord . . . !" Straighthorn said again. "Oh, Lord . . ."

A lifetime flew back at him within a few loud heartbeats.

His eyes closed and at least the Libyans were gone from his view. Instead, he saw a bright light. He felt a salty taste in his mouth, one that made him think—in his fleeting moments of consciousness—of a day that he and his new wife had spent at Dana Point, California.

Mentally, he was sailing now. Higher than any aircraft had ever taken him.

He could hear the enemy soldiers around him, a little chorus of low-life cowards. They were applauding something, and Major Straighthorn, in his delirium, thought he recognized it as the premature arrival of his own death.

He wondered for a long slow second where he would be buried.

Then there did not seem to be anything premature at all, because darkness was all there was and he was so far out of it that he didn't care about never waking up again.

chapter 21

The Ralph Edwards Room was on upper Connecticut Avenue, in an unmarked building that looked residential from the outside, but which had functioned efficiently since the 1950s. It was named for the late host of the TV show *This Is Your Life,* which had been popular when government files first settled here. Each week on the show, a celebrity guest was presented by surprise with his life story. And whenever Laura Chapman thought of the Ralph Edwards Room, she thought of its guardian, Bernard Ashkenazy.

Ashkenazy was a fastidious little man who oversaw the biographic records of the Secret Service. Much of the material in his department was computerized now, but even computerized access was allowed through very few locations outside of Secret Service headquarters.

The building on Connecticut was the main location. Ashkenazy was present that same Saturday, June 20, when Chapman visited. "How are tricks, Laura?" Ashkenazy asked.

"All right, Bernard," she said. "Just need to run some names."

"Run whatever you want for as long as you like. See if I care. Anything urgent?"

"Nope," she lied.

Laura settled in at a computer terminal and did not look up. Then time spiraled. Chapman felt herself back in Chicago seven years earlier, when she briefly worked with Ashkenazy screening Midwestern lunatics against an impending visit to that city by President Bush.

Ashkenazy, white-haired and fastidious, had always struck everyone as a man who had the investigative deviousness for the Service, but none of the muscle. It made sense that he worked with computer files. Ashkenazy dressed like a male model. Spotless impeccable three-piece Italian suits, white shirts, alligator belts, beautiful silk ties.

A flag tie tack in the days after 9/11. A breast pocket handkerchief. He had a hip holster that had been custom tailored by a leathersmith and an always-carried-never-used weapon with a hand-carved ivory handle. The director of Secret Service operations in Illinois once ventured in a scurrilous e-mail that landed in too many unofficial boxes that Ashkenazy was "a don't-ask-don't-tell sorta guy. He should have worked for J. Edgar Hoover, not the Service."

Since then, Ashkenazy had gained the supervision of these files, lost some hair, retained his wardrobe, and successfully sued to get the Illinois director demoted.

Chapman ran several names through the Ralph Edwards database. Secret Service agents and employees. Life stories emerged.

Chapman looked for bumps in the road, and most of these men—except for the odd bout with the bottle, a broken marriage, or a kid in drug rehab—had smooth roads. Ashkenazy notwithstanding, the Treasury Department did not usually hire eccentrics.

For the hell of it, she ran biographies of Larsen and Reilley: the White House PPD.

Larsen was a choirboy, or at least so his file suggested. Much was made of the fact that he sent his mother six hundred dollars a month and that he had played baseball at the University of Montana.

Reilley's file was just as wet a kiss. The only pimple: a DUI bust when he was a junior at Arizona State, subsequently dismissed. Larsen had subscribed to *Penthouse* for six years, but dropped America's second favorite stroke mag just before being hired by the Service. Currently, to satisfy his intellectual side, he received a handful of more conservative publications—*Reader's Digest, Guns and Ammo,* and *Christian Life*—that wouldn't surpass his reading skills.

It surprised Laura not at all that the file kept tabs on who was reading what. In the new "Enemies Everywhere" era, Big Brother did not just watch, he also thumbed through everyone's mail, picked through the garbage, and sometimes listened in on the phone.

Chapman ran her own name.

She learned nothing shocking about herself, but, within her own file, learned about an ex-boyfriend named Gordon and three women whom he had slept with while he was dating her.

She gritted her teeth. Where in hell was this stockpiling and cross-referencing of personal "information" ever going to end? Who came back and sorted out truth from innuendo? No one. They had Gordon's middle name and birthday wrong.

One part of her wanted to torch the Ralph Edwards Room. The other part of her just wanted to complete her work there as quickly as possible and blow the place off.

Ashkenazy coughed quietly. Laura moved onward. She brought up one by one an assortment of Service names she knew, including all those who had recently been assigned to the White House PPD. The procedure ran into the early afternoon and shed light nowhere.

Then she cross-referenced. She ran profile searches within the Service, keying in a few of the hints that had emerged from the file she had read in the Capitol Building. The hired killer may have had some sort of Arabic or Islamic sympathies in his background.

He had blond hair, according to a source, and possibly connections to Miami. Possibly also a two or a seven in his Secret Service shield number.

The database had seven names. Then her computer went bonkers, the screen blinked and froze. A dialogue box from cyberspace presented her with a form called a 602: a request to cross-reference and analyze information.

The 602 stopped her dead in her tracks. For good measure, the printer spat out a hard copy, causing Bernard to glance up.

Goddamn!

She walked the form to Ashkenazy. "What the hell is this?" she asked.

He grudgingly came out of his headphones. "Libyans shot down one of our planes," he said. "Hell's going to break loose in the Mideast. Again."

"What else is new?" she answered.

"Lost a couple of pilots. Blame Israel," he said. "Even when you're wrong, you're right. Or should I paraphrase Oscar Wilde: To lose one pilot is a tragedy, to lose two is carelessness."

"What's this 602 all about?" she asked, showing him the printout.

"Red tape." Ashkenazy arched an eyebrow. "I need authorization from the Deputy Director of the SS or above to put through a 602 request."

"In the past I asked for what I wanted and got it. How long has this been going on?"

"Maybe two years now. Some congressional b.s. again."

"I can look directly into files but I can't cross-reference?"

"That's what the new regulations say. Supposed to make it easier to lateralize information. Actually makes it more difficult."

"That's insane."

"That's why Congress voted for them, I suppose. They're insane, too. Ever see the movie *King of Hearts*? Nineteen sixty-five. French film. Alan Bates played this young soldier who—"

"*Roi de Coeur.* I saw it years ago, Bernard, and I just left the director last night."

"Of *King of Hearts*? Philippe de Broca? I thought he was currently deceased."

"The director of the Secret Service."

"Hooray for you. I'll do the requests Monday morning. It will then take maybe a few days."

"Can't you speed it up?"

"Call the director at home and have him call me."

"I will if I have to."

"Then please do. Otherwise, think Tuesday after three P.M."
He paused. "Unless you want to describe to me what this is
about," he said with a wink, "and I *might* be able to circum-
navigate the Hemisphere software."

But Laura was not inclined to sail around any e-continents.
She muttered to herself, then went and sat down. Concluding
her Saturday time at the Ralph Edwards Room toward 2 P.M.,
Laura also knew that Ashkenazy would emerge from his desk
late in the day to see what she had been investigating. To tweak
the little man, Chapman ran Ashkenazy's name.

She knew Ashkenazy would check, but then be unable to
ask *why* Chapman had pulled up his own bio. Office paranoia feasted within the Secret Service.

She wrapped up, gave Bernard a thin smile, and was set to
depart, no wiser than when she had entered. But Ashkenazy
flagged her down as she passed.

He slipped out of his headphones again and summoned
her to his desk.

"Know something, Laura?"

"What?"

"Secretly, I rather like you. Did you know that?"

The statement took her off guard. Worse, it sounded like a
clumsy come-on.

"I never thought much about it, Bernard," she answered.
"How's that?"

"I'm not playing head games with you, Laura. I know I can
be difficult. You're a good person. You're a real person. You
work hard." He paused. "I have access in here. Files that link
to other files. If I can do anything extra for you, let me know.
Okay?"

"Okay," she said. "Thanks." She was in no position to turn
down an ally in an unexpected place. "I mean, if you can get
those reports by Tuesday. That would be great."

"Count on it," he said. "Have a good weekend."

"I'll be working," she said.

"Ditto."

Half a minute later, she was back outside and into the
Washington heat.

chapter 22

So how could this have happened? Laura Chapman wondered as she sat in a coffee shop two blocks from the White House later that same day. *How could a foreign government have gotten to a member of the United States Secret Service?*

She was indignant that her own agency could have been infiltrated. Secret Service agents went through a stricter screening process than those hired by the FBI or the CIA. How could there be an enemy within the most extensively trained protective security force in the world?

If someone with the Secret Service actually turned on the president, the damage could destroy the Service completely. In many ways the Service had never recovered from the darkest day in their history, the assassination of John F. Kennedy. Never, despite the fact that it had been Kennedy himself who, on November 17, 1963, had prohibited Secret Service agents from riding on the bumpers of the presidential limousine on his upcoming visit to Dallas.

The Kennedy assassination: the worst-case scenario of letting the "protectee" set the rules. Then the investigation that followed—the Warren Commission, with all that "magic bullet," lone assassin b.s.—was a historic low for letting politicians invent a "truth" to foist upon the public. Earl Warren had not believed the findings of his own commission, but he had signed off on them under pressure from Lyndon Johnson, who also had not believed them.

Chapman found a traitor within the Service a preposterous notion. And she was supposed to figure this out alone? At the same time, she knew something else. In the last few years, the Service had fallen in love with technology. Computers, laser scans, and so on. Technology was fine to assist and back up, but infiltrating organizations or finding one lone assassin was tough single-minded dirty work.

Chapman finished her burger and ordered a sixteen-ounce black coffee to go. She watched a congregation of tourists on the sidewalk outside: Fresh open faces. Shorts and T-shirts. Innocence blended with awe. Midwesterners. Flyover-state gullibility.

Laura's thoughts returned to the alleged plot against the president. Any Secret Service agent could painfully learn America's rich history of successful big-time wackos. John Wilkes Booth had murdered Lincoln and a demented loser named Charles Guiteau shot President Garfield. The anarchist Leon Czolgosz put a fatal few rounds into President McKinley.

In modern times, the names were more familiar: Lee Harvey Oswald, Sara Jane Moore, Squeaky Fromme, and John Hinckley. Not one of them dealing with a full deck.

Then there were the assassinations of Huey Long, Robert F. Kennedy, Mayor Cermak of Chicago in 1933 as he sat next to president-elect Franklin Roosevelt, Martin Luther King, and George Lincoln Rockwell. George Wallace was shot while campaigning in 1972, ex-President Teddy Roosevelt was wounded while campaigning as a Bull Moose in 1912. President Truman narrowly escaped being murdered as he entered Blair House in 1950. Did anyone remember the name of the Secret Service agent who died from shots fired at Truman?

And what about a psycho named Sam Byck? In February of 1974, loose-screwed Sam attempted to hijack an airplane in Baltimore to fly it into the White House to kill President Nixon.

Crackpot right-wingers had thrown shots in the direction of President Clinton more times than had ever reached public attention. There was a pattern: Half-crazed or fully crazed loners were the perpetrators in every single case.

The thought gave Laura extra cause for concern.

There was nothing more difficult to track or detect than

the thoughts of a disgruntled individual quietly intent on murder or a paid professional working within the system.

Combine the two, and—

In her seat in the coffee shop, she let out a long sigh. She thought of an unfinished bit of business from the Ralph Edwards Room, reached to her cell phone, and called Director Vasquez's home line. An assistant with a young voice took the message that Laura needed permission to view 602s. Laura then disconnected.

Distantly, in the cook's area, CNN droned on and on about the U.S. aircraft that had been shot down in North Africa.

Well, all right, Laura thought. *The country has its public crisis and I have a private one.*

Her mind wandered again.

Was life always like this? Unseen enemies? One after another? Invisible until the moment they strike?

When the Secret Service was established in 1865, it had no responsibility for protecting chief executives. This, despite the bitterest irony in American intelligence and protective services: The authority to form the Secret Service was given by President Lincoln on the day he was shot.

The agency began with ten men, and its first mission had been to combat currency counterfeiting at a time when more than sixteen hundred private U.S. banks printed their own money. It was not until after 1906 that Congress authorized the agency to expand into a protective force around the president, a response to the deaths of Garfield in 1881 and McKinley in 1901.

Since that time, ensuring the security of the White House, its occupants, and its diplomatic guests has been the chief priority—not always to the pleasure of the protectee. When impending resignation drove Richard Nixon to tears, agents witnessed his emotional collapse. Bill Clinton, when he first arrived in Washington, chafed at the proximity of agents to himself and his family. While Clinton later developed excellent relations with his Presidential Protection Detail, within the first weeks of his presidency he ordered agents away from the residential floors of the White House and had them instead stand guard on the landing one flight below.

And *this* president in the year 2009 was a vigorous man who enjoyed being out and around. Guarding him was a different, more complex task.

And guarding him from a traitor from within the Service . . . ?

This thought gave Laura shivers. Director Vasquez was asking the nearly impossible. How could *anyone* know who the traitor was until the traitor made his move?

Laura left fifteen dollars before her on the Formica counter and went to her car. The afternoon had died and it was now a Saturday evening in June.

She felt overwhelmed and lonely. The black dog wasn't far away. Other women her age had families, husbands, or at least a regular relationship. She had the burdens of a job in which she had probably stayed too long and a current assignment that could only bring her down.

At an intersection in Georgetown she looked out the window of her car and watched couples going to movies, bars, or restaurants. She checked out the sometimes-provocative clothing of the women she watched and the way they captured the attention of the men they were with. She compared their bare midriffs, suggestively short hemlines, and skimpy blouses to the dark Brooks Brothers and Ralph Lauren suits and other monkey clothes that were part of her job.

She would have traded places with any of the women she saw. *In an instant,* she told herself. She felt like a drink.

The light changed. She drove on.

A depressive suicidal urge was upon her for several dreary seconds, but she rejected it. She knew she would have to handle things on her own. Dr. Feldman was not an option.

If only . . .

If only her father hadn't instilled this sense of patriotism and loyalty in her. If only she hadn't been raised in such a conservative family. Maybe she would have been able to cut loose more, to relax, to not take everything so damned seriously.

Damn, indeed!

Laura returned home. She found her smallest suitcase and packed it as an overnight bag. She made a deal with herself. She would stay with this assignment for as long as she could; till it broke her; till she completed it or till it killed her. Whichever came first.

Thereafter she would construct a bold new future for herself. Then she would be able to have a life.

She went to her bedroom closet and turned on the overhead light. She moved a pile of books and clothing from the floor, an array of odds and ends that looked like normal bottom-of-the-closet disorder, but which was actually a primitive camouflage. She leaned down and pulled away a section of floorboards to reveal a discolored plywood panel.

She lifted the panel and came to what she wanted. An iron strongbox bolted to one of the steel supporting beams of the building structure.

She reached to the combination lock on the lid of the box. She spun it deftly to clear it, then entered the combination. The box clicked open. She lifted the lid.

From within, she withdrew twelve .38 caliber bullets and a six-cylinder Colt revolver. In its place, she packed away her Sig Sauer semiautomatic. She also packed away her real driver's license, passport, and Secret Service ID.

She closed the box, spun the lock, replaced the floorboards and camouflage that lived above it. She placed the new IDs in her purse.

She was now Linda Cochrane.

She showered. She loaded the Colt. A short gin and tonic helped settle her nerves.

She tumbled into bed, the recomissioned Colt now at her bedside, and settled in to sleep.

Strangely, nothing disturbed her further this night.

No bad dreams, no uneasy awakenings.

Nothing.

PART TWO

chapter 23

BANGKOK TO BOGOTÁ
JULY 1985 TO AUGUST 2002

The conspiracy against the president began to unravel with a woman named Anna Muang. Her mother had been a Bangkok bar girl who had had an American boyfriend, a soldier who had been stationed at the Udorn Air Base in Thailand.

Anna had been born in 1985. All her mother could ever tell Anna about her father was that his name was Jimmy Pearce. He had been a sergeant in the United States Air Force and had been from a part of the United States where the winters lasted from November to April.

He had been white, very fair of complexion, with a distinctive tattoo on the back of his left hand: a cobra wrapped around an American flag. He had also apparently been careless one day when visiting Anna's mother and had left his dog tags with her. She had saved them.

After Anna had been born, shame fell upon her mother because of her mixed-race baby. No one wanted half-Thai, half-American girls until they were old enough to have a cash value.

Anna was pretty. Very delicate half-and-half features. Her uncle handled the inevitable transaction when she was twelve. The buyer's name was López and he had business between Asia and South America. Occasionally he stopped off in Thailand to acquire teenage girls.

López bought and sold girls the way other wealthy men dealt cars or horses. On a trip to Asia in March of 1998, López procured three young females. Anna's uncle brought her to the Hotel Duroc where López had a suite. Her uncle stripped her for a visual and manual inspection, then her uncle and López haggled over the price before she could dress again.

Her family received nine hundred American dollars. She would always remember the American dollars changing hands. And she had commanded a good price for a girl her age, because her skin was not as yellow as many of the other girls'. It was almost like selling a white girl. Plus, she was a virgin. Or at least she was up until her uncle left her at the hotel for the evening and López deflowered her. Then he returned her to her mother for another week.

The Thai government sold exit visas for Anna and two other girls whom López purchased. Anna came to think of the other girls as her sisters. All three were mixed race.

Two days later, a Spanish-speaking man rounded up Anna and the other two girls. They were told to pack one suitcase of clothes. Anna did, taking a few changes of dress and a few personal items from her mother. Included were the U.S. Army dog tags that had belonged to her father, in case she ever arrived in America and wanted to look for him.

"Or maybe someday, they will lead you to good fortune," her mother said. She packed her daughter a few pieces of jewelry also, gave her a long hug, and said good-bye.

The girls were put aboard a truck and locked in a cargo bin. They were taken to the docks. They waited several hours until they were put aboard a freighter. The Spanish man who worked for López oversaw everything.

Anna could tell the ships apart by their flags, and she knew that most of the flags had hammers and sickles. But the one she went on was different. This ship's flag had yellow on the top half, then one blue and one red stripe along the lower half. She had no idea what that meant. She only knew that most girls were sold to Chinese or Thai businessmen to stock bordellos throughout Asia, where they would work until they were too diseased to continue. She figured that was where she was going.

Anna and her "sisters" worked in the ship's kitchen for all three meals each day. There was an obese matron who was married to one of the men on the ship. The matron looked after them, but did not speak any language the girls knew.

The matron made herself understood with gestures, shouts, and sadistic slaps to the face and buttocks.

Anna knew the crew spoke Spanish, and began to pick up a little from listening. She also knew the crew was not allowed to touch them. Obviously, their new owner was a powerful man, because while the sailors leered all the time none of the crew ever tried anything.

Weeks passed. They were crossing the Pacific Ocean, not going to anywhere in Asia. She began marking the wall by her sleeping berth with a mark for each day. Two months passed on the voyage. Finally they arrived where it was very hot and there were mountains in the distance.

Everyone spoke the same language as the crew on the ship. Anna and the other girls were loaded aboard a truck and driven for two days along bumpy high-altitude roads. Finally, almost as a relief, they arrived at the estate of the man who had purchased her, Señor López.

López had another six girls there that he had picked up in various places around the world. Two were American and blond. From them, Anna acquired a few words of English. It was a harem and they were slaves. But they were not badly treated.

After Anna had first arrived, López often summoned her to have sex with him when he was in residence. Sometimes Anna was asked to come have sex with him and another girl. Frequently, López entertained business contacts from the United States and some South American countries. This was the real purpose of his harem, as he would allow his guests to select "hostesses" for their stay. The girls were moved into guest quarters at night for the men who were visiting. Most of the men were courteous and gave the girls small gifts that they were allowed to keep. A few of the men were rough. Several times, she was obliged to have sex with two men in one day, and one time, during some sort of large gathering, she and two other girls were obliged to satisfy a room of fourteen.

There were always a lot of weapons around and a lot of alcohol and drugs. After a while, it became the norm. A year passed. Then another. Visitors came and went, as did members of the harem. One of the other girls ran away and a pretty young Indian girl named Gita—who spoke no language that anyone there understood—committed suicide.

López also had guards, armed men with automatic weapons, who enforced the barbed wire perimeter around his compound. Sometimes, when one of these guards had done something to earn the particular appreciation of his boss, the guard was allowed to select a girl for a night.

There was one guard named Jean-Henri, who was very light-skinned and who took a special liking to Anna from the moment she arrived. He requested her every time he had the opportunity and grew jealous when she had to entertain guests. He was a rough-hewn but handsome man in his thirties, a former army officer in the Mideast.

A girl who understood Spanish told Anna she had seen Jean-Henri's passport. He was Lebanese, with a French father. She had also learned from the guards that he had deserted his regiment in Beirut because he would not fire on Israeli civilians. Whether the story was true or not, Anna did not know. But the story made sense and Jean-Henri was kind to her.

He spoke to her in a mixture of Spanish, French, and Arabic, which he taught her in phrases as the months passed. It was also Jean-Henri who showed her a pocket-atlas map one night and confirmed where she was.

"You are here," he said in Spanish. He then repeated two words that she had heard a lot. "Medellín. Colombia."

She was a captive on a ranch. She had already figured out what product López provided for his customers. Cocaine.

Jean-Henri slipped Anna candies and fresh fruit when he could. López apparently knew but did not care. He felt it made Jean-Henri loyal to him, as Anna would be his reward for dutiful service.

And so it went for many more months. During this time, Anna estimated that she serviced more than three dozen guests, plus her dear Jean-Henri.

Yet it was not an entirely unhappy time. She had access to

a doctor, who could give medical attention and birth control. She was healthy and fed properly. She received cosmetics and good clothing. She thought of herself as López's servant and Jean-Henri's wife. Jean-Henri spent increasing amounts of time with her and, as months went by, taught her to read and understand Arabic. At the same time, she learned English from the American girls and Spanish from everyone else.

Anna, it turned out, was a bright young woman. She learned quickly.

Then there was one terrible day that would change her life. She knew it was in the summer because it was very hot. All the girls were awakened by a terrible sound.

Gunfire. A lot of it.

Anna went to the window of the room she shared with three other girls and looked out. Their enclave was under attack. After a while, she had stopped thinking of herself as a prisoner here, as this was the only life she knew. So she did not think of those who were invading as her liberators. They were threats.

At first she thought that a rival gang had invaded. Then when she looked closer, a greater fear coursed through her. There were hundreds of soldiers of the Autodefensas Unidas de Colombia, the AUC, a right-wing militia. Anna heard many barrages of gunfire. Then the gunfire came closer and she knew that López's guards were losing to an overwhelming force.

The shooting died down to sporadic outbursts. She heard shouts and screams outside. She came to the window again. Las Autodefensas Unidas were executing all the guards who had surrendered. She saw soldiers drag López and his family out of their residence. López was machinegunned. Next, the soldiers executed his family.

Jean-Henri came out of the mansion by himself, raised his hands, and laid his weapon down. The soldiers laughed. They murdered him at point blank range with automatic pistols, oblivious to the screams of a Thai-American woman watching from a distance.

Then the military went on a hunt through the mansion.

López owned seven girls at the time. The army told each to pack one bag to travel. They obeyed. Then the soldiers took them prisoner. They separated the two American girls from the others and Anna never saw them again. But Anna and four other girls, including the two girls with whom she had left Thailand, were taken to an AUC officers' barracks outside of Bogotá.

They were raped by Colombian army officers for a week. Then, one morning, they were all placed in another truck, taken to a busy section of the city, and roughly pushed out of the cargo area, one by one, many blocks apart, carrying their few belongings.

A big soldier who was a sergeant gave them each a thousand Colombian pesos, the equivalent of about twenty American dollars, and told them to get lost.

"*Vete, vete,*" he said. Another soldier prodded each girl with a rifle until she fled.

It was August of 2002. Anna was seventeen years old, alone and nearly destitute. But she was free.

chapter 24

BOGOTÁ TO MIAMI
AUGUST 2002 TO JUNE 2009

After being dumped on the streets of Bogotá, the slave-prostitutes went separate paths. Anna found her way to a Roman Catholic church, where she received food in exchange for a custodial job on church grounds. She stayed there for two months, learning some more English from American Peace Corps workers assigned to that parish.

Then she heard that a Liberian freighter was sailing from Barranquilla, Colombia, to the Dominican Republic. The ship needed maids and cooks. She signed on.

She had no passport, but no questions were asked, as the

wages were almost non-existent. By this time, however, her one goal was firmly fixed in her mind. She wanted to emigrate to the United States.

She felt a certain affinity for America. Her father had been American. Jimmy Pearce with the strange tattoo. She was half-American. She had been sold for American dollars. And, way in the back of her mind was the notion that she might be able to find her father. She still had those dog tags: a small clue in a vast world. But moreover, Anna was tired of being poor. She had heard good things about America, how a woman could earn money and own things if she worked hard.

She jumped ship in Santo Domingo.

She worked around the port area as a waitress and prostitute. But it was 2004 and she was nearly nineteen years old. She had acquired many smarts as the years had passed and a facility in several languages. She saw that the women who bettered themselves could command higher pay and service a higher class of client.

She shoplifted some better clothes, stole magazines that taught her about the latest fashions, and transformed herself. Soon she was working hotels and tourist spots, making good money. Her clients were now North American businessmen.

She learned that they wanted quick, discreet, intense sex. Many of the Americans were from religious families. She sold them the services their wives would not do for them. She cultivated this trade, improving her Spanish and learning better English. Once she had a Saudi man and earned a two-hundred-dollar tip by bringing him to orgasm in Arabic while dressed as a Japanese schoolgirl.

She had a bodyguard named Tito on her payroll. Tito screened her clients and kept them honest. She kept herself toned through exercise. She stayed clean and did not touch drugs. Because she knew it turned some men on, she acquired a pair of tattoos, a small red rose high up on the flesh of her left inner thigh and a lattice design on her lower back.

For these years, she worked Santo Domingo, close enough to the United States to hear American radio. She saved money. She learned to drive and acquired an old car.

One night she met a man named Miguel. He had an American passport but had been born in Cuba. He was a dark-haired man, moderately handsome, who smoked expensive cigars and owned a small airplane. She knew he was a smuggler.

He hired her for a night and then for a second night, paying her lavishly. He was so pleased in bed that he made a joke about taking her back to the United States with him.

"If you want to take me," she answered, "I'll go. Can you get me in?"

"Sure," he said. "Any state that touches water, I can get you into."

"Florida," she said.

Miguel laughed. "That's the easiest one of all."

"How much I pay you?"

He laughed again. "I make enough money. You can pay me a better way than money."

"Deal," she said.

She knew what the payment would be. She did not mind. Sex was her best commodity. She was used to keeping men happy with it in exchange for what she wanted. To her, it was not illegal, immoral, or degrading.

By now Anna specialized in a special highly commercial product. Herself. Men used force to control women. Anna used sex to control men. She knew that she had become extraordinarily good at it, learning just how to take her time and slowly and sensuously coax a powerful orgasm from a client. With her mouth, with her hands, with any part of her nimble body.

Miguel and Anna departed four days later for America. Miguel had a Cessna 185 seaplane that was moored in a cove south of Santo Domingo. He took off at 9 P.M. and flew with a cheap hand-held GPS system. No lights. Low, zipping in and out of the islands, under and around local radar. It was romantic, thrilling, and terrifying. Miguel asked for a handjob in flight and received one. Then there was one close call shortly thereafter when Miguel swerved wildly to avoid impact with a Piper Comanche that was also flying without lights or markings. Aside from that, the first leg of the trip was a cupcake.

On the first night, they stopped on Martinique, where Miguel picked up packages, dropped others off, and refueled.

That same night, Miguel took her to a bar in the one village. There was a live sex show in a back room. Most people spoke French, but some spoke Creole, others Spanish. Miguel knew the owner. Miguel introduced her as his "new bitch," laughed hard, and got very excited by the sex show and very drunk on homemade rum. Anna had to drag him home and put him into bed.

The next day they ducked around Bahamian radar, flew low north of the Keys, and then, most daring of all, knifed into U.S. airspace through the Everglades just after midnight. Then he roared northward at treetop level before anyone could catch him. All this with no illumination.

"Any lower and the gators will bite my ass," he said proudly, "any higher and I got the DEA to worry about or the U.S. Coast Guard." Then he shot northward forty miles and was home free, setting down on a private lake within the interior of Florida. He stashed his plane in a camouflaged hangar on his own property. Homeland Security be damned; Miguel and his Cessna, his cargo, and his passenger commuted to and from work almost as easily as a suburban commuter, but with less traffic.

Anna had moved from a big-time South American coke smuggler to a small-time local guy. But she was in America now. She began to think. She also remembered her lesson from Colombia very well. She was not about to sit tight and wait for police to come a second time.

She talked to Miguel about leaving. Then suddenly he turned on her. He took her money. After all he had done for her, he said, she could stay there and screw him until she got so old that no man would want to screw her again.

He beat her with a riding crop and had a special leg iron that he left her in when he needed to be away. She was a captive again, and remained one for several weeks.

She examined the iron. Obviously at least one girl had been imprisoned the same way before, because she saw that someone had done a lot of unsuccessful work on the lock.

Miguel was in the habit of going away for two or three days to do his drug runs. During these absences, he left Anna with just enough food and water and access to a television.

"There's no way you could break the lock," Miguel said. "So don't bother trying."

She knew he was right about breaking the lock. But he was wrong otherwise. She lost several pounds. On Miguel's second absence, she slipped her ankle out of the chain. She ransacked his house, took one of his guns, a sexy little .22 derringer that a working girl could pack into a small purse or hide under a miniskirt, a dozen bullets, and five thousand dollars.

As a parting gift, she broke a whiskey bottle, ground the glass into sharp fragments, and sprinkled the breakage between the sheets of his bed. She knew that Miquel liked to slide into bed nude.

Muchas gracias, querido Miguel: Chíngate y adiós.

She stole one of his cars and knifed the tires on the others. She had no idea where she was going, but the highway led to Tampa. There she ditched the car and found a bus depot.

In the bus depot, however, there were frequent departures to Miami. She had heard of Miami, she thought because there was once a television show about it. And that was the next departure.

So she went to Miami. It was March of the year 2005.

She went directly back into the sex-for-pay industry.

She worked with quiet efficient prosperity for four years, sometimes working freelance, other times working out of bars and clubs where introductions to good clients were readily arranged. For months she carried her small gun everywhere and stayed on the lookout for Miguel. But she never spotted him again.

There in Miami, however, she would encounter the opportunity of a lifetime. From her youth on the streets of Bangkok, she had heard stories about the Central Intelligence Agency.

But the United States Secret Service was not something that she had ever known to exist. Making the connection from one to the other, however, would not be difficult.

chapter 25

At Miami International Airport, Laura Chapman rented a car, and was soon on the main expressway that led back past the airport and then to either downtown Miami or Miami Beach.

A hundred and one humid degrees gripped South Florida. Chapman had visited Miami with two presidents—Clinton once in 1998 and Bush 43 four times while he was running for reelection in 2004. One older agent had once described the Miami heat as "akin to making love to a three-hundred-pound woman in a steam room. And she just rolled over and sat on your face."

Laura followed the signs for Miami Beach.

She passed the Orange Bowl to her right, and then, also to her right, the stubby skyscrapers of downtown Miami. She paid a toll. Then she drove along the causeway that led to Miami Beach. On her left was a lagoon with an island, and sitting on it houses that must have cost a minimum of ten million dollars apiece. She shook her head, unable to imagine how anyone could accumulate such wealth, other than by stealing it, inheriting it, or a combination of both.

On her right was the maritime channel—the exit for all ships leaving the Port of Miami—with Caribbean-bound cruise ships awaiting their passengers. Most belonged to the Carnival line, but among them was a different-looking ship, moored permanently: the *Norway,* the former *France,* which the French Line had built with French government money as a final unsuccessful throw of the dice against the jetliner.

Laura drove across the causeway and onto Miami Beach. She turned onto Washington Avenue, heading north, then took Sixth Street, turned right onto Ocean Drive, and turned right again to wind up in front of her hotel, the Park Central.

The Park Central had been built in the '30s in the hope that the Depression would not go on forever. The Depression had lasted a long time, but the Park Central had lasted longer.

Laura pulled up behind a black 1937 Plymouth coupe, a car similar to the one that Bogart and Ida Lupino fled in in *High Sierra*. The car was always there to lend some "deco glamour" to the hotel. Farther up Ocean Drive with the hotels and restaurants on one side and the beach on the other there was a mid-'50s Oldsmobile convertible permanently stationed for the same reason.

Laura checked in quickly.

The furniture in her room was unpretentious but comfortable, done in pale wood. Over the bed was a photograph from when the hotel was new. It showed a group of very pretty young women posing in front of an official billboard saying TWO-PIECE BATHING SUITS FORBIDDEN ON THE BEACH. Naturally, the women were in two-piece bathing suits. But what chaste suits they now were, Laura noted: The bottoms covered the navels, and the very full halter tops only stopped a few inches above the bottoms. It made her think mischievously of a summer day in France many years ago when her boyfriend Jean-Marc talked her, after splitting a bottle of Bordeaux, into taking off her bikini top at a crowded beach. Sufficiently soused, she had obliged. Fortunately, none of the photographs Jean-Marc had taken had ever surfaced.

Laura showered quickly and put on fresh clothes. A navy suit with a jacket, no more than two inches above the knee and room on the right side to keep her weapon handy but out of view. She sighed at the clothing situation. She would be the only woman in Miami outside an office wearing a suit. But pants wouldn't do, she considered them unfeminine. Nor would keeping the firearm in a purse. She kept her cell phone on the left side, turned off.

She glanced at herself in the hotel mirror. She was pleased with what she saw, the right balance between sexy-attractive and confident-no-nonsense, but still displeased at having to wear a suit. Yet, this was the equation she would need today.

She left her hotel and drove back across the causeway to the financial district, where she easily located an Argentine restaurant called La Cabaña on St. Xavier Street, a tiny side street that was half a block from an unmarked FBI outpost. She entered, working off information that had been pre-arranged by Director Vasquez. She sought the nefarious Sam Deal, who, many years ago, before he embarked on his own career in "government service," had been born Sam DeLuccia in a mythical faraway place called Bensonhurst.

Laura spotted Sam immediately at a rear booth, positioned directly under a NO SMOKING sign. He faced front, his back was to the rear wall. Sam was a tall, thick man, mid-sixties and ornery. He was gray-haired, pale-faced, bespectacled with a neat mustache.

His thin yellow-tinted wire-rimmed glasses were low across his twice-broken nose. Sam's thick hands were on the table, unmoving, as if someone somewhere had a gun trained on him. A fresh pack of Lucky Strikes kept him company.

Sam assessed her up and down as she approached, face to ankles. He did not make her as law enforcement till she stood in front of him.

"Ah!" Sam said, by way of greeting. "So *you're* Linda Cochrane."

She couldn't tell whether he recognized her enough to re-call her real name. "Sit, Linda," Deal said. "I remember you. Still look beautiful. I didn't connect the name."

"No way you could have, Sam," she said. Then, from somewhere in her overburdened memory, as she slid onto the bench across from Sam, Laura started calling up some details:

Notably, Sam had been a Casey *wunderkind* in the 1980s.

Notably again: When it came to firearms Sam was a swift left-handed draw. Here he was covered by the right-handed wall. It told Laura that Sam still had his enemies and his enemies still had their memories.

But Laura's knowledge of Sam ran much deeper.

Sam's Nightingales had been formed off-budget as part of an agriculture appropriation—something about the use of pig manure to reinvigorate fields used for growing corn—during the Reagan administration. Their creation had been DCI William Casey's suggestion. Deal had been the obvious choice to emcee the show. Back then, murder, kidnapping, and blackmail were common extensions of U.S. policy on those numerous occasions when all other forms of persuasion had either failed or been blithely bypassed—as, in 2009, they were once again.

La época dorada, the golden age, of Sam's thugs had been the Ollie North era. There were about three dozen men back then reporting to Deal, focusing on the Caribbean, which, in those days, meant Cuba, El Salvador, Grenada, and Panama.

Sam once went along on a mission in Peru in which a "pharmaceutical" warehouse was suddenly caused to explode, but otherwise he was content to sit in Florida and pull strings.

Some of the older Nightingales, guys older than Sam, were longtime hands in Latin America. The standard joke was that the older members had taken their degrees at "Salvador Allende University" in Chile, meaning they had assisted in the CIA assassination of the democratically elected Allende during the Nixon regime's era of dirty tricks. It had not been America's finest moment of promoting worldwide democracy.

Sam's crew had been in eclipse since 2005 when a few of their stunts made the newspapers, such as the time when Sam, to extort information from a Jamaican drug dealer, had shoved the man's hand into a kitchen garbage disposal and turned on the switch.

Though tempered since then, they were again increasingly useful. They could maintain security around an individual by taking out a suspected threat with no time lost through pesky legalities. In their early days, they had had a penchant for taking care of problems after dark.

Hence, their name. The Nightingales.

"Can we have a chat?" Chapman asked.

"Why not, huh?" Deal answered after a moment. His gaze

drifted away from her. His eyes worked the room as he spoke, then returned to Laura.

Sam looked superficially strong and confident. But Laura always noticed the little things when she was on her game. Today, for example: a slight sway of Sam's sturdy hands, a thin line of sweat along his receding hairline. Inside, Sam was as jittery as a spooked cat.

Why?

A slap of Sam's musky cologne assaulted Laura's nostrils, somehow making it past the cigarette smoke. He smiled. His nicotine-stained teeth were like little yellow tombstones.

A waiter appeared. In English, Laura ordered an iced coffee.

There was some small talk, then, "You going to be in town for a few days?" Sam asked. "Do you like to go dancing?"

"Sam, do we talk business? Or do I go back to Washington and talk about cutting Sam off the federal payroll because the senile old jackass tried to hit on me instead of helping us?"

He snorted. "Ow!" he said. "Business is that urgent?"

"Yes. And, I mean, look, I'm overworked like the rest of us, right?" she said. "The sooner I finish this, the sooner I move to something else."

"Sam's listening," Sam said. "I'd be a fool not to."

He cocked his head like a petulant terrier. Laura remembered: Sam was always a diligent listener. Talking was a different skill.

But at least she had Sam's attention. She glanced at her watch. It was a few minutes past five. Oddly enough; the day was on course. She leaned forward slightly and baited him with the softest eye contact she could muster under the circumstances.

"Okay," she said. "Here's today's pitch."

chapter 26

Sam was used to not knowing the full story on his subjects. A busted kneecap was a busted kneecap, a car bomb was a car bomb, and a dead guy was a dead guy. Everything was the sum of its parts; no more, no less.

Laura explained that the Secret Service and the CIA shared a source in Miami.

"Can't hurt to meet in person, the 'asset' and me, can it, Sam?" Chapman asked.

"Maybe," Sam answered. "Don't know and don't care."

In the background, someone had fed the jukebox. Silvio Rodriguez was suddenly singing in Spanish about a unicorn.

"What's *your* problem, Sam?" Laura said, sensing difficulty. "Tell me. Off the record."

Sam leaned back. His eyes were upon Laura, fixed and steady.

On the wall, among the other works of art, was a poster-sized photo of Oscar Bonavena, the late Argentine heavyweight, hooking a right onto the temple of Mohammed Ali.

"See that big dumb Argentine?" Sam asked. "He throws everything he has in the first three rounds. By round four Bonavena can't throw a punch through your cellar window. Ali puts him on the canvas. Bonavena could have been a champion. Instead he's heavyweight roadkill."

Sam paused thoughtfully and continued.

"Ten years later, Oscar's a security goon at a high-rent whorehouse in Nevada. But, see, he's also screwing the wife of the owner, this Eye-talian guy from Brooklyn, and screwing her the best she ever got. How dumb is that? Does it surprise you that the owner knows some guinea wiseguys from Vegas and Oscar gets blown away one night?"

"Probably a bit before my time," Laura said.

"Ever see the great punchers?" Deal asked. "Joe Louis? Sugar Ray Robinson? Ali?"

"Never saw them. But I was dating an actor in Los Angeles for a while. He took me to watch Oscar De La Hoya fight Felix Trinidad in Las Vegas."

"Did you have sex after the fight?"

"Probably."

"Most women get turned on by sweaty guys punching each other."

"I work out on a hundred-pound bag, myself, Sam," she said. "So if the boxing was meant to get me wet, it didn't work. My guy had to do it himself without Oscar's help."

"De La Hoya's a pretty boy," Sam grumbled. "He's got big *cojones* for a Mex, I'll give him that, but he's still a burrito Adonis."

"Sam, where you going with all this?"

"Glad you asked," he said. "Today's lesson is football. Know a bit about *that*?"

"I follow some of the college stuff," Laura said.

"I got a son at home. Ronnie. Named after the great president. Ronnie graduates high school. Top of his class. Captain of the football team."

"Congratulations."

"My Ronnie's smart. He gets into the U of Miami, Florida, and Florida State," said Sam. "Thing is, though, what we're looking for is *a football scholarship* at one of the Florida schools."

"And your son didn't get one?"

"Bingo. And it's something that Langley can do something about!"

"Fix a football scholarship?" she asked.

"It's easier than fixing some of the things *I've* fixed!"

"You have a point."

"Mention it to my favorite Ivy League twerp, Mitch

Hamilton," Sam said. "He's your mentor, isn't he? Tell him Sam is *mucho* pissed off. Sam wants a couple of short-term backhanders coming his way. Now. While I still have an audience."

"Seems reasonable," she said, stroking him slightly.

"Remember the details: Miami, Florida, or Florida State. I hate some of those other SEC places like Ole Miss. Keep that in mind. Oh, do I hate Ole Miss."

Laura asked the reason. Sam dragged on his cigarette down to the final remnants of the butt, then snuffed it. Then he pointed to his nose and the way it triangulated.

"Got hit with a cheap shot when I played for the Seminoles against Ole Miss. No face mask. Busted my nose in the first game of the season, 1965. Put me out for my senior year. University of Missishitty."

"Sam, that was what? Forty years ago?"

"Forty-four. Sam has a long memory for injustice."

"Hurricanes, Gators, and Seminoles. I got it. And you hate Ole Miss."

Sam was mildly impressed. "With a passion." He paused. "So I have your word, also?"

"You have my word. I'll do what I can, Sam. That's all I can promise."

The mood eased under the NO SMOKING sign.

"Good," Sam said after another moment. "Now, what's on your mind? I ordered us some vino cheapo so we could chat."

A waiter with a pleasant light brown face and long arms appeared, swinging a bottle of Chilean Merlot like a spare bowling pin.

Deal had for many years been an intermittent alcoholic. Chapman wondered in which direction the boozy pendulum was swinging today. Meanwhile, Sam launched another smoke.

Laura and Sam Deal fell silent when the waiter arrived and opened the bottle. The waiter poured half a glass for Sam to sample, but Sam waved him away and poured himself a full glass. He poured one for Laura, too, but she stuck to the iced coffee.

A presidential visit was in the offing for Miami, Laura explained as cover, but some of the backwires had been burning up recently with stories of local nuts who were upset that the country was in the wrong hands, or so it went.

"It *is* in the wrong hands," Sam murmured, "and has been since Reagan left office."

"I didn't ask your opinion, Sam. I'm merely bringing you up to speed."

Sam grunted.

Could Sam keep a tight watch on things, Laura asked. She wanted to know about anything that aroused his special notice. Pavement artists like Sam's people would have to think outside the box and play some hunches.

"Washington's barking at its own shadows, again, huh?" Sam said. "Figures."

Sam knocked back the glass of wine in one long draw.

Oh and also, Laura added as an afterthought while she still had Sam's attention, could his people keep the source known as Charley Boy under 24/7 surveillance?

"Who's Charley Boy?" Sam asked.

"Details tomorrow. I'm meeting the source this evening."

"Where?"

Laura gave the address. A beat. Recognition was upon Sam.

"I know the place," he said softly. "You going in alone or you need a back-up?"

"I don't need a date, if that's what you mean, Sam. And the doorman is supposed to watch my back. So what can you tell me about the place?"

Sam snorted and lit another of his repulsive cigarettes.

"Nothing that won't be obvious as soon as you walk in. You wearing some artillery?"

"Do I look stupid?"

"No, but I guess my question was." Sam poured himself a second glass of wine.

"So we understand each other?" Laura said. "You'll take care of the things I asked for?"

Sam shrugged. "I'll take care of things," he said. Sam also

confessed to being officially undermanned, since so many of his people were working private contracts these days.

A few more minutes of pleasantries followed as Laura tried to wrap up with some cordiality. Sam attacked the bottle of wine and insisted that Laura join him in half a glass.

Grudgingly, she did. She was also disconcerted to see that Sam's hand shook a little as he sipped. Was she imagining things again, she wondered. Seeing things that weren't there? Or was she on to a nuance, and if so what was it?

Was Sam slipping, or was she? Or was the world just haywire, as usual?

Sam expelled a fogbank of cigarette smoke.

Two giggling teenage girls came in. A flurry of firm beige skin: clingy denim shorts, colorful bikini tops, and bare flat midriffs. They slid into the booth across from Sam. They spoke Spanish and captured his immediate attention.

Sam turned toward them, fell stonily silent, and listened as his eyes narrowed.

Then he grinned, turned back to Laura, and spoke softly. "Hear their Spanish? They're from Guantánamo. FOB."

Laura could hear their Spanish. The accent did sound Cuban.

"Cute, aren't they?" he said. "They're probably about sixteen." He paused. "You should learn Spanish," he said. "It might help your career."

Sam smiled. Laura bristled.

"Uh huh," she said. "I may need you, Sam. Try to stay out of jail for the next few days."

"Sometimes it's not easy."

Laura rose and turned to leave. Before she was out of earshot, Sam had struck up a conversation in Spanish with the girls.

chapter 27

At sundown, Laura drove to her rendezvous with Charley Boy: a deco-streamlined house in South Beach with the characteristic pastel paint job, pink and blue on white stucco. Three stories on a quiet street, all windows curtained. She eyeballed it from her car, then parked. With reluctance, she pulled her Colt and its holster off her belt and stashed them under the front seat.

She stepped out. Miami in late evening: low clouds and dark thick nasty air. Urban humidity as a bug propellant. The atmosphere dissembled into a steady drizzle.

She went to the door and drew a final breath. She knocked. Solid oak on top of steel reinforcement. Better to stop bullets, she reasoned, better to stop a police battering ram.

What the hell?

Bribes normally stopped police battering rams much better than an oak door. A place like this didn't exist without an extensive police pad or some other connections.

She looked around, wondering where the surveillance cameras were. An amateur might have missed them. There was a miniature set-up on a light post twenty feet to the right side of the door. *So where's the back-up?* She looked in the opposite direction and found its companion piece, a similar little black box with a slit for a lens, fifteen feet up along a palm tree.

A small hole in the door poked open behind a chunk of fish-eyed glass. An eye appeared.

"Robin?" Chapman asked.

The eye stared for several seconds. The hole snapped shut. More ominous metal sounds: multiple locks and chains giving way. Her palms were soaked. There was a special stage fright that could make the steadiest agent dry up and walk away. She faced it here.

Her nerves were shot. Suddenly the idea of standing still in a suit all day, every day, seemed very pleasant.

The door opened. She felt nude without a weapon.

Robin swelled into the open doorway. Six feet three inches tall and tremendously obese. He had a huge moonish face, dark circles under the eyes, a malevolent triple chin. On his left forearm was a long deep scar, and in his left hand he held an old wooden baseball bat, a convenient point of reference: his weight, Laura calculated, hovered near Ty Cobb's lifetime batting average, the high range of the three hundreds. Impressive arms and fists. He wore a light blue rayon shirt that looked like a tent. It had palm trees on it.

"I'm Linda Cochrane," Laura Chapman said. "I'm looking for Charley Boy."

"There ain't no Charley Boy here, lady. So go away."

The Cuban's puffy eyes burned into Laura for what seemed like a day and a half. Actual time lapse: closer to five seconds.

"It's a real estate matter," Laura said after a moment. She gave him a faint smile.

Robin grunted. The heavy lids of the man's eyes lifted. His gaze traveled past Laura's head and shoulders and checked the rain-splattered streets.

No one else.

Satisfied, Robin stepped aside, motioning Chapman to enter. She did, stepping forward carefully. A tsunami of air conditioning washed over her: ninety-six to sixty in point five seconds.

Behind her now, a forty-pound arm with a baseball bat banged the door shut. The double bolts dropped. "Wait for a second," Robin said. "Gotta frisk."

Laura stiffened.

She anticipated his beefy hands lingering too long on her breasts and at her crotch, with nothing she could do to object. Instead, he turned and called to an adjoining area. *"Christiana!"*

From somewhere appeared Christiana, a lithe dark-haired woman in a green silk dress. Burgundy lipstick. Mocha skin, dark eyes, *muy* drop dead gorgeous. Taller than Laura by an inch or two, maybe five ten.

She greeted Laura in Spanish.

The silk was so tight and clingy that it looked sprayed-on. No bra, that much was obvious. Nothing else underneath either, equally apparent.

Christiana carried a hand-held metal detector, a mini-wand with a small disc and another wire sensor at her finger. Best-looking "frisk bitch" Laura had ever seen. Some guys would have gone through airport security five times for each flight if it worked this way at JFK or LAX.

Christiana also wore an emerald pendant on a gold chain, the emerald circled by diamonds. Laura guessed that the pendant was worth her annual Service salary times two and a half. Someone—probably not too far away—was taking good care of sexy Christiana.

Laura raised her hands.

Christiana waved the electronic wand all over Laura, brushing it over the surface of her body. Armpits and ribs, boobs, hair, crotch and buttocks. Between the knees, then upwards and upskirt, touching both inner thighs, skimming her panties, front and back. The search underneath was thorough and intrusive, then descended down Laura's bare legs, frequent contact with the skin, and passed carefully across the shoes. Laura had once had a boyfriend at UMass who had spent less attention on foreplay.

The little gizmo chirped like a parakeet. It didn't like Laura's PID, her bracelet, or her earrings. Christiana gave a neat little *no hay problema* smile each time the wand was unhappy.

Finally she finished. *"Está bien,"* the woman in green said to Robin.

Robin turned. *"Vámonos,"* he said in return.

A jerk of his immense Caligulan head: the visitor should follow. Laura's stomach felt as if it were turning to water.

Past history flooded back: Had she really done work like

this when she was twenty-six? Had she really done state police undercover on narcotics and homicide in Massachusetts? Robin trudged like a lobotomized elephant in a circus parade. Heavy shuffling footsteps through the first floor. She took mental notes so that she wouldn't wonder later if she had imagined things.

The wainscoting was deep mahogany, with a dark rich polish, little portholes here and there to give access to the mini security cameras. The furniture: Whorehouse Eclectic, *molto* steel and glass with gleaming modern stuff in a half dozen different mismatched tones.

The carpets were an explosion of different colors, angular and modernistic shapes. Very South American. The walls had prints and paintings from the Very Unsubtle School of Art: either high-class porn or low-class art, depending on one's tastes.

For starters: a couple of blunt, full color life-size nudes, women sixty-nining other women, and a man at leisure while a nude woman fellated him. The styles were pseudo-Picasso and wanna-be LeRoy Neiman, ending with an all-out black-man-on-white-woman picture, the woman pinned to a blanket, her legs wide open kicking upright in the air like a crab.

In a way not intended, it set the proper mood, although whoever had equipped the would-be artists with paints and brushes had performed a deeply anti-social act.

Robin led Chapman past the artwork to a set of steps. Chapman could hear music. Robin was the watchdog as well as the keep-an-eye-out-for-trouble guy, so he stayed behind while Chapman walked upstairs alone. At the landing, there was a comic knock-off of the Venus de Milo, this one with a pair of wrap-around sunglasses and a jeweled navel; the navel jewel, Laura noted, being another hidden camera.

Clever.

There was another Cuban sitting at the top of the steps, a pot-bellied man with iridescent green socks, and Laura wondered if he was a CIA asset, too. Maybe a pensioner.

The second Cuban looked too damned senior for this sort of thing, so Laura figured he was someone's old man.

Robin's?

He was maybe seventy. He had teeth missing cleanly, as if knocked out with a ball-peen hammer. Post-Batista Havana dentistry or a few good rights to the jaw when he was much younger?

Who knows?

He sat in a cloud of cigarillo smoke and fingered a cell phone as if it were a voodoo doll.

She walked past him into a large parlor and finally made a take on the place: a gambling parlor *con prostíbulo*—with bordello attached—financed by local hoods, the CIA, or an overlapping of both. Being there made Laura feel as much a whore as every other female in the place.

In the center were gaming tables.

Green felt paradise with a touch of hell sprinkled in. Craps, blackjack. A little roulette, a lot of poker. A croupier with a thin mustache at the nearest table flashed a shiny red vest. A matching ruby glimmered in his left earlobe. He called the roulette games in English and Spanish. The felt jungle was busy.

Laura took a quick inventory of the players: men in Hugo Boss and Armani suits. Lots of Ermi, lots of Zegna. Eurotrash at leisure, accompanied by women in Jimmy Choo shoes who were dark, sinewy, and delicious, and most of whom worked there. The women were in various states of near undress. Their eyes were hard and empty. A cascade of voices built in intensity as roulette balls from two tables clicked and circled their wheels. Another detail: one green zero, no double zero. The wheels were Monte Carlo style and gave the players a better break than A.C. or Vegas.

At the far end of the nearest table were a pair of greasy teenage hoodlums, big cobs of money in their hands. They threw around C-notes like used taco wrappers and had New York written all over them. Laura hated them on sight.

More years of experience kicked in.

At the near end of the second table were what looked to be a couple of mob guys with stacks of chips. One of the wiseguys was melancholy faced and lantern-jawed, buttoned up in sharp pinstripes, but he still looked like a bouncer on holiday leave.

Laura's gaze slid from the horse-faced guy to his smaller partner. With a start, Chapman recognized him from her days in Boston when she had been on the trail of a band of counterfeiters who had been dumping ersatz fifties at the pony and dog tracks—Suffolk Downs and Wonderland—in eastern Massachusetts. Their engraving had been good. But President Grant's eyes had been too narrow on the bad bills. He looked like someone's Japanese grandpa.

She searched for a handle, a name, then pulled it out of the air. Teddy Barbieri.

Teddy B. Teddy hit the 3F trifecta: frizzy haired, frazzled, and fucked up. Laura's investigation had ended with a trial, but no conviction. She had, however, made things hot enough so that Teddy's engravers had skipped to a western jurisdiction. The same product started to turn up in downstate Illinois three months later.

Chapman ignored her old acquaintance Teddy and hoped he didn't recognize her. She did, however, feel several eyes upon her, a single woman entering a room like this. She wondered: Did she look too much like a cop or not enough like a hooker?

She scanned the ceilings. The place had dozens of inverted little black surveillance cones. There was not an inch of floor space that wasn't electronically scanned.

Roulette balls rattled. There was a scramble of bare female arms and legs. A hot number—twelve black—came up at two tables simultaneously. To the side were slot machines that were not as heavily attended but were busy nonetheless, mostly single men pumping Susan B. Anthony dollars into electronic oblivion.

The old Cuban with the Easter Egg socks and missing teeth appeared at Laura's side. He yanked rudely at her sleeve. "Hey! *¿Qué quiere usted?* What you want?" the old man demanded.

"Charley Boy," she said below the din.

"*¿Qué?*"

She shouted into his ear hole to be heard. In Spanish, "*Busco a* Charley Boy!"

The Cuban gave a lazy nod. Then, "*Aquella chica es* Charley Boy," he said.

The Cuban indicated an elfin female at the closest bar, one of two women tending the smallest of the three watering holes. Her age was in the mid or low twenties, Laura reckoned quickly, and she was pretty and sensual in the style of a quick exotic cat-house professional.

Laura looked and could barely put a lid on her surprise. "*That's* Charley Boy? *¿Aquella chica?*" she said.

"*Sí,*" Green Sox affirmed.

Charley Boy was dark haired and Eurasian, about five one and compact and very female. Her hair was black, straight, and touched her shoulders. She wore a tight black velvet dress that was low up top and high down low. The hem barely left her decent, which was the point.

Laura sat down at the end of the bar that Charley Boy was tending. Charley Boy gave Laura a fast smile and slapped down a cocktail napkin in front of her. Laura needed to work fast. She had to get Charley Boy out of this place and talking before some hood tried to pick her up.

A moment of truth was at hand. Laura had a world of important questions.

Anna Muang—or Charley Boy as she was now known here—had most of the answers.

chapter 28

"What do you like, lady?" Anna Muang asked from across the bar.

Anna had an accent. Southeast Asian singsong.

"You can get me a beer," Laura said. "Whatever's good and cold."

"Cold beer," Anna repeated, all business. "*Sí, señora.*"

Anna turned and bent low to a long cooler behind her. The backside hemline of her dress did peek-a-boo tricks. She fished a Corona out of ice. She turned back again and deftly opened it. She poured it into a tall glass garnished with the useless lime and threw Laura a fast cold smile.

"Ten dollars." Anna's most concise English so far. "Plus nice tip for me, okay?"

Chapman reached into her wallet. The American taxpayers ponied up a ten and a five to buy a drink in a whorehouse. "Keep it," Laura said.

Anna tucked the tip into whatever tiny lower-half undergarment she was wearing. Then she made a production of wiping the bar clean.

Laura glanced around. There were a few girls sitting idly by, waiting for dates for the evening. Two of the girls—one a surprisingly young and pretty redhead with pure Anglo features—were already watching her, wondering.

Laura looked back to Anna.

Anna lit a narrow brown cigarette that looked like a twig. A cheap stinker from a pack that had no tax stamp on it. She held it like a peashooter, fingers across the top. The grip was a habit that she had picked up since she had come to Miami and started hanging around with Cubans. It turned on a certain segment of their clientele, the guys looking for something tough and trashy for the night.

She took one puff, set the butt in an ashtray, and did not touch it again. The stinker began to slowly incinerate itself.

Laura started her pitch: "I'm Linda Cochrane," she said. "Please call me Linda. I was sent by Mr. Martin in Washington. I think we have something to talk about. Real estate."

Several seconds slid smoothly past. "I'm Charley Boy," Anna said softly, a half sigh of relief in her tone. "I was expecting you. Now I got to talk to Señor Victor."

Anna left from behind the bar and quick-stepped across the room on tan compact legs.

Laura quadrant-scanned, checking all corners of the room without noting any one more than another, without seeming to be interested.

Uh, oh! Teddy B. was watching her, or seemed to be, probably wondering where he remembered her from. She turned slightly away and kept a hand to the side of her face.

She watched Anna. She spotted the boss.

Señor Victor was a large man who sat in the southwest corner, his back to the wall. Laura had not seen him earlier because he had been surrounded, mobbed up in more ways than one.

The boss had a nasty angular face. Gray hair, rose-tinted glasses. He must have been sixty-five and looked like a latter-day Santo Trafficante. He kept company with a pair of younger strong-arms who were at his table. Anna went to the main man. He placed a hand on her black velvet rump as she spoke to him, then ran the hand admiringly under her dress to her bare hip. Anna leaned to him, placing an arm around his shoulders as she spoke into his ear.

Señor Victor mostly listened. Midway through what Anna had to tell him, the main man's gaze traveled the room and settled upon Laura.

Their eyes locked for an uncomfortable instant. The other pair of *cubano* wiseguys at the table turned. The look: a Miami wiseguy blend of lust, curiosity, and suspicion. They glared at Laura, assessing her in every way from a legal

threat to a quick trick. Their gaze remained aggressive and
steady. She stared back.

Finally, the head honcho nodded slowly and gave Anna an
approving squeeze on the ass. Anna gave Señor Victor a kiss
on the cheek. Laura wondered how often a girl had to screw
the boss to keep a job in a place like this. Anna turned and
walked back to the bar.

"Señor Victor says it all right. We can go," Anna said. "I
make up time tomorrow."

Anna ducked behind the bar for an instant and grabbed
her purse. She grabbed Laura's hand and pulled it. Her touch
was gentle.

"We need to go *now*," she said.

Anna wanted to be out of there, it seemed, before anyone
could change his mind. It appeared like a good approach to
Laura also, who felt Teddy Barbieri's eyes on her as she left.

In the back of her mind, Laura wondered again: With so
much running together, was this another reason a "she" had
been picked out for this job? What was the larger picture and
where did she fit into it?

The two women left together.

chapter 29

Anna owned a zippy little BMW Z4 roadster that was in the
back parking lot. Canary yellow and hot-to-trot. It looked
brand new but had a pair of dents in the rear left side. Laura
went to her own car and retrieved her Colt from under the
front seat. The cars rendezvoused in front, just in time for
another violent thunderstorm.

They drove in tight single file, one behind the other, Laura following. Laura had to run two red lights on wet roads to keep up with Anna's BMW. Laura wondered if Anna had a license or insurance. Her manner of driving argued against it. But then the drive was over and she was at the nondescript vintage 1953 two-story stucco house where Anna lived. There was a huge scar on the front where graffiti had been white-washed off. The building, like the rest of the neighborhood, looked to be on the down staircase.

Laura made sure her weapon was ready as she parked. Every warning instinct was now on red alert. She stepped from her rental car and joined Anna on the sidewalk. Anna fished though her purse for a key while Laura acted as a sentry.

"I live with other woman. Rose. Rose work with me," she said. "You see Rose earlier?"

"Maybe. What does she look like?"

Anna described Rose as a pretty American girl with flaming red hair and very white skin.

Chapman recalled seeing such a girl at the bar. Rose said that the men who patronized their club referred to Rose as Vanilla-and-Strawberry. When she undressed, Anna explained with a laugh, that's what they got.

"Uh huh," Laura said.

"Rose is not at home now. She got an all-night trick," Anna said. "Rich guy. From Caracas."

Chapman followed Anna inside her home. Subconsciously, Laura's hand started to flirt with the handle of her Colt as she stepped into a darkened hallway.

Christ, what's happened to me? Laura thought to herself, feeling herself break a new wave of sweat. *Never had nerves like this before.*

The black dog was suddenly having his moment.

Damn! Serves me right for staying in the White House and not being out in the field for all these years! I should have transferred out when Bush left office.

They took a dozen steps through a darkened entry alcove. Laura did not like the feel of it. Gut feeling time again. Something was immediately imminent.

Instinct: Laura drew the weapon.

Anna turned on the light and ---

Something fast, black, and large—a physical living shape!—leaped from the sofa in their direction. Laura felt a fear that shook her whole body.

Laura's hot wet palm moved with astonishing speed. She whirled with the weapon, trained it, was about to blast away and—

"Hey, hey, hey!" Anna laughed. "It's okay, okay?" she said. "It's Juan Perón."

Juan Perón was Anna's Doberman, given to her, she explained, by a romantic old Argentine admirer. Anna gently pushed Laura's weapon harmlessly aside, finger to barrel.

Slowly, Laura lowered her artillery and tucked it away. A wave of anxiety withdrew.

"You're a jittery lady," Anna said.

The dog licked Anna's hand.

"I guess I am."

Anna kept the big friendly Doberman as a pet and as a life insurance policy. A few pats and a big warm hug for Juan Perón from Anna. The dog's tail looked like a fifteen-dollar Davidoff and was going like a metronome.

"I call him JP for short," Anna said. "He's my buddy and bodyguard."

Anna hugged her pet. Anna began, "The real Juan Perón was—"

"I know who he was," Laura said.

"Evita's man," Anna smiled.

JP took a couple of sniffs at Laura, rooting at the new guest's crotch as Laura sought to push the animal away. A little of this and the beast was satisfied.

"Coffee?" Anna asked.

"Excellent," Laura answered. "Thank you."

Anna unzipped the back of her dress and disappeared down a hallway to the kitchen.

Laura glanced at her watch. It was past midnight. She sat in the first-floor living room and tuned in to the sounds of the kitchen. Dog food being put out for JP. Coffee cups on the counter. Clicks from a coffee maker. Then Anna scooted upstairs, tiny feet on narrow steps.

In the living room, the shades were down. Laura wondered if the CIA had dropped a wire on this place. She wondered where it was. And if they hadn't, why not?

Then she took in the living room furniture.

Seventies contemporary. Partridge Family retro. Crappy stuff punched out from wood pulp. A semi-circular red couch, badly worn, in the center. The chair she sat on was Naugahyde—canary yellow, like a New York taxi. Two standing lamps and a slatted coffee table. On it, one book, badly worn. Picasso's erotic drawings, with a cheerful artistic in-your-face female nude on the cover. Laura wondered if Anna ever grew tired of sex, whether she liked or hated it.

Underneath the table was a big round well-worn shag carpet, looking much like a giant lily pad, except it was royal blue and there was no frog. Laura's keen eyes drifted back to the drawn shades, looking for details, things right, things wrong, anything that made an impression. Part of the shade was uneven, allowing a one-inch visual access to the room where they sat.

Easily enough room to put a bullet through, Laura thought to herself.

She rose, crossed the room, corrected the shade, and sat again. She hadn't felt so wired since she'd been a much younger woman on her first White House assignment. Traveling with President and Mrs. Clinton, Laura had often been mistaken for a friend of Chelsea, which suited Laura's purposes just fine.

Laura looked again at the furnishings. Another question: Why was Anna living in such a place with the money that she was making? Then it hit her. Anna was always ready to up and run on short notice. She banked her money. Why spend on furnishings that she might leave behind?

Laura heard a toilet flush on the second floor. Moments later Anna was back on the staircase, descending.

Laura waited. Anna stopped at the kitchen first.

More rustling with cups. Anna came around the corner

into the living room, carrying a tray with coffee and milk. She now wore a blue UCLA sweatshirt and white denim cut-offs, very short, very tight, with bare feet.

Anna smiled sweetly. Laura blinked at the transformation.

Anna could have passed for a graduate mathematics student. The prostitute lit another small black cigarette. Laura found herself starting to like Anna.

"Where do I begin, Linda?" Anna said, her first perfect sentence of English in two hours.

"You told a story to my associate in Miami," Laura said. "Tell me the same story."

Anna blew out a long stream of smoke. She folded her hands on her knees and began.

JP heaved a dismal sigh and curled up at her feet.

chapter 30

MIAMI
JUNE 22, 2009; 12:34 A.M.

It had been less than two weeks ago, Anna said. June 10th. She remembered it very clearly because it had been a Wednesday. Wednesday nights in the sex business were often busy.

She had been at the club when she had caught the eye of three men. She had never before seen them: two dark men and one lighter taller man, who Anna said was a blond American.

The other two were foreign, she insisted, at least by birth, maybe Israeli, maybe Iranian. Or at least that had been her first guess.

She knew a few things about émigrés, she said, and was pretty good at spotting a man who was looking to have a good time by taking his pants off.

The boys were having their fun working the slot

machines, playing poker, winning a little, losing it back. From the bar, Anna watched the proceedings.

Next, Anna rambled. She felt she was at the end of the line with prostitution. She said she wanted to get out before she got too old or got killed. Sooner or later, one would happen.

Gradually, a softer side of Anna emerged. Why couldn't she enjoy a home like everyone else? She loved children, she said, little girls in particular, and would never sell them into the life that she had been sold into. Why couldn't she meet a man and have a couple of girls of her own?

Laura had a few words of sympathy for her. "I know what you're saying," she said. She would have liked children herself sometime, she offered, and a twinge ran through her.

Laura let Anna ramble, wondering what she might say that might someday be important. She began to speak of the soldier, Jimmy Pearce. Her father.

Once Anna quit prostitution, she said, she wanted to find her father. She didn't want anything from him, she said, and didn't feel he owed her anything. But she wanted him to know that he had a daughter. He was the reason she was alive, she explained. So she owed him at least that. Life was good after all, Anna concluded philosophically, and worth living.

"You think I'd be able to find him?" Anna asked. "My father? Jimmy Pearce?"

"Don't know. Difficult. This is a big country," Laura answered, quietly wondering if Jimmy would *want* to be found, if he were still alive.

Anna disappeared upstairs again and returned with something that had not been part of the story that had been presented so far: the U.S. Air Force IDs.

The dog tags. Sergeant Pearce. She dropped them in Laura's hand.

Laura held them long enough to see that name, but not to note anything else.

"Thailand? You know about America and Vietnam and Thailand, yes?" Anna asked.

"My father served in Vietnam," Laura said. "Two tours,

plus." Another feeling of unease swept over her. The tags felt heavy in her hands. "He must have worn tags much like this."

Anna nodded. She took the tags back protectively. She slid them into her purse, which lay on a table nearby. "You can help me someday, Miss Linda," Anna asked. "Find my father?"

"Maybe," Laura said. "Maybe if we have time and the occasion. You help me now, I help you later. How's that? I promise. We need to deal with other business first."

Anna smiled. She had a pretty face. When she relaxed, when she was happy, despite everything there was even a suggestion of innocence. "That's good," she said.

"So what happened next?" Laura pressed. "On the evening of June tenth?"

"The evening get late," Anna said. "The men get horny. Very drunk and horny again. The three of them. I know what that usually means."

By that, she meant that the same trio wanted to share a girl for the night. The three of them with one female. They were celebrating some deal they had struck, Anna said, and their way of closing out the transaction was a gang bang.

Robin lurched upstairs to strike a deal. He asked them which girl they might like.

"The little Chinky-looking one," she heard one of them say.

Anna had bristled, said nothing, waited and wondered how much she could earn.

Robin approached her with the formal offer.

She said she would do it for two thousand dollars, cash paid in advance, which meant she would stay till eight the next morning wherever they were staying. She set her price high figuring that they might cheapskate out.

They did not.

The men pooled the cash from their wallets. Anna left with the two foreign ones a quarter hour later. On the way, she stopped at an ATM and deposited her money. That way they could not take it back from her. And frankly, she said, they scared her right from the beginning, and she wondered why the third man, the blond man, wasn't immediately accompanying the other two.

"They didn't by chance go to the ATM *with* you, did they?" Laura asked.

"No. They stayed in the car."

"Pity," Laura said.

"Why?"

"The camera at the ATM might have gotten a picture of them," Laura said with disappointment. "Too bad."

Anna agreed. It was a shame. And perhaps no coincidence.

"And where were you in the club when all this was happening?" Laura asked.

"Top floor. Same place as you met me."

"Weren't there surveillance cameras all over the ceiling?"

"I suppose."

"Then shouldn't we have pictures?"

"Maybe. Ask Robin."

WTF, Laura thought. She couldn't figure why someone hadn't asked *el cubano gordo* already.

"I will," Laura said. Then Anna continued.

"We go to The Tides Hotel. Miami Beach. Very chic. Expensive," Anna said, impressed in spite of the fear she had felt at the time.

Laura knew the place, having been there during the Clinton visit. It was on the other end of Ocean Drive from the Park Central she was staying in. A few blocks away but in a different world of price and clientele, with a vast and elegant cream-colored lobby with a high ceiling, and the 1220 restaurant, named after the hotel's address.

Each room at The Tides had an ocean view, with curious touches like a piece of real slate with natural jagged edges for people to chalk messages to whomever they were sharing the room with, and a telescope on a tripod for ogling people on the beach. Along with a more sedate class of guests, The Tides was a favorite of South Florida diamond pinkie ring guys.

Anna kept a low profile in the elevator. When a working girl serviced the glitzier hotels she had to be discreet. Otherwise she would be sharing her fee fifty-fifty with the house detective.

"Do you remember the room number?" Chapman asked.

Room 1544, she said, which checked with the story she had previously told.

An FBI buzz through the hotel's records had already confirmed that the room had been rented under a fake name via an ersatz Alabama driver's license. The bill had been paid in cash.

Then Anna added something which hadn't been in the OPI report. Before the CIA had paid out a cent to her in Miami, they had asked her to sit down for a polygraph. They had brought in an expert from New York to work on her.

"Mr. Lewisohn," she remembered.

Chapman noted it and was busy correlating facts again.

Anna had marched through the polygraph minefield with honors. Such was probably the source of the expert agency opinion and analysis that had appeared so cryptically in the OPI reading. No wonder Case Officer Richard McCarron had vouched for her bona fides. He was regurgitating what his lie detector people told him.

"The three men," Chapman pressed. "Tell me about the evening."

Anna continued. At first there was nothing memorable about any of the three men. She went to the hotel with them, undressed completely, and settled into the bedroom. She was instructed to turn the light off. Obviously, none of the men wanted her to get a good look at them. That was a little silly, she recalled, since she had seen two of the men, the foreigners, very clearly already. So she figured it was the blond man, the American, who was sensitive about being recognized. At the time though, she didn't think much of it. It wasn't that unusual.

The two foreigners came to her first, one by one. The blond man came third, the lights being completely off when he came into the room. None of them talked much. Only one of the foreign men got rough; he wanted to slap her across the buttocks a few times before he had sex.

She successfully serviced all three. When the first round was over, it was only 2:30 A.M. Anna lay on the bed for a while, knowing they would be coming back to see her over the course of the night. The men's voices in the next room were loud. They had been drinking since eight in the evening and were pretty well plastered by now, sitting around in underclothes.

Because they had been cheap bastards and hadn't promised to tip her, she decided she would have a quick look through the blond man's suit jacket and pants, which he had left slung over a chair in the bedroom.

"Maybe a big fat wallet," she said, wistfully thinking back on the opportunity, "and he never miss an extra eighty or hundred dollars!"

Chapman took it as iffy behavior, without considering the lack of morality therein.

Anna went to his jacket and patted it down.

Nothing in the jacket except a couple of fresh cigars.

She moved to his pants and cruised through the pockets. There was no wallet, per se, but—as if she had smelled it— there was a roll of greenbacks in a thick blue rubber band, separate from the rest of the money. She flicked through it quickly: a thousand dollars in fifties.

But what troubled her was that the bank notes had bloodstains on them, and that did make her cringe. It was in keeping with her feeling that he was a very bad man. So she quickly scammed six of the less-stained fifties and put the rest back.

Anna grabbed her purse again and showed Laura the fifties, stains and all. Anna was superstitious about spending them and had tucked them away for an emergency.

Laura pounced. "I need to take a couple of those," she said.

Anna didn't follow.

Laura reached to her own purse and pulled out one hundred fifty dollars. She handed it to Anna. "I want to do DNA tests on the money," she said. "And any other lab test possible. It'll help us track the blond man."

"Oh. Okay." Anna peeled off three soiled fifties. They made the exchange. The other fifty-dollar bills looked clean.

"Hang on to the rest of them," Laura instructed. "I may want to run more in the future."

Anna nodded and returned the other fifties to her purse. Emergencies could always be close at hand.

Then she found something else in the hotel suite, she said, resuming her story.

It was a small black leather folder. She was familiar with what things like that contained because she had had her run-ins with corrupt police over the years. So the discovery made her wary. She figured if he was a policeman he probably had a gun and could get away with anything he wanted to. So suddenly she was very anxious to dress and get out of there.

But knowledge of a policeman's sex habits can be useful, coming from the other direction. She wanted to know if he was a Miami cop, and if so, where he was stationed.

The information might someday be helpful.

So she opened it.

"I saw a Treasury Department badge. Secret Service. United States of America."

"Tell me what it looked like," Laura asked.

"Silver badge," she said, describing it accurately. "Blue letters. Gold trim. It said Treasury at top, Division of Secret Service at bottom."

Chapman felt a surge deep within her, gut feeling and anger, mixed with disbelief.

Yes, by God, she told herself, this is a credible witness and in this world anything is possible. She knew that from this point on, she would be moving forward, not back.

She suddenly felt very thirsty. Very very thirsty, indeed, and she knew the reason was fear. Fear of what she was going to hear, fear of what she was going to learn.

And fear of what the Service might be unable to deny.

chapter 31

"Was there a number?" Laura continued. "On the badge?"

"A number, yes," Anna said. "But I can't remember."

Too bad, Chapman thought.

"I was looking for name," the call girl said.

"We don't have names on our shields," she said. "Just numbers. And a laminated ID card to go with the shield."

"Yes," Anna said. "I looked for name, but I never saw one."

Laura wondered if Charley Boy would submit to hypnosis. They could try to dredge the number from her subconscious. It was a possibility for the future.

It was Anna's impression that there were five or six numbers and that there was maybe one 7 and one 2. Maybe, she stressed. That helped a little, but arguably the shield could have been a forgery. Who was to say yet that this blond man was really Secret Service? Laura noted the numbers and assumed she would try to work the angle eventually. But it was an unreliable detail.

"And I don't suppose you examined further to get a name?" Laura asked politely.

"No. No name," she said.

In fact, as Anna remembered, that was when the main event began. She was standing there nude going through the blond man's suit when she tuned in to the noisy conversation among the three men in the next room.

Their words stopped her in her tracks.

It frightened her so much that she quickly put the leather case back where she had found it. "They were talking in Arabic," she said to Chapman.

"*Arabic?* Even the blond man?" Laura asked, recalling the report she had read in D.C.

"All three voices were in Arabic," Anna answered. She added a reverential reference to Jean-Henri, her murdered Lebanese lover in South America. "That's when I started to listen good," Anna said. "Things started to fall into place! Arabs. Not good for Americans!"

"Right," Laura said. The understatement of the last two decades.

The two dark men, Anna said, spoke the language fluently. The blond man spoke the language of the Sahara fluently, but with an American accent. Very quickly, Anna caught snippets of their conversation in Arabic.

. . . five million dollars, the payment . . .

. . . deposited in the Cayman Islands, St. Andrew Trust, Grand Cayman . . .

. . . payment for successfully murdering the president of the United States . . .

. . . the blond man, the Secret Service agent, would be the man to do it . . .

"They plot together!" she said. "They plotted to kill president. Oh, they scared me!"

Anna said she had caught further phrases. The American had forced booze upon the Arabs. So the Crescent Moon boys were talking too damned much, which was just great:

. . . assassin would walk into the Oval Office and pull the trigger . . .

. . . no one will suspect the killer . . .

. . . to do it on next national holiday . . . July Fourth . . .

. . . his death would be fitting act of war against America . . .

They were laughing when they said all those things. Those were the only direct quotes she could remember, although she was very insistent on what she had heard. Anna could understand Arabic better than she could speak it, she explained.

Chapman nodded. "You said earlier, though, that you thought the men could have been Israeli. Or Iranian?"

"I thought that originally. But when I heard them speak, I changed my mind."

And this was, Anna admitted here to Laura, exactly the type of situation she had been praying for. What Anna wanted was the new immigrant's holy trinity: money, a U.S. passport, and a new identity. What she overheard had value, she realized immediately, if she parlayed it correctly. Much more than she had made that night, even taking into account the extra fifties scammed from the wallet of a hired killer.

So she had gone to the U.S. Attorney's office in Miami, she explained next.

An investigator there sat her down before the FBI. From out of nowhere, another man contacted her. A team of two men in suits; one was the thinker and the other was the muscle guy. They took her to an unmarked office in a Miami skyscraper.

Laura recognized it as Agency even if Anna had not.

There she told her story again, this time to Richard McCarron, an Agency case officer.

Anna had an astonishing recall for details, something Laura respected. Taken over a point relentlessly from different angles, she never covered a point in any way but one. She was the perfect witness. She had little malice, no fantasy, no personal opinion, no overriding moral judgment. There were just facts, things that had happened, and her knowledge of them.

Laura asked several more questions, working Anna's story forward and backward, seeing if anything suspicious or inconsistent would emerge.

How long had she stayed with the men, for example?

Till 8 A.M., Anna said. Then she had hurriedly departed.

"Would you recognize the blond man again?"

"Difficult. Never got real good look."

"What if I assigned a police artist? Computer composites? We could create a picture."

Anna shook her head. He had behaved, it seemed to Laura, like a bit of a rapist: He'd had his sex but had never left a good look behind.

"The dark men. The foreigners. You'd recognize them?"

Anna nodded. She would assign the police artist to the other two, then.

"Could you help us with names?" Laura asked next.

"I never know names."

"Did you ever see any of them again?"

"Not yet."

"Do you know if any of these men had been to Robin's club before?"

"No. They were new. I never saw them before."

"Then how did they know about the place?" Chapman asked.

Anna laughed. Most of South Florida knew about the place, she said. It might just as well have been in the guidebooks.

"But if Robin was at the door," Laura answered, "he must have known *someone*."

She shrugged her narrow shoulders. "Ask Robin," she suggested.

Laura would have, but the FBI already had, according to the documents in Washington. Robin had not proven a terribly helpful witness. It was quickly gaining currency with Laura that the porky doorman had three times the weight and half the IQ points of Anna.

Life, she had long ago learned, was frequently like that.

Anna said the club had drop-ins all the time. Anybody who could wave around a fistful of twenties could find the place. If Robin liked the looks of the drop-ins, they entered. If he did not, or if they didn't pony up the proper baksheesh, they could stew in the Miami humidity.

Chapman was suddenly startled. A lock snapped open on the front door of the house.

The door opened. Anna froze. Laura's right palm settled on her Colt.

She looked to Anna and fell silent. *All clear or not?*

JP, who had been seated at Anna's feet, lifted his head and went on orange alert.

There followed a calm conversation in English at the front hallway, a man and a woman.

For an instant the lovely Rose, the redhead girl with the pale face and green eyes, appeared in the doorway to the living room; baby blue mini dress, long sleek chiseled legs, and calf-high boots. She stood looking at Anna. "Hi, baby," Rose said.

"Hey, girl," Anna answered.

Rose had $1,500-a-night written all over her. She looked at Chapman suspiciously, then decided Laura was somehow okay, much like the way a den mother might be okay. Laura meanwhile sensed conspiracy everywhere and wondered if Rose was a CIA asset, also.

"We just talking," Anna said to her roommate. "This is my friend Linda."

Laura raised a friendly hand.

Rose acknowledged with a slight wave. "I came by to pick something up," she answered.

There was magnolia in Rose's speech. She was Deep South. Alabama, maybe.

The "something" was in the medicine cabinet of the downstairs bathroom.

As Rose disappeared, a reed-thin man with a trim mustache—her high-rolling escort—slipped into view. He wore a dark silk suit. He eyed Anna and Laura lecherously, said nothing, then retreated to wait in the front hallway. He looked Mediterranean.

Laura's hand stayed near her weapon. One never knew.

The wait was not long. Within two minutes Rose and her john were out the door again. Laura heard the lock snap smartly back into place, then heard the car start again and disappear into the sweaty night.

Anna looked back to Chapman and forged through the rest of her account. The dialogue continued for another forty minutes. Then it finally hit a dead end.

"Anything else?" Anna finally asked.

JP leaned back against her bare ankles, seeking affection. Anna patted her companion's head. "Just one thing," Chapman said.

Laura dug from her jacket pocket the cell phone that Mitch Hamilton had given to her in Washington.

"I'm going to phone you at least once a day. Keep this with you and keep it turned on."

"Sometimes I forget," she said. "Or it don't fit with my dress."

Laura was already shaking her head. "It's not negotiable," she said. "Are we paying you?" She didn't wait for an answer. "If we are, you have to play by our rules."

Anna sighed and grudgingly accepted it. She input Laura's number into the new cell phone.

Anna asked about her money and when she would be getting more. Laura explained how the finances were not her department, but she would pass the inquiry along, same as the one from Sam about the football scholarship.

The president's life is threatened and already the profiteers are lining up, Laura thought to herself. *Already it's an industry.*

Anna's small black cigarette died. After another sip of coffee, she lit another. A few minutes later, the interview ended in a small cloud of friendly smoke, and a few minutes after that, Laura stepped from Anna's front door.

It was past 2 A.M. She placed one hand on her Colt. Her fears were the size of the city now, her gut tensions and paranoia enjoying new lives.

She walked to her car.

Her footsteps resonated. Harsh beams from industrial-strength street lamps flittered across trees and parked cars. They cut nasty intimidating shadows, each of which, to her fertile imagination, offered a kaleidoscope of threats. There was a ticking of moisture on leaves overhead.

The sidewalks were deserted and wet, the air sticky. When she was no more than a few paces from her car, holding the key in her left hand, there was movement from underneath.

Laura's entire body thumped. She expected her life to end.

Her right hand drew her weapon as a stray cat scrambled

away. Laura froze, then settled down as rapidly as she could, assimilating everything in a nanosecond, seeing that there was no threat, only paranoia.

She put her weapon away and looked around to see if anyone had seen her.

Oh, God, did she need a session with Dr. Feldman when this was over! Her sanity could crash at any time and she was the only person who knew.

Or was she? Did someone out there sense it, know it, too?

She stood perfectly still. There was no one anywhere. Not in an alley, a doorway, or a window. And yet she still had this notion of being watched.

She put her weapon away, unlocked her car, and slid into the driver's seat.

She turned on the ignition.

Car bomb tonight? Will my upper torso land thirty yards down the street while my legs stay in the car?

Interesting question. She waited for the answer.

The motor ran smoothly.

No big bang. Not tonight.

She wondered if her blond assassin existed or whether Anna was the best spinner and scam artist she had met in her life. And why in God's name had this case landed on her?

Blond assassin?

So far, he was a little like Elvis. She heard a lot about him, and it was alleged that he was out there, and there had been "sightings." But she hadn't quite met anyone who could prove that he was real—least of all herself.

So if he *was* out there, where?

chapter 32

"Yes, ma'am," the blond assassin said to the hostess named Tiffany.

"You're as lovely a woman as I've ever seen." He gave her a huge smile. Then he reached into his wallet, under the stern brown-eyed gaze of his two dining companions, and made a show of folding a pair of crisp bills into the woman's bikini shorts. In return, Tiffany smiled.

Her eyes sparkled at the compliment. The money was appreciated, too.

The blond man was having an evening for himself. The location was Diamond Lil's, an expensive upscale restaurant and strip joint that liked to flatter itself as a "gentlemen's club." The term "gentleman" applied to any man who could get himself into a jacket and tie and pay the admission.

Lil's was a glitzy joint that had recently opened in a refurbished warehouse area. It operated in an old brick mansion, run by a couple of connected guys named Tony and Sal from New Jersey.

The hostesses, like Tiffany, served huge drinks, steaks, chops, and grilled seafood while clad in bikini shorts, stockings, high heels, and rhinestone tiaras—hence the perpetuation of the diamond motif—and then took part in the topless stage show. Then they would return to their assigned tables after a show to serve more drinks and pick up tips.

The show did not have much of a plot and displayed more flesh than a Las Vegas revue. A guy got processed for a meal and a great show here for usually about a hundred fifty bucks, including lots of close-up visual contact with the employees. There was always room for a lap dance, but nothing more.

Tiffany was a perky brunette and had a smile as wide as the state. She liked the friendly blond man in the dark suit who was seated comfortably in a club chair. He chatted her up each time she brought drinks to his table. Once when she looked over he was alternately looking at her and inscribing something inside a Diamond Lil's matchbook.

That happened all the time. On-the-make married guys writing their phone numbers in matchbooks, hoping to score after the show. Tiffany's real name was Carol Susan Mackowiack and she was a church-going Methodist. Where, she wondered, did these guys get off, anyway? Looking was fine. Touching was a no-no.

The two other men with him were darkly complexioned. She could not make out what they were. Pakistanis, she guessed. Turks, maybe. One of those "in-between" things: not dark enough to be black, not light enough to be white. Tonight, she didn't really care. The blond man was drinking a whiskey. The two darker quieter men had ordered ten-dollar soft drinks.

She was from Saginaw, Michigan. Her dad had been an auto worker. By being a topless waitress in a swank place in Dallas, she made in an evening what her dad used to make in a week.

Michigan: Well, that was a world away, though she thought of it quite a bit. Her mom knew the type of place she worked and her dad didn't. Her mother was worried that she would never meet "a marrying type of man" in a place like this. Her dad would have flown down to Dallas and beaten the hell out of her if he found out. She lived in fear of her dad discovering.

When her younger sister came to visit, she had to swear her to secrecy. After all, Tiffany thought of this as just temporary, a way to put together a solid bank account over a few years. It wasn't a lifetime. It wasn't a career choice.

So what Tiffany did know was that she had to get on with her business, keep her tables happy and not ask indelicate questions. The blond man was handsome, the best looking of the clientele that night. Tiffany had passed by their table for just long enough for each of the two foreign men to slip twenty-dollar bills into her bikini shorts. The blond man—obviously American—slipped a pair of fifties, it turned out later.

This was definitely a man, she decided, that she wanted to get to know better. A man who spent a hundred bucks just to look at a woman, well, how much might he spend once he knew how happy she could make him? And better yet, Tiffany figured, the man had plenty to spend. She figured he was in oil or computer technology or something.

Then she found something else in between the two fifties. It was the matchbook that she had seen him working on earlier. Inside it, he had sketched a drawing of her in pencil.

Tiffany's shoulders and face. A remarkable likeness. The man had a sensitive side. And with the drawing was a note saying, "You're beautiful. I'm only in town for one more night."

She loved the little sketch. It was lovely. Highly flattering.

She knew she wanted to act on it. But did she have the nerve? Lil's was definitely a look-but-don't-handle operation. Did she have the nerve to date a patron?

Diamond Lil's closed at midnight. Tiffany packed her change of clothes into an overnight bag and walked to the parking lot thirty minutes later. The blond man was standing there alone.

"Hello," she said, surprised but wary.

"Hello," he answered.

She had a cigarette going and put it out.

"You're very beautiful," he said. Then, as an afterthought, "I'll leave right now if you want me to. But I'm staying at the Sheraton Renaissance five blocks away."

He smiled. He was pure charm. Slightly Southern accent. She couldn't quite place it.

"How do you know I'm not married?" she asked. "Or have a boyfriend waiting?"

"I don't," he said. "I thought I'd take that chance." He paused. "Should I ask?"

"You just did."

"What was the answer?"

She looked him up and down. "I didn't tell you to go away, did I?"

He smiled. In many ways, a killer smile. "My name is Kevin."

"I'm Tiffany."

"I know."

"I don't go home with men I meet at work," she said. "And never in my life have I gone to a hotel with a stranger."

He opened his hands with a friendly gesture. "I'll leave if you want."

She kept her distance from him while she thought about it.

"Why don't I follow you in my car?" she suggested. "If I change my mind, I'll go home. If I don't, I'll follow to your hotel. If we go upstairs, I still might change my mind and leave."

"Fair enough," he said. "You know how beautiful you are. You don't need the ego trip."

She looked at his car. A brand-new Lincoln. Okay, so it was probably rented. It was still a brand-new Lincoln.

"You're not a married creep, are you?" she asked.

"I'm not married and I'm not a creep," he said.

"What type of work do you do?"

"I'm an independent contractor. Private security. And I'm good at it."

"You probably are," she allowed.

"Come along," he said. "We can just talk if you want."

He wore a beautiful suit and tie. It said money, but not in an ostentatious way.

Her heart started to do funny things. Never in her life had she encountered a man anything like this. Never. She watched him climb into his car, then she slid into hers.

chapter 33

The blond man had a large suite, one with a huge bed and a bathroom with a massive tub and shower. Tiffany felt comfortable, though Kevin had been a stranger a few hours earlier.

He ordered a late supper for her and let her relax. As she unwound, he did some work on a laptop. It looked to her like he was responding to business messages. All this time, he maintained a pleasant conversation with her.

It was a spur of the moment thing, she decided afterwards. But when she stood and a voice within her told her it was time to leave, she let him embrace her and kiss her.

"You're still free to go," he said.

"I really never do this. I'm embarrassed."

"Don't be," he said. He kissed her again. "I've already seen you undressed."

"Not completely."

"I'm looking forward to the rest."

She thought about it. "So am I," she answered.

She went into the bedroom with him. He turned the lights out right away, but did not release her hand. He pulled her into bed with him and she did not resist.

In bed the blond man was strong and gentle, as if he appreciated her, cared for her, and had known her for a long time. He climbed on top of her expertly and she gasped when he thrust powerfully into her. He was a good lover, large and incredibly exciting. She felt that he filled her better than any previous lover had. It was the best sex of her life, she decided. She guessed that she might have sensed something special when she had fallen into bed so quickly with him.

She also knew he carried a gun, because she saw it during

the night when she got up to use the bathroom. But this was Texas; she saw guns every day.

She was, in fact, much more surprised to see some sort of police badge that she had never seen before. He must have been an official lawman in his security work. That reassured her, yet she made a point of not asking. She had lost men in the past by asking too many questions.

She knew enough to give a new lover his space. Yet where did he get such money on a lawman's salary? That question had no good answer.

Something strange happened, however. Something unusual that she would remember.

After they had made love for a third time, Kevin got up and fetched himself a beer from the mini-bar. She lay on the bed watching him, feeling very comfortable, highly fulfilled, and extremely tired. By this point, she just wanted to curl up next to him and sleep.

Naked, with a gorgeous build for a man in his mid-thirties, Kevin stood at the plate glass window and looked out over the city. Tiffany admired him. He had gorgeous arms and shoulders, a flat stomach, sturdy legs and, the center of her attention, a hefty package, the centerpiece of which had just given her a string of orgasms unlike anything she had ever experienced.

Now he smoked a small cigar.

"Don't know if you can see Dealey Plaza from here, do you?" he asked softly.

"Is that in Dallas, hon?" The smoke smelled expensive.

"It's where the Texas School Book Depository used to be."

"School books?" she asked.

"The building from which Kennedy was murdered."

"*John* Kennedy? You mean, the president?"

He glanced back to her. "Not that leftwing bitch Teddy," the blond man said.

He paused and worked thoughtfully on the cigar. "Ever heard of someone named Jack Ruby?" he asked.

"No." A pause, and she added, "Was he part of the Kennedy killing?"

"Sort of."

"Wasn't there a policeman killed? Was he the policeman?"

"The cop was J. D. Tippett. J. D., as in Jefferson Davis. Tippett was a Ku Klux Klan guy. Most Dallas cops were White Knights in the sixties. Tippett was supposed to shoot Oswald but Oswald shot him first." The blond man smiled. "It worked out better that way for Tippett's widow."

"I'm confused. Who was Ruby?"

"A Jewish gangster who ran a strip club. Used to be a bagman for Al Capone in Chicago."

"Oh." She shook her head. "Who killed Kennedy, anyway? Anyone ever find out?"

Kevin seemed philosophical late at night, but was versed in his fine points of history, particularly when it came to taking out a world leader.

"It's still a mystery," he explained. "Maybe Castro: payback for trying to kill him. Maybe the Mafia: The Kennedy family double-crossed the mob. Maybe the Russians, just for the hell of it. Maybe some white supremacists, who didn't like the civil rights crap. Maybe the Teamsters, 'cause Bobby Kennedy was after Jimmy Hoffa."

"Who?" she asked again. "Bobby and Jimmy What?"

"The point is, do it right," the blond man said evenly. "Hide everybody's true identity and motivation deep enough and you leave behind a long list of suspects. No one ever knows."

"Do what right?"

"Murder the president."

Tiffany shuddered. "I don't know about that stuff," she said, "and I don't really want to."

"Good girl," he said. "It's smart not to know too much."

She sat up. The sheet tumbled to her waist. She leaned on an arm as she watched him.

The blond man's attention drifted back out the window as he finished his cigar. Dealey Plaza was four blocks away on the opposite side of the hotel, now a federal landmark. The sixth floor of the school book building, from which Lee was believed by some to have clipped JFK, was now a museum.

"Terrible thing," Tiffany said, trying to recover. "An American president being murdered like that," she said.

Then the blond man snorted a little laugh. "Yeah," he said. "Terrible."

His reaction disturbed her more than anything. He was a lawman and he was not revolted by the act of assassinating the president? Maybe the guy was a weirdo, after all, Tiffany decided. A little sick. For a couple of seconds, she was disappointed and felt herself turn against him.

But then the cigar was finished. He came back to bed. She started to drift into a very deep slumber and she rolled away from him. He pulled her close to him and wrapped his powerful arms completely around her.

There was one quick moment of alarm when she felt his hand on her neck and something far away in her psyche flashed a danger signal and reminded her that girls who jumped into bed with strange men were sometimes strangled after the act.

But, "Sorry," he said. "I didn't mean to scare you."

Instead, his hands went lower and held her bare breasts as she drifted off. She returned quickly to a comfort level that she had rarely known so soon with a man. She couldn't understand why she felt this way about Kevin because deep down, he scared her.

Well, maybe that was part of it.

chapter 34

PRESIDENTIAL PALACE, TRIPOLI
JUNE 22, 2009; 9:07 A.M. GMT

General Mohammed Omar Mesdoua was in all his glory. The little tyrant had governed Libya for two years. Constantly, he sought ways of outdoing his predecessor, Muammar Qaddafi, verbally trashing the West and foisting his "Pan-Africanism" upon his neighbors. Today, he stood in the press room at the presidential palace and denounced American aggression.

On the sidewalks outside, Qaddafi had fled in his underpants an early morning in March of 1986 as American bombs dropped on his doorstep. The Libyan power structure had never forgotten the humiliation, even when they had retaliated by blowing up the Lockerbie jumbo or when the unpredictable Qaddafi tried to kiss and make up during the Iraqi fiasco in 2004.

Today, General Mesdoua wore a crisp khaki uniform. He affected the same crazy look as his predecessor. His voice sounded like fingernails on a blackboard: an irritating nasal brand of desert-rat Arabic as he maintained "the United States and its gangster allies and forces" were waging a war against the Arab and African peoples. And he had proof, he insisted. Proof.

Every once in a while during the press conference he would pause to let his press attaché, an American-educated Libyan named Bahrim Shahadi, translate into French and English. Two dozen members of the foreign press had assembled on short notice. Most had learned to take anything official with a mountain of salt. But still they listened. And still they reported.

By now the news had flashed around the world that an American aircraft had engaged in yet another aerial dogfight against Libya. Independent sources maintained that both sides had lost an aircraft. The United States had only confirmed that an engagement had taken place. But observers also knew of a huge air-sea rescue operation in the Gulf of Sidra just north of Tripoli.

As Alan Savett of Reuters said to Lisa McJeffries of ABC News, as he waited for the tyrant to start speaking, "You Yanks are *not* in those waters on a fishing expedition. You *must* be looking for something. One of your aircraft, perhaps," Savett suggested, angling.

"I don't make foreign policy," Lisa replied, "and I don't have better contacts than you."

"Oh, I doubt that very much, my dear," the Englishman said

with a snort. "A woman with such blinding beauty as yours in *this* hellhole?" Savett was a large, lean man, fifteen years older than Lisa. He was brilliantly intellectual, a classical scholar and, like many intellectuals, personably unbearable. He was a self-styled computer geek and an amateur photographer. He was known to augment his own written reports with self-congratulating photographs of himself, many of which made him look much goofier than he actually was. But his main claim to his posting in Tripoli was his overt pro-Islamic bias and fluency in Arabic. Reuters had assigned him to Libya not long after Qaddafi fell from power, leapfrogging him over several more deserving correspondents. The rumor was, the Libyans liked him so much that they had requested him.

Savett was a British national, but his mother had been a secretary at Aramco. His father had been an Egyptian-born petroleum geologist. He was a University of Leeds graduate and had been head of the Islamic Student Union there. Meaning, his public sympathies were decidedly anti-West and his reporting often had the odor of his biases. He also had been coming on to Lisa McJeffries for the six months she had been in Libya—not that it was not already difficult enough for an attractive thirty-five-year-old American woman to work that beat.

She always sought to ignore him. To the rest of the Western media in Tripoli, he was deemed a pain in general. He received special treatment from the government because of whom he worked for and how he felt. To Lisa, he was much worse than the normal undesired suitor.

"Any *idea* what happened out in the gulf?" Savett pressed.

"I don't know anything more than you do, Alan," she said. "Probably less."

"Be nice to me and you *would* know more," he said.

She ignored the remark. Savett forced a jaunty smile and turned his attention back to the press conference, a digital camera hanging off his belt.

He had noticed an ominous trend recently. Increasingly, the newly formed National Police Corps administered these events. Red Berets they were called, as they were outfitted in red berets, along with forest green uniforms, the same color as the flag, and plenty of firepower. As in any totalitarian state, one did not solicit private engagements with them if one were wise.

In Western Europe, leaders of fifteen governments had already condemned the United States for flying so close to Libya. Privately, a few of those same governments applauded the missions. They were as happy as socialist pigs rolling in socialist shit about the air surveillance of the Libyans. The Christian population of Europe had been decreasing rapidly in the first decade of the twenty-first century while Muslim immigration had surged, as had the increasing Islamification of the continent. Anti-American and anti-Semitic sentiments had increased, which did not displease many native Europeans, until their own traditional cultural symbols—crucifixes, wine, beef, bratwurst—came under social assault.

The leaders of "traditional Europe," those who held to traditional values, lived in fear of the networks of militant Arabs within their own boundaries. Nor did they wish to make the recon flights with their own air forces. It was typical European diplomatic double-speak:

When the United States is involved, the Americans are meddling in European affairs; when the United States is *not* involved, the Americans are isolationists and failing to take a leadership role. Always blame the Americans. Even when you're wrong, you'll always be at least partially right and— no hard feelings, pal!—they'll still send dumb tourists with dollars.

Alan Savett was one who, in print at least, proclaimed the new European demographics—the new "Eurabia"—with great cheer. It was to him just a matter of correcting history.

If the French had failed to defeat an invading Muslim army at the Battle of Poitiers in A.D. 732 . . .

Savett once wrote in *The Times* of London before being personally canned by Rupert Murdoch,

... all of Western Europe would have eventually succumbed to Islam. We would all be reading the Koran now and professing the sanctity and truth of the holy revelation of Mohammed. Instead, this will come to pass closer to A.D. 2032, a mere thirteen centuries later, at which time we shall be obliged to drop the oppressive 'A.D.'

In the wrong quarters, Savett and his opinions could wear out a welcome rather speedily. Sometimes in the right quarters, too. On another occasion, he wrote:

... The Americans in the Middle East provide a perfect parallel to the British of the 1920s. They are dedicated, heavily armed, and remorselessly on the wrong side of history. Why cannot Washington understand that history is often propelled by violent minorities? Why, when the American colonial insurrection of 1776 was exactly such an example?

As members of the press came to attention, General Mesdoua started making motions with his arms, spinning them as if to lure journalists forward.

"I say, what's this, now?" Savett asked, watching Mesdoua's limbs rotate.

"It looks like he wants us to come up and kiss him," Lisa McJeffries said. "You go first, Alan. Your credentials are better. Go ahead. All four cheeks."

"I'd rather kiss you, Lisa, darling," Savett retorted.

"File it under 'never,' Alan," she said.

"I will win your heart eventually, Lisa," Savett promised.

Other journalists were also baffled over what was going on. But the dictator indicated that his two dozen laptoppers should follow him into the adjoining chamber.

"Come. Follow me," General Mesdoua exhorted in English. *"Venez. Suivez-moi!"*

"In English or French, that's Matthew 4:18–22," Savett mumbled, intentionally playing on the words and the context. "Follow me. The general wants to make us 'fishers of men.'"

"What are you talking about?" Lisa asked, highly annoyed.

"Nothing," Savett answered, smirking. "My reference was far too oblique for an American audience. I apologize."

"Jesus Christ. You're the most obnoxious man I've ever met," she muttered.

The dictator's lackeys herded the journalists behind a rope. Mesdoua made a grand gesture to an awaiting police captain, a nasty thug in a red beret. With the crimson crown, dark aviator sunglasses, and a sharp nose, the captain looked like a woodpecker on Methedrine. The captain pulled away a drapery.

The correspondents gasped en masse.

Beneath a ten-by-twenty-foot color portrait of Mesdoua, there were two gurneys. The gurneys bore the bodies of two American aviators, still in blood-stained uniform.

Captain Jack Kendall.

Major Gerald Straighthorn.

"Both dead!" Mesdoua pronounced proudly. He took a prissy little bow and appeared pleased with himself.

"Told you," Savett whispered to Lisa. Savett was quick with his camera. He snapped twice, then a third time for good luck.

"Oh, my God!" she said.

Lisa averted her eyes quickly from the gruesome spectacle. Savett remained focused, taking notes while never taking his gaze off the funereal display.

chapter 35

PRESIDENTIAL PALACE, TRIPOLI
JUNE 22, 2009; 9:34 A.M.

General Mesdoua started to applaud. Another elite guard thug appeared and forcefully shoved each body, indicating that the two Americans were dead. The reporters gawked for several more seconds, some looked down and began to write. Lisa looked back up. Three who were accredited took photographs. General Mesdoua quick-stepped smiling into the photo op.

"Two American air pirates!" Mesdoua said in Arabic, accompanied by a running translation of his words by his man, Shahadi. The tyrant clapped his hands more and continued.

"They died when their plane crashed," said the press spokesman. Shahadi spoke good English. He had attended Boston University for two years on a scholarship for foreign students.

"Time is up, thank you," Shahadi said.

The dictator clapped twice, a different cadence this time. Then soldiers pulled the curtain back in place. The two Americans sure looked dead, all right. The navigator was torn up with scars. His head was crooked. Same as the colonel's beret. The other body had a bandaged wrist.

"Were they both dead on impact?" someone from *Agence-France* asked.

"Dead on impact," said Shahadi.

The dictator beamed. He interjected that it was a great victory for Libyan self-defense forces and the world of Islam, Allah be praised.

"Dead when they hit the water?" Lisa McJeffries asked.

"They did not survive the downing of their pirate aircraft," Shahadi answered.

Lisa McJeffries persisted. "But the American on the right had a bandaged wrist."

"Yes? Please?" Shahadi answered.

"Obviously, he did not leave his base with a bandaged wrist," McJeffries said. "Why would he have received medical attention if he died on impact?"

"He was dead on impact according to Our Esteemed Leader, the prime minister," Shahadi said. "That is all the information I have on the American bandits. The downing of the invading aircraft was a great triumph for His Excellency, the president of Libya, and the people's self-defense forces."

"May we take a closer inspection of the bodies?" Lisa McJeffries asked.

"That will not be possible."

Savett turned conspicuously to Lisa. "Oh, for God's sake, woman. The pilot is *dead,* can't you see? The Libyans did the humane thing, bandaging an injury in preparation for burial."

"I asked *them,* not you, Alan!" McJeffries came back sharply.

Savett folded away his note pad. He slid his pen into a leather folio, a gift from the palace. "It's disrespectful, your line of questioning," he said. "You can be such a *sunt* sometimes, that's a 'c' with a cedilla."

"Alan, get away from me," she said.

"With pleasure," he huffed.

"No further questions on this aspect of the incident in the Gulf of Sidra," said Shahadi.

"Have arrangements been made to return the bodies to the United States?" asked Kevin Halloran for CNN.

Mesdoua chimed back in. The only thing about him that was world class was his swagger, and that was in full bloom by this time. More high-pitched bullshit in Arabic: "In keeping with Islamic law," the general said, "the American bandits will be buried in unmarked graves on the soil they came to desecrate."

Shahadi translated.

"The bodies are not being returned?" Lisa McJeffries asked.

"Why should they be?" answered the dictator in Arabic. Shahadi translated for her

"International law would suggest—" she began.

Furious, impetuous, the dictator cut everyone off and went into a polemic.

Shahadi kept the commentary running. It would have been comic had there not been two bodies on gurneys and a general mobilization going on among the Sixth Fleet.

"International law!" the translator howled. "Ask the American president about international law! Unmarked graves. Tomorrow. No changes."

The dictator raised his hands in the air and shook them.

No one from the Western press could tell if the gesture was in celebration or if he were imploring the heavens.

With that, the tyrant was finished and so was the press conference. A team of soldiers wheeled away the gurneys. A second team shunted the press from the presidential palace.

Lisa McJeffries continued to make notes. Savett tossed her a glance as he prepared to depart and file his own account back to the U.K.

"My own opinion," he snorted loudly, "is you Americans received what you deserved."

"I'm not interested in your opinion, Alan," she said.

"You'll be exposed to it anyway. You're not the world's policeman, you're the world's arrogant self-righteous bully boy. And those pilots deserve to lie in the sand."

"You disgust me," she said. "You're such an overt apologist for this regime. You ought to be ashamed of yourself."

"When your cowboy presidents stop provoking unnecessary wars, and the majority of your people stop voting for them, we can discuss who's the apologist," he shot back.

The exchange was sharp and in full view of the rest of the correspondents. Lisa flipped Savett an upraised center finger.

But the next major move and response was in the hands of Washington. All she could do was report. She and the other correspondents were on the air within a quarter hour.

chapter 36

DALLAS, TEXAS
JUNE 22, 2009, 7:38 A.M. CDST

When Tiffany awoke, the man she had slept with was gone. So was every trace of him. It freaked her out. She had the horrifying notion that he might have stiffed her with the hotel bill.

When she went into the bathroom, however, her fears

were put to rest. He had left a note on the mirror. In beautiful bold handwriting it read,

> *Tiffany,*
>
> *You were great. I hope we'll do it again sometime soon. The bill is settled downstairs, although the account has been left open. Feel free to order breakfast and stay till noon checkout time.*
>
> *Sorry I couldn't stay. Business elsewhere* ☺.
>
> *Lovingly,*
>
> *KG*
>
> *PS: If you should suddenly come into a small amount of "found money" some time soon, buy something I'd like.*

She sighed, though the last sentence mystified her. *Found money?*

She confirmed from someone at the front desk named Mark that the bill had indeed been settled. So, might as well enjoy this. She ordered breakfast and took her time leaving.

At noon, overnight bag in hand, she attempted to drift unnoticed through the lobby to leave. The hotel watched their patrons more carefully than that, however.

Someone from the front desk called to her. "Ma'am? One minute?"

She froze, knowing that this had just been too good. A young man with a Northern accent came to her.

"I'm Mark," he said politely. "We spoke earlier?"

"What is it?" she asked, now expecting there to be a problem and to get socked with the bill, or worse. She scanned the lobby, wondering how they knew what room she had come from.

"Ma'am, Mr. McKinley overpaid," the clerk explained. "He's due a small refund."

Mark held a small brown envelope with cash in it.

"Mr. McKinley? Oh," she said. "You mean Kevin," she

said, trying not to fumble, not to reveal that she had been his one-nighter. "Yes, he mentioned that he might have."

"He said you should take the change with you," Mark said. "He said you'd either hold it for him or use it the way he suggested?" It sounded like a question. Maybe.

"Sure thing," she said. "He's like that."

Mark grinned.

She took the envelope. Mark wished her a good day. When she was out by her car, she opened it and found cash in the amount of $187.56.

Tiffany considered going back into the hotel and asking if "Mr. McKinley" stayed there often. But that would have thrown the wrong light on her. So instead she accepted it.

And she would buy herself something. Accepting cash would be wrong. Accepting a "gift" was different.

He was a piece of work, this Mr. Kevin McKinley, Tiffany concluded. And when she arrived home in Fort Worth twenty minutes later, she made another small discovery.

Her name tag from the club, the one that said TIFFANY in black on a sparkling silver background, was missing. She knew she had clipped it to her bikini bottom, as she always did. And she remembered packing it up when she assembled her things to leave work.

So either she had lost it, or, much more likely, Kevin had gone through her bag. He had taken it as a souvenir.

One part of her was glad. She wanted him to have it, his personal way of claiming her. Another part of her, upon further thought, was cautious.

Was he some sort of creepy fetishist who had sex with women and collected their name tags? And what else had he taken?

That thought made her check her wallet immediately.

Nothing missing there. But her cards and licenses had been rearranged, as if someone had shuffled through them, then put them back. Only one person could have done that. "So," she mused, "he knows who I am and where to find me. Not just at the club, but at home."

This was a trickier issue. She remembered all the arguments

with her mother, that the men who came to these clubs were never to be trusted in relationships. So was this a good thing or a bad thing that Kevin had looked for personal information?

If he were on the up and up, he could have asked her those questions. Yet, maybe he had just wanted to let her sleep. After all, he had had every opportunity to rob her, but didn't.

These issues troubled her all day.

As she bathed at home later and prepared to do some shopping, her thoughts coalesced.

She came to a conclusion. A very firm one.

It was a good thing that she had gone with him to the hotel and had gone to bed with him. And it was a good thing that he knew her name and where to find her.

Kevin McKinley was one of the only true gentlemen she had ever met at her "gentlemen's club." And so she had done exactly the right thing to entice him back.

There was no other way it could be. Sometimes in the past when she slept with a man she felt dirty afterwards. Soiled and used. Not this time. This had been just what she needed.

She felt good. The sex had been outstanding. And she hadn't felt this giddy in years. And the more she thought of it, the more she liked her Kevin and the less she was afraid of him.

chapter 37

MIAMI
JUNE 22, 2009; MORNING

The next morning, Laura showered and had breakfast brought to her hotel room at nine. She dressed in a white blouse, dark green skirt, and a navy jacket. Small gold hoop earrings that she had once bought for herself at Cartier in New York. Laura might have been a banker, until she clipped her cell phone onto her left hip and holstered her Colt on the right.

In the center of the lobby was large coin-cluttered fountain, presided over by a giant steel sculpture that was said to represent the Americas but, as it seemed to her, described nothing more than a cosmic muddle. Perhaps both statements were true. There was no music, mercifully.

The hotel bar was named Casablanca. Not surprisingly its dark walls had framed photographs from that movie. Subdued lighting gave it a movie-theater quality. The Casablanca was not in the Park Central itself, but in an annex next door which had once been a separate hotel named the Imperial, and which was reached by a passage from the lobby.

The barman was busy opening his register when Laura entered. He gave her a polite double take. "Morning," he said. He had an accent.

"Morning," she said in return.

The barman gave her a strange look. Did he think she was bringing some sort of trouble or complication with her? She ordered a ginger ale and told him she was meeting a friend.

From under the bar he produced a chilled bottle of Canada Dry. He set her up with a glass of ice cubes. Four dollars.

She thanked him and glanced at her watch. Two minutes before ten. Segments of Anna's story from the preceding evening flitted through her mind. She turned them over, relentlessly looking for inconsistencies, but found none.

The bartender turned on a television. A special report concluded about the crisis in Washington and North Africa. Regular morning programming resumed: a local bilingual game show in English and Spanish that featured fat people in shorts trying to win hundreds of dollars.

Laura's contact, Richard McCarron, wasn't here yet. *No one* was there yet, other than Laura and the barman.

Laura ran a brief test. She phoned Anna. To her relief, a sleepy-voiced Charley Boy answered the cell phone that she had left behind. Anna was very much alive and unharmed. She started to tell Laura about the man she had had two evenings earlier, a young television producer from Hollywood.

Laura indulged and listened. The irony struck. She had

signed on in a career of personal protection and here she was in Florida listening to a hooker describe her work.

"I'm glad you had a good evening," Laura said finally.

"Very good evening," Anna said.

Laura rang off and put the phone down. At least the small stuff was starting to click into place, and, truth was, she had already developed a bit of affection for Anna.

Laura's thoughts returned to the conversation they had had the previous night.

What had she learned? What new questions had been raised?

What were the facts? What were the issues? How did Anna's account mesh with what she had learned in her own briefing?

Laura's only question about the venue itself—the joint where Anna worked—was whether the set-up money for the joint came from the U.S. taxpayers. She assumed it did. The wiseguy who ran the joint was a typical Agency asset, though apparently Anna hadn't known that much when she first went to work there.

So if the gambling house was an Agency place, was it a coincidence that Anna had come to work there? Was it a further coincidence that someone bent on killing the president would have wandered in?

Strangely enough, within context, that part made sense. The club was an efficient front, an ear to the local ground. The Agency ran a number of such places around the globe. Was this any stranger than previous generations? In the past CIA money had financed Students for a Democratic Society at the University of Michigan, LSD research in New York City, and *Paris Match* in France to keep non-communist Western opinion alive in Western Europe.

So what did a few brothels matter here and there?

Then again, in the last quarter century, the CIA had failed to anticipate the fall of the Shah in Iran, the collapse of the Soviet empire, the 9/11 attacks on America and the lead-up to the Bush 43 war in Iraq. They had alleged nuclear weapons where they were not and missed them where they were. And that was just the big stuff. Why trust them on any-thing?

Disgruntled, Laura also processed other information in the back of her mind. The records of the Secret Service bureau in Miami had not shown any unusual movement for the days in question for anyone believed to be a potential threat to the president.

Daily monitoring—those boys and girls who sat at computers all day and kept tabs on the local nutcases—had established nothing unusual.

The FBI had also run a check of flights in and out of Miami for early June, flights that went to the Middle East or connected to it. They had scanned lists of passengers for suspected terrorists and their known passports. They had run cross-checks with a newly, but grudgingly, cooperative CIA. Again, nothing had turned up and they had run fingerprint and laser retina scan checks all over the United States.

Still nothing.

Strange. Strange, Laura thought, that *nothing* was turning up.

What *had* turned up, however, when some source in the Caymans broke into the local bank computers, was the June 10 entry for five million dollars in the St. Andrew's Trust Company, Ltd. of Grand Cayman.

The deposit stuck out like a beacon that day, 1:45 P.M., and it had been carefully laundered through a neutral bank computer in Costa Rica. Here was exactly the bank named in Anna's narrative and exactly half the amount of money promised. It did not take a genius or a mathematician to suspect that the killer had been paid half now and would receive the rest when his job was done. *If* the owner of the account was actually the assassin Laura sought.

The account was under the name A. Lincoln.

A. Lincoln: *Yeah, right!* Laura stirred her ginger ale with a plastic straw. The old sick joke returned to her. *But aside from that, Mrs. Lincoln, how was the play?*

And "A. Lincoln"?

Fake as a three-dollar bill. But Laura wondered if the

killer had a historical predilection of some sort, consciously or unconsciously. Lincoln was the first American president to be murdered. Was Chapman reading in too much? Did the killer have a macabre sense of history? Was the killer well educated? Were her gut instinct and paranoia homing in on something?

The address given had already been run up by the FBI. It was in Texas and non-existent. It bore no relation to any other fake address or idea that had already surfaced in this investigation.

Dead end, dead end, dead end.

There was already a frightening touch of professionalism to the enterprise as well as some heinous symmetry. It scared Laura anew. What this pointed to, if it pointed to anything at all, was that this was a conspiracy among the very few. Half a dozen persons? Maybe fewer? The only thing visible was the invisibility of the participants.

Where would Laura pick up a trail if none existed?

Yet from the tidbits of bank information, Chapman wondered if she could draw some conclusions. Five million dollars was a whopping sum to place somewhere as window dressing for a plot that did not exist. Even in the day of watery four-dollar ginger ales, five mil was a chunk of dough. So she now went on the assumption that the money had been paid for a service. It made her wonder what the recipient had done with the money.

Then there were the little associated details, the little smirks in the face of authority. A bank account set up to finance the murder of the American president named for Lincoln, the most revered of the slain presidents.

A coincidence? As noted, Laura did not like coincidences.

And similarly, why a fraudulent address in Texas?

Was the killer perhaps a Southerner, a Texan even, who made up the bogus address from knowledge of the area? Maybe.

But John F. Kennedy had been murdered in Texas. Another coincidence?

Why Texas? Or why *not* Texas? Had the killer recently been in Texas? Or was there any such thing as coincidence? Was there any way to know?

She sat very still at the bar, far away in thought.

Then something else hit her. The registration at The Tides. *Jay W. Booth.*

As in John Wilkes Booth? Another coincidence? No, not at all. Now she was *certain.* The killer was so sure of himself that he was mocking anyone foolish enough to try to track him.

She felt her anger rise.

A. Lincoln. Jay W. Booth: Screw you!

Laura's gaze swept the room, hit the doorway, and slammed to a halt. A trim, handsome man of about six feet, slender and athletic with dark hair, entered and glanced around. He was in a suit, with a pale yellow shirt and blue patterned tie. He was a man her gaze would have settled upon with a bit of longing any day. But this morning there was an ulterior purpose.

Gut feeling again: Richard McCarron. Her CIA contact.

The man spotted her at the same moment. Their eyes locked. He approached her and immediately she noticed, incongruously to his dark suit, that there was something large and white on his right hand.

Instantly, she wondered what he was hiding. What sort of weapon.

Momentary panic.

Then when he drew closer, she saw that it was a cast and a bandage. Then again, as he drew nearer still, what if it wasn't?

Her own right hand moved closer to the edge of her jacket. It settled on her weapon as he stood in front of her. She gripped it.

"Laura?" he asked.

"That's me," she said.

"I'm Rick McCarron."

It took a moment, but her hand relaxed.

He watched the movement and smiled.

"You planning to take me out before I have a chance to talk?" he asked smoothly.

She let both hands relax onto her lap.

"Sorry," Laura answered. "I *am* jumpy."

"Aren't we all these days?" he asked. "Aren't we all?"

Gut feeling vindicated. More relief washing over her. This *was* her contact.

"Let's talk," he said to Laura, glancing to the barman. "But not right here."

chapter 38

MIAMI
JUNE 22, 2009; 10:16 A.M. EDST

"I'd offer you a handshake," he said as they settled into a booth in a corner out of the barman's hearing range. "But . . . as you see . . ." McCarron showed the cast and shrugged.

"Is there a story behind it?" Laura asked.

"I'd offer a lie about a forcible arrest," he said, "but it was actually Sunday softball. Sprained a thumb. The cast comes off in two days."

"You sure you didn't punch out a water cooler? Or a regional director?"

"Wish I had. Got charged with an error, too. Playing third base. That's what really hurt. That, and the fact that the ball was hit by my secretary."

McCarron had a boyish face, though he must have been forty. His shoulders were broad and powerful. His only jewelry was a gold Movado watch with a leather band; no bracelet, no rings. Nothing strange.

He ordered a coffee and made some small talk. After the coffee appeared and the barman vanished, he turned his brown eyes back upon her.

"So," he said. "How did it go last night? Sam and Charley Boy? Talk to me."

"Sam's a sleaze and Charley Boy is a credible witness, at least so far," she said.

McCarron smiled. "How do you know it isn't the other way around?"

"Gut instinct."

"That's nice. Got anything more substantial than that?"

"Do we ever?" she asked.

"Sometimes."

"I knew Sam was a sleaze before I came down to Miami," she said. "So if I'm wrong, I mean, I'm only half wrong. I'm going by instinct on your source because I don't have any way of corroborating anything other than what's been given to me."

"So am I," he said. "Going on instinct. Sam's not my favorite individual either. But, God knows, he seems to have a pipeline into everything within five hundred miles of Miami."

The barman, seeing their lack of interest in the television, switched to another Spanish-language game show, this time in brighter colors with trimmer, better-looking contestants.

McCarron leaned back from the table. "I'm on a fine edge on this case," he said. "The FBI had a file on this, but they've passed on it. They've decided it's nothing and have nothing active on it. Or so they tell us. I don't buy what they're saying, so I'm staying with it."

"Good. I'm glad."

"You don't have issues with me staying with it?" he asked.

"Issues? I'm delighted. You're one of the first allies I've found."

He broke a small smile again. "I was afraid you were going to claim jurisdiction and ask me off the case. So I'm relieved, too."

"I'm not territorial like that," she said.

"Five years ago I wouldn't have been able to touch this case with a cattle prod," he said, "but under National Security

Reorganization if the FBI doesn't want it, I can follow up at my own option. With me?"

Laura was.

"If I give it back to them, they'll deep-six it," McCarron said. "We won't know how our case is proceeding until we hear gunshots in the White House."

"I'm surprised they're letting you touch it. Usually the FBI is more territorial."

"Not much they can do about it," McCarron said. "Under NASRO there's more latitude than there used to be. They have to deal, so do I."

They spent a half hour comparing notes. McCarron, if he could be believed, was reading tea leaves as much as Laura. But at least they had that dead end feeling in unison.

"Who's taking care of security on Charley Boy?" he finally asked. "My office can't."

"Sam says he will."

"And Sam's sober these days?"

"Probably not very often."

"You're a bright woman, aren't you?"

"Why do you say that? I haven't said anything."

"That's what I mean. You're just letting me talk."

"You're not so slow-witted yourself," Laura answered.

"That's the nicest thing anyone from Washington has ever said to me." He paused. "Then again, Washington doesn't talk to me much. That's why they parked me in Miami."

"Something you did?"

"I'll tell you about it sometime. You'll probably sympathize."

He smiled slightly. She felt a thaw, also. She was starting to like Mr. Rick McCarron.

"I'll give you my cell phone number," he said. "Secure line, scrambled on a two-second delay. Let me know what I can do for you." He wrote out the number. "Memorize it, okay?"

It was the new Miami area code: 565.

She looked at the number and worked the rest of it into her head. A three-five-seven exchange with a seven-eight-zero-eight.

She handed back the number. "Got it," she said.

"That fast?"

"It's only three numbers."

"I'm impressed. Come work for me someday."

"Maybe you can come to D.C. and work for me," Laura answered.

"Ah. Who knows?" he said with a laugh. "I might like that. Anything else?"

"You have my cell number?"

"Mitch gave it to me."

"Then I think that's it," she said. "When I get back to Washington, I'll take inventory on everything. You'll hear from me. I know I'll need your help."

"You'll get it," he promised.

McCarron disappeared into the hotel lobby. Laura went back upstairs to pack.

The only thing left on her to-do list was Sam again, the only thing resting between her and her flight home. And Sam, as she reminded herself, was always a bitch and a half. She braced herself and she too wondered if Sam would be sober when she found him again.

chapter 39

MIAMI
JUNE 22, 2009; 4:03 P.M.

For some reason, the paranoia kicked in again as she was leaving the Park Central.

The rendezvous point on Monday afternoon was La Veranda, an outdoor café on Ocean Drive, open, bustling, and adjacent to a grand hotel. It was across a busy street from the beach, with a view of the sand and Atlantic Ocean. Laura walked there in twelve minutes.

She found a seat at an empty table for two, fifteen minutes

early for a 4:30 meeting. She sat with her back to a wall. She could see in all directions. She watched the bench across the street on the beach side, still keeping a keen eye on comings and goings. Two men appeared and sat down on the bench shortly after she took her place at the table.

They didn't talk, but stared across at the café where she was seated.

Her paranoia heightened. What vibes was she picking up on?

The two men were joined by a girl with long brown hair. She carried a straw beach bag. From what Laura could see from about fifty feet away, the girl was very pretty. She wore a white blouse, a very short pink skirt, and sandals. She had long tan legs, perfectly shaped. The men looked at her and struck up a conversation. The girl looked non-committal. She sat down on the bench. The girl must have been about twenty and Laura liked her look.

A waiter came to Laura's table. Laura ordered a tropical iced tea. The waiter vanished.

A few minutes passed. A bus came along across the street. Laura kept watching. The men boarded and the girl didn't. Was she avoiding riding with them because she sensed potential harassment and she preferred to take the next bus?

Or did they know each other and she had conveyed a message?

Was the beach bag filled with beach attire, books from a college class, or a change of clothing so she could remain on surveillance?

Was the girl a model, a college student, a pavement artist, all of these, or none of these? Was she comfortable looking so pretty, or did she find herself too often pestered because of it?

In her mind, Laura named her Estela. Little fantasy scenarios took over. Estela took out a paperback book and began to read. But Laura noticed, the girl never stopped facing the café.

Still no Sam. Maybe someone had shot him overnight, Laura mused idly.

Estela remained at the bus stop. Minutes ticked away.

Laura watched to see if she would occasionally flip a page. She did at regular intervals.

Laura hauled herself back into reality.

The waiter returned with the iced tea. Eight bucks, counting the 25 percent tip automatically added.

On a menu card on the table, Laura saw the price list for the "specialty drinks."

The Florida Hurricane	$20
The Jaws of the Alligator	$20
Sex with a Stranger	$22

She shook her head.

How 'bout one called *Death of a President:* $10,000,000?

Laura looked across the street again at the azure sea, the lithe brown girls and boys walking along the beach, both genders stripped down to barely anything in the formidable Florida sun. Along the roadway, cars cruised; ordinary cars and expensive BMWs, Mercedes, and Porsches, as well as the occasional real—and beautifully maintained—antiques, two- and three-toned cars from the '50s and earlier. Some of the drivers were scanning for pick-ups, while others seemed to enjoy showing off their rides. No one anywhere in sight, aside from her and the café's staff, seemed to work or entertain any personal responsibility; money flowed as readily as if it came off a printing press at home.

And how? From what source sprang such wealth? One sure didn't buy into this lifestyle by working for the government, not if one had any principles.

She ruminated about the nature of the blond assassin, if he existed, if he was truly out there. Ten million dollars. *That* would buy him a lifestyle like this. But if that was his motivation, how could he ever hope to escape?

Again, something somewhere didn't make sense. This wasn't an airline hijacker seeking a thousand virgins in paradise in return for his earthly martyrdom. This was a man somehow seeking to do a job and escape.

Wasn't it?

What was wrong with this picture?

She was so hooked into the perplexities of this case now that she couldn't dismiss it, even for a minute. It was with her now until she either resolved it or it killed her.

Estela continued to hold her gaze.

A husky close-by male voice said, "Hello."

The voice was silky and jarred her again back to the present. It startled her.

But she had dropped her guard, so much so that it could have cost Laura her life. Jolted, her hand flew toward her weapon but never arrived. A powerful male hand reacted much faster. It clamped on her wrist and held it firmly.

She looked up and stared into a pair of dark brown eyes that lurked behind yellow-tinted lenses.

chapter 40

MIAMI
JUNE 22, 2009; 4:43 P.M.

"This seat taken?" Sam Deal asked.

"Hello, Sam," she said. She moved her wrist against his thumb and broke his grip.

Cautiously, he released her. Sam pulled out the chair across from her. Her thoughts had been riffing so far away that she had not seen him coming.

He sat down. "You had a faraway look," he said.

"Did I?"

"Well, your thoughts weren't in this café, that much was clear. I know a distant look when I see one."

Sam signaled to the waiter, who seemed to be familiar with Sam's drinking preferences. The waiter brought a bottle of Glenmorangie and poured Sam a double Scotch straight up, ice water on the side. Sam gave him three crisp tens and declined change.

"So?" Sam asked, turning back to Laura. "Last night? Anyone get shot, anyone get laid?"

Laura gave Sam as much as he needed to know.

"The contact's a woman; we feel she could be in danger," Laura explained. "She's resistant to protective custody so she needs to be watched. That means you have to put some of your best people into the place where she's employed. Have you done that yet?"

"I'm getting a crew together."

"Sam, it needs to be done *now!*"

"Don't worry. The place is fully padded up with the local police. How do you think the Republicans keep winning in Florida if not for places like that?"

Laura let Sam's suggestion sink of its own weight.

"Robin at the door will let you know which of the girls she is," she continued. "Can you get someone on it tonight?"

"Probably."

She felt a constriction in her stomach. "I need something better than 'probably,' Sam."

"Probably," he said again.

A leggy dark-haired woman strolled by in a tan miniskirt and a Columbia University T-shirt. She was pretty and carried a Fencing Dude bag. Sam watched appreciatively.

"This whole neighborhood has sure changed," Sam said. "It used to be nothing but elderly Hebrews waiting to die. That girl there with the Columbia shirt. She's a fencer. That's why she has great legs."

"Sam, would you pay attention, please?"

"Oh," he said. "Sorry."

Then, before her fuse burned down further, Sam allowed that he would go over and babysit, himself, if necessary. That mollified Laura. A little of the inner tightness untangled.

Laura flicked her gaze across the street. It was almost five o'clock. At least two buses had passed. Estela hadn't moved.

"You ever been under surveillance, Sam?" Laura asked.

Deal made an unattractive guttural sound, clearing his throat. "Is there any time I'm not?" he asked.

"Do you have watchers now?"

"It's always possible," Sam answered. "I'm sure there are people out there who would like to give me two behind the ear."

"It's my guess one of us has a team today. Watching."

"Sure," Sam agreed in a tone that sounded more facetious than anything else. "Why wouldn't I be under surveillance? I'm an old white guy who goes to church and who's put in a lifetime of faithful patriotic service. But I hold some political opinions that aren't on the edge of fashion." He paused. "So I'm toast."

"That's not the point," Laura said. "You're taking it in a different direction."

"I answered your question. And why do you ask? What the hell? *Whose* surveillance?"

"You see that girl there on the bench across the street?" Laura asked, indicating. "She joined a couple of men, one of whom tailed me when I walked from the Park Central. They moved on, but she's been there for thirty minutes. What's she watching? You or me?"

"Maybe both."

"It doesn't unnerve you?"

"Why should it, even if I believed that you knew what you were talking about?"

"Would you at least *look* at the situation?" Laura pleaded.

Sam sighed. He scanned the street and eyed the girl across Ocean Drive.

"If she was watching, she wouldn't wear a damned pink skirt," he said. "Man sees that, he remembers it all day, as well as what's packed into it."

"She's carrying a bag," Laura said. "A woman can get out of a skirt and into a pair of jeans in thirty seconds."

"Maybe."

"I feel eyes on my back, Sam."

"Maybe it's because you're a good-looking girl. Get with the program. Men like to watch." He paused. "Maybe that's your problem. You're a tight-ass."

"Thanks for your career advice, Sam. I'll file it right there with the time you told me I should learn Spanish."

"Just being helpful. And you *should* learn Spanish."

A moment passed and her anger started to match Sam's irritation point for point. Sam poured himself another double Scotch and immediately knocked back the top half of it.

"Anyone ever tell you that you might be a little bit nutty?" Sam asked. He paused and smirked. "Oh. That's right," he said, twisting the knife. "You've *frequently* been told you're a bit psycho. That's part of the problem, isn't it?"

She bristled and opened her mouth to answer. Sam finally lost it.

"Think I forget a face?" Sam snapped. "Think I'm such a piss-poor amateur that I wouldn't have looked at the CV for Insane Laura Chapman as soon as she turned up yesterday waving her Linda Cochrane shit? I don't forget faces. I must have laid five hundred women in my life, and to this day I can tell you the names of every one, as well as who had what tattooed on her ass or her tits and who made a lot of noise when I did them and who didn't. Same way, if we popped a little Faribundo Martí guerrilla group in El Salvador in 1984, I know whether it was fifteen point two kilometers southwest of Soyapango as opposed to fifteen point three miles southeast. Get it, Laura? I'm *alive* because I remember things, and if you really want to know, this is not women's work what we do here, it's men's work and you should get your ass out of it."

Laura finally realized that Sam's second double was probably closer to the second half of the same bottle. Worse, the nearby tables were sharing Sam's performance.

"Shit!" he said as a benediction. Top of his voice. It quieted the room.

She felt the blood rise to her face, the colors in her vision heighten, and her sense of moderation begin a quick journey to oblivion. But she kept it in check.

"Get your own watching teams established and put them on Charlie Boy *now*," Laura said, quiet but terse. "Now, before there's a catastrophe. Hear me?"

"Sit down. Stay. Have a peppermint martini. I'm buying."

"I'll talk to Mitch about the football scholarship. Now do

your job, you asshole. I hope you remember this conversation."

"Sure," he said finally. By now, people at farther tables were gawking.

Laura threw some money on the table and stalked away. When she arrived back outside in the heat, and broke away from La Veranda, she finally stopped and stood for several seconds, trying to calm down.

Across Ocean, another bus arrived. Laura watched the girl in the pink skirt close her paperback and finally board the bus.

Great! Then it's me being watched, not Sam! Why else would Estela leave? I've now been passed along to another.

Laura walked back to the Park Central and checked out. A dark mood gripped her. It wasn't that Sam had intimidated or scared her. Worse. He was unreliable. She would have to replace him as soon as she could.

She was at the airport an hour later and caught an American flight to Washington. As her aircraft lifted off, it was 8:56 P.M. Eastern time.

For Laura's purposes June 22 was all but gone.

chapter 41

OKLAHOMA CITY
JUNE 22, 2009; 9:24 P.M. CDST

As Laura's flight bumped through turbulence over North Carolina, the blond man whom she sought was a hundred and fifty miles from Dallas, also on his way north.

When the fuel gauge on his Lincoln told him that he only had a quarter of a tank left, he rolled into a truck stop off Interstate 35, on the northern edge of Oklahoma City. In another few miles, he would hit the junction of Interstate 40 and turn eastward toward Washington, D.C.

He was a world away from the Mexican cesspool where he had murdered two men and from the indulgent pleasures of Dallas.

The blond man wore a dark suit and a light blue shirt and a good silk patterned tie. The American Southwest was hot in June, however. When he walked into the restaurant area of the truck stop he wore his weapon in his ankle holster so that he could leave his jacket in his car.

At the newsstand in the truck stop, his eyes narrowed.

The Dallas Morning News bore a screaming headline about the American aircraft that had been shot down off North Africa. Apparently Washington had been abuzz with this topic for the last twenty-four hours. There was a picture of the new president on the front page of the newspaper, huddling with some generals, some admirals, and some wealthy guys in suits.

"Asshole," the assassin muttered.

The blond man grudgingly picked up a copy of the paper. He would need to know every nuance of the president's schedule. To carry out his mission, he would need to remain flexible.

Which reminded the blond man. He needed to make a phone call.

He no longer trusted his cellular phone, so he found a phone booth. Convenient. So few pay phones existed anymore. He pulled the door shut and, using coins, called a special number.

A voice came on the other end of the line. "Yes?" it asked. Southern inflection.

"Me. How are things going?" the killer said.

There was a split-second delay in response, one that the blond man did not like. "Good thing you called. Somehow they found out about you."

The killer stiffened. *"What?"*

"There's a leak somewhere."

"Impossible."

"Someone in the Secret Service has been assigned to your case."

"Who?"

"Don't know the name. But we have a picture. Go to the safe Web site. I'll scan the picture in when we get off the phone. I'll leave it up for ten minutes. Take a look."

He thought further, but reacted calmly. "Do they know what we're trying to do?"

"Yes."

"Do they know the date?"

"I don't know."

"Do they know exactly who they're looking for?"

"No. But they're looking at everyone in the Secret Service, now and past."

"Damn! I don't think they'll find me, but that's not good. Tell me what you *do* know."

For the next five minutes, the man at the phone barely moved as he listened and spoke, a hand cupped near the mouthpiece of the phone. A film of sweat broke on his forehead, but there was no other no visible sign of his furious displeasure. Occasionally, he asked a short terse question.

Finally, he emerged from the booth. By then, he had lost his appetite for food. He walked back to his car and fueled it.

He paid the cashier with a crisp fifty-dollar bill—one with a few bloodstains across Grant's beard—and returned again to his car. He moved from a fuel lane to an isolated parking place. He tried to figure out what had happened and what he should do next.

He turned on the car radio to a country music station, but kept the sound low. He smoked a Marlboro, drawing heavily on it, and his thoughts deepened.

He took stock.

Had one of the foreign men he had been traveling with somehow betrayed him?

Impossible, he concluded. To betray him, they would have betrayed themselves and would have invited him to murder them both. Not likely. Plus, he would already have been arrested.

Someone in Mexico?

Barely possible, plus he had left a very cold trail in Mexico. Someone in Florida? He doubted that, too, though there always could have been an FBI snitch in the Florida mob. And eventually, someone would miss the Salvitalian.

Someone attached to the transfer of five million dollars into his bank account? Not possible, either. No one involved with the transfer knew what it was for, other than the original sources who had hired him. They certainly would not have talked.

Someone in the bank in Grand Cayman? Not possible, either. Everything was computerized.

So what was he missing? It made no sense!

How could this have happened? Another question emerged. To proceed or abort the plot?

To flee would embroil him in a dispute over the money already paid. He was not anxious to give it back, not five million dollars. So he would spend the rest of his life trying to evade armies of blockheaded gunmen who would look for him. No national border would be safe. He didn't mind being a martyr, but he didn't much feel like living in a cave.

Money like that could only draw a crowd.

His eyes scanned the truck stop. With disgust, he surveyed the people at the gas pumps or by their trucks or working within the rest area. Men and women in grungy jeans and dirty shirts, spiritually exhausted and bankrupt, old beyond their years. And the young people in their clothing fashions taken from the degenerate races. And their moronic idiotic music. What a thoroughly corrupt society this was, morally bankrupt.

The blond man was of Anglo-Saxon stock. He had been born in a state of the old Confederacy and had grown up in the heartland of America. He had watched his parents raise him, lose their business, grow old, lose their health, and die without ever having had the life that was out there to be had in America for those who were clever enough to get it.

Capitalism had failed them.

So had their religious leaders.

So had their American dream.

Who knew? If he succeeded, in fifty years he would probably be hailed as a patriot and a hero.

His eyes scanned the truck stop further. Every third person he saw seemed to be some sort of dark-hued immigrant. Africans and South Americans were everywhere, it seemed to him, driving new cars, spending money indiscriminately, bringing along their loose morals and lesser religions. They had three, four, five children apiece, these infidels. They reproduced like inbred rabbits and restocked the American war machine. When would it all end?

He hated America very deeply, the blond man did, what it had become right before his eyes. The West, led by America, was sick, greedy, and depraved, pushing forth a crusading arrogant foreign policy of an international bully. The late much-beloved Ronald Reagan, in the eyes of the killer, embodied the great paradox of America: wonderful ideals, yet an enthusiasm to pursue policies that went against those ideals. Mr. Reagan talked of freeing people from tyranny, while at the same time supporting guerrillas terrorizing Nicaraguan peasants, menacing the peaceable Islamic states of the Middle East and supporting a rogue like Saddam Hussein as he was gassing the Iranians and the Kurds. These were perfect examples of America's mendacious duplicity, as was the country's support for expansionist Zionist Israel. George W. Bush, the son, talked of a war on terror, then brought precisely that to the Middle East, lying to the world about the pretexts for war while causing the deaths of tens of thousands of Iraqi civilians.

Anger and resentment boiled in the blond man. Where in the name of the Almighty was the world headed if warriors didn't take things into their own hands? The man in the White House was an apostle of the American expansionism that the blond man so hated. The world would be a better place when Americans understood how vulnerable they were and how no one was safe from retaliations to its near-century of arrogance.

It did not bother the blond man if he became a martyr, himself. If he were able to strike a blow against the president, wouldn't the Almighty be pleased? Sometimes, God spoke directly to the blond man and he would stop everything to listen.

The voice from the Beyond was always so clear! The great cleansing would begin with the first blow against America's leader.

When one could believe, one did not always need to think.

The bitterest moments, Americans would soon realize, lay ahead.

Now the blond man asked himself a final question.

If Washington and the White House were expecting an assassination, he would be attacking a command post that had cranked up its security to the highest possible level.

Escaping afterward would not be a problem. But could he still make the initial strike?

He pondered this for almost a quarter hour, smoking two more cigarettes as he sat in his Lincoln. Then he decided he could succeed. There was very little within White House security with which he was not intimately familiar.

He had a longer history in the place than most of the people who were there now. And they could scan the lists of security personally from now until Judgment Day and no suspicious eye would ever settle on him.

Never!

He made his final decision. He would go ahead.

This would be more complicated and dangerous than he had planned. But, he told himself, he would succeed anyway.

He glanced at his watch again. His contact must have had time to scan a picture onto a secure Internet site by now. He accessed the site. He waited as a picture took shape.

His heart surged: anxiety mixed with recognition. His eyes went wide.

In astonishment, he studied a photograph of a woman he knew.

Laura Chapman!

He knew who Laura was. She had been at the White House for several years, never moving up, never moving down or out. He thought of her as a typical Secret Service spinster.

His anxiety gave way to partial relief. They hadn't assigned the case to one of their top people! While Laura had put in some good years on the Presidential Protection Detail, she was still a desktop technician. In short, her presence on an investigation signaled that it was off from the mainstream. And then there were the psycho vibes surrounding Laura. Who could completely believe her? She had, in summary, distinguished herself in the small ways that agents distinguish themselves, faithfully reporting to duty, never tripping up on anything easy. But there had never been a big case that she had broken, or a major investigation that had gone her way.

Women were lesser beings, anyway, meant to be subservient in the eyes of the Creator. And in one way or another, they were all whores.

Still again, the task before him was not easy. And he would have to be very cautious with every step, leaving nothing to chance. Even a maverick theoretician like Laura Chapman might get lucky and ruin his plans.

He shut down his laptop. He thought furiously, working his assignment forward and backward, going back to his initial problem.

The greater problem. The leak.

How had the opposition caught wind of him?

He walked himself through every memory along the way. The only time he had spoken aloud to his financial people had been in Florida and in Arabic when they were all busy getting laid. And there had been no one anywhere near except—

Then, like a flash, it occurred to him.

Right there at The Tides! That little Chinese girl must have picked up something. As he racked his memory it was the only time that he had spoken aloud with his financial people with anyone in earshot. How a little Chinky could understand Arabic perplexed the blond man. In a hundred years he would not be able to come up with an answer to that.

But, oh, my God, how careless he had been!

Five minutes later he was on Interstate 20 pointing east. Better late than never.

He would make sure there would be no more careless chatter in the future.

chapter 42

Laura Chapman, awake again after minimal sleep, stared at the television set in the living room of her home. Increasingly angry, she watched the CNN replays as Omar Mesdoua pontificated over a pair of American bodies.

Laura sipped from a tall mug of ginseng tea and uttered a low profanity toward the Libyan dictator. God, how this stuff sickened her! She wondered how the new man in the White House was going to react. The president had made a few brief remarks and a press conference was already scheduled for that morning.

Chapman averted her eyes from the television and returned them to the files in front of her, ones that she had brought home from her office at the White House.

These files addressed her more immediate problem: protecting the president from a homegrown traitor. The ginseng gave her a friendly lift.

Then she stood and dressed and went to her car. But as she drove into the District from Virginia, something astonished her. She could not find any pattern in the traffic that followed her. She stopped in the pull-off lane once to see if such a move could smoke out a watcher behind her.

It didn't.

She couldn't spot anyone on her tail this morning. Not having one was sometimes more confusing than having one.

Okay, she reasoned.

First she couldn't figure out why she was under surveillance. Now she couldn't figure where it had gone.

Then she realized:

Her car had been idle while she had been in Florida:

enough opportunity for someone to plant an electronic tracker into it. Now that she thought of it, there was now probably also an eavesdropping device in the car. And all the more damning, the CD case from Queen's *Greatest Hits* didn't seem to be between the seats anymore, either.

Had she dislodged it? Or had someone else?

The answer was clear.

Sneaky bastards! My apartment has probably been bugged, too!

All right, she decided.

If that's the way they wanted to play it, she knew *just* the way to fight back, and would deal with it this evening. She made a note to herself.

chapter 43

WASHINGTON
JUNE 23, 2009; 9:30 A.M.

Tuesday morning, the new president hit a political trifecta: a great opportunity to look presidential, impress the public, and show that he was not going to take any crap, either.

At a meeting with members of the Federal Reserve Board at the White House, he showed up and shook the proper hands. He expressed complete confidence in his secretary of the treasury and the economists who ran the nation's financial interests.

He had his picture taken at the head of the table and excused himself after a quarter hour, fifteen minutes longer than Ronald Reagan ever stayed. Economists bored the current president. Their ramblings on finance always seemed uncertain and heavily laden with theoretical bullshit.

"A toy balloon," the president once pointed out, "is also an example of inflation, as well as an apt analogy for monetary theory. Both the toy balloon and economic theory are filled with hot air and vulnerable to any nasty little prick that unexpectedly comes along."

Today's economic meeting was different, however, thanks to the crisis in North Africa. The president had met with his money people at 8:30 A.M. as scheduled, then slipped away to stage an impromptu press conference.

Almost every recent American president had had his *bête noire,* the national enemy who was looking to get punched out. Kennedy had had Castro. Johnson had had Ho Chi Minh. Arguably, Nixon hadn't had one, but he had had *The Washington Post* and the Watergate Committee, instead. Ford and Carter had had Khomeini. Reagan had Qaddafi; Bush Senior had had Saddam Hussein. Clinton had needed one, but he had had the latter-day Reverend Dimsdale, Kenneth Starr, instead. Bush 43 had had bin Laden in addition to all the Oedipal baggage involving Bush 41 and Saddam. Going back far enough, Lincoln had had Jefferson Davis, and George Washington had had King George III.

Now the current man had Muhammad Omar Mesdoua. As might be expected, the new president was steamed over the events in the Gulf of Sidra.

Two reasons.

First, as a military man, he was incensed that an American aircraft had been attacked and that the remains of two American flyers were being held. There was an ugly echo of the MIA situation from Vietnam and Iraq: Two thousand sets of remains were still unaccounted for after decades in the former, and eighty-five still MIA in the latter.

Second, the president had been planning a goodwill trip to Africa in July, a trip that was not being made any easier by Mesdoua's messianic Pan-African agenda. Now that trip was jeopardized by events in the Gulf of Sidra and a suggestion that African nations would have to take sides between Libya and the United States.

So at 9 A.M., the president went before the nation to address the events of the last twenty-four hours. The president had ordered, he explained this morning, a massive maneuver by the American Sixth Fleet in the Mediterranean to seal off

Libya by sea. He had also secured a blockage of all air service in or out of Libya until this crisis was resolved. Any nation who chose to challenge the air blockade would be met and diverted by fighters from the United States Air Force. The blockade was effective immediately.

The president then demanded two immediate actions from the Libyans. The first was the return of the bodies of the two American aviators. The second was the dismantling of any new weapons—such as the missile system that had apparently brought down the Warhawk the previous day.

The Libyans, the president said, had two days to deliver the remains of Major Straighthorn and Captain Kendall into the possession of the Swiss consulate in Tripoli. Otherwise the United States would assume Libya had no intention of complying with the president's demands.

Mesdoua further had seventy-two hours to turn over information on any weapons systems or missile placements. If that was not done, the United States was prepared to take out anything that U.S. intelligence could identify as possible missile sites.

Then, time for questions from the White House press corps.

"Mr. President, in the case of non-compliance by the Libyans," Harold Finnegan of CNN asked, "and in the case that the United States seeks to enforce its objectives militarily in this situation, what would be the acceptable price in terms of American lives lost?"

"*One* life lost is unacceptable, Harold," the president snapped angrily. "And in the case before us, we're prepared to act unilaterally to put the entire armed forces of Libya back in the stone age," the president answered. "Clear? *The stone age.*" He then added, "And as for Mr. Mesdoua, he will be toast. The combat will not end as long as that man is left in power. *Clear?*"

It was already clear. But the president made it clearer. He walked to a side table in the press room where some remnants of staff breakfasts had hastily been pushed. The president picked up a slice of burnt toast and held it aloft.

Then, as photographers fired away, he crushed it, crumbled it, and let the crumbs drop to the floor. Then he put his toe to the crumbs, ground them into the carpet, and strode purposefully from the chamber.

chapter 44

WASHINGTON
JUNE 23, 2009; 9:33 A.M.

Tuesday morning, not yet 10 A.M.

Laura sat in a stuffy temporary office in the Longworth Building, Room 476-S, borrowed from Mitch Hamilton, who had requisitioned it for her from a congressional friend.

She had a computer terminal and access to her new clerical assistant, Vanessa Stone, a tall thin girl in her late twenties.

Vanessa had a green streak in her black hair. She wore a knee-length skirt that revealed a *papillon* tattoo on her left ankle. There was a spider tattoo on her neck, and heaven knew what was in between, insects and otherwise. She sat at her desk in an outer office sipping cranberry juice when nothing else was happening. In deference to the air conditioning, which only barely worked against the sweltering day that was again brewing in the capital, Vanessa kept very still.

Laura was quietly amused by Vanessa's appearance. If stuffy old Mitch Hamilton could have seen what he sent over.

Laura asked Vanessa to access the Secret Service current personnel records and compile a spreadsheet of all male agents with a 7 and a 2 in their shield number. This was Vanessa's first assignment and she set to it immediately. Laura would have asked her to compile a list of blond agents, also, but the list would have been useless. Anyone could dye his hair.

Laura clicked off a television that sat in the far corner of her office. The press conference of the president, the man she was trying to protect, had just concluded.

She had not voted for the man. She knew him personally, as he had been around the White House for years. She knew about his private instabilities and tantrums. She had never assessed him to be emotionally or intellectually up to the challenges of the presidency. The voters, who were carefully shielded from the man's many deficiencies and inner lack of balance, had decided otherwise.

She thought about what she had just seen on her television screen and its possible link to what she had been assigned to do. A curious notion struck her. Could there be a link?

Time to take an official inventory:

How many foreign countries would like to have a power play in which the American president—no matter who he is—gets snuffed?

Chapman could flip open any U.S. passport to the third page, see which blighted Third World stinkholes Americans weren't allowed to travel to, and see what power-mad maniac might have started the chase of paper and blood that led to the file that sat before her.

Who would have had ten million bucks to throw at the job?

The usual suspects, in other words.

The Libyans. The Iraqis. The remnants of Osama bin Laden's foul little network.

The North Koreans.

The Israelis? No one in Washington ever wanted to admit it publicly, but Tel Aviv was always on the short list of suspects whenever anything went haywire worldwide.

Some diehard Cubans still worshipping at the shrine of the late Fidel Castro?

Maybe.

A handful of Balkan crazies, some renegade former-Soviet states and some South Americans. Bogotá had fallen to the Revolutionary Armed Forces of Colombia in 2008, for example, and a man named Simón Trinidad had gone from prison to a cabinet post overnight. One day a narco-terrorist, the next day a diplomat. There was no underestimating the persuasiveness of Andean cocaine and the white powder wealth that came with it. A plot had been afoot by narco-terrorists to kill George W. Bush on a state visit to Colombia in early 2005. So there was even a precedent here.

Laura tried to assimilate all the factors into Charley Boy's story, keying upon the recurrence of the Arabic language. No answers emerged.

Another pattern of duplicity reappeared before her, an-other explanation: there *was no* plot. The whole thing was a set-up. Chapman was doomed to failure. Everyone was going to *make sure* a woman could not succeed in these circum-stances. Then they could destroy her personally the way they had destroyed selected women in the military, in Justice, and the FBI, and create a case for never allowing "skirts" in posi-tions of responsibility.

Laura leaned back. She rubbed her tired eyes. She blew out a long sigh and dismissed the nonsensical conspiracy theories against her.

Time to suck it up. Time to get going.

But how to proceed? More impossibility:

Taking rigorous precautions around the president would tip the Service's hand to the purported assassin. So she, Laura Chapman, would not be able to investigate in the tra-ditional way, because the offices of investigation might have been compromised by the assassin.

Chapman could not officially place anyone under surveil-lance or monitor electronic mail because those would require the involvement of the Secret Service's Internal Investigation unit, and anyone there might be suspect, too.

Nor had Chapman any immediate authority to interro-gate other officers or limit access to the White House or to the president. To do so would raise a stink, create numer-ous lifelong enemies, find its way into the press, and—once again—alarm the assassin immediately. She felt as if she had been asked to walk through a minefield.

How then, could she possibly succeed?

God! What she wouldn't have given to kick back with a joint right there in the office.

Cursing quietly to herself, she glanced at her watch. She had a meeting scheduled with Mitch shortly. Okay, okay. Might as well get a few things done first.

She pulled out her phone. Another quick check-in. Charley Boy answered and was on her way to work. One of her regular clients was in town, Anna said. He was a wealthy Frenchman in the textile business and always brought her a piece of jewelry.

Laura sighed. Situation normal, whatever normal meant these days. Anna gave chatty sex reports—past histories and predictions of the imminent future—as readily as other people gave weather reports or baseball scores. It would have amused her more if the stakes weren't so high.

Laura then launched a few other inquiries. She had a contact with the FBI—a woman who had helped her twice previously—whom she phoned. Could another informal check be run of the ledgers at The Tides in Miami? She wanted to see all the names for the dates surrounding the time that Charley Boy had been there with her big blond john.

Never mind whether any names looked familiar or keyed any other links. She wanted to see the whole list. If there were a killer out there, eventually he would make some small mistake.

Laura also had an international banking contact over at Treasury. Was there anything that she could do that might scare up a little inside info on the deposit that had been made at St. Andrew's on June 10, 2009? She knew previous attempts to trace it had been unsuccessful. Could it be given just a little higher priority, a bit of a boost, she asked when she called.

This was not a routine inquiry, she said to both her contacts, and she couldn't completely explain why it had such priority. But it did have the highest urgency and neither recipient of her call was to mention that Laura had communicated with them.

This request was met twice with a knowing silence and a promise that attention would be turned to Laura's request that very morning.

The third call was to Miami. Rick McCarron. He wasn't answering so she used secure e-mail instead. The club in South Beach where Anna worked: What could Rick tell her about the ownership and funding? There might be something there. Anything. Looking for a killer who had no name, no significant profile, one had to grasp at straws. Other points: the surveillance cameras in the ceiling of the casino. Were images accessible for the date that Anna had first met the blond man and his two cohorts? Similarly, could bank records in the Cayman Islands be examined again? Where had the five million dollars gone?

This was all CIA turf. What could Rick provide?

Next she retrieved the three bloodstained fifty-dollar bills that she had obtained from Anna, handling them with latex gloves. She studied the bloodstains.

Laura had learned to pay attention to the unusual. If the DNA on the money was a match of any sort, she could at least link someone to Anna, even though it might have been a bank teller who sneezed on a client's deposit.

Maybe that someone could tell her something.

Nothing to lose.

Son of Sam, the infamous .44 caliber killer, she always recalled, had finally been busted over a parking ticket.

She placed the money in a separate evidence envelope and placed it in her purse. She would deliver the banknotes in person to the NDNAR. They were only a few blocks away on Connecticut. Waiting for, or trusting, a courier was not an option.

She glanced at her watch. Ten thirty-two A.M.

Then a call to Florida. An FBI artist was to contact Anna and possibly put some computerized headshots together for the two foreign men who had hired Anna, if not the blond man, also.

Shortly before noon, Vanessa presented Laura with the 7/2 spreadsheet she had asked for early, complete with bios. It was thick.

"How many names on the list?"

"Between five and six hundred, I'd guess."

"Good. Thanks," Laura said.

Laura asked Vanessa to find and contact the Mr. Lewisohn who had handled the polygraph test that the FBI had given Anna in Miami. No harm in double-checking his conclusions. Authorization papers would be needed so that Lewisohn could speak to Laura. Laura gave Vanessa a phone number for the FBI in Miami where she could begin her inquiries about Lewisohn. Vanessa started immediately, quickly proving to be a highly capable assistant.

Concluding her calls, Laura went to her car.

There were further appointments to keep.

She went first to the National DNA Registry, dropped off the three fifty-dollar bills, and inquiry request forms. Then she proceeded to Washington's most popular current tourist attraction.

chapter 45

WORLD WAR II MEMORIAL
JUNE 23, 2009; 12:43 P.M.

Laura met Mitchell Hamilton on a bench at the edge of the World War II Memorial.

Laura liked the memorial. With its facing arches and its circle of granite pylons—one for every state and territory that existed at the time of World War II, plus the District of Columbia—bearing bronze wreaths, and its wall of gold stars, one for every four hundred service members killed, it gave a sense of peace, and of closure to events and sacrifices that belonged to a long vanished world.

Its best feature was the Rainbow Pool, which had been on the site since the 1920s. The memorial had angled fountains around its periphery that when seen from just the right angle in relation to the sun refracted the light and created miniature rainbows.

When the monument had been inaugurated in 2004 architectural critics had generally slammed it as retrograde architecture, for it could indeed have been designed in the '30s. But the surviving veterans—there were about a quarter of a million World War II veterans still alive at the time—had loved it, and so had the general public.

Hamilton was there first, seated on a granite bench, reading *The Washington Post*. When he saw Laura he stood and greeted her.

"Let's walk," he said. They strolled together in the monument park. "So?" Hamilton finally asked. "How are things?"

"I'm doing okay," she said. It was already a hot morning, getting hotter as midday approached. Washington in late June, not a breeze to be felt.

"You're following the headlines? From Libya?"

"It's hard to avoid them," she said.

"If it's not one damned thing, it's another," he said.

A gaggle of loud tourists passed them, one of them wearing striped shorts, a blue vest, and an Uncle Sam top hat. Washington could be a town of strange sights and stranger behavior.

As they walked, she was conscious of Mitch's stride, how it was nowhere near as brisk as it had been the last time she had walked with him. Time or age or the weight of the world or *something* always caught up with everyone. She wondered when it would catch up with her.

"Okay. Miami and Sam. Charley Boy. What did you think?" Mitch asked.

Over the course of the next half hour, Laura brought Hamilton current on her trip to Miami. She also detailed the so-far dead-end she had reached prowling through Bernard Ashkenazy's nefarious files in the Ralph Edwards Room, though she was also due back that same afternoon to retrieve her 602s.

Hamilton listened quietly. He looked uncomfortable. And again there was a flurry of scattered thoughts in Laura's mind. At the forefront: Was there something big, some Rosetta Stone that would key her into a baffling world that she could not yet decipher?

She had woken up entertaining that notion.

"So in the end," Hamilton said, "we think there might be something out there, some enemy within the Service, or formerly within the Service. But we still don't know?"

"That's correct."

"Charley Boy's story makes sense to you?"

"Within context."

"You find her credible?"

"I'm having the same problem as everyone else. Her story is credible, but are we interpreting it properly? We have a credible story, some conclusions, and not a whisker of evidence to support those conclusions."

They walked onward several paces before Hamilton answered.

"Director Vasquez won't like your conclusions," he said.

"My job is to find an accurate resolution, not one that pleases the boss," she said.

"Exactly," he said, almost like pronouncing a blessing. More slow strides and then he added, "So stay with it, then. Uncover something if there's something to be uncovered."

"I'm trying. It's a great assignment for a paranoid who's losing her mind, isn't it?" she asked. "I mean, couldn't be better, could it?"

"No," he answered with a slight snort. "It couldn't."

He placed a hand on her shoulder. Laura wondered if it lingered a second or two too long. "You said it, I didn't," he said, making a joke of it, but not entirely.

"And there's something else," Laura said at length. "A final issue with Sam."

Hamilton waited. "What might that be?" he asked.

"Do you know anything about football scholarships?" Laura asked.

"Ah. This has come up before."

"Why not give him what he wants?" Laura suggested. "If Sam's kid is as much of a thug as he is, he'll make some Division One football factory happy."

"Sam's always asking for something extra."

"This will be easier with Sam's cooperation," she pressed. "Come on, Mitch. Give me something to work with."

"The line has to be drawn somewhere. Anything else?"

Greedy Sam or not, Mitchell's response bothered Laura. She knew that whatever "department" of the government it was that could rig a pigskin scholarship, Hamilton could at least try to strong-arm it. He had almost half a century of favors to call in.

It was not that he was unable. He was just frankly unwilling.

Why?

Hamilton had nothing new to offer, either, other than concurring with Laura's theory that something strange was going on out there and it might touch upon the Service. But what was it?

Laura embraced him as they parted at the south parking lot behind the Executive Office Building.

It was only when Laura was driving over to the snake pit known as the Ralph Edwards Room, making her return appearance, that some early pieces of the puzzle slid into place.

She recognized what was bothering her. Two things, those unseen somethings that no one else picked up on but which tore her apart several times a day, each clawing at the other.

Conflicting notions:

Mitch is my best friend in this operation, a prince, a trusted ally from way back and the only person I can rely on, she concluded, this sentiment on the down staircase.

That, juxtaposed with, *He's been in Washington too long and has turned into a career doublecrosser like all the rest of them. I can't trust him, either,* which was a feeling that was wrestling its way upward.

Laura returned to the Ralph Edwards Room in the afternoon.
Ashkenazy provided her with results from her 602 requests.
She went to a computer screen.

A search of prior and present Secret Service employees had
yielded four hits. Artinian, Arman; Cambrerra, Richard; Northy, Edwin; Wilder, Jeremy. She went through the profiles.

1. Arman Artinian was retired from the service and was
currently an electronic securities analyst for a bank in Glen-
dale, California. He hadn't missed a day of work in three
years.

2. Richard Cambrerra was still active, assigned to a Se-
cret Service office in Seattle. He was number two in the unit.
His log sheets were impeccable. He had been nowhere near
Miami.

3. Edwin Northy was also still with the service. Laura
knew the agent. He had been on the White House detail for
six months in 2007. He had been injured in a skiing accident
in January 2009 at Vail, however, and was on medical leave,
having undergone two knee operations. He walked with
crutches these days, was thirty-one years old, and was an un-
likely suspect.

It took Laura an hour to review these three files and make
a supporting telephone call to confirm their accuracy. At the
end of the calls, she was nowhere closer to her blond man.

Then came the fourth.

The fourth subject was Jeremy Wilder, an agent who had
been in the service from 1999 until 2006. He had left under
favorable circumstances to take a job in private security.

Wilder's father had worked for Aramco in Benghazi and

his mother had been a nurse. Therein lay an Islamic connection. Unlike the other three hits in the 602s, he was also blond. The Secret Service file contained a photo of a handsome man in his thirties. He looked like a morphed photo of young Robert Redford, with a trace of Owen Wilson around the nose.

There was a list of women Wilder had dated. Snoopy Service personal files again. Everyone's file seemed to have crossed the desk of at least one evangelical Christian: Relationships were always listed as vice.

In Wilder's last year on Uncle Sam's payroll, there were no fewer than twenty-seven women's names listed, a remarkable number of them Spanish and five that were clearly Asian. But what raised Laura's interest now was that not only had Wilder spoken fluent Arabic but his file indicated that he had also been a free spirit within the service.

Wilder had frequently been on diplomatic assignments in New York, escorting Middle Eastern diplomats around town. Agent Wilder was also reputed to have taken on a three-card monte dealer who had fleeced a Canadian diplomat outside the Plaza Hotel in New York. When the dealer refused to return the money that had been scammed, Wilder had arrested him.

Continuing through Wilder's file, Laura felt her interest accelerate. Then, playing devil's advocate with herself, she wondered if a man who dated twenty-odd women in a year would mess with prostitutes like Anna. Something didn't quite hang together.

Laura put the point on hold and read further. The address given on Jeremy Wilder's most recent passport application was in Westbury, New York.

Long Island. Or, as her college roommate from Hempstead used to pronounce it, she recalled with a whiff of a smile, Lawn Guy Land.

She kept pushing. IRS records indicated that Wilder drew a salary of $214,000 the previous year from QualCo Security Systems in Manhasset, Lawn Guy Land, a company that this same report insisted that the former agent had founded.

Security work. That raised an eyebrow, and his salary, roughly three times Laura's, raised a wave of envy. She refocused. His driver's license echoed the same address.

But recent calls to his home had gone unanswered. A phone inquiry at QualCo yielded the fact that no Mr. Wilder currently worked for that enterprise. It was not unusual for a security company to deny the existence of one of their directors or guiding geniuses so she put the corporate denial on hold. Or was the security firm a front? Something else to check.

What struck Laura as slightly out of joint, however, was the fact that Wilder had not filed his taxes that April 15, but had filed for an extension, instead. When a man does something outside his normal pattern, Laura was trained to take note.

Why an extension now when never before? And what about income?

It was about that time when her incipient suspect might have been reaping in a transfer of big bucks in the Caymans. The details were circumstantial, but enough to hold her interest.

She continued.

Wilder had never been assigned to PPD at the White House, but he had been there countless times. Dates were included in the file. Wilder had also worked with several people who had done the PPD, meaning he knew the system. Then again, security changed all the time at the White House, getting tighter and tighter until it threatened to strangle the people it was supposed to protect. There was a reason that President Clinton had once referred to the White House as "the crown jewel of the American prison system."

Laura's mind was in fast forward now, pondering, trying to locate further angles.

Since White House security changed all the time, how could an "outsider" plan to penetrate it? The only way was with inside collusion. And even then it would not be easy.

Laura sighed. For all that the databases could provide, for all the modern methods of gathering, assimilating, and analyzing intelligence, someone still had to apply brain-power, shoe leather, and make common sense deductions. Today, here, with eleven days to go, *she* was that someone.

She leaned back from her computer screen.

What was this information telling her? Or *not* telling her?

She clicked back onto Wilder's picture and accessed his bio, wondering if there was something personal there to build upon. There was not. He was single, thirty-two years old. Both parents were deceased.

Square one: Laura needed to confirm Wilder's where-abouts without letting him know he was under suspicion. If he were the potential assassin, the slightest hint that anyone was on his trail could cause him to alter his plans, run, or lie low for years and re-emerge when the case had grown cold. Or throw the assignment to a back-up shooter of whom they knew nothing.

She signed out of her terminal.

"Find anything useful?" Ashkenazy inquired as she rose from her work station.

"Probably not."

"Typical," he said. "No one ever leaves this room happy."

In her sweetest voice: "Am I allowed to print photos off a 602, Bernard?"

"Absolutely not. Strictly prohibited. I could have you fired."

"Can I do it while you're not watching?"

"Of course you can. Wait for a moment while I kill the se-curity camera."

From memory, Bernard input a code into his keyboard. He nodded to a printer-scanner on a work station adjacent to his desk. Laura went to it and found her print-out photo-graph of Jeremy Wilder. It was dated May 2006. Three years old; it would have to do.

She gave Bernard an appreciative wink and left the Ralph Edwards Room. It was already past five in the afternoon.

chapter 47

When Laura left the Ralph Edwards Room, she felt eyes on her again. She walked past her car and into a CVS pharmacy, pausing to see if anyone followed.

No one appeared to.

She left the store quickly via an exit on K Street. She ducked quickly into a small Vietnamese restaurant and took a table that had an unobstructed view of the front window.

When several minutes passed and she sensed no street watchers, she accepted a menu, reached for her cell phone, and called Mitch Hamilton.

"We might have a place to start," she said.

"Bravo."

"See what you can find on a Jeremy Wilder. Former agent, worked the White House. Big good-looking blond guy, speaks Arabic. Maybe you can launch a search through Homeland Security. Passport records. See whether he's in the country or out. If you initiate, I'll follow up."

"Homeland Security," he snorted. "Hopeless."

"There has to be someone over there who can help us."

"Any motivation for why this Wilder might be the man we're looking for?" he asked.

"None that I see, but he went missing a few weeks ago."

Silence on Hamilton's end. She could visualize him writing notes.

"Excellent," he finally said. "Stay with your cell phone and I'll get back ASAP."

"Thanks," she said.

He rang off. Laura collected her thoughts and her confidence.

For the first time in days she felt hopeful. Maybe she was nowhere near as close to a nervous breakdown as she imagined.

She ordered food. It turned out to be excellent. But Laura was too jittery to enjoy it. She kept waiting for a phone call to come back from Mitch Hamilton. She stalled and lingered over tea, watching couples at other tables, wishing she had someone to linger with. It was an unlucky time in her life to be alone.

No return call from Mitch. She paid and, toward seven o'clock, walked slowly back to her car. The day's heat had subsided, but was still present. She reminded herself of what she had promised herself that morning and her suspicions about some sort of device having been planted in her car.

Time to do something about it.

chapter 48

WASHINGTON, D.C.
JUNE 23, 2009; LATE EVENING

Laura drove to an Exxon garage on North Capitol Street, ten blocks from Capitol Hill. A gallon of gas maxed out at $4.79 in the District proper. This station charged $4.99 for the cheap stuff. A C-note would fill the average SUV, one reason why more electrics and hybrids were on the streets of the capital this summer.

But Laura liked the station for reasons other than fuel economy. Discreetly, the garage performed maintenance on all sorts of government vehicles, including the personal vehicles of Secret Service agents. It was a station blessed with special talents.

She arrived a few minutes past eight. She walked to the business office. A tiny Indian woman named Kalpurna tended the register.

Two mechanics were in the garage past the cashier's desk, laboring to the blasting accompaniment of pneumatic drills, jacks, and eighties and nineties oldies from WUSA FM.

Fortuitous timing: One of the guys was Vladimir, a stocky bearded man, a Slav by way of Dubrovnik, who worked with his partner Zarko. They were the Starsky and Hutch of the jacks, lifts, and lug nuts. Zarko rarely spoke and gave the appearance of being seriously deranged.

A few months earlier, Laura had watched as a Jeep Cherokee had cruised into the shop. The Balkan boys stripped the Pennsylvania plates off the Cherokee practically before it stopped rolling and hustled the male driver and a female passenger to a souped-up white Acura with a Tennessee registration that was waiting, doors open, engine running, in the rear parking lot. The Acura was set to drive away, which it did with no conversation between any of the parties involved, the girl sitting low in the front seat.

Vlad had worked on Laura's Lexus in the past, though nothing as entertaining as the Cherokee-Acura turnabout.

Two customers were paying for gas as Laura walked in. She stepped back outside and phoned Anna in Florida. Anna answered. She was safe, at least for now. Laura was under no illusions, but that situation felt stable. She wondered if Sam had followed through with protective watch. She phoned him, too. No answer. She grimaced. That meant there was another call to make, but it wasn't one she could do from here. Maybe, she mused, she should put Rick McCarron on Sam's case. That might have a better geometry.

She stepped back inside the station. Vladimir, on a mechanic's dolly, rolled under a black 2009 Dodge Gallactica with deep blue tinted windows, the pimpmobile of choice in current Washington. Finally, Kalpurna looked to Laura. "Yes?" she asked.

"I need someone to take a look at my car," Laura said to the cashier.

"For what?"

Laura had dealt with Kalpurna before. Her two most salient features, other than size—or lack of it—were a quick temper and bad breath. Laura treated her gingerly. "Maybe I could explain directly to Vlad?" she asked.

Kalpurna shrugged and motioned in the mechanics' direction with her small dark head.

Laura walked into the garage. A wall calendar from a motorcycle company, featuring a fully naked girl on a Suzuki, reminded Laura how much she had now invaded a male preserve.

At the sight of her approaching footsteps, Vlad zipped out from under the Gallactica. He wore green overalls on top of a Los Angeles Lakers T-shirt. Zarko glanced twice at her and kept working. There was an ominous stillness and quiet to Zarko that gave Laura a creepy feeling.

"Hello, Vlad," she said.

Vlad smiled. A big grin. His lower left incisor was missing. "Hey. Miss Laura! I thinked I recognize you." With Vlad, every language was foreign.

"Just from my ankles?"

"Ankles and . . ." He laughed and motioned to his leg above and behind the ankle.

"Calves," she said, assisting.

"Calves," he said appreciatively. Zarko, seeing the conversation, cut the decibel level of the music by half. "Vlad love a beautiful woman's calves."

Vlad's words rose up from the floor along with his gaze. He spoke with a deep voice. "Vlad have good memory for beautiful women and their lower legs," he said.

Vlad had had a special crush on the rest of Laura, too, ever since the day he noticed that she carried legal firepower. Sexy, smart, great legs, native-born American, and carrying a professional-strength 9 mm automatic. She was Vlad's perfect type of chickie.

"I know you're busy, Vlad," she began, "but how long would an electronics scan take?"

"For you? Your personal own car, and this would be now?"

"For me. My own, now," she affirmed, indicating the Lexus.

He looked at her and her car. "Not long," he said. "Someone

spy on you? Shame. Boyfriend? You tell Vlad who, give me address and, *hey,* Vlad take care of *that* for you."

He pounded a huge filthy fist into a huger filthier palm. The sound of the impact filled the room along with Aerosmith.

"Not a boyfriend, Vlad. But thank you for your concern."

"Then *who?*"

"Who spies on any of us, Vlad?" She motioned first to the surveillance camera in the garage, then to the Capitol, visible beyond the open garage door. The mechanic laughed.

"Yeah. All over now, everybody same like goddam Soviet Russians."

"Yup. Like goddam Soviet Russians," she agreed cheerfully.

Vlad grinned, turned to Zarko, and spoke in Serbo-Croatian. Zarko laughed. Vladimir had been a spy gadget specialist in the old country. She reckoned that Zarko had been one, too.

"Scan it?" Vlad asked again, turning back to her. "Complete car?"

"Exactly."

"I do! Now here when I finish which I am, almost done," he said, clarifying.

"Thank you," she said.

Vlad wrapped up the pimpmobile. He moved it to a parking spot and rolled Laura's Lexus into the garage. He went to work with a small electronic gizmo that looked like a stripped-down Geiger counter. Zarko moved over to help.

Laura sat in the waiting room, paging through magazines, one eye on a television. Still no response from Mitch Hamilton. She concluded that there would not be one this evening.

Half an hour passed. A moment of transitory truth neared.

"Miss Laura?" came the voice. Vlad's. Somber.

She turned. Vlad had something in his hand.

"You found something?" she asked.

"Something," he smiled. He held up the case from the

Queen CD. "You been looking for?" Vlad asked. "Under back seat. Slide, maybe?"

"I was looking for it, yes. But it's not what worried me." She gave him half a smile.

Vlad stepped closer. He was a big man, a full head taller than she and double her weight. And he smelled bad. *Boyfriend: Imagine,* she mused, *unleashing Vlad on an ill-behaved former suitor.* The thought amused her, as did the notion that Zarko, who was even bigger, would probably come along on the expedition; Zarko to hold, Vlad to whale away, or maybe just for the amusement value of thrashing someone. She filed that one in the back of her mind. Way back.

"The car completely clean," Vlad said. "No bugs, no snoop stuff. No bad shit. Nothing."

"You're *sure*?"

He straightened up and gave her an expression that said he was. From the garage, over Vlad's shoulder, Zarko watched from a distance, large brown eyes intent and focused.

"Thank you, guys," she said. "Great work."

She tipped Vlad an extra twenty-spot for each of them.

Vlad grinned. "Hey," he said. With a dirty hand, he found a business card. He turned it over. Holding a pen the way someone might hold a candle, he drew a phone number on the back of the card. "You ever need any extra work, protection, the like, you call us, all right?"

He handed the card to her. She looked at the number. "I'll keep it in mind, Vlad," she said. "Thanks."

Vlad gave a nod of his massive head.

Laura visited Kalpurna in the cashier's cage. She paid and went home. Her car was sanitized, but there was still plenty that did not add up.

There was no van outside this night, she observed toward midnight. No cable company, no phone crew. She settled slightly. She turned her lights out and waited a few minutes. Then she found her favorite little foil package under the mattress, and indulged in a puff or two or three.

More made up pot-head doggerel formed itself in her run-away mind, with giggly apologies to the sixties folk scene and Peter, Paul, and Mounds:

> *No-good men on paper*
> *Involved in murd'rous stuff*
> *Bring me home, strung-out, depressed,*
> *So I can't help but Puff.*

She suppressed another loud giggle.

Don't laugh too loud. You know your home is bugged. Don't let them know what you're doing or what you're thinking. Can't give the opposition any weapons to use against you.

She snuffed out her smoke. She washed her ashtray, sending the residue down the drain. She stashed her supply back within the mattress.

She thought of Jeremy Wilder just before she drifted off. Maybe, just maybe, she had turned the corner. As she eased into sleep, June 23 became June 24.

chapter 49

FAYSHAHID, LIBYA
JUNE 24, 2009; 9:23 A.M. GMT

Two trucks turned off a desert road and drove a hundred fifty meters into the empty sand. The driver of the first truck blew his horn and the second truck, a Fiat, came to a stop. The driver of the first, wearing the uniform of the Libyan Home Guard, stepped out into the blazing morning sunlight of the northeastern Sahara.

He waved and signaled. He cursed in Arabic and pointed. This, he said, was as good a place as any.

The workmen in the second truck were a team of gravediggers: four of them, young men in white. They jumped out into the hundred twenty degrees carrying shovels. The army officer clapped his hands, telling them to work fast. The sun roasted them. There would not be water until they finished.

They rapidly dug two trenches, about four feet deep each.

From the rear of the truck they pulled two long objects. To a satellite in the sky, the objects would have looked like rolled-up carpeting. Human bodies look that way sometimes.

The graves were ready in twenty minutes of furious shovel work. A photographer in the first truck, also in the Home Guard uniform, recorded the event on a digital video camera.

The workmen didn't lay the wrapped objects in their graves, they threw them. Then they pushed and piled sand back on top of the burial site.

There was an assortment of rocks in the van, also. The diggers quickly planted these across the tops of the graves. For a while at least, the heavy stones would keep nocturnal scavengers from disturbing the human remains. All this time, the photographer was working his camera from the front of his truck. He missed nothing.

There were no words of farewell, no benediction. Just disposal of what appeared to be corpses.

The workmen piled back into their truck, the military people theirs. They drove back into Tripoli and were home within the hour.

They enjoyed a great feeling of accomplishment.

chapter 50

TRIPOLI, PRESIDENTIAL PALACE
JUNE 24, 2009; 11:12 A.M. GMT

Mohammad Omar Mesdoua stood again at the podium of the press room. There were no bodies to display today. His soldiers and his press attaché Bahrim Shahadi ushered foreign journalists into the chamber. Then Mesdoua made a nodding motion and a low growl. He had written a ten-page statement for himself and was planning to stick to it.

First, Mesdoua sounded off for a half hour in Arabic on Western oppression of African and Arab peoples. American-educated Bahrim Shahadi passed around poorly translated copies. Lisa McJeffries of ABC read the English text as Alan Savett of Reuters sat closely nearby. Alternatively, Savett took a pair of photographs, studied Lisa's knees, and listened to the Esteemed Leader.

Then Mesdoua oozed into a recycled plea for African and Arab unity against the American aggressors. And finally third, Mesdoua approached the central part of his statement.

The new Libyan sea-air "self-defense system" would remain and the president of the United States could, in the words of the Libyan leader, "burn in his Christian hell with his two air pirates." And by the way, the bodies of the two American aviators had been buried in unmarked graves in the remote desert. The Libyan strongman offered a final touch, sarcastically wishing the new president "a very happy and most memorably enjoyable July Fourth."

There was something else new that day, too.

The room was ringed by members of Mesdoua's newly formed National Police Corps. Their leader, a surly little man, Major Housahodi, stood a few feet behind President Mesdoua. Quite disturbingly, Savett noticed, at one point during Mesdoua's remarks, Major Housahodi was talking to the press attaché, Shahadi, and staring at Savett.

Savett offered a weak smile in return, continued to make notes, and fantasized about being between beautiful Lisa's legs. Even if he were the subject of conversation, there was no point to bask in the attention of the National Police. Secretly, he wondered how long he could survive in this posting.

When Mesdoua finished, the Esteemed One stared at the members of the press who were present. Then he turned and departed.

No questions were allowed. When Savett raised his camera to take a single picture, he was forbidden. Armed police with red berets dismissed the foreign press corps.

Mesdoua returned to his private quarters in the palace. He had dates and yogurt for breakfast, followed by a small cigar made in the Dominican Republic. He waited to see his speech covered on al Jazeera at noon. He then placed a call to the American embassy in Tripoli. He invited the ambassador to meet with him at the presidential palace as soon as possible.

"There are ways," President Mesdoua expounded, "that this crisis that the Libyan people have not created can be made to cool down."

The American ambassador spoke for seven minutes and duly reported the conversation to Washington.

chapter 51

WASHINGTON, D.C.
JUNE 24, 2009; MORNING

As the situation in North Africa deteriorated, Laura sat in her new office. She had been there since seven that morning. Her suit jacket hung on the chair at her desk, her Sig Sauer was carefully holstered on the right of her light blue blouse. It occurred to her that morning when she transferred her IDs and packed up the Colt, that she had never fired a single shot in the line of duty. Odds were, she never would. So be it. It was a good record to keep intact.

By 8 A.M., Mitch Hamilton still had nothing to report on Jeremy Wilder. Nor had the NDNAR reported back yet.

Mitch had promised to shake up a few contacts of his own. The same back channels would work in reverse to report if any activity were seen at Wilder's home or workplace, or whether his motor vehicles—there was a Mercedes and a new Ford registered in his name—were active.

Braced against Laura's computer screen was the headshot of Wilder that she had obtained from Bernard. Laura knew she had to get the image to Anna as quickly as possible. Positive identification would help loads. It either was Wilder or it wasn't.

But as usual, there were problems:

She couldn't run the image through the Secret Service in Miami, that would leak the existence of her investigation. She didn't trust Sam. *Who the hell does?* That meant she needed to trust Rick McCarron. Could she? Ninety percent of her said yes. Then there was that other voice within her. *Should* she?

She could electronically transfer the photo to him. But if there were a breach of security through his office, her case was blown. This was a decision she had to make correctly. And soon. She also had to tread carefully on assistance from the CIA. They still were not chartered to work domestically, only to share information. Not following the rules could get Rick McCarron reprimanded or worse. And then there was the CIA's reputation for lousing things up, even following the reorganization of 2006.

She checked her secure e-mail at 8:10 A.M. Nothing of relevance. Mitch Hamilton was attempting to obtain tracking from Homeland Security: Had Jeremy Wilder used his passport to leave the country? Homeland hadn't replied yet, though the request was marked urgent.

Typical. They promised a one-hour turnaround and usually took days.

She sighed. No one was moving with the speed she needed. No one!

Laura fired back an e-mail to Hamilton.

"Can't you go to the head of the Agency?" she wrote. The head of the Agency was a former governor of Indiana, a political appointee, and the heir to a politically connected direct-mail marketing fortune.

Laura's cynicism kicked in. From previous experience, she knew the former governor had no idea how his agency functioned.

Not much more progress with the FBI artist either, the one who was going to attempt composite pictures of the men

Anna had met at The Tides. "Jesus," she muttered. Wasn't there *some* way to get people moving? As a concept, was urgency an old-fashioned thing?

At 8:59 Vanessa arrived, sipping a latte, a bran muffin in a plastic bag.

At 9:15, Laura's FBI contact e-mailed. The contact had obtained booking records for The Tides in Miami for the months of May and June.

"Fantastic work!" Laura wrote back.

"Don't ask me how I got them," the source returned. ":-)."

The records were by attachment.

Laura scanned.

No name jumped out. She ran a software check that compared names of hotel guests with Secret Service employees past and present. Several hits of similar names, but nothing that looked like an actual match.

Laura continued to work the list.

She isolated guests for the night of June 10 and created a list of guests with Arabic names or passports from Middle Eastern countries. The former list had eighty-seven names. The latter had forty-six. She printed out a hard copy.

Jesus. The whole world to look in and I don't even know who I'm looking for. No Jeremy Wilder, of course, on any list. That would be too easy.

She wondered if The Tides still had a surveillance tape from June 10. She e-mailed her FBI contact and floated the question. Could such a tape be made to magically appear?

The morning began to pass.

Mitch Hamilton phoned. The director of Homeland Security was playing tennis that morning at a private club. His cell phone was off. Mitch said he would stay with it.

Meanwhile, the passport division at Homeland couldn't locate their initial request from the previous day and had, with apologies, started another.

Laura slammed down the phone.

"Christ, this is impossible!" she muttered to herself, cooling slightly. A killer might be set to strike in ten days and it could take two weeks to wade through all these agencies. *God*

Almighty! What was the description that John F. Kennedy had given Washington: a city of northern charm and southern efficiency.

What next, what next? Think of something outside the bureaucratic box.

A thought came to her.

A few former boyfriends had surfaced in convenient places. Some had followed similar paths into law enforcement. One, Brian Copeland, was now Detective Brian Copeland of the New York State Police, stationed in Long Island.

Laura had followed Brian's career via the alumni directory. This was a good time to renew old acquaintances. Save a president and reconnect. No law against it. Brian's posting was four miles from Jeremy Wilder's last known home address. Beautiful.

Well, no hard feelings after all these years, she hoped.

She phoned Brian Copeland at his office. She was lucky enough to catch him at his desk. After the perfunctory greetings and catching up, she explained where she had worked up until the previous Friday. Next she explained what she needed, but not exactly why.

Sgt. Copeland fell very quiet and listened. He did not ask many questions. He knew she would not be able to answer most of them.

"Give me a little time to see what I can do," he said. "Are you still gorgeous?"

"I weigh two hundred pounds, I'm gray, my teeth have fallen out, I have a large infected goiter on the left side of my neck, and I drag my right foot," Laura said.

"Same here," he said. "And I have a pretty good memory of what you *do* look like."

In the midst of everything stressing her, she felt herself blush, wondering exactly what he was picturing and from which occasion of trysting.

"You're still a flirt," she answered.

"That's right. And I'll drive by the Wilder address today," he said. "How's that?"

"Solid," she said. "I owe you."

"No you don't," he said.

It was as good a gambit as any. But again it would take hours or maybe days before anything might pan out. And hours and days were in decreasing supply.

Worse, late morning, the gut instincts kicked in again. She had a bad feeling about Wilder, a sense that she was rambling down the wrong path.

The black dog starting to whimper. Incipient depression. A small bark.

A nasty question posed itself, direct from the dog: What had she done with her life? She had given the best years of it to the United States Secret Service and they probably couldn't wait to get rid of her.

Well, screw 'em all!

This was a major case even if she was the only one who thought so. She would succeed with this! She knew what she was doing.

She made a decision: Trust Rick McCarron.

Vanessa scanned a copy of Jeremy Wilder's picture and sent it electronically to McCarron. She included the hotel listings for The Tides. Maybe he could run them across whatever directory of miscreants the CIA kept locally.

Who knew? Throw enough lines in enough lakes and eventually you hook something.

Her insides felt as if they were going to spontaneously combust. It was 1:35. She had been there for five hours.

She had to get out. Lunch. She would go out. Maybe lightning would strike. Maybe she would get lucky.

But she knew the truth about luck. It didn't exist and a woman had to make her own.

She checked out of her office at 1:47 P.M., not knowing whether to feel hopeless or just plain incompetent.

chapter 52

The president of the United States sat with his arms folded at his desk, watching the infuriating images from North Africa on the forty-eight-inch flat wireless TV on the wall.

At the sofa in the near corner sat Michael Ostenfeld, the White House chief of staff, a former Wall Street banker. Standing near the president was Robert Lynch, a former Wisconsin senator who had never served in the armed forces, but who was now the secretary of defense.

The president watched Omar Mesdoua wish him a happy July Fourth.

The live report concluded. The network talking heads took over. The president reached to a remote control switch and zapped the power from the television. For a moment, no one spoke.

The president's eyes flicked from Lynch to Ostenfeld back to Lynch, then back to Ostenfeld, the chief of staff.

"I don't know about you, but I've had enough," the chief executive said.

"That makes about two hundred and fifty million of us," Lynch said.

"What do you think? Those two flyers? Think they're really buried in the desert?"

"It looked that way," Ostenfeld answered.

Lynch was silent but the downturned gaze indicated agreement.

"How is our intelligence in that part of the world?" the president asked. "What do we know about what's doing on the ground?"

"Could be better, could be worse," Ostenfeld said.

"What's that mean?"

"They got those underwater SAMs in place without our knowing."

"How the *hell* did they do that?" the president asked angrily. "You telling me they put in an underwater missile system and we didn't even *know* about it? How does that happen?"

"Previous administrations. Restraints on the CIA."

"Why is it every time I want to do something around here, someone uses the phrase 'previous administration'?"

Ostenfeld knew better than to answer.

"What did they steal? The technology or the hardware?" the president asked.

"First one. Then the other."

"Damn it!" shouted the president. "They do things like this," he said, rambling forward, "and they count on the fact that we'll react with a sense of decency. Exactly the type of civility with which they haven't acted." He paused. "It's like what's happening in Europe. These Muslims move into democratic countries and have no regard for the democratic institutions that protected them. Then they want to have their own little fascist state."

He was furious. And when he was furious, he was used to venting.

"They crash planes into our buildings, they plant bombs. They sabotage mass transportation," he said. "They kidnap our citizens, they shoot down our aircraft. I'm tired of it. I'm not going to preside over an America that turns into the pitiful ineffectual giant."

"Yes, sir," Ostenfeld said.

"That was the phrase Nixon used, wasn't it? 'Pitiful giant.' Or something like that?"

"I believe so, sir."

"Nixon," the president said. "Even when he was drunk he knew what he was doing."

He paused. Both Lynch and Ostenfeld knew not to speak.

In the first month of this administration, one woman, just below cabinet level, was fired two weeks after being confirmed by the Senate for interrupting a private rant. Lesson learned.

"Two weeks ago I thought Teddy Roosevelt could be my role model," said the leader of the Free World. "I sometimes ask myself what Eisenhower would have done. I don't care about the party. I care who had balls. And smarts. Today I'm thinking more towards Bismarck. They don't respect the lives of our soldiers, maybe we don't respect the lives of their civilians."

"I don't know much about Bismarck, but I'm certain you have a point, sir," Lynch said.

"I have tons of points," the president said. "And I plan on making all of them."

His eyes drifted out the window to the Rose Garden, then back in again.

The president was already shaking his head. "Damn! Can you phone Jamison at CIA and find out who he's got in place in Tripoli? We need to know some things."

He looked at Ostenfeld, who took the cue and left the Oval Office to make the call personally. Then he glared at Lynch, who finally spoke.

"Actually, sir," Secretary Lynch said, "the Libyans met with our ambassador and—"

"Oh, they did, did they?"

"Yes, sir."

"Well, here's something else that's famous. Know what Bismarck said? Or maybe it was Churchill? He said, or whoever said it said, that war was too important to be left to the generals. Well, my feeling is that when they shoot down one of our planes and kill our boys, the response is too important to be left to the diplomats. What do you think of that?"

"Very apt. Brilliant."

"Recall our ambassador. Now." The president paused. "No discussions. Not here, not there, not anywhere. He won't want to be on the ground in Tripoli, anyway."

"Yes, sir."

Secretary Lynch quietly left the Oval Office, closing the door behind him, avoiding any interaction with either of the Secret Service agents, Larsen and Reilley, who stood guard outside and who had heard everything.

chapter 53

WASHINGTON, D.C.
JUNE 24, 2009; AFTERNOON

With renewed dedication, Laura continued her journey through all records at her disposal. Bernard Ashkenazy had sent over another few hits off his remorselessly slimy 602s. Long shots, every damned one of them.

Into her computer, she fed security codes that would allow her to access new information from Bernard. Sometimes Laura's eyes took an unfocused pattern as she asked herself the same redundant questions.

Who? Why? What motivation? Money alone? Laura doubted it. *Ideology? Islam? Race? Please, God, could I please find just a small clue somewhere?*

Poking into the private lives of one's peers was something she would not have wished on anyone. She held her breath:

Samuel James Lutella, retired from the Service, but formerly White House PPD. Sam Lutella had a wife (Carole) who liked sex with two men at once. See cross references Richardson, Gregory; Bloch, Emil; Mosher, Frank.

Laura guessed what the cross references would tell her in terms of Mrs. Lutella's daisy chain relationships. She checked and had her suspicions confirmed. Sam Lutella, now divorced, had been fishing in Oregon for two years. Carole Lutella, she of the voraciously polygamous instincts, now lived in Scarsdale, New York, with her new husband.

There was a picture of Carole, or rather a series of them. She was thirty-two, looked eighteen, and dressed like a frisky thirteen-year-old. A dream date for an aging pedophile.

Laura continued in disgust:

Mason George Sampson, current Secret Service, assigned to Manhattan. Former United States Navy lieutenant. Once had an affair with a girl named Irina Klebnakova. Dancer. Kleb-nakova's father currently a missile technician in the Ukraine, believed to be former KGB.

Laura paused on this for a moment, recalling that a missile had, days earlier, punched a U.S. surveillance aircraft out of the sky over the Gulf. Laura noted the reference and continued. One coincidental false lead was enough to send an investigation in the wrong direction for weeks.

Linda Billingsly, clerk, White House detail. Husband heavily in debt and recently left her. Two teenage daughters . . . Family falling behind on home payments and credit cards . . .

Michael Maculis, former PPD, now Houston, has sister teaching Marxist economics at UC-Berkeley. Sister is also a lesbian activist . . .

Laura continued reading, shaking her head. It was just one well-balanced dysfunctional American after another. What the hell *was* "normal" anymore?

The files did not just have the dirty laundry on government employees; the files had the smut, as well. There should have been a special category for innuendo. Typical of the new wide-ranging "Christian Taliban" within the government, Laura noted with contempt.

Somewhere out there people with guns and grenades are planning to kill, and we're making notes on people's sleeping arrangements.

She continued past 3 P.M., through a take-out iced coffee courtesy of the green-streaked Vanessa, whom she sent out into one hundred degrees of Washington summertime.

Her phone rang. It was Laura's female friend, the FBI contact. The hotel's registration records in Miami had been a favor from a friend who worked for the parent company, the contact explained. They were easy to filch through the marketing department. Video surveillance was another matter. A court order would be necessary. Should they attempt to get one?

"No," Laura answered. "Hold off on that. At least for now."

There followed shortly thereafter a call from Mr. Henry Lewisohn, the FBI's polygraph expert in Miami. Lewisohn was cordial with a heavy New York accent. He went over Anna's polygraph. The bottom line remained. "She might be mistaken on certain details," Lewisohn said. "But she believes she is telling the truth."

Laura thanked him and hung up. Mildly distracted, she spent the next half hour looking at the 7/2 list, prepared earlier by Vanessa. It shed no further light on anything.

Nothing from Homeland Security. Nothing from the ND-NAR. She lay down the list and pushed back from the desk. She did not have the proper tools with which to work quickly.

The phone rang.

Vanessa's voice from the outer chamber. A returned call. "A Sergeant Copeland. New York State Police?" Vanessa announced.

Laura double-clicked the phone line. Her one-time lover. "Hello, Brian."

"I don't have much," he said. "But it might help a little."

"Fire away."

By gently abusing the authority of the New York State Department of Taxation, Copeland had learned that the last paycheck issued for Jeremy Wilder at QualCo had been in May of that year. Further bureaucratic abuse yielded more: the most recent check had been a large one.

"Four hundred fifty-eight thousand dollars, Laura. Generous compensation for private security work," Copeland suggested. "Most likely a severance payment from his own company."

"Jesus," she muttered. She felt impoverished on her Service salary.

"I know, I know. We're both fools, working for the Feds, working for the State," he said. "Selling our youth for peanuts."

"Yeah," she said. "Right." She tried to assess the information. "Why would he take severance from his own company?" she asked.

"If he sold the company or retired from it," came back the answer, exactly as Laura thought of it, too.

"Who's been paying money to his company? Any angle there?"

"Can't get that without a court order," Brian answered. "Maybe someone in the IRS in Washington can help you better."

"Maybe," she said.

Brian had also attempted to snoop in the state pension department, but was reluctant to pursue. Not that he couldn't. Any fool with computer dexterity could get any state info desired. But he did not want to leave electronic fingerprints that could lead back to him and then to Laura.

"So where's Mr. Wilder?" she asked.

Sgt. Copeland then offered her a final gift.

"I did the in-person snooping for you," he said. "I live in East Islip. So I drove by Wilder's address in Westbury."

"You're a prince. What did you find?"

"His name's off the mailbox. New people at the address. But he's still listed as the owner. Meaning the tenants probably pay rent to him. Should I follow up and ask what they know?"

"Not yet," she said. "If he's our man, I don't want to alert him with anything suspicious."

"I get it," he said.

They hung up. She sighed.

An image of the elusive former agent Jeremy Wilder was coming into focus, but only in absentia. She knew where he wasn't. He wasn't in the Service. He wasn't home. He wasn't at or with his company anymore. So where was he? And what he was doing?

She returned to the end of Bernard's 602s. More crap for the back end of the afternoon:

Leon Grimes, eight years in Service. Currently under psychiatric leave, feels department has bugged the pear trees in his
garden in Maryland.... Contributed $5,200 in 1999 and
$7,800 in year 2000 to United Evangelical Ministries of Or-
lando for overseas Christian services. UEM is shell corpora-
tion and has no actual overseas ministries. Subject (Grimes)
is in debt from contributions and most likely unaware of the
fraud....

Chapman sighed. In the old days of vetting it had been
simple: Who's a Red? Who's a queer? Who's got a bastard
child somewhere? Who did hard drugs? This was different,
an Inquisition for the new millennium. God, she hated this!
What purpose did these files serve?

WTF?

The phone rang again. Another friendly: Rick McCarron,
announced sweetly by increasingly efficient Vanessa. Laura
picked up immediately.

Rick, bless him, had something.

The picture of Jeremy Wilder that she had transferred to
him meant nothing. No recognition. He could take it past
Charley Boy whenever she wanted. But something else curious had clicked. "June ten at The Tides Hotel," McCarron
said. "Two names registered are Israeli agents."

"What?"

"Lev Bilsky and Haim Schumann," he said.

She accessed her own list of registrees at The Tides and
found the names. Both had British passports and claimed
home addresses in London, which was how they had escaped Laura's initial notice. They had both checked in on the
eighth and checked out on the twelfth.

"Think these could have been the two men with our blond
man?" McCarron asked.

"What type of Israeli agents are they?" Laura asked.

"Our records list them as Mossad guys."

"Jesus," she whispered. A kaleidoscopic view of possibil-
ities opened before her. "Charley Boy says the two men with
Blondie were speaking Arabic," she recalled aloud.

"Charley Boy could be lying. Or mistook Hebrew for Arabic. They're both Semitic languages. Confusion is possible."

"C.B. speaks good Arabic, remember?" Laura answered.

"Then maybe we have a strange coincidence."

"I told you I don't like coincidences," she said. "And some Israelis speak Arabic."

"Agreed," McCarron said. "Everything's connected until we prove it's not."

"Maybe the Mossad guys are there keeping an eye on exactly what we're now watching. Strange," Laura suggested.

"On one hand, yes. On the other hand, two Israeli guys at a hotel in Miami? They could just be on vacation."

"I don't believe that any more than you do."

"We're on the same page," he said.

There was a heavy silence on the phone. Laura worked the angles, waiting for the details to tumble into order. Motivation? Where was it? What was going on? There were two Mossad agents in the hotel while the murder of a U.S. president was being discussed.

Coincidence?

"Can your office vet anything on this one?" she finally asked. "With the Israelis?"

"I can try. It will take time. It has to go through channels. And then who knows if we get an honest answer?" He added that he had already requisitioned airline records in and out of Miami for that week. That he could have within twenty-four hours, he promised. It might be beneficial to know where Bilsky and Schumann were coming from and where they went.

She thought about it. "What's in your files?" she asked. "Could we get photographs?"

"I'm working on it already," Rick answered. "Then we take them to Anna."

Laura set down the phone again, having no idea in which direction this threw her investigation. She did know she was pleased with Rick. So far.

She was still considering the Israeli discovery half an hour later when Mitch Hamilton phoned again. No luck on locating Jeremy Wilder, Mitch said. The blond former Secret Service agent had disappeared off the face of the earth.

chapter 54

MIAMI
JUNE 24, 2009; 11:35 P.M.

Anna was tending the bar at the club late in the evening when her gaze rose. She looked past the wiseguys, past the Russians, past the cologned investment bankers out for some South Florida slumming, past the rattling roulette wheels and the crap tables and—from a distance of fifty feet—locked into a return gaze from the blond man's clear blue eyes.

He was not a ghost, not an apparition.

Maybe other people saw things that were spiritual or that weren't there, but Anna was grounded in the real world. She knew exactly who she was looking at. It was *him*. In the flesh. This was the blond man who had taken her to The Tides Hotel with his two dark-hued friends.

The one she had overheard. The one she had reported to the FBI.

It was a moment of sheer terror.

He smiled at her. She turned away.

But at last she had gotten a *good* look! That FBI artist who had been bugging her for the last day or two, well, now she would have something for him! Then again, maybe not. If the blond man was back, he was back for her.

She grabbed her purse from under the bar and disappeared into the ladies' room. She went into a stall, opened her purse, and found her pistol: a small .22 caliber Italian job, serial number conveniently removed, but it would have its impact when needed. She loaded it.

She sat down in front of a mirror at a dressing table and steeled herself. She had been in worse situations than this in her life and wasn't going to be anyone's compliant victim now.

She freshened her lipstick and her eyeliner.

She returned to the bar and struck up a conversation with two men who had just sat down. She scanned the room and didn't see the blond man anywhere. Now what was going on?

Anna moved away from the two men for a moment and reached again for her purse. She pulled out the phone Laura had given her. She called up Laura's number and was about to punch SEND, then stopped.

What about her Frenchman? Where was he? She didn't want to surrender a good trick and if he showed up, he would protect her. Should she wait?

No, she reckoned, the main thing was to get out of there as quickly as possible.

But to where and how? Two options: She could dart home, grab some things, and hide out. She eyed the two men. She could offer to go with them for the night and thus have a pair of escorts while she was working. Possible. But what if these two men were with the blond man?

Anna went to the quiet end of the bar.

She surveyed the place again and did not see the blond man. The casino was busy. She kept looking for him. The incident took on a hallucinogenic effect.

Had it really happened? Had she *really* seen him?

His two buddies were nowhere to be seen, either.

She asked Robin, who answered with a shrug. There had been a blond man or two that evening, he said. One man gambled for about an hour, Robin said, lost a few hundred dollars, and left. The other man took a Spanish girl back to his hotel. So what? It happened every night.

Anna trusted no one now. Only JP, her Doberman.

She had lived by her wits since she was a girl. She had survived this long not because of other people, but in spite of them. So she would put faith in no one else this night.

How did she even know, she asked herself, whether her new friend Linda was not setting her up to be killed?

Anna made her decision.

She would go home and lock herself in. She would arm herself like a warrior. The next day she would cash out at the bank in the early morning and head north. She would tell no one where she was going and she would trust no one other than herself. She had always wanted to visit New York City and she figured she could successfully disappear there for a while.

It all made sense.

She borrowed a blond wig, platform shoes, and a long coat from another girl who worked there. She told Robin that a man had threatened her earlier in the day and she needed his help.

"Help how?" he asked.

"Just leave with me, please, okay?" she said. "I give you special reward tomorrow." She made an "O" motion with her lips, a flick of the tongue tossed in. Robin appreciated her way of thinking. He wasn't averse to dipping his enormous pen in the club's inkwell.

Robin and Anna left together shortly after 1 A.M., Anna keeping her face obscured and letting Robin guide her to her car. Then Robin waddled to his evening car, a neon-blue Impala. She did not see any of Linda's surveillance people, but she didn't see the blond man either. She felt a small surge of relief. At least she was away from the club.

They drove to a hotel on Collins Avenue; Anna leading, Robin following. She waited for a few minutes in the lobby, then went back to their cars and Robin led her to her home.

The streets looked clear when she arrived. She looked carefully before she went inside.

She entered her home through the back door. The place was completely dark.

Rose was not there. JP was. That was a good sign. No one could be hiding in the house without the dog knowing. JP was now, more than ever, her life insurance policy.

Anna did not put lights on, but rather found her way through the premises in the dark.

She was good at getting around without lights. Her spirit was emboldened. She locked all the doors and windows. She kept JP with her.

Robin remained outside and vigilant for half an hour. Then she heard his car start and heard him leave.

She sighed appreciatively. The big guy was more than a mouthful, but she would give him his reward the following evening.

By now, it was past 2 A.M. on the morning of June 25.

Anna owned a larger pistol that she kept under the negligees in the top drawer of her dresser. It was an old protective device for a working girl, keeping a piece of artillery in a place where she might be grabbing something seductive for an ornery customer.

This pistol was a Browning 9mm, a big weapon. It could blow a hole the size of a melon in a man. Just what she needed. She had never fired it, but she kept it loaded.

Just in case.

More precisely: Just in a case like this.

It could save her life. She would use it if she had to.

She changed into her comfortable off-hours outfit, the cut-off jeans and sweatshirt that made her look like a graduate student. She tucked the Browning into her shorts pocket so she could carry it from room to room. Her heart was beating like a runaway metronome now, but at least she had a sense of survival.

She assembled a suitcase, still working in the dark.

All she would take with her was jewelry, a few changes of clothing, and her dog. She wondered if when she got to New York in a day or two she could escape this working life she now had.

Again, the thought made her feel good. In New York, she would know no one. She spoke enough English now to get a real job. She had thousands of dollars stashed away. And maybe down the line she could get in touch with these CIA people again and they would pay her some more for the information she had provided. And she wanted that U.S. passport they had promised her!

At age twenty-four, yet another fresh start. Third and final. Well, it was better than a dead end in Thailand or Colombia or any of the points before or after.

And well, she concluded, she would worry about the details later, too. The main thing was getting out of here alive. Then she could reinvent and reorganize her life. She could find a straight job, a man, she hoped, and have some babies. Suddenly, her future seemed very bright to her, if she could just survive this night.

She glanced at the clock. Almost 3 A.M. now.

On the long road from Bangkok to Miami over the course of a decade, she had learned about self-survival. There was no way she was going to make a mistake now.

Then, as she closed her suitcase, she froze.

Had she heard something downstairs?

Or hadn't she?

She looked at JP. His ears perked.

Danger!

Then it happened.

Not just a small second noise from downstairs, but an enormous one.

A crash! The sound of big-time glass shattering and then the sound of a man coming through the window, hitting the floor and running.

JP snarled protectively, bolted, and hit the stairs.

Anna screamed. She thought of Jimmy Pearce and her Jean-Henri. She wondered whether one or both would be waiting for her in the afterworld.

She drew the big Browning and went to the top of the stairs. She heard JP bark and snarl and she heard screams, as if the dog had gotten a piece of the intruder.

And then one of those moments followed in which life either stops completely or continues on for another forty years.

The moment passed very quickly.

chapter 55

That same evening, as lights blazed all over the capital, Laura Chapman stood in the window of her office in the Longworth Building. She focused on the brightly illuminated dome of the Capitol. Her arms were folded neatly before her but her thoughts were all over the planet.

As a history major at the University of Massachusetts, she had taken academics seriously. She had always wanted to *understand* history, not just *know* history. Now, she had difficulty knowing the modern world, or at least finding logic within it.

Why did her nation give millions of dollars to regimes that abetted America's enemies? The previous week Jordan's King Abdullah II had lectured America about everything from the West Bank to Iraq to the role of women in society. The recipient of nearly a billion dollars in annual American generosity, he had for years closed his borders to refugees from the West Bank. The humanity of his stance compared almost equally to Kuwait's decision in 1991 to ethnically cleanse its Palestinian residents.

Saudi Arabia, the incubator of a decade of guerrilla terror against the United States, was considered equally restrained because it subsidized terrorists covertly rather than publicly.

Thousands of American troops—who had been promised they would be home by 2008—were still stationed in the dangerous Middle Eastern deserts. They were prevented from venturing into Iraq, which had expelled all U.S. troops in 2008, and were not to hunt down the final few hundred Taliban and al

Qaeda warriors in Afghanistan. Instead, American female soldiers remained veiled as American guns, planes, brains, and democracy protected the corrupt sheiks.

She sighed. *What a complicated world!*

Many lights burned late in the Capitol. Laura stared downward at the traffic on Independence Avenue. Traffic tended to desert the District after dark. But tonight, with the Libyan crisis in progress, there were more cars and press vans circulating than usual. Instinctively, she wondered if the assassin she was seeking was in one of them.

Several hundred yards away from her, at the intersection of Independence with First Street, SE, a lone district policeman gently moved his arm to keep traffic flowing.

There was a subtle ballet to what the policeman was doing.

He was *conducting* traffic, the way a man would conduct an orchestra. He kept it flowing. The effort was orderly, calm, serene. Laura envied the uncomplicated simplicity of the man's job. She also knew that the policeman would probably have envied the perceived glamour of Laura's.

Closer to the Capitol, in the driveway leading to the front of the building, there were four other federal guards. Laura watched them from her office. Three men and a woman. Their job was to back up the policemen on the peripheral roads—Independence and Constitution avenues, and First Street, and to make sure that no unauthorized vehicles entered the Capitol grounds.

Again, order and simplicity.

A vehicle either had a permit or it did not. If it did, it could stay. If it did not, it got the heave-ho. Everything was clear. Hidden within the shadows and booths surrounding the building were other officers—reinforcements, back-ups—who would respond immediately as needed.

The situation below her was unlike her office. Here nothing was clear and she had no back-up. Chapman was scared as hell that it would happen yet again, the tragedy of twenty years ago returning for an encore performance: Someone would die on her shift!

Like Walter McKiernan, the swimmer, long ago when she had been a lifeguard.

Gut feeling, all over again. *Someone's going to die.*

She wondered if it would be her.

Well, bury me in a nice place if it is because I'm giving every fucking thing I have to this job. Hell, I drive by Arlington all the time. That's a good place.

God! Where the hell did THAT thought come from?

That's the third time recently I've thought about being buried at Arlington!

Three times lucky?

Arf, arf. Here came the Black Dog again.

Her mind surged defensively back into the present day. Her eyes swept the distant streets. A lone man stood at a curb, gazing up in her direction.

Is that him? The assassin? Looking for me? Seeking our day of reckoning?

The man turned and walked away, seemingly in response to her thoughts.

Just a tourist? Or was this her suspect *right down there,* taunting her? Planning?

Damn it to living hell, she thought again.

Somewhere in Laura's world there was something that was not as it seemed: an agent of the president's protective service who was set to kill him, a retired agent, or a bogus agent who would penetrate security? The particulars of life did not get much more duplicitous than that.

Strange geometric patterns of deceit crept into her mind and then took possession of it. She knew why James Jesus Angleton, head of CIA counter-intelligence during the Cold War, had gone quietly insane in his final years, seeing conspiracy in everything from the arrangement of cereal boxes in the Wal-Mart to the way the orchids bloomed in his garden at home.

She glanced at her watch. Eleven thirty-two P.M. She had been brought into this case one week earlier. There now remained one full week till the eve of July Fourth.

She was convinced that somewhere out there was an assassin who had to be stopped.

She was on the verge of a complete collapse, physically and mentally.

She glanced again at the policeman on the mall, fluidly conducting traffic, his support all around him if problems arose, seemingly oblivious of the hell breaking loose all around him.

She envied him anew.

PART THREE

chapter 56

In her bedroom, the feeling was as palpable as a hand on her shoulder while she slept, shaking her awake. One of those damnable feelings again. A vehement premonition.

From sleep, Laura bolted upright in bed. *Oh, Lord! Miami! Anna!*

There was no logic to it. It was just another one of those things she *felt.*

She threw on the light in her room. Anna had not called in that night, either. Laura fumbled with the cell phone.

A flashback to girlhood:

When Laura had been a little girl, she had watched a World War II movie on television. An old black-and-white flick. In it, a soldier is about to be killed by the Japanese, all of whom looked like little Tojos. Right at the moment that the bayonet was about to go in his gut, his fiancée back home bolted up in bed because she knew it was happening.

There was no way that the woman in the movie could know, but across seven thousand miles, she knew anyway. Laura understood those moments because she had them; she saw and felt things that others didn't. And she was having one now.

An awful one.

She punched in Anna's number, broke a fierce uncontrollable sweat, and waited.

chapter 57

The cell phone rang insistently in Anna's purse. It stopped and then rang again.

The blond man reached into Anna's purse and picked up the phone.

He glanced first at the display, showing what number might be calling. The word RESTRICTED appeared. No surprise there, he reasoned. No man wants his favorite hooker calling at home. But who else would be calling at this hour, he reasoned further, than a guy with a wicked hard-on?

Curiosity got the best of him. He pressed the SEND button. He said nothing, only listened.

He was surprised to hear a female voice on the other end of the line.

"Anna? Anna, are you there?"

He held his silence, wondering who this was.

Laura repeated. "Anna? Anna, are you there?"

His response was as free of intonation as he could make it. "Anna is here," he said. "But she's unavailable. Who's calling?"

"Linda. Cochrane."

"Looking for your husband?"

"I want to talk to Anna," Laura said.

"It won't be possible," he said. "Try tomorrow."

"Where is she?"

"Servicing a client."

"Who are you?"

The man laughed. "The client. So leave us alone."

The assassin clicked off. Then he turned the phone off completely.

He knew he couldn't return it to her purse. So he dropped it into his pocket. It might prove useful for a day or two, then he would destroy it.

He turned back to where Anna lay waiting for him, gagged, hands bound, and he smiled.

chapter 58

ALEXANDRIA, VIRGINIA
JUNE 25, 2009; 3:56 A.M.

Laura phoned back, but received voicemail.

An ensuing call yielded the same. Then another.

The next call was to Rick McCarron. Middle of the night or not, she didn't care.

Get out of bed, Rick. Wake up! Answer my fucking call, God damn you!

No answer there, either.

She tried Sam Deal.

Somewhere Sam was snoring—or snorting—peacefully.

No Sam, no Deal.

Laura held her cell phone in her hand, resisting the urge to fling it. Where in Christ's name was everyone when she needed help? *Good God Almighty!*

She tried to control herself. She tried to tell herself, calmly, that maybe, just maybe, Anna *was* with a customer and maybe she would materialize the next day.

Maybe.

Maybe, like hell! Laura knew! She had been having these feelings all her life and she knew when she knew.

She looked at the clock. How quickly could she get to the airport?

chapter 59

Laura caught the first available flight to Miami that morning. Seven fifty A.M. She had a car waiting at Miami International. She would have driven into the city at a mad speed, except every expressway was clogged. She drove the fastest crawl imaginable.

She did not hit the city till shortly after 1 P.M. Several calls to Sam failed to find him.

Ditto, Rick.

Where to go first? The club was closest.

If Anna were around she might be there, even though it was afternoon. But when Laura arrived there, no one had seen Anna since she had left with some anxiety the night before. And by the way, asked one of the pit bosses that worked the second floor, where was Rose?

"No one see her today, either," he bitched, "and we short by *tres muchachas bonitas.*"

He eyed Laura appreciatively but stopped short of making an employment offer.

Now the inevitable reality hit Laura like an express train. She turned, bailed, and went to her car. She cut out of her parking place as quickly as she could, tires wailing.

She stopped at three red lights, then cruised through them as soon as it was safe. She was Linda Cochrane again, on assignment. Screw the stop signs and the red lights. Her Virginia State Police credentials would make short work of *los polis* in Miami.

She drove like a maniac and skidded to a halt in front of Anna's.

The front door was unlocked. Signs of forced entry. A broken window nearby.

Oh, no!

She drew her pistol and turned the handle, using a tissue on her hand to keep her prints off the door. She pushed the door open with her foot.

She stepped into the front landing.

The air conditioning rumbled on full blast. The place was like a meat locker.

Laura stealthily moved into the living room. She could hear something very faintly.

Something human. Something in a deep dark emotional state. Upstairs.

Laura prayed it was Anna.

Gut feeling: She knew it wasn't.

"Hello?" Laura called out. "Anyone?"

No response.

She moved to the steps. Her Colt was out and ready for business.

"Hello?" she called again. "Anna? Anyone?"

No one on the first floor.

But now she did see—*Oh, my God!*—bloodstains on the floor.

More on the steps.

Breakage to the walls, combined with bloody streaks.

Shots had been fired here.

Oh my dear God!

There had been a struggle. Crime Scene 101/Homicide; fall semester at the Massachusetts State Police Academy. Not good.

She moved halfway up the steps, sidestepping the blood.

She knew now what she was listening to: a woman crying. Deep long grievous pathetic sobs. The sobs of tragedy and hopelessness. The wailings of death and grief in any language.

"God Almighty!" Laura muttered. She already knew what she was going to find.

She moved to the top of the steps. She knew the way from

the previous visit. She went toward Anna's bedroom. The door was partly open.

The crying was louder.

She came to the door and looked into the room.

Rose.

Vanilla-and-Strawberry in T-shirt and tight micro mini-skirt. She cried uncontrollably.

Anna's roommate was sitting on a big canopied bed. Her face was in her hands and her skirt was up around her thighs. Rose knew Laura was there and paid her no notice. Nothing could happen that was worse than what already had.

Laura lowered her gun but kept it against her skirt, right side. She looked across the room. A pile of clothes lay on the floor. A whole wardrobe, and, for that matter, a tart's working wardrobe, amidst scattered suitcases that never got packed.

Reds, electric blues, and blacks. A nun's outfit, a Dallas Cowboys cheerleader's outfit, and the black velvet micro dress in which she had met Laura for the first time.

Plenty of negligees and stockings. A pink leather mini with matching vest.

Splashy short sexy things, give-a-guy-a-quick-ejaculation stuff, all scattered in a heap, and a big dead dog named JP not too far beyond that, its skull crushed by a large caliber shot.

The closet door was open and Laura knew: That's where the real horror was to be found.

She stepped toward it.

The door was ajar toward her. The blood had flowed out from the closet onto the beige carpet by about a yard. Laura had seen crime scene still pictures of things like this.

But never in person. Nothing this bad. Not until now.

Laura turned the corner and looked into the closet. Her eyes focused. She felt herself sway and backpedal half a step, fighting an intense gagging reflex at the same time.

"Jesus Christ," she said. "Oh, no, no . . . !"

She gazed in shock and disbelief at the nude mutilated body of Anna Muang.

Anna had been gagged, stripped, and tied up in the closet, her arms extended in a cross; she had been wired at the wrists to a couple of coat hooks. When Laura summoned up the stomach to look down, she saw that the dead woman's feet weren't touching the floor.

Sick, vengeful, and unspeakable. Fanatic. Borderline depraved.

Laura cursed violently. She had seen homicides before, but never anyone she had known.

Anna had cigarette burns on her breasts, stomach, and thighs, as if someone had wanted information before killing her. Whether or not she had given it was anyone's guess.

Laura's guess, spunky fighter and brawler that Anna had been, was that she might have used a free instep to whack a guy in the crotch, or at least try. That had probably made it worse.

Two deep slashes had killed her, one to each wrist.

She looked for a bullet hole. She did not see one.

He—or they—had tortured Anna and let her bleed to death. Anyone with the slightest sense of mercy would have shot her. It probably took her two hours to die in agony.

Laura recoiled again. Fortunately, her stomach was empty.

She would now have to call the local cops. If all went well, they could keep this as a local killing and not crowd out her own case. She thought of calling anonymously but that would never work. She needed to oversee whatever information was gained by a homicide investigation.

Anna had wanted a passport, a hundred grand, and a shot at the middle class white bread U.S. of A. dream. Instead she had gotten bled dry in a closet.

She heard Anna's chirping voice again in her mind, addressing her as "Linda." Something made Laura feel genuinely filthy. Anna hadn't even known Laura's real name. She was just part of the whole deceptive charade that had been her life.

"Jesus on the cross," Laura whispered aloud. Her eyes were wet and stinging.

Her words roused Rose. The next thing she heard was a commotion behind her. Rose was coming at her with an empty Absolut bottle, upraised and held by the neck.

Laura raised a hand fast to block the initial thrust, then knocked the bottle away from her. It shattered on the bloody floor. Rose started pounding at her with her fists, demanding over and over again, amidst sobs, "Why? Why? Why?"

Laura caught Rose's arms, turned her, and shoved her away. Rose staggered and retreated to the next room. She collapsed into another round of noisy hysterical tears.

And of course, Laura did not know, herself.

Why? Why, anything?

Why did the sun even bother coming up each day on a world like this?

She felt like going back to Washington and saying the hell with all this, it just is not worth it, and I want a little art, music, and love in my middle years instead of blood, guts, gore, conspiracy, and bureaucratic bullshit!

But she could not go backward. And damned if she knew how she would ever move forward, either. She stood amidst the carnage, the bad decor, and the sobbing, feeling completely alone and having no idea what to do next.

Her Colt was still in her hand.

She holstered it and removed her jacket.

She turned, sucked up her courage, suppressed her disgust, and walked to Rose in the next room.

Whoever had done this, Laura told herself, would pay.

chapter 60

MIAMI
JUNE 25, 2009; LATE MORNING

Laura went to Rose and sat down next to her. She placed an arm around her and retreated into convenient lies. She identified herself as Linda Cochrane, Virginia State Police. She showed the two fake IDs and, not surprisingly, both passed Rose's cursory glance. Then it must have occurred to Rose that if Laura was a police detective, she, Rose, must have been a suspect.

"I would never . . . have hurt her," Rose said. "She was my friend."

"I know that." Laura held Rose tightly, then released her.

"Do you know who she was with last night?" Laura asked.

Rose shook her head, eyes crinkled in tears, the sobs barely under control.

"A man was here late. Maybe three A.M. Could you help me on that?" Laura pressed.

Rose couldn't.

She had been taking care of a recently retired U.S. Foreign Service officer at his hotel, she said. He was a steady customer, an urbane and amusing retiree, who was trying to talk her into joining him on a cruise to Europe on the *Queen Mary 2* to celebrate his sixty-first birthday. Rose hadn't arrived here until maybe a quarter hour before Laura and was now overdue at the club.

"Okay. I know how horrible this is," Laura said, holding Rose's free hand. "But you need to leave Miami immediately. Do you have a safe place to go?"

Rose thought about it. She had a mother in Atlanta, she explained. Buckhead, a good neighborhood where she had attended an outstanding Christian high school and left after eleventh grade. The people she grew up with thought she worked at Disney World in Orlando and made top money dressed up as Ariel, the Little Mermaid. Rose still had her Georgia driver's license. She showed it to Laura, who copied down the address.

Rose said she would go up there for two weeks.

Laura said this was good thinking. Several weeks, Laura suggested, might be an even better idea. And that free cruise to Europe, if Rose could snag it from her would-be sugar daddy, was an offer any working girl in her current position might consider.

Laura continued: "I want you to be safe, Rose. Do you have money to get to your mother's place?"

"I got plenty of money."

"How will you travel?"

"I . . . have a car," Rose whispered.

"Do you feel capable of driving?"

She nodded. "I need some cigarettes," she said.

Inside Laura was exploding; on the surface her kindness and patience with Rose, her tranquility, astonished even her.

Rose was very still for an instant. Laura feared she had immobilized into shock. Then Vanilla-and-Strawberry reached for the Kleenex box, wiped her eyes again, and Laura resumed.

"Pack. Then I need to make phone calls. There will be people arriving. Police of various sorts. Authorities who won't identify themselves. Maybe others. People will ask questions that you won't wish to answer. Do you understand what I mean?"

Rose nodded. She knew.

"Then there will be forensics people. Photographs. Fingerprints. A DNA search."

Rose cringed.

"Do you have *any* idea who might have done this?" Laura pressed.

Rose shook her head adamantly.

"Was there anyone Anna was particularly afraid of?"

Most of her boyfriends were good to Anna, Rose said. Appreciative.

Laura showed her the photo of Jeremy Wilder. "Ever seen this man?" she asked.

Rose took a long look, working her nose with paper tissue. She shook her head. No.

"Think hard. *Very* hard," Laura pressed. "Your own safety depends on it. You've never seen him? *Not once?* You've *never* been with him?"

More head shaking, left to right and back again.

"I won't be angry if you know him. You won't be in trouble. But I *must* know."

Rose shook her head emphatically.

Gut feeling again: Laura believed her.

"What about foreign men? Middle Eastern, perhaps. A pair of them who travel together?"

She saw that at the club all the time, she said. Nothing unusual about it.

"Okay," Laura said, getting nowhere.

Laura glanced around. Then she asked, "I gave Anna a cell phone a few days ago. Do you know where it is or where she might have kept it?"

Between sobs, "She kept her new phone in her purse."

"Thank you. Now assemble your things. I'm sorry, but you need to be gone very quickly."

Laura stood. Rose didn't budge. She had finally gone catatonic.

Laura gently lifted her to her feet. *"Go!"* she urged. "You have to. You don't want to be here when the Miami Police arrive. I'm doing you a favor. Go *now, please!"*

Laura pushed her onward. The frigid A/C continued the meat-locker effect.

Rose struggled out of her paralysis and into her room to pack.

Laura went downstairs. She pulled on the latex gloves she always kept in her purse. The JIC pair. Some women carried a condom in their purse, just in case. Laura carried prophylactic latex gloves, just in case. She often wondered who had better priorities.

She looked for Anna's purse and found it. She dipped in, latexed.

Kool cigarettes, and some of the small black cancer sticks that Anna favored. Birth control pills, a wallet packed with money, Cherry Soda lipstick, makeup, a comb and brush. In a side pocket within the purse, another small stash of money.

Laura was happy her hands were latexed: Three fifty-dollar bills off to one side in a rubber band. From the roll that had been spatter-stained with blood?

Who knew now?

And what the hell was the blood all about? Menstrual or murder? The damned NDNAR still hadn't reported, the idiots. But were these the same bills she had seen previously?

Likely, Laura decided. Highly likely.

Laura tucked the money back where she had found it. Then also, to her amazement, Laura found a Filipino passport, old and worn: Anna's picture beside the name of Asua Togudo.

To Laura's keen eye, the passport was fraudulent. It was not even a distinguished fake, but it would have gotten Anna out of the United States in an emergency, if not quite back in.

There was more clutter at the bottom of the purse that Laura didn't examine. But no cell phone. Laura closed the purse. She could examine the contents more thoroughly later.

Laura sat down on the sofa where seventy-two hours earlier she had de-briefed her witness. Now she was picking up the pieces after a murder.

She pulled out her own cell phone.

The first call she made was to Sam Deal.

No answer. No surprise.

The second call: Rick McCarron, who did not answer, either.

The third call: Anna's cell number. It kicked to default voicemail.

Fuck!

Laura listened to the footsteps of Rose above, hurriedly packing. She thought of the male voice that had answered Anna's phone the previous time.

She tried the number a second time. No dice again.

Wherever the phone was, no one answered.

Damn it all to hell! Zero for three on the calls.

Worse, Anna's phone was not ringing anywhere nearby.

Several minutes passed. Laura sat and waited. Laura tried Sam and Rick again.

Predictably, nothing. *Damn! Where* are *they?*

She wondered, *Together? Wouldn't that be something?*

Sounds: a woman's footsteps on the stairs. Rose had changed to tight jeans, sandals, a kelly green tank top, and an aqua Miami Dolphins cap. She had big owlish round dark glasses to hide the crimson in her eyes. She carried a denim shirt. She had a bag and was ready to travel.

"Good," Laura said, looking at her. "Very good."

She embraced her again.

"Now you better get going. I have to call the police. There's going to be a lot of trouble."

Rose went through the door. Laura drew a breath and called 9-1-1.

She reported the homicide. She clicked off and worked on her tears.

Inexplicably, Rose dawdled outside at her car.

Laura couldn't figure out if Rose had difficulty saying good-bye or if there was something else. Laura's paranoia surfaced: Was she sure Rose didn't know more than she had revealed?

But Laura was on her own radar and the redhead wasn't setting off any alarms. Not yet, anyway. Laura went to the window, pushed the shade aside slightly, and peered out.

"Get moving, Rose," she whispered. "Get moving!"

Finally the engine turned over. Vanilla-and-Strawberry disappeared as Laura noted the license plate number. Once again, just in case.

Rose missed the first of six police cars by less than a minute, which, all things considered, was lucky for everyone.

chapter 61

TRIPOLI
JUNE 25, 2009; 5:45 P.M. GMT

A quarter of the way around the globe, the local police were equally busy.

Alan Savett, the Reuters correspondent in Tripoli, sat at his desk, tapping the keys at his computer terminal, finishing a cup of tea. In an ashtray, a cigarette smoldered. Acrid

Egyptian tobacco: a vice he refused to give up unless a doctor found a spot on his lung.

He reread his evening column and was pleased with himself. His dispatch had replayed a theme that he had sounded
much of the week, namely that the United States had once
again created its own mess in world affairs. Those Puritan
cowboys had learned nothing in seventy-five years of non-
diplomacy in the Middle East and probably would learn
nothing this time, either.

Then, with infinite care, he attached a new set of recent
digital photographs. His photo mix was always important.
Satisfied, he checked his work. Convinced that even the
smallest pixel dots were in place, his hand went to the right
side of his keyboard.

He pressed the SEND button. His column, widely read by
Muslims in Great Britain and the rest of the English-
speaking world, zipped across cyberspace to his editor's terminal in London. It would appear in print and on the
Internet within another five hours, even if many of the photographs did not. "There," he said, pleased with himself.
"Finished."

He leaned back and stubbed out the remnants of his cigarette. He glanced at his watch. He had no plans for the evening. Tripoli wasn't London and even among the press corps
there was not much of a social scene. Partying with babes in
burkas was not an option.

Then his telephone rang. He answered in Arabic.

"Mr. Savett?" asked a voice in English, heavily tinged
with an accent.

Unidentified callers always jolted him. And Libyan accents put his sweat glands into overdrive. Libya could be an
Orwellian place. But Savett had long mastered the technique
of keeping cool under pressure.

"Yes, this is Alan Savett. Who, may I ask, is calling,
please?"

"This is Major Housahodi of the National Police Corps of
the Libyan Socialist Republic," the voice oozed. "How are
you this evening, sir?"

This was an individual with whom Savett had never spoken before. Not on the phone and not in person. Savett's mind raced. He placed the name and suddenly, within his Turnbull & Asser shirt, it felt as if it were raining. Housahodi was the commander of the palace police and rumored to be overly ambitious within the current Libyan power elite.

Major Housahodi was speaking as if he were reading. And why *was* he phoning?

"I'm very well, thank you for inquiring, Major," Savett answered. "And how are you?"

In Arabic: "Are you at home tonight, sir?"

"Well, I wouldn't very well be answering if I weren't, Major," Savett answered, remaining calm. "So for what reason do I have the pleasure of receiving this distinguished call?"

"Have you reported information about us this evening?"

Savett was not clear how that was meant.

"Well, yes, I do three times a week, Major, I believe you know that. And one of my reports is transmitted on Saturdays, but you know that, too, since your people have the very indelicate habit of monitoring this Internet outlet."

"Very good, sir," Housahodi said.

"*What's* very good, Major?"

In Savett's chest, more palpitations. There was nothing good about this call. Not the time, not the tone, not the content, not its unsolicited nature.

It quickly occurred to Savett that the call had perfectly coincided with the sending of his evening dispatch. London would expect nothing more from him for two days.

"You will stay there and we will come for you," the major said.

"I beg your pardon, sir?"

"Tonight there will be a story you do not report."

The major rung off.

Savett put down the phone and stared at his computer terminal. Then he moved to his window, knowing how the Libyans worked, knowing what he expected deep down. He was not surprised to see a detachment of Royal Guard marines, armed with automatic rifles and sidearms.

More red berets than he could count. Not a civilian in sight.

He had no illusions. They were there for him.

"Oh, my Lord," he muttered slowly. There was no escape when things went the wrong way in a country like this. He had written favorably of the Libyans for so long, boosted their star in the world, and now *this!*

He might have known how it would turn out. He should have known a long time ago that he was playing with fire. He thought back to the moment a few days earlier when he had seen Major Housahodi stare at him and discuss him at the press conference.

Savett wondered where his mistake had been.

Perspiration pouring down from his brow, the Englishman sat back down at his computer. He would quickly punch out a message to London letting them know who had called and where he was going. That was innocent enough, even to the Libyan censors.

He attempted to bring up the Internet connection. Furiously, he hit the keyboard. He knew he had no more than a few minutes before he might disappear.

He wrote that he was possibly being taken into custody by the Special Police, Major Housahodi himself doing the honors, and—

His screen went blank. His hosts had snuffed the satellite feed that led into the building.

"Oh, bugger," he muttered to himself. "Oh, shit, indeed." Joseph Stalin, the role model upon which all modern dictators could be judged, could not have done it better himself.

Savett froze where he sat and waited. He picked up his cell phone and it, too, was as dead as those two American flyers had looked.

Several more minutes passed.

Savett heard footsteps in the hall. A few seconds later: the knock on the door.

A complete gentleman at such times, he rose and pulled on his suit jacket. When he opened the door, the major was there in person, beaming, his red beret slightly crooked.

"Mr. Savett?" he asked in English.

"That is I. Yes?"

"It is my honor to meet you in person."

"I'm honored as well, Major. Would you care to speak Arabic?"

"Of course." The red beret bowed graciously. "If you prefer. But there is no reason. I lived in London for several years. I attended comprehensive schools near Bishop's Gate and read history at the University of Bristol. So English is not a problem."

"So I am now aware," Savett said. "I commend you."

"May I come in?"

"Would I stop you if I said no?" Savett asked, eyeing the armed men behind him.

"Not for very long," Major Housahodi said.

"Then by all means, welcome."

"Thank you."

The major entered Savett's apartment, followed by six heavily armed national policemen. He slowly surveyed the room, moving around as if he were in a store. "Do you know anything about a term in English, 'steganography'?" the major finally asked.

"I believe I've heard the term somewhere. Refresh my memory."

"I was hoping you could tell *us*," the major said. "It is a tool of espionage."

"Is it, now?" Savett answered.

"So you cannot help us on that?"

"No, I cannot, sir." The sweat poured off Savett now. The major was fingering books and material on a table in Savett's living area. The police chief's attention momentarily settled on a silver-framed portrait of a young man, about twenty-two, handsome and mocha-complexioned.

"Would this be your son?" the major asked.

"It is. Yes. And how did you know I had a son?"

"Is he a good son? Do you hear from him often?"

"Sadly, very rarely. He has his own life which does not intersect with mine."

"And where is he? Where does he live?"

"He's finished with his studies and has chosen to live in the United States."

"America?" Housahodi answered, an eyebrow raised. "How do you feel about that?"

"I miss my son considerably," Savett answered nervously, "and wish he lived much closer. But where he lives is of his own choosing."

The police chief set down the photo. "I have a family, myself," he said. "I have a cousin who lives in Toronto. A very lovely woman who is a Canadian citizen."

"Imagine that," said Savett.

"What about the term 'Chiron'?" Major Housahodi asked next.

"Chiron?"

The major eyed the journalist. "Yes. Come now. Don't act so puzzled, please, sir. We know a bit about you. You read classics at Cambridge. You know the name."

"Chiron was one of the centaurs in Greek mythology," said Savett. "A kindly centaur. He educated Achilles, particularly upon the harp. Later Chiron saved the life of Achilles' father, Peleus, as well as restoring his sword."

"We are looking for a Western spy in Tripoli, a CIA agent who goes by the code name of Chiron," the major said sharply. "It occurs to us that you have a knowledge of such names."

"As would anyone who studied classics, Major. Unfortunately, I cannot help you identify your spy."

"You are unwilling to or you are unable to?"

"Unable, sir. I would help you if I could."

"But there are only so many foreigners in Tripoli who would be familiar with the classics of the ancient world," Housahodi suggested. "Aside from myself, of course, who greatly enjoyed the Greeks while studying in England." He paused. "How many? Maybe a dozen?"

"Perhaps. So then you must be certain to go ask the other eleven."

The major gave Savett a long hard look that conveyed

disappointment. "Of course," he said. "So now you will please accompany us to police headquarters?"

There was a violent tumbling feeling in Savett's stomach. "Police headquarters?"

"Yes. Voluntarily, I would hope. A few more questions, please."

What had he ever done that these people would read as disloyalty or subversion? Beyond his immediate fear, he was genuinely confused. But he also knew the long history of pesky journalists who had just plain disappeared over the previous decades.

Argentina. Chile. China. El Salvador. Iraq. This place.

"Of course," Savett said. "I understand."

But he didn't. And his emotions were in turmoil. His column had been relentlessly pro-Libyan and pro-Islam for years. What in hell *was* this? This part of the world was so damned treacherous and unpredictable, but Savett already knew that.

There were now eight uniformed policemen with the major, all of them carrying Chinese-made rifles. Exactly the same number, Savett noted with an extra cringe, as a Libyan firing squad.

With a correspondent's instincts, Savett was still making mental notes. What he was aware of now was that the National Police were taking no chances with him.

Their mission was to bring him in and *that* they would do without fail. Much as he would have liked to, there would be no chance to use his camera this time.

chapter 62

The ranking officer on the murder scene was Sgt. Clarence
Foster, a wiry no-nonsense black man in his early thirties
with tight salt-and-pepper hair.

Laura's Virginia State Police shield hung on the breast
pocket of her jacket. Foster glowered and did not react well
to it. "You have a valid permit for that weapon?" he asked.

"Sure do," she answered.

"I'll remind you: You're not in Virginia."

"I have a permit to carry out of state. Federal."

Clarence Foster had an attitude. Laura had long experience
with attitudes. "Show me," he said. "Then we're copasetic."

From a small leather billfold, she produced the plastic ID
that Mitch Hamilton had produced back up north. She
handed it to Sgt. Foster.

"It's your city," she said. "I just visit it."

"You got that part right." He scrutinized the permit. "Virginia? Lieutenant Linda Cochrane?"

"Want to call it in and check it?" she offered.

"Damned right I do. Lieutenant."

"Be my guest."

He looked at the ID again, then at Laura, then back to the
ID, which he turned over. He glanced at the backside, looking for something wrong.

"Don't feel yourself flattered. I check everything," he said.

He gave her ID to a detective, who retreated to a corner
with a cell phone.

"What happened here?" he asked.

"Follow me upstairs and I'll show you."

Sgt. Foster followed. They arrived at the closet.

"Oh, Christ," Foster said.

He averted his eyes for a moment, then looked back. "So who was this?" he asked.

"I have an ongoing investigation," Laura said. "She was a witness."

"State of Virginia?"

"More or less," she said.

"Something unusual about this case?"

"You're catching on fast," she said.

Foster's assistant returned with a closed cell phone and the ID. "She's good," he said.

Foster took the ID from the detective and handed it back to her. "Let's get past the bullshit. What's going down here?" Foster asked.

"Think Virginia, then think about another 'district' a little farther north," Laura answered.

"So Virginia carries you on their books, but you just could be working federal. Is that it?"

"Might be."

"Uh huh," he said.

"It's your jurisdiction on the homicide. But I can use your discreet help."

They stood alone, discussing. "I hear you," Foster said. "What do you need?"

"Run this as a normal homicide," she said. "When and if you find anything, let me know first. I need every fingerprint and every piece of DNA that you can find. Keep it low profile in the newspapers if you can."

She paused, watching CSI people flood into the chamber.

Sgt. Foster looked back at the body again while Laura continued.

"Somewhere on these premises," Laura explained, "there may or may not be a cell phone. A Nokia Generation 21 with a blue case. If you find it, which you probably won't, I need it and I need any fingerprints on it. I also will need an autopsy report. But even after the report, I want the body held at the medical examiner's office indefinitely."

"Indefinitely?"

"Short term, I hope. Possible?"

"Special paperwork. Within four days. Otherwise the remains go to the crematorium. That's on you, the paperwork."

"You'll get it."

"If you louse it up there's nothing I can do."

"You'll get it," she said again.

"The victim have any next of kin?"

"Not readily available," Laura answered. "But I'll work that angle eventually."

He nodded. Then, adding up all the components, Foster asked, "Mind if I ask? What's so special about what's going on here?"

"I hope you don't mind if I don't answer."

"I didn't think you would." Foster sighed. He nodded slightly. "I'll do what I can for you," he said. "Strikes me that you're a pretty good law enforcement type. I appreciate that."

"Thank you, sergeant. Thank you twice."

They exchanged contact info. As Laura left the room, medical people came in with a gurney.

Laura spent another thirty minutes trying to find Anna's phone. No luck. When Laura left, she carried Anna's purse with her, holding it as if it were hers. Illegal seizure of evidence maybe, but she could make a case for it, federal jurisdiction over local, and who cared right now, anyway?

There was much to do that afternoon. Time to move on.

chapter 63

MIAMI
JUNE 25, 2009; 1:02 P.M.

Laura walked out of Anna's home and smack into the suffocating Florida heat.

She steadied herself. She felt the sweat glands pop all over her. She went to work.

Several cars of harness bulls from the Miami PD set a perimeter. Yellow tape all over; like a giant jaundiced spider had gone berserk. Blue strobe lights in every direction.

Flashing, flashing. A mini war zone.

Police radios crackled into the scorching air.

Laura found Anna's car, the little Beemer. Yellow, same color as the crime scene tape. What an irony. Anna was color-coordinated in death.

The BMW was outside the MPD perimeter.

Several cops watched her. Sturdy young guys in blue short sleeves. Powerful tanned arms and the sturdy T-square shoulders of gymnasts. Spanish names, hard eyes, lantern jaws. Shields glimmering. Big black weapons at their hips.

She flashed her Virginia shield at them, invoked Foster's name, and drew nods when she indicated that she was going to spend quality time with Anna's car. The non-stop sweat made her skirt ride a little higher. She gave the boys some leg to look at to keep them happy, felt a cooperative karma settle in, and went to work on the dead woman's wheels.

Laura circled the car.

No one squawked. They were amused by the Anglo female cop.

The presence of the car told Laura that Anna had probably arrived by herself, then been murdered in her home. That was consistent with the broken window and the damaged door lock. The suitcases upstairs and the clothes all over told Laura that Anna had seen something and had raced home to pack.

Where had Anna seen something? Most likely at the club. That's where she should have been that night. A working girl works.

Speaking of penetration, it was time to get into the Beemer.

Then it was latex glove time again. Off came her jacket. Her blouse was sticking to her. The male uniformed officers formed an audience. Laura borrowed a slim jim from the cops' tool chest and up came the door locks in five seconds. Impressive.

Laura opened the driver's side and an alarm cried bloody

murder. Two hunky Miami cops came to Laura. Nameplates: Hernandez and Soto.

Young guys, crisp new uniforms, maybe rookies: a combined age of forty-seven. They could not wait to assist.

Surprise time: Laura turned and gave them a smile. Then she spoke Spanish.

"Un carro de cuarenta mil dólares y se puede entrar sin llave en un dos por tres," she said. *"Y por una chica, además."*

They laughed and were fascinated all the more.

"¿Me pueden echar una mano?" she asked.

The boys were happy to lend a hand. Hernandez helped pop the hood. Soto slashed the alarm wires to the battery. The siren stopped in mid-scream and folded up like a three-dollar beach chair.

"Gracias, amigos."

Canned heat. The inside of the vehicle was a torture chamber. A girlie-girl air freshener assaulted Laura at a hundred twenty degrees. Laura gagged on the cloying perfume and opened the other side for some crosscurrent.

She eyeballed the insides. She saw nothing of interest.

She poked around. Still not much, latex fingers melting on Naugahyde.

On the shotgun seat, scattered CDs. Vietnamese pop music with some salsa sprinkled in. A map of Miami. Did Dr. Anna do house calls? Interesting point. Laura had never asked.

The glove compartment was locked.

Laura turned to Officer Soto: *"¿Me puedes prestar un destornillador?"*

Soto obligingly handed her a screwdriver. She jacked open the glove compartment with one quick yank. Not much there, either. Registration, two hundred dollars, some coins. A knife disguised as a pen. Some condoms, ibuprofen, emergency tampons, and a melted lipstick.

Laura retreated from the sweat box, closed it, and went back inside the house.

Foster arranged for Miami Homicide to tow the car in and impound it. They would do a forensics work-up and hold it. More DNA scans, overall a fishing trip.

Laura waited until the police wrecker arrived, just to make sure.

More Cubans. Tow truck guys. A couple of oily unshaven men in cut-off shorts and no shirts. *Los descamisados.* She watched Anna's Beemer go nose-up on a hook, like a giant yellow marlin. She noted the license plate of the truck and the location of the garage.

Details, details.

She moved to her own car, which was also outside the perimeter. She turned on the ignition and cranked the A/C hard. Oh, God, what a relief.

In her car, she broke out the cell phone and tried Rick Mc-Carron and Sam Deal again, but again came up with a double *nada.* And worse, a familiar feeling was creeping back upon her, as if *she* were the woman now under surveillance, now that Anna was dead.

Gut feeling. It had crept up on her fast in the last few minutes.

Not just from the young Miami bulls who were watching her, but distant eyes upon her. A gut feeling again. Intense. Strong. The mystery cleared up fast.

She glanced at the passenger side mirror and spotted another vehicle.

A massive Chevrolet Alaskan rose up out of the heat vapors on the pavement, the largest SUV ever built. It came to a fast rude stop next to her with a skidding noise, nose jutting inward, intentionally blocking her departure.

Big man, big car. Big problem? The driver lurched out. *WTF?*

Laura's hand slid to her Colt and stood by for clarification.

The huge man lumbered. Nothing subtle. A red plantation shirt that could have doubled as a tent. Large enough to house a Cambodian family of six. Big bare arms. Tan slacks.

Shrek on an acid-trip vacation.

The big doughy face melted into familiar features. From the club, she recognized Robin.

Robin had been on her afternoon revisit list. He had anticipated.

How? Why?

She lowered her window halfway. Miami humidity rolled in.

Robin came to her window, leaned downward, and filled it. A carpet of gray-black chest hair overflowed his neckline. He was sweating like a pig. She could smell him. His eyes prowled her own too-open neckline, explored, then rose to meet hers. He sought conversation.

"*¿Qué?*" Laura asked.

"*Tenemos que hablar,*" he said.

"*Hablamos,*" she answered.

"*En el club.*" A nasty pause. "*¿Quieres venir conmigo, o prefieres seguirme en tu carro?*"

"I'll drive and follow," she said. "You lead."

Robin hulked up to full height. Five foot fifteen. Then he turned, froze, and kept his big hands where everyone could see them.

Soto and Hernandez again, keeping tabs, close behind Robin. Hernandez with his hand on a cannon.

"*¿Está todo bien?*" Soto asked.

"*Sí, todo está bien,*" Laura answered. "*No hay por qué preocuparse. Gracias.*"

She was okay and Robin was okay, too.

Laura's eyes rose and for once she made the specific surveillance. Second floor of Anna's, Sgt. Foster peering downward, something in his hand to his ear.

Hernandez said something into a walkie talkie. Sgt. Foster squawked back.

"*El sargento Foster nos ha autorizado seguirles,*" Hernandez said.

"*Perfecto,*" she replied.

Robin gave a shrug. He may have been friendly, but didn't look it.

Laura raised a hand and gave a wave to the second floor. Foster cued back.

They began the drive to South Beach.

It was nice to have back-up.

It was even nicer to have *hermanos*.

chapter 64

Off hours at the nameless club in South Beach.

Blasting daytime heat outside; A/C enough inside to keep a penguin smiling. No customers. No music, no rattle of craps tables or roulette wheels. No sex for sale. Cleaning staff mostly. Pine-scented roulette wheels. The occasional sound of a vacuum cleaner created a background as Robin led Laura to a small den on the first floor.

Robin pulled a chair to a table and sat. Laura did the same. Robin broke out a fresh pack of no-apology unfiltered Chesterfields and lit a smoke. He offered one to Laura. She declined. Not her type of leaf.

There were people in the kitchen, Robin said from within a small white cloud, so sandwiches were possible, as were cold drinks. Laura took advantage.

Robin took on the countenance of a big concerned bear. Laura felt a thaw. He *did* seem to be on her side.

Soto and Hernandez, meanwhile, sat outside in their sector car. Last thing they needed was to be seen walking into this place in uniform during off hours. Bad career move. Who knew who else was staking out the joint?

Sandwiches appeared. So did some iced tea. Laura felt herself coming around on this place, though not enough to apply for employment. Robin closed the door, switched to English.

Time to talk. Back to English. "So what happened? Anna?" Robin asked directly.

"Anna's dead," Laura said. "Murdered last night."

"I know."

"How did you know so fast?"

"Word gets round fast."

"I'm sure it does."

Robin grunted angrily.

"Exactly how did word get around?" she pressed.

"Police radio," he said. "Who killed her?"

"Don't know that. But I'll tell you what I can," she said.

Laura talked carefully, spilling what she could. Robin listened.

Laura sensed that whoever had murdered her, the perp would not want to deal with Robin first.

Anna had been, Robin recounted, a popular girl in the place, and not just in a business sense. Management liked her, so did the staff. For a waif from Bangkok, she had connected all over.

"Classy little lady," Robin said in a rare stretch of eloquence. "Then like that, suddenly she's gone. Shit like that has never happened. Most people who come here, it's boys' night out, but they show respect for our girls. We got the pick of the litter here with girls, you know?"

For the taciturn Robin, the statement was on a par with a Nobel acceptance speech.

"What happened last night?" Laura asked.

Robin's huge eyes darkened. He told how Anna had come to him last night and said she'd been having a problem with "a blond man." She had left early and hastily. Robin volunteered that he had gone and watched over her path for as long as Anna had requested.

Laura sensed emotion, a lot of it, within the huge doorman, but he never openly betrayed it. He went through the expressions of sympathy and the desire to help. As Laura had guessed, Robin spoke of his wish to find her killer and—as an example of how he would like to help attain justice—"crack open the bastard's head with an ax."

"Uh huh," Laura said.

She knew she would have to vet Robin's whereabouts the previous night. But he wasn't acting like a suspect.

"I don't want to be presumptuous or nothing," Robin continued, "but if that's the type of thing you need to take care of stuff, breaking someone's head open, you let me know."

It was an easy promise for Laura to put on file.

"Actually," Laura said, "there *is* something else, too."

Robin's eyes narrowed. He extinguished his first Chesterfield. "Name it."

"Surveillance cameras. What do you have from last night? Or three weeks ago?"

"That's why I brought you here," he said.

"I'm listening."

"We keep records. Who comes in and out. Minicams. Digital," Robin said. "There's a storage computer in the basement."

"How far back do you have?"

"We erase after one week," Robin said. "So I can't help for earlier in the month. But for last night, I have video surveillance of the door and the staircase."

"That's good. It would tell me who came in and who came out. Are there any gaps?"

"No. And it's time tabbed to the hour, minute, and second."

"Excellent."

"You got a PID, don't you?" Robin asked. "I remember from when you first visited."

"You have a better memory than you admit," Laura said.

"You I remember because of . . . you know."

He shrugged. The shrug meant Washington. And the request for her PID meant that he could download his surveillance pictures into it and she could carry them back to Washington.

Good deal. Happily gone were the days when PID stood for pelvic inflammatory disease.

"I understand," she said. "Take a look at this. Maybe your memory can help again."

Laura showed him the picture of Jeremy Wilder. He took a moment to study it and Laura grabbed that moment to eat.

No sign of recognition from *El Gordo*. He shook his head. She pushed the point.

Robin claimed to have had more than a hundred visitors the previous night and he had the appearance of telling her the truth. Plus, why would he lie? That thought troubled her, too.

There was a gentle knock on the door. Robin answered with a grunt. The door opened, Laura looked up. A dark-haired girl eased into the room, her movements as fluid as those of an eel.

A pretty face. Familiar. Perfect twenty-two-year-old body. Tight blue cut-off jeans with a parrot appliqué on the left side rear. A snug floral shirt with a lot of pink. Open neck, no bra again, and a different pendant this time: a massive ruby the color of blood.

"Hello," the girl said, easing into a seat at the table.

The flashy pendant was the giveaway. Laura recognized her. The frisk girl.

"I'm Christiana," she said.

"Of course. I remember you," Laura said.

For half a second, the girl's gaze hit Robin's. The big man gave a go-ahead. "I'm Robin's assistant with entrance security," Christiana said.

"I remember that, too. You stuck an electronic wand up my skirt."

Robin smirked. Christina smiled.

"Robin asked me to show you something," she said.

She held her right hand aloft. No wand this time. But Laura saw the sensor that she had noticed last time, the small silver disk on her finger, attached to a fine wire, almost imperceptible.

"It takes a DNA sample," Robin said.

Laura, astonished: *"It does what?"*

"When I run the wand over everyone I do at least one brush against the skin," Christiana explained. "That gives me a DNA sample, which goes into our server."

"Our customers don't mind so much when Christiana does the touchy-touchy," Robin said. "If I did it I'd be getting kneed in the *cojones*."

Laura nodded. "We know everyone who's ever been here,"

Robin said. "We know when and who they came in with. We don't make a point of checking everyone but we can if we want."

"So you have a file of everyone who's ever been in here?" Laura asked.

"Plus the date. And who they was with," said Robin.

Laura leaned back in her seat, stunned. "So you could tie your own records into the national DNA bank, casino records, airport security systems, Homeland. Any of it?"

"I couldn't," said Robin. "But *you* could."

"You're right," Laura said. "I could."

It made sense.

Her mind raced ahead. If she could get interdepartmental cooperation, the DNA samples from this place could make her case or show her how much off course she was. Or, racing ahead further, if Jeremy Wilder was on file, which as a Secret Service employee he obviously was, all she would need to do was run his DNA across the records of the club.

"So what can you give me to take away?" Laura asked.

"I hope your PID has a lot of memory," Christiana said.

"It does."

Robin took Laura's PID and carefully slid it into a pants pocket. He left the room, the door again open. Christiana remained behind to babysit. No point in having some strange woman from Washington wandering around the place.

A small brief conversation ensued between the two women.

Christiana was a recent graduate of NYU, she said. She had done some modeling in New York and Miami. Mostly lingerie and bathing suit catalogues.

Laura was in no way surprised.

"Tough career choice," Laura said.

Christiana's desire for a modeling career had brought her to South Beach, with its fashion photography scene. She had wound up needing a steady job between shoots. She had a BS, she said, in criminology and wasn't doing badly with it. She liked working security in the club, she said. She maintained that she had the best job of any female in the place.

The other shoe dropped a few minutes later.

Señor Victor—the Trafficante clone—arrived, flanked as always by his two bodyguards. Christiana sprang to her feet when she saw him, then went to him and climbed into his arms. Señor Victor embraced her and gave her a long squeeze that confirmed Laura's suspicions about the pendants and the other glittery appendages of Christiana's life.

Robin returned.

Christina disappeared with her boss. Without being judgmental, it was nice to see a recent college graduate doing so well.

Robin quietly returned the PID to Laura. "It's loaded," he said.

Laura was back out on the street by five, her skirt clinging to her legs from the humidity. She retreated to the air conditioning of her own car. Then she picked up her cell phone again.

She called Anna's number, just in case. Wherever it was, it was turned off or unattended.

No answer.

She tried Sam. He must have been on a serious bender. Again, nothing.

Then she again tried Rick McCarron. To her astonishment, he answered.

She asked for a meeting again, as soon as humanly possible, same place as last time and told him to keep a watch over his shoulder as he traveled.

God, what a day so far!

But at least, she felt, she might have turned a corner.

chapter 65

For Laura, "as soon as humanly possible" turned out to be that evening, midway between seven and eight. Casablanca, the bar of the Park Central, was only dimly lit, presumably to give it an air of intimacy. Laura was there early for a 7:30 meeting and waited over a gin and tonic. She selected the same table she had shared with Rick McCarron once before. It had the right karma.

At a nearby table, a pair of men in Technicolor slacks and open-collared shirts drank Coors from bottles. Alternately, they munched peanuts and kept looking at Laura. She dreaded when one would come over and attempt a coarse seduction. She could feel it coming.

She felt spiritually exhausted. Sam Deal had remained AWOL all day. She began to wonder whether Sam was lying somewhere in an alcoholic haze, a pool of his own blood, or an infelicitous combination of both. She wondered which she preferred.

Odd images jumped to mind: Sam letching over the young *guantanameras bonitas* at La Cabaña, Sam's oft-busted nose going in three contradictory directions, Sam's syrupy cologne, Sam inveighing against Ole Miss football, Sam being damnable undependable Sam.

Rick McCarron strode into the bar and directly to her table. Out of the corner of her eye, thank God, she saw her other two admirers turn away. He eased into the seat across from her. His hand no longer bore the bandage.

He was wearing another sharp suit. Deep navy. It showed off his square shoulders. His shirt was pale yellow and she wondered idly what was under it, then wondered how he could afford it on the salary of a CIA case officer.

"Sorry I'm late," he said.

"That's the least of my problems today."

"At least you have a drink," he said.

"Sure, and I'll have a second gin and tonic after you order it for me," she answered.

A waiter appeared. Rick complied. For himself, he ordered an aged bourbon straight up. Somewhere in the back of her mind she felt a tiny warning signal start to sound, but couldn't tell which one it was: personal or professional.

"Well?" he said, looking around. "Bring me up to date."

"Our witness was murdered last night. Right under our noses."

"Jesus! Who? Charley Boy?"

"You didn't know?" she asked.

"No. How would I?"

"You're the case officer. Why don't you know?"

"I thought Sam was on protection."

"Sam blew it and to make matters worse I can't find him."

He looked shaken. "Oh, Christ . . . !" he said. "Tell me what you know."

Rick McCarron sat very still and took it all in, interrupting only to ask small details. As the minutes went by, she noticed that McCarron did have this one nervous tic: tapping a forefinger slowly on the table when he was alarmed. The finger tapped periodically through her account and then at the end, rapidly.

McCarron's deep brown eyes met Laura's as she described the situation that she faced in Washington. Eventually, she brought her explanation to a conclusion. McCarron was very still. Even the finger that had been intermittently tapping had come to parade rest.

"And you know what I think?" Laura asked. "As soon as I take this to someone higher up in the service, they're going to say *anyone* could have killed Anna. 'She was a hooker.

That's what happens to hookers. Can't trust them anyway.' Know what I mean?"

"She told us the initial story and was in a position to help," he said. "She also passed the polygraph. She was credible."

"You know that and I know that," Laura said. "But no one else wants to believe it."

Laura sipped more of her drink. She watched the man across from her. And something else was at work inside her, too. She felt more pull for avenging Anna's death than protecting the president. At least the two destinations were on the same track.

She finished her second drink. The image of Anna in the closet would not go away, and a buzz was setting in. She was also starting to wonder a lot about Rick McCarron and knew she'd like to run his name across the Agency's files sometime soon, too.

The waiter appeared, McCarron gave him a nod.

Another round of drinks arrived. The warning sirens in the back of her mind were closer to an alarm now. She hadn't had dinner. The gin was settling in very pleasantly, the highlight of a horrendous day.

She wondered if Rick had saved her from the crude seduction attempts of the Coors-from-the-bottle lotharios at the nearby table. Well, she reasoned, Rick would be smoother and if she felt frisky enough and if he said the right things, she might accept.

Sure, it was still a little on the fantasy side, inspired by the smoothness of the Tanqueray, but Rick had a certain hot quality, or several of them, actually.

The idea of letting him make love to her had its growing appeal.

But then suddenly some inner defensiveness rose, responding to those alarm signals again. She would have liked him to seduce her and at the same time she would not like him to seduce her. It made perfect sense in a contradictory world.

So she raced back to the professional issues at hand. She

looked steadily at him. Her gaze must have been heavily on the accusatory side, for after a moment he smiled and spoke.

"What?" he asked.

"Where were you last night?" she asked. "About the time Anna was getting butchered?"

He gave her a hesitation she didn't like.

"Well?" she asked. "It's not that tough a question."

He hesitated again. Then, "I had a date," he said.

"Great. Can I meet her?"

He thought about it. "Why don't you just ask me what you *really* want to know," McCarron said. "Then we can be done with it."

"Okay, I will." She looked him point blank in the eye. The booze helped. "Did you kill Anna?" she asked.

"No."

"Do you know who did?"

"No."

"Do you have any idea who might have?"

"No."

"Anyone at the CIA?"

"Not that I know of."

"Should I believe you?"

"Yes."

"Would *you* take a polygraph?"

"I'm insulted, but if it helps you settle things in your own head, whenever you'd like."

She held his gaze again, waiting. Now he was angry.

"All right," she finally said. Somehow, her glass was empty again.

"You're a little paranoid, aren't you?" he asked.

"More than a little."

A quarter minute passed like half an hour.

"So, what do you think?" he asked. "Do you believe me?"

"I believe you," she said.

"Why?"

Now was her own turn to pause and answer defensively. "Gut feeling," she finally said. "I trust my instincts. I trust

what my inner voice tells me. I trust what I pick up on.
Does that sound crazy?"

"No. That can be useful, too," he said.

He sipped more bourbon, finishing his second round.
The waiter appeared and tried to keep his glass going. Rick
declined, then looked to Laura, who also indicated that she
wanted no more alcohol, three in an hour was just fine.

"Look," Rick finally said. "Do you need my help or not?
My guess is you do."

The gin had found its mark. Something within her nudged
her in the wrong direction. "I'm not working with anyone,
Rick," she said. "I don't trust anyone, so I don't work with
anyone. I have a job to do and I need to do it alone. That's all
there is."

She stood.

"Thanks for your insights," she concluded, "I'll be in
touch."

She took one stride to leave and felt his hand take her wrist.
Again something primal flashed through her. She wondered
which direction this was going.

"Let go of me, Rick," she said.

"When you need the help," he said, "give me a call. You
can't do this alone."

He released her.

"And it's ironic you should ask me if I killed her or knew
who did," he said. "I was going to ask you the same series of
obnoxious questions."

"*What?*"

"It would make some sense. Secret Service solves the case
internally, covers its own mess, then makes sure the one witness could never tell the story. You knew right where she
lived, she would have allowed you in and then Sam's people
could have finished the assignment."

"That's outrageous."

"So is your paranoia."

"I was in New York," she said.

"Lucky for you or you'd be a suspect. You need to get a

grip on yourself before you can get a grip on this case. It's that simple."

A long pause between them.

Distantly Laura was aware of the two Coors brothers connecting with some bosomy twenty-somethings at the end of the bar. They already had their arms around the girls.

"Good night," she said to McCarron. "Have a nice life."

She turned and walked from the table to the door, from Casablanca to the elevators, never looking back, but feeling Rick McCarron's gaze upon her the entire time.

Gut feeling time again. Strong. But this time she was confused. Was it a strong attraction or a strong suspicion, or was it both?

Or were there no differences between the two?

In the elevator, the door closed and she sank against the wall, needing nothing now so much as a chance to think and a chance to sleep. But she did not get that either. Not immediately.

Her cell phone rang the moment she walked into her room. She looked at the caller ID.

Sam.

Oh, God! And I'm already half stewed.

She drew a breath and picked up.

"It better be good, Sam," Laura said.

There was a pause, then Sam was purring in her ear.

"A couple of problems," he announced.

"Talk to me, Sam," she said coldly.

"First, no Charley Boy at the establishment you mentioned."

A beat, then, "There's none now, *no*," Laura said, seething.

"Well, I can't exactly guard someone who's not there anymore, can I?"

"Sam! You're supposed to be the expert in that area! What the hell's going on?"

Sam was on the defensive pronto.

"I went over there myself tonight! An hour ago. Address you gave me!" Sam shot back. "Big fat belligerent asshole at the door. Threatened to knock my remaining teeth out when

I got pushy. Told me there was nobody there by that name. No Charley Boy. No Anna."

"She was there when I told you to get on the case, Sam!"

"So, excuse me! I got manpower problems! I'm suddenly down to two operatives from my usual dozen. Both of them are married guys who have day jobs and don't want to hang around whorehouses at night. Get some better funding for us. When Colonel Ollie was in business . . ."

Finally, she exploded, a cracking, raging, intemperate voice. *"Sam, my witness was murdered! What happened and what do you have to say for yourself?"*

Silence from Sam, then an exasperated sigh, as if witnesses got snuffed all the time, which, in his world, they often did.

"No shit?" Sam asked.

"No shit isn't even the beginning of it, Sam! You owe me big time and you owe big time to the girl who's in the freezer at the Dade County ME's office."

"Listen, I—"

"No, you listen now, Sam! I'm calling the shots here! Stay available and I'll let you know when you can make things up. And your bulked-up kid can flip burgers at the University of McDonald's until you redeem yourself on this end. That's all I've got to say."

If Sam protested, Laura didn't stay on the line to hear it. She clicked off. She slammed the phone down on her bed, so angry she was shaking.

It had been a day of horrors and Sam's call had only been the final one.

A final gin and tonic out of the mini-bar helped her sleep, but not by much and not for long.

chapter 66

Thursday night at Diamond Lil's was slower than usual. Tiffany hardly had her heart in her work. Kevin, or whoever he had been, was definitely a man she wanted to know better.

Every previous day this week for Tiffany, and all of this day, too, there had been thoughts of Kevin. Then came work. What a bummer to report to Diamond Lil's for the dinner shifts at 8 P.M. Every evening brought plenty of admirers, but no one special.

He had left her no idea who he was. Nothing, other than a name. And men often changed their names when they were with women out of town. She would have checked credit card receipts to see if anyone named Kevin had paid on the night that she had met him, but his table of three had paid cash.

Same as at the hotel, she noted. Was he hiding something?

Not knowing anything about him gave her a funny feeling. Conflicting emotions. She had had her share of lovers in the past, but always—in high school, in job situations, from meetings in bars through friends—she had at least known her guys a bit before she slept with them.

Not this time, though.

It made her think: What did she know about her most recent lover?

Not much. She forced herself to think harder.

The only little hints that she recalled from his conversation—aside from that weird bit about John F. Kennedy—had been the hint that he might be going to Miami, Florida. And she recalled him saying that he had just come from Mexico. When she thought back on his companions, she could not

recall anything about them, either, other than that they seemed
to have been from the Middle East.

Iranians, probably, she told herself. Maybe Turks. They
hadn't uttered a word in her presence so it was tough to tell.
She never would have admitted it, but Iranians and Turks were
two of the groups she most disliked. The Iranians were creeps.
They would never look her in the eye. They would only stare at
her bare breasts. She dreaded them, actually, though the Turks
were worse. They'd always be trying to paw her on the ass or in
the crotch while they tucked money into her shorts.

Eight P.M. turned into nine on Friday. She had four tables
to wait on and performed in one fifteen-minute topless skit
behind the bar. The tips were okay that night, but it was
mostly Nascar types in colorfully overdone jackets. Somehow, she could not get passionate over a man with a Penzoil
advertisement on his sleeve.

There were a lot of Stetsons that night and one table of
Chinese who gawked like hell but at least kept their mitts to
themselves.

God, what a way to make a living, she pondered. Maybe
one more year of this, max. Then she would move to some-
place warm and become a schoolteacher.

She thought again about Kevin, even more during the second show when she worked six tables. Heck, even if he were
married, she could deal with being his mistress for a while as
long as it took her out of this place. She hoped that she might
see Kevin again that night. But one never knew and he had, in
fact, checked out of the hotel. One thing reassured her, though,
as she put on a robe and stepped outside on a cigarette break
toward 11 P.M.

Her clientele was very simple. Guys who were satisfied
came back for more. Sometimes when a girl least expected it.
And Tiffany was very confident that wherever Kevin had gone
that morning, he had probably been very satisfied.

Three times in a night, no charge.

If that wasn't keeping a man happy, she didn't know what
was.

So she kept her eyes open. She had a hunch she would see

him again. And she decided, as she got down to the short final carcinogen-packed stub of her cigarette, that her Kevin was a good guy, despite her suspicions. If she were lucky enough to ever see him again, she would throw herself at him. She would let him know that she was a woman he could depend on against all adversaries and in all situations.

It was that simple. She felt like she now belonged to him and was mildly humiliated to be parading around half-naked in front of strangers. Maybe, she decided, she'd quit this job sooner than expected. Like this weekend.

But what if he *hadn't* looked in her wallet? What if he didn't know where to find her? No, she would have to hang on here for a while.

At least until the next time he returned.

chapter 67

THE OUTSKIRTS OF TRIPOLI
JUNE 26, 2009; 1:23 A.M. GMT

In the basement of the police station, a chair scraped the concrete floor. A murmur of voices followed in Arabic. Seven Libyan police officers were seated at a long table. Heavy breathing came from the British subject in the chair ten feet in front of them.

Five hours and counting: the interrogation of Alan Savett. The inquisitors took shifts, all except Major Housahodi, who sat in the center of the table and guided the inquiry.

Savett was not without his sense of history and literature. The room had a glow and feel out of Kafka—Savett's subconscious floated to *The Trial*, where the hero never had the chance to confront his accusers—with some *Darkness at Noon* sprinkled in. A retro exercise in psychological terror.

Savett sat on a wooden bench before his inquisitors, unable to tell the size of the room, the height of the ceiling, or the color of the walls. He had been brought in with a blindfold, forced to sit, then his manacles and blindfold had been removed. The bench was worn—obviously others had occupied it previously—and bolted to the concrete floor.

There was one pool of light, flooding from a brutally bright table lamp directly in front of him, its shade tucked down to shield the eyes of the policemen at the table. The light was aimed directly at Savett. The men behind the bench were in darkness.

From the table, Major Housahodi spoke again.

"Really, Mr. Savett. You have nothing to fear if you share the truth with us. And you have everything to gain. Come. You have proven you are a reasonable man with patriotic intentions. Even idealistic. We respect you for that. But now you must share the truth with us."

"I already have," Savett said.

"Your parents are Muslim. You cannot be our enemy."

"I have told you many times this evening, Major, that I am *not* your enemy."

"Yes, yes. But you have also not told us the truth we seek. *Who is Chiron?*"

"I don't know," Savett insisted.

"What is steganography?"

"I don't know, other than what you've told me."

The light from the lamp was so intense that it heated the room, giving the cellar dampness a sticky humidity. Savett had not been allowed water or food since departure from his comfortable apartment. His mouth felt like the desert.

"You have contacts with the Americans," Major Housahodi said. "How? You pass information to them. You profess Islamic ideals in your writing, but your personal philosophy is very Western."

"That is absolutely untrue."

A different voice now from the darkness. Arabic: "Come, come, Mr. Savett. We *know* the truth." A pause. "You have engaged in espionage against the Islamic Republic of Libya for many years. Confirm for us what we already know."

"I cannot do that," Savett said in Arabic. "I do not wish to lie to my hosts in a country which, until this dreadful evening, has treated me with charity and kindness. Praise Allah."

The major again, back to English. "We have documents, Mr. Savett. We have proof."

"If you have documents," Savett implored, "show them and I will prove they are untrue."

"Come, come, Mr. Savett. *What is steganography?*"

"I've never heard the word in my life," Savett said.

"You insult us when you lie to us," came the response. "Tell us about Chiron. Is he an educated individual, much like the mythical beast from whom he draws his name?"

Despairingly, "I don't know," Savett said.

"We can use physical coercion, Mr. Savett. We can use drugs. We have electrical devices with sharp copper clamps. Must we attach one to your penis to have our answers?"

Savett shuddered and shook his head. The answer to everything was no.

"I have seen what happens when one of the little copper claws is attached to a man's penis," the major said. "The end of the reproductive organ burns off. The man never again takes his pleasure from a woman. Will you suffer a fate like that, or will you cooperate with the National Police?"

"I do not have the answers you seek," Savett insisted.

In the darkness beyond the brutal light, there was again the sound of a chair moving, wooden legs scraping on concrete. The location of Major Housahodi's voice changed also. Savett reasoned that the physical torture would soon begin.

He wondered how long he would last.

He was a journalist, not a soldier. He reasoned they would break him very quickly as soon as the torture began, and he reasoned further if that was the case, why resist at all?

"You are an extremely stubborn man," Major Housahodi said with a long dismal sigh. "We know things that you cannot deny."

"Sir, you do not know much of anything. But you apparently imagine quite a bit."

The major—or his corporally disconnected voice—was

exasperated. "You would make things so much easier if you had told the truth. So be it. We will work with what we have."

The big light went out. Everything was dark.

Savett blinked away the pain in his eyes as best he could. He felt movement behind him, then hands on his shoulders. His bowels nearly released when he realized that he was possibly about to be decapitated.

Then a gentler light went on. The hands on the shoulders lifted and nothing happened.

Savett opened his eyes painfully, squinting. He tried to orient himself. Moving forms turned into human beings, men in police uniforms.

The first thing Savett identified was Major Housahodi. The major raised a gloved hand and signaled to his minions.

Four new sets of hands worked on Alan Savett. As the two larger soldiers held him in restraint, two who were almost as strong undressed him. They pulled off his shoes first, checking them for any hidden devices, then casting them aside.

Savett struggled and cursed them, but the more he fought the young Arabs, the more it amused his captors. They removed his shirt and slacks, then his underwear. He was naked. His wide belly swayed as he resisted. One of the men working in front of him grabbed Savett's testicles with his bare hand, clamped, and tightly squeezed.

Savett bellowed, but was incapacitated. Then the soldier released and gave Savett a quick punch in the same location. Savett bellowed again.

The major walked to him. "Very, sorry, sir," the major said with a slight bow. "But you have not been cooperative."

Savett's genitals ached as they had ached once in his youth when he had been squarely hit with a cricket ball. There were tears in his eyes.

"Who is Chiron?" the major asked again.

"I don't know! By God! I do not know!"

Then, to his astonishment, his captors dressed him in desert regalia: the robe and the headgear. Terror turned into surrealism. His guards joked with him. They gave him a mild mint tea, slightly chilled, with some bread and some dates. It was like a ten-minute time-out as Savett endeavored to stand up straight again. He was able to drink, but eating came with difficulty.

One of the soldiers told a crude joke in an Algerian dialect and motioned to his own genitals as he told it. Something about a eunuch at an Italian whorehouse. The other soldiers laughed. Savett was in too much pain to enjoy it.

Then, just as abruptly, back to business.

The major supervised. "Precautions, please. I apologize," he said. "We will be moving again and you are not yet free to go."

The soldiers clasped manacles on Savett's wrists and ankles, though his hands were allowed to remain before him, rather than behind his back. He would not be throwing any punches and he would not be running anywhere. Not soon, anyway.

Then they walked him back outside into the night. All Savett could think of were the recent images on Libyan television of the burials in the desert. He was being taken somewhere to be finished off.

"I don't know why you are doing this," Savett insisted for the final time. "I've always been an ardent proponent of your regime and your leader."

"You will have your answer shortly," the major said.

"I demand that you inform my employers where you are taking me."

"No one can know where you are going," one of the major's men answered.

They took him to a Land Rover and pushed him into the back seat. Soldiers climbed in on each side of him and another sat in the flat area behind. The major rode in a different Land Rover with guards. They took off across a highway that seemed to wind through a sandy nowhere.

The major's vehicle led the way, Savett's vehicle followed, and very quickly the journalist was aware of the headlamps behind him, suggesting that there was a third vehicle, if not also a fourth.

The small caravan—or was it a cortege?—moved rapidly across a highway through the desert. There was little other traffic. Savett was not sure at first why he had not been blind-folded.

Then, with a shudder, he thought of a reason. He had not been blindfolded, he conjectured, because nothing he saw would ever be of any use.

He would not be making a return trip.

chapter 68

THE DESERT SOUTH OF TRIPOLI
JUNE 26, 2009; 5:02 A.M. GMT

As the small caravan of Libyan police vehicles drove across a desert highway, Alan Savett remained an unhappy detainee. He entertained the idea of pushing his way out of the vehicle to escape, but knew the effort would be pointless. Even if he had not been shackled and could have run, his captors were younger and swifter. They would easily pounce upon him.

And where was there to go in the desert? He would not last into the next evening without water. His life flashed before him. Execution or incarceration, he concluded. Execution would be swift and incarceration would be long. He wondered which he should hope for.

They drove for more than an hour. The trip was bumpy and uncomfortable. Every time the Land Rover hit a bump, Savett's large cramped body bounced and landed hard. His gonads pulsated with pain with each crash landing. Fatigue gripped him like a python. He wanted badly to sleep, but if he were to be executed, if these were his last sentient moments, why waste them?

There was little conversation, and what there was came between the driver and the policeman behind Savett. Mostly they discussed a weekend they had spent at a brothel in Athens.

More distance covered, more time passed. Savett knew a few things about the stars. He tried to keep track of time and direction, but failed. He couldn't see the sky well enough to orient himself and the instrument panel on the dashboard of the Land Rover was dark.

He silently cursed his employers. Someone must have betrayed him somewhere. That was the only explanation. He would have set himself on revenge in the afterlife but he didn't believe in the afterlife. There was little in which he could find solace at this moment.

Finally, two hours out of Tripoli, Savett saw lights in front of the convoy. The lights came up quickly and the next thing Savett knew, more bereted policemen were opening gates. Their convoy was entering some sort of high-security compound. The tires no longer sounded as if they were on a sandswept highway, but rather well-conditioned concrete.

That told Savett that the installation was new, probably the result of the various factional rivalries within the Libyan government. The vehicle rolled to a stop within a compound with high walls. Savett carefully studied the location. From the electronic gear above the treeline, he guessed it was some sort of radar installation. He theorized that it could have had something to do with the downing of the American aircraft.

But if so, why had they brought him here?

A flurry of voices. Lots more bright lights.

Savett squinted. It felt like the middle of the night, but the sky was lightening.

Their arrival was the center of attention. Was this all just for him, Savett wondered. Car doors opened. Major Housahodi appeared from the lead vehicle. He now seemed indulgent of his enforced guest. He offered a hand of support as Savett disembarked. The major took Savett by the right arm and guided him into what was obviously a building of high security, controlled by the National Police.

"We are here," the major said.

"Here" sounded ominous. Savett said nothing. The major gestured to his guards, who removed the cuffs and shackles from Savett without explanation.

"You are making a hideous mistake, Major," Savett said.

"I do not make hideous mistakes," the major answered.

The major walked Savett into the main structure. The front hall was sparsely decorated, but had a vast bakara carpet and Libyan flags. It was also air-conditioned, which came as a jolt, and there was a distant smell of cedar.

"Follow, please," the major said politely.

The major marched Savett into the adjoining chamber, a policeman guiding each of Savett's elbows. The guards closed the door.

Savett saw a man reclining on a cot in a comfortable room, reading, of all things, a copy of *People* magazine. The man sat up when he saw he had visitors. He set aside the magazine.

The man had an Anglo-European face. Savett knew he had seen him before, but in his crushing fatigue and his fear, he couldn't place the details.

This man, Savett, and Major Housahadi were the only people in the room.

Savett had seen some strange things in his life, covered some odd stories, borne some strange assignments, and kept some tight secrets. But as the reality of what was happening slowly sank in, he realized that he had never *ever* seen anything quite like this.

"Go ahead," the Libyan major said. "You are a man of many words, Mr. Savett, and many various truths. Speak. Tell this man who you are."

Savett, still wearing his desert robes, stepped tentatively forward, his reproductive equipment still throbbing as if someone had slammed them in a car door.

The little major beamed. Savett addressed the stranger on the cot and extended a hand.

"Hello. I am Alan Savett. I am a British journalist. Reuters News, Tripoli."

The man accepted the handshake and stood. He had facial lacerations and many visible bruises. "Oh. So you speak English?" the injured man asked, eyeing the native robes.

An American accent assailed Savett's ears. Prairie state flat. Clipped and military.

"Yes, I do. Reasonably well, I might like to think," said Savett.

The American seemed calm, out of pain, and in good health, considering. Savett's eyes dropped to the man's left hand and focused on the bandages.

Suddenly the shock of full recognition was upon Savett. It hit him with a jolt unlike anything that he had ever felt before. He couldn't help himself.

"Oh, my dear sweet Lord!" Savett said. *"I cannot believe this!"*

"I'm Major Gerald Straighthorn," the other captive said. "United States Air Force. I'm a hostage here."

"You're alive?"

"Seems so. Nobody's more surprised than me."

"But—?"

"They tell me I was injected with something. Kept unconscious for two days. I'm also told the Libyan army wanted to execute me but the National Police intervened. All I know for sure is that I'm here. Wherever here is."

"We're in the desert south of Tripoli, I would guess. At an installation maintained by the police, not the army."

Major Housahodi nodded.

Straighthorn continued. "That makes sense," he said.

"Why?"

"It seems also that my new best friend, the major here, has got a plan to send me home," he said. "And if you're the Brit reporter, you're part of it."

"What?"

Savett turned to the chief of the Libyan National Police, his face a picture of confusion.

The little major beamed and spoke to Savett. "You are surprised?" he asked. "If you are, that is highly good. Because if you are surprised, we can proceed. Allah be praised."

"Praise Allah," said Savett.

"Goddamn," Major Straighthorn said. He shook his head. He looked directly at Savett.

"You know what's going on here, don't you?" Straighthorn said. "The National Police are about to take over the country. The major here is planning a coup."

chapter 69

Laura returned to Washington on the first flight out of Miami on Friday morning. She went directly to her office, arriving at the Longworth Building before 8 A.M. She brought with her the souvenirs from Miami, including Anna's purse, stashed in a cloth folio.

It would have been convenient to blame Sam Deal for allowing Anna's murder but Laura held herself accountable.

The black dog barked. And why not?

"Go away," she muttered. "I'm too busy for you. Forward. Got to move forward."

Where in hell to even begin when one's best material witness has been killed? After another moment's thought, Laura reached to the desktop terminal in front of her.

She downloaded the information from the gambling club/whorehouse in Miami from her PID into a secure file on the desktop. She would not have time to examine the information until later in the day. Other things needed to be put in motion first.

Vanessa arrived one minute before 9 A.M. and stepped inside Laura's office. Laura did a double take. Vanessa's outfit today included a long A-line skirt with diagonal stripes. And the green tint in the hair had turned to a deep red.

"Did the trip go well?" Vanessa asked.

"No. A lot of bad stuff went down." She paused. "Someone got killed."

Vanessa made a sorrowful, consoling expression. "Sorry. What can I do?"

"Ever deal with a medical examiner's office?" Laura asked.

"A couple of times. I grew up in Baltimore. When I was in high school, you know, kids I knew were always getting shot. Couple of them got murdered."

"I see," Laura said. "Phone the ME's office in Miami. I need a body held for thirty days. I need a court order, so get me the paperwork. I need to sign everything and return it today. Also, before you do that, phone Passport Control at Homeland Security. See if you can find someone who can talk on the telephone and think at the same time."

"Anything else?"

"Yes." Laura picked up her own phone and found the stored number for Yee, Charles, Mitch's telephone man who had designed the ersatz Nokia. She gave Vanessa that number, too.

"See if you can get Mr. Yee on the phone for me, also. Tell him that it's urgent."

Vanessa nodded, closed the door, and went to work. Laura could hear her on the phone as she spent more tedious time prowling through the "7/2" list, seeking enlightenment.

Again, none was forthcoming. The two possible digits of the assassin's Secret Service badge were receding in possible helpfulness. It had been easy to accumulate a list of agents with those numbers in their shield, but an examination of those agents was yielding nothing.

Twelve minutes later, Vanessa had a young clerk named Steven on the phone at Homeland Security. Laura patched into the call and spoke to him.

Once again, Laura gave an inquiry number and an authorization number and asked how the results were proceeding for one Jeremy Wilder. After a stretch of dead phone time, Steven replied that the inquiry number had never been entered.

"I've requested it twice myself," Laura said, anger building.

"Sorry. We have a lot of new people. Some are unfamiliar with information searches."

"I thought that's basically what your agency does. Information searches," Laura said.

"It is. What can I say?"

Before Laura blew completely, Steven explained that he was a recent graduate from Antioch College, himself. But he was learning the Homeland system quickly and would personally fast-track the inquiry if Laura could send him the proper security codes via secure fax.

She faxed him the codes immediately, adding requests also for the two British subjects, the alleged Israeli agents Bilsky and Schumann, who had been registered at The Tides. Then she hung up, commencing another wait. Washington bureaucracy, she knew, could kill off the best intentions of even the brightest new recruit.

She followed with another call to her friend at the FBI, making a similar inquiry about Bilsky and Schumann. Knowing their whereabouts would help. Talking to them might help more. Finding them, of course, would be the trick, as would convincing them to cooperate. They might have diplomatic immunity. She would have to proceed cautiously.

By mid-morning, Vanessa had the forms Laura had requested pertaining to the Miami homicide. Laura filled out a request for a court order to hold Anna's body at the medical examiner's office for a month. She faxed it to Dr. John San Pietro, the medical examiner of Dade County, and duplicated it with a request to Judge Joseph Guardado of the Fourth Circuit Court in Florida. Twenty minutes later, she received a response. The remains of the deceased, Anna Muang, were now held for an extra ten days, pending the completion of the forms.

On the same call, Laura was frustrated to learn that an autopsy had not yet been performed. She phoned the office of Sgt. Clarence Foster to attempt to speed the post mortem. Foster was out of the office. A clerk in his precinct said the message would be passed along.

Increasingly, this was an electronic and paper chase. Laura knew that modern manhunts were often episodes of persistent electronic searches, tedious dissections of stored information. But there would always be street smarts and shoe leather involved. She knew that the endgame of this search, if indeed she ever got that far, would be person to person. She was anxious for the moment. After all, she had only seven days.

She had also begun to brood upon a certain contradictory point: If a potential assassin planned to walk into the Oval Office and shoot the president, how could he hope to escape? And if he had no hope of escaping, what was the point of the ten million dollars?

Judge Guardado's clerk returned Laura's call at 11:07 A.M.

The judge had signed the request to hold Anna's body. Laura received the fax back and forwarded it to the Miami ME's office. Then Steven at Homeland Security phoned back. He had found recent movements for one Jeremy Wilder of the given address in New York State. He had hit records for Bilsky and Schumann, also.

Laura sat with pen in hand, held her breath, and wondered if this were the miracle she had hoped for. As Steven spoke, she took notes.

Bilsky and Schumann had spent one week in Miami and flown back to London, also from Miami, traveling British Airways both ways. They had entered the United States on June 5 and departed on June 12. Their stay had been unremarkable. Homeland Security had no records of any business they had conducted in the United States.

"Okay," Laura said. "What about the American?"

According to flight manifests at JFK International Airport in New York, Steven said, Jeremy Wilder had flown from New York to Mexico City on American Airlines on June 6, 2009. He was confirmed aboard that flight and had used his U.S. passport.

As Laura processed this information, wondering how it tied to Anna's possible meeting with him in Miami on June 10, Steven continued.

"Since you seemed interested in this individual," he said cautiously, "I took the request a little further. Bent the rules a little. I hope you don't mind."

"Not at all." She smiled. "What did you find?"

"Mr. Wilder's return booking is open," Steven said. "He

has a year to use the back end of the ticket. And he doesn't appear to have purchased another from any other U.S. carrier. So as far as U.S. passport control is concerned, he remains outside of the United States."

"Which doesn't mean he couldn't have reentered under another name with another ticket," Laura suggested.

"No, of course not," Steven said. "If we were set up to do laser eye scans at all the airports we'd know for sure," Steven said, "but that's still five years away. We have them at major airports like New York or LAX. But anyone wanting to avoid the LES could always come in through, say, Charlotte or Phoenix, where we're not set up yet."

Steven was telling her nothing she did not know already. But, if Wilder was her suspect, several questions shot through her mind almost simultaneously.

What was he doing traveling to Mexico and disappearing?

Had he been in Miami four days later, on June 10, or not?

Had he met with Israeli agents during that time, or not?

Had he been in Miami to murder Anna on June 25, or not?

Had he come back into the United States on a fraudulent second passport?

Was he building his alibi in advance that he was out of the country when Anna was killed or when the president was shot?

And the biggest of all: Was he really the man she was looking for?

"What about other airlines out of Mexico City?" she asked. "Anything there?"

"I'm roadblocked there," he said. "It's Mexico. You might try another 'agency' on that."

"I might, indeed," she said.

She thanked Steven and was about to ring off. Then he spoke again.

"May I suggest another possibility?" he asked. "It might be worth a try."

"Sure," Laura said.

"Since I've launched this much of an internal search," he said, "it's a simple matter to file a Domestic Entry Inquiry tagged onto the first search. I can do that if you can get an empowered officer of your investigative department, whatever that is, to sign off on it."

"I'm authorized to sign, myself. What do I need?"

"Form HSA/DEI-4322. The Web site will let you download a copy." As usual, even in emergencies, the government ran on permission slips.

"What would it accomplish?"

"It would alert you ahead of time if Mr. Wilder is on a flight coming into the U.S.," Steven said, "assuming the tracking system catches the inquiry and assuming Wilder travels under his own name. It doesn't give you authorization to detain a suspect, it only alerts you. And I didn't suggest this, you initiated it yourself. Right?"

"Of course I did," she said. "Thank you."

"I'll wait for the paperwork. Good luck."

She hung up, shaking her head.

Clever young man, this Steven.

She downloaded the document, signed it, and gave it to Vanessa to process.

Then she sat at her desk and tried to assimilate and process her latest information.

She glanced at the clock.

Almost noon. What next?

Her eyes traveled the room. Her gaze locked onto the folio that held Anna's purse. Laura donned latex gloves again and opened the purse. She had a side table with a clean uncluttered surface. She spread Anna's possessions around to see what they would tell her.

Initially, they told nothing. A working girl's travel kit: lipstick, cigarettes, two stashes of money, eyeliners. Laura's fingers rooted around the interior of the purse, settling upon a clunky rattling item. She pulled it out and was surprised to find herself holding a set of USAF dog tags.

Jimmy Pearce. It took a second, then the name resounded for her. Anna's American father, according to the story she had told.

But why had Anna had the tags?

Was she in touch with Pearce? Where *was* Pearce? Alive or dead?

Were the tags real? They looked it.

Laura sighed. One more avenue to travel.

She deposited them in an evidence bag and dropped the bag in her own purse.

She scanned the rest of the items before her, begging for a story to come forth. None did. Tracing down the origins of the false Filipino passport could take months. She studied the three remaining fifty-dollar bills from the six Anna had lifted from the blond man's wallet. If there were bloodstains on them, they were microscopic. But why not give these to the lab, also? She should have taken all six from Anna in Miami, but would correct that oversight now, even if it meant another trip in person to the NDNAR.

She placed the money in another evidence envelope. Then she reassembled Anna's purse and filed it in a cabinet in her office, locking the cabinet. She went back to her desk, downloaded the DNA records from the club in Miami, and transferred a request to NDNAR via secure Internet.

By then it was one o'clock.

She made another decision. She phoned a number in Miami.

This time the man she wished to speak to picked up on the other end.

"McCarron," he said.

"Good morning, Rick," she said. There was a pause. "Still on my side after I told you off?" she asked.

He laughed. "It stinks when you lose a witness. I understand. So now tell me what you need and let's get to it."

"That club on St. Xavier Street. Who bankrolls it? It seems to be an Agency operation so the Miami bureau must have something."

"Couldn't Robin tell you something?"

"Robin only works there. Same as Anna."

"What about Mitch?"

"I'd rather know what your office in Miami knows," she said. "And anything you can get me on Sam Deal's funding might be interesting, too. I should have asked you in Miami."

"I'll make inquiries," Rick answered. "I'll even pull a few strings. Anything else?"

"How about air travel records out of Mexico City?" she said. "Homeland Security doesn't have records from Mexico for non-U.S. carriers. So I thought your employer might."

"Got a name?"

"Wilder, Jeremy." She spelled it out and added the address in Long Island. "Any kind of retina scans for him for anywhere in the world might be good, too."

"I'll call you back this afternoon," he promised. "But first I have something. I was going to call you and let you know. Bilsky and Schumann. Photographs. Want them?"

"Oh! The Israelis. Damned right."

"I'm sending them electronically when we get off the phone."

"Beautiful," she said.

She set down the phone and entered the proper codes in her desktop. And as she waited, another emotion boiled up within her. She realized she had a higher personal opinion of Anna than of the president. Well, by God, if she couldn't catch a killer for the chief exec over in the White House, she could nail a murder suspect in Miami.

The thought helped her keep the black dog at bay, at least for the time being. Meanwhile, a few moments after she had again put in a complicated series of access codes, the images of two purported Israeli agents took shape on her monitor.

She settled back, took a slight breath, and stared at them.

The blond man's associates? Or not?

Personally and professionally, she didn't like the look of either of them.

Meanwhile, across the United States, overnight polls gave the president an approval rating of 88 percent on his handling of the crisis in North Africa. The consensus among American voters: time to deliver a receipt to the Libyans. They shot down our aircraft, they pay.

Most Americans were ready to volunteer someone else's family member to do the job.

chapter 70

In the early afternoon, Rick McCarron phoned again.

"Your Wilder guy," McCarron began, "knows how to cover his tracks."

Laura sighed. "Details?" she asked.

"We have a source with Mexicana Airlines," McCarron said. "The same individual who flew New York to Mexico City on June sixth connected the same day to Ixtapa–Zihuatanejo on a domestic flight, then came back again the next afternoon to Mexico City. Then on the morning of June eighth, we lose him. He connected to Havana."

"Damn," she said. "Havana?"

"Even though relations with Cuba exist again, we still don't get much cooperation there. Our receipt for forty stubborn years of cigar embargos."

"So we can't tell where he is?"

"Standard technique. You can travel to Havana through Managua, too. No records are kept. Convenient for anyone who doesn't want to leave a trail. If your guess is that he didn't stay in Cuba, he could be anywhere now. He's had, what, two and a half weeks?"

"About that," she said.

"If he used the airline of a country not friendly to us, that covers him even better. Cubana Air would be perfect, as well as convenient, for anyone who dares to get into an antique plane. They fly everywhere. Montreal. Rome. Moscow. São Paulo. Take your pick. Wilder could be in the South Pole by now or he could be downstairs sitting in your car with a gun across his lap."

"Thanks, Rick. Is that a specific warning?"

"No. Just being realistic."

She sighed. He continued.

"You could, or *we* could, check the arrivals records for other airports, but we're starting back at square one without a day or a specific city. And who knows what precaution he would have taken entering another country? If he has a second passport, he has effectively disappeared."

"Can you run the name anyway?"

"Sure. But it may take weeks."

She grimaced. "Run it anyway." She could hear the weariness in her own voice. "What else? How are you doing on the financing question? Who runs the club on St. Xavier Street?"

"Don't have an answer on that yet. Working on it. Same with Sam Deal. Elusive stuff."

"Damn. Okay." She sighed. "Thanks again."

"Don't sound so depressed."

"I'm at wit's end on this," she said. "Plus it's Friday and I feel like I'm nowhere."

"That's always the way it is right before you break a case open," he declared in an evident attempt to soothe. "How you doing on Bilsky and Schumann?" he asked.

"Just getting set up."

Laura hung up with McCarron and returned to the tracking software that Mitch Hamilton had provided. She had a program that could input faces and images and then apply those images and compare against surveillance tapes: another painstaking process in an imperfect system that would take days. If the software found a match, it would conjecture a hypothetical certainty of the match, ranging from 75 percent to 99 percent. Anything anywhere close was worthy of close attention, at least in theory.

She could only look for one potential match at a time.

She had input Wilder, Bilsky, and Schumann, but had so far only begun to scan Wilder against the surveillance tapes of the club in Miami.

Shortly after 3 P.M., Vanessa had Charles Yee on the phone. Laura picked up. Yee, the telecommunications expert at the CIA in Langley, was helpful. He had digital voice records of every conversation made on the bogus Nokia 21 that Laura had given to Anna. He transmitted those records back to Laura across the Internet. With further authorization, which Vanessa arranged that afternoon through Robert Vasquez's office, Yee could also initiate a voice match search for any existing records in Agency files.

"What about tracking on the phone?" Laura asked. "Isn't there a homing device?"

"The homing mechanism is activated for twelve hours after each call, incoming or outgoing," Yee said. "There's been no recent activity."

"So if I call again, it would reactivate?"

"Unless the phone has been destroyed, yes."

"Would whoever has the phone know it has a homing modem?" she asked.

"Did the recipient of the phone know?"

"No."

"Then it's invisible. It would only be apparent if the current owner were a techie and took it apart. Even then, you'd have to be familiar with your nano-chips."

"Follow up on it, could you?" she asked. "I'll try calling it again."

"Are you working a major case?" Yee asked.

"Let's say I am. Why do you ask?"

"You might want my after-hours number, then," Yee said. "A hot case has a way of behaving strangely at inconvenient hours."

Laura thanked the efficient Yee, took the number, and rang off.

Immediately thereafter, Laura called Anna's number. The line was still in service, with the phone turned off. Laura left no message. Then she repeated the procedure to be sure.

She returned to her desktop computer. She accessed the telephone records Yee had just sent. She quietly reviewed her own brief conversations with Anna, mostly surrounding what client Anna had been embarked on servicing on the evenings in question.

With both sadness and anger, Laura listened to her own final conversation on that line, and the words of a possible assassin, as they had come across the audio transcript.

LC: Anna? Anna, are you there? **(Pause)** Anna? Anna, are you there?
V1: Anna is here. But she's unavailable. Who's calling?
LC: Linda. Cochrane. . . .

Laura cursed violently. She wished she could pour herself a drink right there in the office.

During the next hour, Laura continued to try for facial matches in the surveillance tape from the club and continued to fail. The afternoon died, as did another hot Washington day.

Friday afternoon morphed into Friday evening. Laura dismissed Vanessa at 6:30. But the surprises of June 26 had not ended.

Charles Yee was working late, too. He phoned at 6:54.

The homing mechanism in the fake Nokia had awakened. For reasons that escaped everyone's comprehension at the moment, the phone was traveling westward through Louisiana. It was in the Shreveport area, Yee explained, and was moving slowly, as if in an automobile.

"Is the phone with the first person to whom it was given?" Yee asked.

"No. The first person had a bad accident. The device was stolen."

There was a pause.

"Ah ha." Yee said. "Maybe that explains the strange behavior. I've been watching the movement for an hour," Yee said.

"What are you seeing?"

"The phone is on Interstate 10 passing through the Shreveport area, heading west. Whoever has it seems to be driving to Texas."

"Son of a bitch," she said in a low voice. "Thanks."

She made her final call of the day, again to Miami, where she tracked down Sgt. Foster at yet another hot sweaty summer homicide.

"I could use my own FBI contact for this," Laura said, "but I'll owe you another favor if you can use yours."

"What have you got, Agent Chapman?" he asked.

She explained, as much as she could.

Four minutes later, Foster made a call to FBI headquarters in Miami, who forwarded the request to another bureau in New Orleans. In conjunction with a homicide in Miami, agents were to follow the tracking tones on the indicated cell phone and take into custody anyone in possession of that same phone.

Laura sat quietly at her desk for another five minutes, wishing she could oversee the tracking herself. Somehow, she reasoned, that way she would know it was being done properly.

Her final act of the workday was to pick up the phone again and request a face-to-face meeting with Director Vasquez at his earliest convenience. Laura was unable to speak with him in person, but did reach his appointments assistant, who suggested the meeting for the next Wednesday morning at the increasingly familiar World War II Memorial.

"I understand. The venue's fine but the time is no good," Laura said. "I need sooner."

"There's nothing sooner."

"With all due respect, please make something sooner."

The assistant went off the line for several minutes. Then she returned with a Monday afternoon slot at 5:30. Same location.

"Much better."

Laura thanked her and rang off.

chapter 71

The president, seated at his desk in the Oval Office, continued his conversation in a softer tone, but not a conciliatory one. The audience was his secretary of defense, Robert Lynch.

"The other day when we met, the Joint Chiefs' meeting," the president said, "I did not want to bring this up. When I took office, I had some major briefings with the Pentagon people. The advisors with the silver oak leaves. People I've worked with a lot in the past. Someone said something about a plan called Project Swift Sword?"

A small silence descended on the chamber. The secretary nodded his head.

"Oh, yeah. That one. I'm familiar with Swift Sword," he said.

"How long would it take you to review it?"

"Maybe an evening, Mr. President."

"Good. Give me your opinion tomorrow. And not a word to anyone else. All right?"

"It can be done," the secretary said. "But I think Swift Sword was devised for situations more out of control, though, was not it? More extreme?"

In a flash the president soared from mildly angry to apoplectic.

"That's for *me* to decide! They've shot down our reconnaissance plane. I don't believe that both our men did not eject. They've executed our airmen. They refuse to give bodies back. I want to hit these sons of bitches so hard that it takes them fifty years to recover!"

The president reached to a note pad on his desk. Beneath the presidential seal, he wrote down the names of eight countries around the world that had been, in the eyes of American diplomatic historians, points of nuisance for the United States for the last twenty-five years.

The president handed the list to the secretary.

"Swift Sword addresses all eight of these venues, does it not?" the president asked.

"As I understand it, it does," Secretary Lynch said.

"Libya is on the list of eight, is it not?" the president said.

"It is."

"If we use Swift Sword, we need someone to lead the operation, don't we?"

"Obviously, Mr. President."

"I know just the individual."

The president reached for another piece of note paper. He wrote down a name. He walked to the door with his secretary of defense.

He opened it. Two Secret Service agents, Joseph Yeomans and Jason Sharp, already on the balls of their feet, rose a little higher, a little straighter. Their pulse rates always quickened when the president was in view.

"I'll see you tomorrow morning," the president said to Secretary Lynch.

At a desk a few feet away sat the president's personal secretary, Mary Corliss, a pretty Alabama woman of forty-four who had worked for him for a dozen years. Like all personal secretaries for previous presidents, from Evelyn Lincoln to Rose Mary Woods to Betty Currie, she was loyal and trustworthy almost to a fault. She knew her boss's every whim and command.

"I want to talk to a Colonel Ferris Small, USAF. He's stationed in Sardinia. That's in Italy. Or near Italy." He paused very slightly. "His number is on file. Find it."

"Yes, sir."

The president retreated into his office and closed the door. Neither Yeomans nor Sharp budged or batted an eye.

chapter 72

Laura left the Longworth Building shortly after 7:30 P.M. and drove to the National DNA Registry. There, using her Secret Service ID, she filed another request for analysis of the blood-stains on the fifty-dollar bills she had found in Anna's purse. She inventoried the three banknotes, marked the request for urgent analysis, and put a follow-up request on her first inquiry. A sleepy-eyed clerk advised her that twenty-four hours might be the quickest turnaround. Laura stressed that she needed the results vetted against the national registry. This too, she was advised, would take extra time.

From there she drove back to M Street where, just before closing time, she revisited the Ralph Edwards Room.

"Ah," Bernard Ashkenazy said, raising eyebrows at the sight of her. "The prodigal daughter returns. And shouldn't you be out on a date, it's Friday night, is it not?"

She scanned the room. Empty other than the two of them. She approached his desk and sat on the edge of it. She watched Bernard's eye drop to her bare knee and back up eye-to-eye again. "Bernard?" she asked. "Remember how you asked if you can do me a favor?"

"I never said that," he said. "But suppose I had. What would you need?"

"Would you be able to track down a retired American soldier?"

"Former soldiers are usually easy. Why don't you ask the Defense Department?"

"This needs to be in confidence. I trust you more than Defense."

"And why wouldn't you?" he asked, not seeking an answer. "I don't cheat on my budget or bomb people indiscriminately." He shrugged. "If I made a few phone calls and crossed a few wires, added eye of toad and tail of newt," he said, "should be easy."

She reached into her purse and pulled out the dog tags from Anna's purse.

She handed them to Ashkenazy.

"Ah," he said, examining them. "Sgt. James William Pearce. Roman Catholic BR 32 456 817." He eyed them critically. "Post-Vietnam era, I'd say. The alloy changed in 1983. These are maybe twenty-five years old."

"About that. Yes."

"Is the man dead?" He squinted at the tags. "This Pearce warrior?"

"I was hoping you could tell me."

"And this is all you have?"

"Pretty much."

"Well, let's see what Bernard can do," he said.

Ashkenazy took the name and the number. He also pulled a small digital camera from a drawer and snapped a series of pictures. Laura retrieved the tags and slid off Bernard's desk and thanked him. She was back out to her car five minutes later.

The difficult part of her day concluded, she was off to the gym on Eighteenth and M streets, attempting to hold to her Friday evening physical training.

She was deeply into distant thoughts as she went to her locker, from Miami to Mexico to the White House, to a stolen cell phone traveling across the American South. She undressed completely, as if shedding her work clothes had peeled away part of her professional burden.

Note to self: a week at a spa when this is over. Bermuda, Jamaica, or even Southern California would do just fine, thank you.

She pulled on fresh underwear, including a new sports bra, a clean T-shirt this time, USSS discreetly on the breast, and blue track shorts again. Tonight she used a headband and a wristband, also. She felt like a tough workout. She needed the release.

She worked the punching bag first. She hit it vigorously, working it for a full twenty minutes, even more pleased than the previous visit. She toweled off, went back to her locker for a fresh T-shirt, changed, and then was out on the street.

She felt agitated but a bit pumped.

Heat and humidity, I don't care! she mused to herself. She walked out into the long hot fade of the capital's evening. Night had finally fallen. She ran by the more-than-ample street lights. She knew the route she wanted.

She ran up Connecticut, across the Taft Bridge over Rock Creek Park, then right across the Duke Ellington Bridge to Adams Morgan, then down Eighteenth, to M. Four miles, plus a few hundred feet. She looked at her watch when she stopped. She was pleased.

Forty-one minutes. She had hit her personal accelerator. And she wasn't even winded.

She went back to the gym. She toweled off, pulled a sweatshirt over her damp T-shirt, and walked to the firing range next door. She checked in with her USSS ID. No waiting tonight. Someone two lanes down was working with a Glock 9. Someone in the other direction was pumping away with an old-fashioned Colt 38, a target version. Sometimes, *damn it,* her hearing and other senses were *too* sharp.

She donned the safety lenses and ear muffles, then entered the shooting galleries.

She took her place on a firing line.

The targets were those of human-form assailants at twenty-five yards, bull's-eye circles over the hearts of would-be human targets. She fired seven rounds quickly.

She brought the target forward.

Much better than a week earlier. No shots off the mark. Two on the fringe of the chest circles, two nearby, three toward the center. Solid hits in a real-life situation.

Kills.

She repeated. Wow. She was on target this evening,

literally. She repeated the procedure eight times. She holstered her weapon. She pulled off the glasses and ear protection.

Then it happened again: The gut feeling that had been away for a few days was suddenly back. The feeling of being on view, of being watched.

A male voice from nearby startled her. Made her jump. It seemed to come out of the walls.

"Hit anything, Laura?"

She whirled.

Reilley from the White House PPD.

He was seated on a bench behind her, toweling down. He ran a towel across his head and shoulders. His T-shirt, same style as hers, was white and soaked. She guessed he had gone for a run, also, then done his own time on the firing line.

"How long have you been watching me?"

"Don't flatter yourself. I'm just surprised to see you. I thought you were on leave."

"I *am* on leave."

"Leave or special assignment?"

"What's it to you?

"Just curious. You're still on the authorized list at the White House," he said.

Indignation rose to her defense. "So what's so damned unusual about that? If you know the first thing about White House security, you know that one's clearances always remain in effect when one's on leave."

"Or special assignment," he said. "Why do they do it that way?"

"How the hell would I know?" she answered. "Look. I haven't retired, I'm coming back, and I don't miss you, okay?"

"Right," he said.

His eyes drifted across her chest, then settled upon her more recent targets. His eyes gave nothing away, not what he was thinking, not what he was noticing.

"Rumor says you'd gone bonkers again," Reilley said. "Psych leave. Second of two strikes. Three and you're out, you know. No room in the Service for a crazy woman with a weapon."

"Rumor can screw itself," she said, reloading her weapon. "Can and should."

"New crop being rotated in, you know," he said.

"What?"

"PPD at the White House. We're getting sixteen new people next week. July first."

"Isn't that normally done at the end of July?" she asked.

"Normally, yeah. Not this time. No one knows for sure who's rotating in or out."

"Whose idea was that?"

"It's under the signature of the director."

"Vasquez?"

"That's the man. What we hear, however, is that the sixteen coming in are replacing fifteen that are going out. The extra one would replace someone who just went out on leave or who is on special assignment. In either case, that would mean that you're being replaced, too."

"I wouldn't know," she said.

"I'm just giving you a heads up."

"I mean, I so appreciate it."

Reilley finished toweling. He offered his hand. "Hey, no hard feelings, right? I mean if you don't come back or I'm transferred out, good luck."

She accepted his hand with less than complete enthusiasm. "Sure," she said. "Right. Are you rumored out?"

"No, they tell me I'm staying." He glanced at his watch. "Hey. Got to run. Got a woman waiting at Clyde's," he said.

He moved toward the exit.

It wasn't only anger that built in Laura this time, it was confusion.

She pulled the ear guards and protective goggles back on and lined up a final target.

She squeezed off seven shots. Six of them missed completely.

"Damn!" she snarled.

Angrily, she packed up her weapon. If a few barbs from Reilley were enough to rattle her, how well, she wondered, would she ever shoot in a real situation?

chapter 73

Laura watched the final minutes of the late news as June 26 came to an end. The crisis in North Africa was taking the bulk of the air time this evening.

A new surge of depression rolled over her.

How was she ever going to get a grip on this case? How was she ever going to determine whether a killer was out there at all?

The assignment was impossible.

She had no idea where to go with this investigation or who to trust. She knew well that certain cases capped agents' careers and other cases destroyed them. In her situation, she saw all the artillery being wheeled into place for the latter. Her hunch was that the replacements at the White House would rotate her out. She was back where she was two Fridays ago, groping around in professional darkness while moves were being made that nudged her career toward oblivion.

And then there was the matter of an assassin who was out there. Maybe.

The black dog barked. She poured a drink. The drink helped quiet the big dark mutt. Then, with the lights off, a little toke from the stash of m.j.

She stood and sleepily trudged into her bedroom. She carelessly unhooked her Sig Sauer from her belt. She showered, dried off, and stepped out of the bathroom. She liked the feel of being clean. She pulled on her sleepwear.

She crashed into bed. She had even been too tired to entertain her favorite paranoia, pushing back the blinds and watching for the watchers.

If she had done so this early morning, she would have seen a familiar van stop in the usual spot down the block. The cable TV folks again, on one of their usual midnight calls.

Sure!

She would even have seen a man get out of the van and approach her home. If she had looked carefully, she might have even known whether or not she recognized the man. She might have had some inkling as to his intentions.

Maybe.

But none of this happened because she was exhausted and slept soundly.

But only for the next eighty-five minutes.

chapter 74

ALEXANDRIA, VIRGINIA
THE HOUR OF THE WOLF

Laura sat upright in bed. She thought she had heard something. Ever so gently, in the next room, the front door had opened.

She counted her heartbeats as they came in rapid pairings. Eight . . . ten . . . a dozen . . .

The most ominous sound in the world. She lived alone. How could she possibly have forgotten to throw the chain and bolt the door? Her heart raced so fast that her chest hurt. Her sweat glands were in overdrive, her entire body was overheating. Her heart thundered.

The door gently closed. Next, footsteps.

She had a visitor.

She reached to her bedside and silently clasped her Sig Sauer with her wet hand.

All right. Day of reckoning, night of reckoning.

She stood quickly. She edged toward the doorway, the

weapon extended. The next room, her living room, remained dark. A new drenching wave of sweat poured off her.

Okay, let's have it. Let's get this done.

She turned the corner.

Darkness. The living room was the way she had left it.

No movement. No voice in the darkness. Nothing at all.

So why had she heard the door close? Someone leaving? A second visitor?

She edged a few more feet into the room. One hand on her weapon, the other hand found the nearest light switch. Her weapon was still out, surveying the potential battlefield.

And if there is an intruder, where is he? Living room? Kitchen?

Her fingers came to rest firmly on the light switch. She threw it.

The room illuminated. A blaze of harsh yellow. Then, in a moment that had no proper measurement in real time, everything came together at once.

The form of a man sitting on her sofa, moving his arms and his head, turning toward her!

His voice.

The recognition of his face and voice in the nanosecond before she could fire a shot.

"Laura . . . ?"

She screamed, then exclaimed aloud: "Good God! HOLY JESUS!"

"Hello," the visitor said calmly.

Her eyes were like saucers. Her finger froze on the trigger of her weapon.

If she were seeing the actual dead, the shock could not have been greater.

"Holy. . . . Oh, my God, I—"

"Don't shoot me," Robert Chapman said. "It won't do you much good. It's against Service protocol, it won't do me any favors, and it's not a nice thing to do to your father, either."

He smiled at her. A big warm grin. No fair.

Her fear, her sense of terror, teetered on the edge of a knife.

"I'm seeing things," she said, suddenly angry. "And *what the*—? You scared the living hell out of me! Don't *ever* do this again!"

Her father shook his head. "Sorry, sorry," he said. "And you know we have to do it this way. Calm yourself, would you? Sit down. I can help you."

But she didn't move.

"Where did you come from? Where have you been?" she asked.

"Can't really tell you that."

"Of course not," she muttered.

"Look here," he said. "Put your weapon down and *talk* to me. How many appearances like this do you think I can make? Put your weapon *down* and let's see how I can help you."

There was a pause that seemed like an hour. It was like a hole in real time.

"Like how?" she asked.

"Start by helping yourself. Cut down on the booze. Get rid of the marijuana."

She stiffened. "If you know so much, help me professionally, too."

"Then put that weapon away before you shoot yourself by accident," he urged again. "Want to end up in Arlington? Sit and talk to me. Tell me what you need to know. I can help, Laura, I can help."

He held out a hand, indicating a place at the opposite end of the sofa from where he sat.

She placed the Sig Sauer on the table before them.

Outside, a car quietly passed, throwing its headlights across their windows. Or maybe it had been a van. Or maybe she was imagining it. She didn't check.

She turned back toward him. He hadn't changed much in the years she hadn't seen him. Hardly a day. But some men are like that, almost freezing at a certain age.

"Excellent," he finally said. "Now. What do you most need to know?"

"I think there's an assassin out there," she said. "Am I right or wrong?"

"Think you got this far with no brains and no ability? Trust your instincts."

"Sometimes I can't."

"Trust your *gut*!" he insisted. "When did that ever lead you astray?"

She couldn't think of a time.

"What about Sam?" she said, her mind a clutter of tangled suspicions and doubts that were barely formed.

"What *about* Sam? I know all about Sam and his type."

She held him in her gaze, relentlessly, as if he might disappear if she blinked.

"Where does Sam factor in?" she asked. "What part does he have in this?"

"You expect me to know?"

"I expect you to offer guidance."

"Exactly as you suspect," he answered. "A key part. And I assume what Sam has told you so far has been essentially true. But . . ."

"But not complete?" she asked, finishing the notion they shared.

"Why in heaven would Sam tell you the complete truth?" he answered. "His career was built upon deception and lies."

"That's what I thought."

"Then act," he said. "And do it with confidence. Sam speaks the complete truth when the situation is forced upon him. Never before. Go after Sam and then follow the trail from there."

"Pretty much what I thought," she said. "Pretty much as I suspected."

Her father shook his head. "Then I don't know why you needed me," he said. "Point?"

"Point."

She sat for many minutes, pondering the matter, her father next to her. At one moment, he raised an arm and wrapped it protectively around her. Sometime later her father rose. He kissed her on the forehead and departed.

Thereafter, she remained where she was for several minutes more, before returning to sleep in her bedroom.

chapter 75

Under ordinary circumstances, Alan Savett might have been pleased to have so much interview time with Major Housahodi, Chief of the National Police. But these were not ordinary circumstances, riding across a bumpy desert highway for the second time in twelve hours.

The sweat within Savett's robe made it cling to his ribs and back. And then there was a Libyan police lieutenant with body odor and halitosis who sat next to him, an arm affectionately upon his shoulder, the other hand holding a pistol.

And worse, Savett was having trouble staying awake. They were driving him back to . . .

Back to where? To Tripoli? To his apartment?

He had no idea. And he also knew that part of the game they were playing with him was to wear him down.

And why?

What was this talk about a coup in the midst of a national crisis?

Why did they think he was a spy?

What was his life worth in this context?

He wished he had cleared out of this North African hellhole months earlier. Or days earlier. Or maybe just, as his tired mind tried to reason, *hours* earlier.

Savett had no idea who to believe, what truth or cover story to cling to and, biggest question of all, how to get out of Libya alive.

The major rode on the shotgun side of the Land Rover. Front seat. He began to hum after a mostly quiet and uneventful drive. Then, without turning, he addressed Savett.

"How long have you been in the employ of CIA?" the major asked in English. "And what do they pay you?"

"I don't receive money from the Americans, Major, I told you that."

"*How* do they pay you? Money on deposit back in UK? Switzerland? Future financial considerations?"

"We've been through this, Major. I—"

Savett had been a witness to interrogations of this sort. A wearying process that gradually would erode resistance from its victim; a laborious catechism of statement-questions swathed in routine and repetition.

But then, just as Savett expected it to continue, the major broke away from it.

"Do you remember a Soviet leader named Gorbachev?" Housahodi asked.

"Of course I do. Very noble fellow. He followed Andropov and preceded Yeltsin. *Glasnost. Perestroika.* I believe Gorbachev is still alive and lives in New York."

"He does, sir," the major answered. "You are correct. Much like Aleksandr Kerensky did after he was driven out of Russia by the Bolshevik Revolution." He paused for a moment. "Do you feel he was important to the fate of his country?" the major asked.

"Kerensky or Gorbachev?"

"Gorbachev."

"Of course, he was."

"Libya needs a Gorbachev," said the major, as the bumpy trip continued. "Do you understand what I mean?"

"I'm not sure that I do."

"Libya was once an important place in the world," Housahodi said. "The Romans called the African continent, or the part of it they knew, Libya. The name Africa was given by the Carthaginians to the territory around Carthage, and was applied to all of the known continent. It was retained by the Romans when they made the Carthaginian territory a Roman province after the Third Punic War."

He paused, gazing ahead into the night. The vehicle bounded onward through the sandy highway.

"The Roman province was expanded with colonies until it stretched along our northeast coast from Cyrenaica to the Atlantic," the major mused. "The wealth of Roman Africa was derived chiefly from the export of vast quantities of grain."

"And unfortunately in the third century AD, the Holy Roman church spread its corrupting influence rapidly in our province," Savett answered. "But if your point is that Libya once held an exalted position in the world, there is no argument from me. And you impress me with your worldview and your scholarship, Major."

"I suspect it is no better than yours, Mr. Savett. For example, if your life depended on it, as it might, could you name three Roman senators who were African by birth?"

"Cyprian, Tertullian, and Augustine."

Housahodi turned to face his prisoner. "Your knowledge is formidable. This is why we must reason together, and why I dearly wish not to execute you. You are educated as a classicist, as well as an Islamic historian."

"I appreciate your kind words and any mercy you can extend."

The major frowned dismissively. "We have shared with you our secret. We have shown you the American airman. Now you must share your secret. We wish to communicate with your American handlers."

"I have *no* American handlers!"

"What is steganography?" the major asked.

"I don't know. The study of whales?"

"Who is Chiron?" he demanded next. "Who is the Western intelligence agent who calls himself Chiron?"

"I have no damned idea."

"Do not be foolish! No cooperation with us will be foolish, unless—!"

The major turned to his driver and, suddenly furious, switched back into Arabic. "I have no more patience!" he barked. The only subsequent phrase Savett caught was "take him out and shoot him."

The van pulled to the side of the highway. No other cars in

sight. Eerie heat, an eerie setting as all the light came from headlights of three military vans.

The side doors opened and policemen marched Savett about a hundred feet from the vans. The major quietly followed. A team of men with rifles flanked the journalist. The grim lieutenant with the halitosis prodded Savett along.

So this is where it has all led to, Savett thought to himself as he was roughly pushed-pulled along. *Execution in the desert by those whom I've been defending in print. They'll probably leave my corpse here to rot, then go back to the city and rip through my computer. What will they find then? Will they understand anything they are looking at?*

His heart pounded violently. His whole body was running with sweat.

What did I do wrong? Where was my mistake?

Final moments. Probably.

To Savett's horror, there was a sturdy post positioned in the sand, obviously used in the past for executions by firing squad. There were stains on it and small craters. Blood and bullets.

When they pushed Savett up against it and tied him, he nearly lost control of his bladder.

What was left for him? What was there to say now?

They strapped him tightly to the post.

"Still time, Monsieur Savett. Will you cooperate?" Major Housahodi asked.

Monsieur. What sort of last-minute Third World diplomacy was this, calling an Englishman "monsieur"? The entire planet, as Savett had frequently observed in his dispatches, was mad.

"I don't know what you want me to tell you," Savett said.

"If you cannot contact the Americans for us, you have no value to us," the major said. "So we shoot you. If you can contact the CIA for us, in your usual manner, then we do not shoot you."

Again, the Alice in Wonderland quality of journalism in Libya. "You're telling me that if I *am* a spy, my life will be spared. If I'm not, I will be executed."

The riflemen took their places.

"Exactly."

"And how then would I prove that I'm a spy and save my life?" Savett asked.

"Tell us. From where do you make your transmissions?"

The soldiers raised and readied their rifles. Savett assessed his chances for survival as thoroughly as he could.

"My home. In Tripoli," Savett chose to answer. "Exactly the place that you took me from."

"Then you would be willing to make a transmission for us? From your home?"

"You would have to reconnect my Internet terminal," Savett said.

The soldiers stood before Savett, silhouetted in the vehicle lights like a small dangerous line of trees. The major gave a gesture to his riflemen. The entire team took aim.

"With the Americans? You *admit* that you communicate with the Americans?"

"Yes, sir. I do."

Savett waited for the shots. None quite yet.

"And so you *could* communicate with the Americans for us?" the major asked.

"If it pleases the major," said Savett.

"What is steganography?" the major inquired for a final time.

Savett weighed his response. His reward: either a barrage of bullets or freedom. ·

"Steganography is," Savett began slowly, "the black art of encrypting a message within a microscopic pixel for use on a computer screen. The pixel," he continued, "can contain several volumes of information, sometimes of a highly secretive nature."

No response.

On a roll, surprised to find himself still alive, he continued. "The information, when transmitted with millions of other pixels in a digital photograph, would go universally unnoticed . . . except by those privileged few who knew where to look and how to decode."

"And who is Chiron?" the major asked quietly. "Who is

the spy, the agent of the Americans, code named Chiron after the gentle centaur?"

A long long pause, then a response from the Englishman. "I am Chiron," Savett said. "I have been an American spy for six years."

"Ah ha," the major said with finality. "And you are telling the truth now?"

"I am," Savett said.

"Fascinating," the major answered. "Fascinating."

"No more fascinating than how you might have known about it," Savett answered.

Savett braced himself for the inevitable volley of bullets. Seconds went by. Still nothing.

He heard a distant wind, a faraway aircraft, and a shuffling in the sand of some of the soldiers' feet.

The major laughed. "Release him," he said in Arabic to his soldiers. "Time is short. He will now be of great value to us."

chapter 76

ALEXANDRIA, VIRGINIA
JUNE 27, 2009; MORNING

Before 7 A.M., Laura awoke again. Her weapon was in place beside her bed, only slightly dislodged. Her psyche, however, had been dislodged more thoroughly.

For several minutes, as was her habit on weekend mornings, she lay awake but motionless, listening to the sounds beyond her apartment: A distant lawn mower. An occasional car passing. A dog barking down the street. Then her attention rose and settled into her living room where she had engaged her father in conversation during the darkest watches of the night.

Was he there now? In daylight? She couldn't imagine that he would be.

She drew a breath. She took her weapon in her hand and walked to the door of the bedroom. She was alone again. Her eye drifted to the chain latched on the door. She went to the kitchen and made coffee, an egg, and an English muffin. A vague sense of unease misted around her. Then she pegged the cause: the conversation with Reilley at the gym.

Transfers coming up. At first it unsettled her. Then she decided there was nothing she could do about it. There was only the assignment before her. That, and the advice from her father.

She ate breakfast and drove to her office at the Longworth Building. Traffic was predictably lighter than usual. She was in her office by 8:15.

The first thing she did was check secure e-mail. She found items of importance.

Someone working late had pegged an initial ID for the DNA on Anna's money. It belonged to a Vincent Rivera, twenty-eight, of Coral Gables, Florida. Rivera had a short rap sheet, but nothing distinguished. He had been arrested twice in his life, once as a juvenile offender, the second time at age twenty for receiving stolen property from a Best Buy burglary in West Palm Beach. Nothing further on him. He had either stayed clean since then or his record had been expunged. His future, however, did not look rosy. Within the bloodstains on the bills were microscopic bone fragments and brain tissue. The DNA from both matched Rivera also.

Laura fired off a return e-mail to her FBI contact: Could anything further be found?

Then a second e-mail had come from the NDNAR forty-six minutes after the first. No DNA match had yet been found for Jeremy Wilder within club records in Miami.

Then more from the FBI: More frustration—no voice prints on file matched those that she had recorded of the man with Anna the night of her death.

She felt restless, going nowhere fast.

She sighed and tried to figure what the two messages had told her. Vincent Rivera. Her latest mystery man. Great. Who the hell was this? For all Laura knew, Rivera had done

Anna once and been on his way. Or never even met Anna. Or he had given money to someone who had given it to someone who had given it to Anna. From such stuff were dead ends made.

She placed a call to Rick McCarron in Miami. His private number. No answer. Sure, too damned early. Good-looking single man, she grumbled. Probably out getting laid. She patched into voicemail and left a message. Her real quarry this morning was Sam Deal.

Her father's words echoed: "Why in heaven would Sam tell you the complete truth? His career was built upon deception and lies."

What an epithet. She would have loved to have carved the words on Sam's tombstone. But Laura had matters to settle with Sam. Better he should stay alive until business was concluded.

She eyed the phone. She tried Dr. Yee at communications support and Sgt. Foster in Miami. Once again, Saturday morning and no one was answering anything.

And a week from that hour would usher in the morning of July Fourth.

Nervously, she eyed the phone. No callback from Rick.

Try again? No! Too soon to badger him again.

Alternatively, she drew up huge sections of the case as it sat before her and began to dig.

She worked forward and backward.

There were no flashes of light, no explosive revelations, nothing forthcoming in Service files or her notes from Miami or the details of Anna's death. Scanning randomly through Service personnel files again, she found no "ideological penetration" of Islamic extremism into the Service, nor, working the theory in reverse, anything to link the Israelis Bilsky and Schumann to any Service employee. Forward and backward she went through everything until there was no difference between the two routes; the same voyage, the same perplexing destination. All this while her mind teemed with doubts of her own efficiency.

Deeply engaged in a quiet office, she pressed forward.

She spun Sam and his Nightingales into government records as far as they could go, pursuing countless cross references until she gradually gained the notion that she was holding up mirrors to mirrors. She worked with special high-access codes that had been given to her by both Mitch and Director Vasquez.

Toward 11 A.M., almost by accident, she hit something curious that had escaped her previous probes. Using the words "deal," "sam," and "security" in a deeply covered joint search, she found a file sending her to "Agriculture; Allotments; 1987," under the further reference of SOUTHERN SECURITY/Plátanas.

She might have passed over the file completely—she knew already that Sam's Nightingales were formed with federal agriculture funding—but there was a subset on the file labeled "unique product." And she knew "Southern Security" meant Sam.

Or at least it could.

"Plátanas" more than likely meant nothing, other than someone somewhere had a sense of humor.

But when she clicked on the link, her screen illuminated like an Italian neighborhood at Christmas. Before her was a window that contained warnings and instructions: If any government employee were to happen across this file, they were to immediately

DEPART WITH THE FILE NON-ACCESSED

Then, as she stared at the screen for several seconds, her computer shut down.

She retraced the route that had brought her to that site. But whoever had designed the site had thought of nosy folks accessing by chance. The site had launched a cyber "attack mole" in Laura's direction that had already eaten the information pathway that had taken her there.

But she remembered most of the route that she had traveled. She tried the complete path three times before she had it. Then, quickly before the site could disassemble again, she clicked on the box for her top security access code and entered it.

The screen went dark again, then came alive. Now she had another file, one that had eluded her in the past. It read:

DEAL, SAM (né Deluccia, Samuel Anthony Michael); Southern Security (Nightingales: *Ruiseñores*) 1988-200_; financing arrangements; supplementary estimates to Secretary of US Treasury / customer satisfaction / cost evaluation / bounty / wider exploitation / geographical operations. LIMITED AUDIENCE; DCIA(x)

And there her access code stopped her cold. She took a screenshot and transferred it to her PID. Just in time. Her access crashed again.

This time when she tried to retrace her route the file had already been moved. Or deleted. She was not going to find it again. She wondered how long it might take before some gatekeeper within the site would be notified of her visit. She wondered who would next call on her in the middle of the night.

Paranoia again? Or a healthy fear?

Laura's immersion in her work was so complete that when the telephone rang at twenty-eight minutes past eleven, she had to give herself a moment's pause to remember where she was. But then she picked up, shorthopping the third ring, and found herself on the line with Rick McCarron in Miami, which, she liked to feel, was an increasingly good thing.

"Getting anywhere?" he asked.

For a moment, she was startled. Suspicion rose and gripped her again. Was *Rick* the gatekeeper and knew what file she had just accessed?

"Why did you happen to call just now?" she asked.

"Because I got your message five minutes ago and it took me that long to run through the other messages," he answered. "Why?"

A little relaxation gripped her.

"I found an intelligence file on Sam that I can't access. It seems to be buried very deep."

"I would think it would be," he answered.

"What did you find out about Anna's club? Its funding? Give me anything on Sam."

"Actually, I have nothing to report," he said. "Nothing of any significance is turning up in any of our accessible files, and believe me, I've pulled the highest strings I could in this office. Sam's off the normal books and so is the club. *Way* off."

"What does 'DCIA(x)' mean attached to a file?"

"Is it an Agency file?"

"It looks like one."

"Then it means two things," McCarron answered. "First, and I did not tell you this, it means the file touches on operations that are outside the CIA's official mandate and available only to the director or anyone to whom the director gives special access."

"What's the second?"

"The second is that you have no chance in hell of getting at it. Nor do I. I'd have to get a CIA deputy director to read the file and brief me verbally."

"Okay. Maybe if—?"

"It would take weeks, Laura. Better to get him drunk and sleep with him, maybe."

"Not funny, Rick."

"Sorry. I apologize."

There was a pause. Then Rick continued.

"Look, you've got questions for Sam," he said. "So do I. More than Sam would probably care to answer. Maybe we'd like to ask Sam ourselves. In person. Tomorrow morning. Ten A.M. I've set a meeting. Can you be in Miami again?"

"You don't like Sam, do you?"

"Does anyone?

"Think it's worthwhile? Confronting him in person?"

"I wouldn't suggest it if I didn't."

"You're not just trying to lure an unattached female government employee to Miami for a Saturday evening, are you?" she asked.

There was a pause. "It crossed my mind," he said.

"I'll bet you talk women into a lot of things," she said.

"Maybe," he answered.

She glanced at the vacant computer screen and the tables and files in her office that had so far yielded so little. Then she glanced at her watch and a calendar.

"So can you get here?" he asked.

"I can," she said. "I can do that."

"Want me to meet you at the airport?"

It was her turn to pause, then to resist slightly. "No. I'll get to the Park Central myself. I'll see you for the meeting with Sam."

"You're sure?" he asked, sounding slightly disappointed. "After all, as you just noted, it *is* a Saturday night and—"

"I'm sure," she said. "And let's try to stick to business, okay?"

He gave the location, the Blue Dolphin on Collins Avenue, and rang off with what Laura took to be a sudden chill.

chapter 77

TRIPOLI
JUNE 27, 2009; AFTERNOON

Blown as a CIA asset in Tripoli, Alan Savett was now home. He sat at his computer screen and attempted to save his life. On his keyboard, as Major Housahodi and several armed national police stood guard, Savett composed a message to be carried as an emergency.

It took shape upon the screen of his monitor:

PERSONAL FOR DCI AND IMMEDIATE SUPPORT: DECIPHER IMMEDIATELY. URGENCY CATEGORY A.

ON 6/26/09 CHIRON WAS GUIDED BY LIBYAN NATIONAL POLICE TO STATION IN DESERT, EXACT LOCATION COORDINATES UNKNOWN. AT THIS LOCATION

CHIRON WAS PRESENTED WITH USAF COL. GERALD
STRAIGHTHORN, INJURED IN ESCAPE FROM AIRCRAFT
OVER GULF OF SIDRA, BUT ALIVE. (LACERATIONS TO
FACE AND SKULL OBSERVED, RIGHT WRIST IN CAST)
REPEAT: STRAIGHTHORN ALIVE AND IN SATISFACTORY
CONDITION AS OF NIGHT OF 6/26/09. HIGH SOURCE
IN NATIONAL POLICE (HEREAFTER CODENAMED "AJAX")
HAS TOP SECRET REQUEST THAT CHIRON NEGOTIATE
WITH AMERICAN INTELLIGENCE AGENTS TO COORDI-
NATE TRANSFER OF STRAIGHTHORN BACK INTO U.S.
CUSTODY. SOURCE "AJAX" MAINTAINS THAT CON-
TACTS IN TUNISIAN EMBASSY, TRIPOLI, WILL ASSIST AS
INTERESTED THIRD PARTY. AJAX IS POLITICAL ADVER-
SARY OF COLONEL MESDOUA AND WISHES TO STAGE
COUP IN COMING WEEKS. AJAX DESCRIBES SELF AS
"LIBYAN GORBACHEV" AND WILL IMMEDIATELY DE-
LIVER CAPTURED AIRMAN SAFELY TO THIRD PARTY OF
ISLAMIC NATION AS GESTURE OF GOOD FAITH. AJAX
WISHES IN RETURN AMERICAN ASSISTANCE FOR SUC-
CESSFUL COUP TO TOPPLE CURRENT GOVERNMENT
AND FINANCIAL ASSISTANCE TO ESTABLISH MODER-
ATE PEACEABLE ISLAMIC STATE IN LIBYA, SYMPATHETIC
TO WESTERN COMMERCIAL INTERESTS. CHIRON WILL
BROKER ARRANGEMENTS AS NECESSARY. URGENT
AND IMMEDIATE RESPONSE REQUESTED FROM DCI
WASHINGTON, D.C. >>> SITUATION HERE EXTREMELY
FLUID AND PERILOUS. STRONGLY SUGGEST B/T/W NO
MILITARY ACTION DIRECTED AT LIBYA AT THIS TIME AS
AJAX ASSERTS ELEMENTS OF ARMY FAITHFUL TO HIM
AS WELL AS NATIONAL POLICE. POSSIBLE TO REMOVE
ANTI-U.S. DICTATOR MESDOUA WITH BARELY SHOT
FIRED. URGE STRONG CONSIDERATION OF THIS
SITUATION.
TR&F54>7Ua CHEERS, CHIRON

Savett leaned back. "How is that, Major?" he asked.
The major read over Savett's shoulder. "So now I'm Ajax?"
"You are."

Housahodi thought for a moment and nodded slowly. "Which one?" he asked. "I studied my classics at the University of Bristol. The hero of the Trojan War or the Locrian Ajax who violated Cassandra during the sack of Troy?"

Savett blinked twice. "I continue to underestimate you, Major. My apologies. I had in mind Ajax son of Telamon, the Greater Ajax, the courageous warrior who rescued the body of Achilles. Not Ajax, son of Oileus, who raped Cassandra."

Another pause, then, "Excellent," the major said. "Excellent. Now will you encrypt?"

"Now I will encrypt."

"The steganography?"

"The steganography," Savett confirmed.

Savett always kept an extra report or two to send in an emergency. He pulled one from his computer archive and brought it to his computer screen. Then he accessed and attached a pair of photographs also conveniently on hand.

Savett's computer was highly specialized and unique. It was a complementary match for another computer in Langley, Virginia, on the third floor of Central Intelligence Agency Headquarters. As Savett drew from memory and entered a code that brought forth the encryption function, his computer generated pseudo-random number sequences from a secret "seed" number by applying elaborate secret mathematical operations to that base. True randomness would have been preferable, but the steganography function created something close enough to it to suit his purposes. Within the transmission was another code which allowed the receiving computer to discern the seed number and decipher the message.

The Englishman used his encryption software to scramble his message, then applied it into the steganography software. The major, watching, blinked as the message switched into encryption, then shrank into a tiny blue dot which morphed into a picture of the lumbering Savett strolling in the Park of the Ancient Prophets.

Then Savett sent the dispatch. A moment passed. He turned. "Congratulations, Major," he said. "Today you are the victor and I, unhappily from my point of view, am the vanquished."

"But now what?" the major asked. "What happens now with Washington?"

"Well, I suppose, now we wait," said Savett. "We're dealing with the Americans. They are highly unpredictable, have little sense of history, no understanding of other cultures. Worse, they frequently have moronic individuals in positions of decision who have little idea what they're doing, and even less inclination to consult with someone who might."

"But you work for them?"

"I didn't say I didn't like them. I'm rather fond of them, in point of fact. Even with all their apparent flaws."

"I see."

"And they pay me generously," Savett said. "But that doesn't change how they are. They're like an elephant setting out to save a nest of ducks. They'll trample the mother and father duck, then feel remorseful and sit down on the nest to say a prayer, crushing the rest of the baby ducks. But their overall good intention really was to protect the ducks."

The major nodded. "For the most part, I reluctantly agree with you," he said. "So we wait. Meanwhile, I leave some policeman with you."

"Am I under arrest?" Savett asked.

"No, not under arrest. You are, instead, under guard. Indefinitely."

"Is that good or bad and what is the difference?"

"It depends on what you make of it. And what response we get."

"Allah be praised," said Savett.

"Allah be praised," the major agreed.

chapter 78

The rest of Saturday afternoon Laura dedicated to the long cruel journey through every file at her disposal, hard copy and computerized. But the case before her taunted her, and, like the smile of the Cheshire cat, facts often appeared to recede the closer she approached them.

She found herself exhausted by 6 P.M., spiritually and physically, and ready for another trip to National Airport and a return to Miami, a next step that she welcomed and dreaded at the same time.

Further, Laura sensed for the first time that her interest in Rick, which she had so far been denying, was possibly a mutual thing.

Well, let him wait if he wants me. The waiting will make it all the better. I have things to deal with, she mused to herself.

Sam, for example. Sam.

chapter 79

Back in Dallas after the drive from Miami, the blond man parked in the lot of a small white Methodist church in a quiet neighborhood off Mockingbird Drive. He sat for a moment, made sure he was still unobserved, and entered the church through its front door.

It was unlocked and empty. He walked down the center aisle. He waited. He broke a sweat again; not because of the oppressive heat, but because of his deep faith.

He waited for a message, a dialogue, from *his* God, the one who so frequently addressed him directly. He thought of the two Islamic fundamentalists who had helped fund him and he thought of the huge sums of money sitting in the bank account in his name in the Cayman Islands.

Yes, he told himself again, someday he would be hailed as a hero. A martyr.

He closed his eyes and leaned forward, then came to a near-kneeling position that almost put him into a light trance. He leaned forward in prayer, shutting out the blond-haired blue-eyed Jesus that graced the stained glass behind the altar.

Praise be to the Almighty. A few moments passed and, as if on cue, God was now talking to him. He pondered his situation and sought spiritual guidance for what to do next, what would happen next.

To go on was to court further dangers, to put himself and his mission increasingly at risk until the Day of Judgment came on July Fourth. There would need to be more death along the way.

One here in Dallas, one perhaps in Washington before the main event, if Laura Chapman stepped in the way.

Well, no matter. Killing women was easy for the blond man. They were gullible and expendable. Their deaths did not matter when his reward would be so great in the afterlife. His faith told him that.

Insha'Allah, as his Islamic patrons might have said.

God willing, as his Christian brethren insisted.

Speaking of the Almighty, God had been chatting him up recently.

Definite visions. Definite guidance.

Like right now. God told him to move some of the money along to other fundamentalists who shared his beliefs and his goals. All right. He could do that with a few keystrokes.

God also told him to go forward with his plans against the president. It was a brief conversation and the blond man was the only one who heard it.

His heart surged: anxiety mixed with joy.

The anxiety gave way to relief.

He rose and left the house of worship.

He walked calmly back to his rented green Nissan, at peace with himself and his Creator. Now he surged with joy over what was before him.

He opened a small duffle bag that he carried. In it, next to his handgun, was a prayer book and—he had almost forgotten—the cell phone he had taken from the whore in Florida, the one who had betrayed him.

As he looked at the phone, a horrible thought was suddenly upon him. What if there were a tracking device within the phone? This thing was poison. Time to trash it.

He opened the phone and examined it. He knew a bit about how these little cellular monsters worked. He pulled the guts of the phone out if its chassis. He found the SIM card, where a tracking device would most likely be implanted.

The card was sealed in a thin transparent plastic film. He tore at it with a finger. It dropped from his hands down between the front seats of the car.

He held the SIM card. He twisted it and tore it. He stepped out of the car and dropped it onto the hard concrete of the parking area. He rubbed the heel of his shoe onto it, shredded it, and obliterated it. Then he picked it up, took it to a trash can, and dropped it in.

He turned on the ignition of his car and drove into downtown Dallas. There he discarded the chassis of the cell phone by throwing it piece by piece into the sewer.

He knew the club where Tiffany worked would be too busy on a Saturday night for him to complete his business in Dallas. But Sunday night would be perfect.

He found a moderately priced hotel in the center of the city and checked in, carefully bringing almost all his belongings in from the car. Aside from venturing out for dinner, he would spend the evening quietly in prayer and meditation. He was very much on his own now and no one could possibly pick up his trail while he stayed in one place.

chapter 80

VIRGINIA TO MIAMI
JUNE 27, 2009; EVENING

On the flight to Miami that evening, Laura sat with a book across her knee, gazing out a dark window. She tried to make sense of one of the more troubling aspects of the case.

If Sam held the key to the case, or *a* key, how had she been onto him so quickly? If denouement was so close at hand, why had she been steered to Sam almost immediately?

Was it too much of a coincidence? If it were, she was convinced she was following the wrong investigative path. She had grappled with this in the back of her mind for a week, with no answer taking shape. For the first half of her flight, the solution remained just as elusive.

Then suddenly she nailed what passed for an explanation.

South Florida and Latin America were Sam's bailiwick. Home of the *Ruiseñores*.

Anna had appeared at the club in Miami and Anna had died there. It only made sense that Sam could steer her in the right direction. Nothing much happened ex-officio in that area of Florida without Sam or some of his people picking up some information.

That was it. Or was it? *Was* it too simple?

Was that why Hamilton and Vasquez had steered her toward Sam to start with?

Well, either way, she had plans for Sam. She was confident that Sam had things to tell her that he had no intention of revealing. She was a woman and had her ways of getting men to loosen up and start talking. Seduction could take many forms. Idly, her mind running away on a tangent, she entertained the image of undressing for Sam and having sex with him.

She cringed.

She shifted her position in the seat to get comfortable and dismiss the idea of going to bed with Sam. When she moved, the attention of the man next to her moved briefly in her direction. She donned headphones to avoid a conversation.

The flight arrived on time. She checked in on phone messages. There was one from Charles Yee, her cell phone tech and tracker from Langley. She called him back right away. Anna's phone was behaving erratically, Yee explained. Something had happened and the signal was now frozen.

"What do you mean, frozen?"

"Not moving. Stationary."

"Goddamn!" she said. "He's thrown it away. Or destroyed it."

There was a silence. "Maybe, maybe not. I'll try to reactivate by satellite."

"What about the FBI?" Laura asked. "It shouldn't be asking too much for them to intercept the car carrying the phone."

"Haven't heard from them yet," Yee said.

"I mean, it's not like I have a lot of time," she said.

"I know, I know. I'll do what I can."

Yee promised to update her regularly through the weekend. Laura deleted the message from her phone and hoped the FBI people out of New Orleans were doing the proper follow-up. Somehow, however, she suffered a sinking depressing feeling.

Anna's phone was probably as dead as Anna.

Fifty minutes later, Laura checked in again at the Park Central. She had a comfortable corner room with a view of the ocean on one side and another view up Ocean Drive with its art deco buildings on the other. It was wonderfully romantic, but she was by herself.

This night, she went to bed alone and slept comfortably with no intruders.

chapter 81

Almost 9 P.M. on a Saturday and Martin Thayer was deeply engrossed in a computer war game on his desktop monitor.

Thayer, in his early thirties, sat in a cramped cubicle in the CIA's old Langley Building, monitoring dispatches from covert sources in five North African countries. None had come in since nine that morning. Thayer was bored out of his mind, glancing at his watch. On slow weekend evenings, he was permitted to leave by 10 P.M.

His floor was quiet. None of the other cubicles in his section were active.

A small MAIL flag flashed onto his screen. He blinked at it for a moment.

Then he accessed it. He read a coded e-mail.

There was a source in Lebanon wishing to phone immediately from the U.S. Embassy in Beirut. Unusual. That meant using an STU-3, a secure telephone. STU-3s were not on everyone's desk, least of all the desk of a junior political analyst. They were kept in a secure room and were operated with a special key.

Thayer shut down his game. He locked his monitor and keyboard, standard for anyone who was moving from his workstation. He walked down the hall to a special room with a red door.

The SecCon Room. Secure Conference. Each floor had a couple.

His pass card and laser retina scan allowed him entry. It even made him feel important, which was unusual for Thayer. He normally felt like a small unappreciated cog in a big machine. His negative attitude toward his job had been simmering more than ever recently.

Thayer sat down at a desk. The desk had the STU-3, which for all its security did not look a whole lot different from an ordinary telephone. There were also notebooks and pencils.

He punched in a number that connected him to a corresponding secure phone in the embassy in Beirut. An operative he had never spoken to answered on the other end.

"Ready for me to go secure?" Martin Thayer asked.

"Ready."

On both ends, each participant pushed a button, sending their subsequent dialogue into electronic tones that were incomprehensible to anyone other than the two of them, but which came out on their ends as computer-toned dialogue.

An Iraqi-born Israeli spy and his American wife had been shot dead getting out of their car in front of a restaurant in Beirut hours earlier, the caller said. Two of their accomplices were being hunted by Palestinian gunmen and had fled to Rome, where they would still be in danger.

Would the Agency be able to arrange immediate protection at Aeroporto Leonardo da Vinci and immediate transit out of Rome to Costa Rica?

Thayer's response was brief. "I'll convey the request," he said. Then he rang off. Saturday evenings were not propitious times for such intrigues. No one was in a mood for problems.

Thayer found the section officer on duty, an amiable career man named George Jenkins. Jenkins sat in his office and looked up from the opinion section of the Sunday *Washington Times*.

"Hey, George?" Thayer asked.

"Now what?"

Thayer explained. Jenkins listened.

"Send it along the proper routes," Jenkins finally said.

"It sounded urgent."

"Everything sounds urgent," Jenkins answered, barely moving. "Do what you can. Is there other stuff on your screen?"

"Not currently."

"Then stay with this."

It took Thayer half an hour to find a duty clerk for Beirut. The man's cell phone wasn't answering. It then took another forty-five minutes for the duty clerk to find the regional officer by a second cell phone. The regional officer, reached at a restaurant in Georgetown with his mistress, okayed a security and transit request for the operative in Rome.

By 11:15, Thayer was back behind the red door making a second call on the STU-3 that connected to Cairo. The transaction went smoothly, though tensely. Tickets were issued by Lufthansa to Madrid, with a connection to San José.

Thayer leaned back from his desk, glanced at his watch, then left the SecCom room with a yawn.

He passed by his cubicle. By now it was 11:38. No point to continue the war game. And he had no desire to tediously scan for further messages. The day had been long enough. Fifteen hours on a Saturday, sixty-two hours for the week. Financial cutbacks in U.S. intelligence being what they were, there was no one to come in to relieve him.

He went back to his section officer and found him still reading the newspaper.

"Hey, George, can I leave?" Thayer asked.

"Did that problem get taken care of? Beirut, was it?"

"As far as I know."

"Nothing else on your screen?"

"Empty last time I looked."

"You working tomorrow or someone else doing Sunday?"

"Not me. Must be someone off another desk."

"Enjoy your day off." Jenkins raised a hand and motioned amiably toward the door. "Dismissed. Go."

Thayer exited with an appreciative wave. It wasn't that he had great plans for Sunday. He didn't. But he was exhausted.

Had he gone back to his desk, however, and reopened his work station, he would have immediately seen the urgent request from "Chiron" in Tripoli, a steganographic transfer that he would have been obligated to download and forward to his superiors immediately.

Instead, Chiron's message flashed relentlessly but without attention in cyberspace. And it would continue to do so till Thayer's work station came to life again, whenever that would be.

Sunday, Monday, or whenever.

chapter 82

MIAMI
JUNE 28, 2009; 11:02 A.M.

The Blue Dolphin Hotel was on Collins Avenue, one block back from Ocean Drive and the beach. Its open-air terraced restaurant stretched between it and a neighboring hotel that had been taken over as an annex. In the middle was an island bar, surrounded by tables, both in thick dark wood, surrounded by potted palms. While most of the restaurants on Ocean Drive were run separately from the hotels behind them, this was the Blue Dolphin's dining area for its customers. Some late risers were taking Sunday breakfast as Laura and Rick McCarron arrived almost simultaneously.

They found places at a table for four on a quiet far edge of the terrace, Laura laying a blue leather folio on the table. The morning heat in Miami continued to build, but the terrace was cooled by shade and by newly installed air conditioning that blew cold air from the indoors out to the patio. At their request, a very young waiter—he must have been seventeen and a recent arrival—brought them coffee and a plate of breakfast rolls. He wore a name tag that said JUAN and he struggled slightly in English.

The cups, plates, and coffee pot were of a Limoges-style cream-colored porcelain with a single blue dolphin upon each.

Laura turned to Rick. "We're working together, it seems. Tell me a little about yourself."

"What's there to tell?" he asked.

"Anything that I don't already know," she answered. "How's that? Pick anything."

"Recent CV," he said. "Came out of UCLA in 1996, degree in Latin American studies, minor in Spanish. I needed a job and took some interviews. Did the Foreign Service exam, got hired, met some people. Did a two-year tour in Mexico City and another one in Bonn. That brought me back to Washington."

"Good assignments," she offered.

"When I was in Washington, I heard about other openings," Rick continued. "I didn't feel like taking my next assignment, which would have been in Kenya. Central Intelligence hired me in 2000. I was in Langley for three years, London for two, and have been in Miami since."

"Not bad assignments."

"Someone must like me, somewhere," he said.

She admired his dark eyes, his sturdy shoulders, and the way he wore his suit. "I wouldn't be surprised if someone did," she said. "What do you do for fun?"

"Watch baseball. Football. I'm certified at scuba. Had a great trip to Bonaire two years ago."

"Sorry I missed it."

"You dive? You're certified?"

She flipped open her wallet. It was a relief to go past the Secret Service ID and proceed to her diving certification. "Never did Bonaire, but I've done Mexico, Panama, and Hawaii."

"Your turn," he said as she put the wallet away.

"My turn to what?

"Tell me about *your*self. The professional Laura and the private Laura."

"Me? I'm a bore," she said. "Sixteen years in the Secret Service, some in the field, some at a desk," she said. "Eleven years at the White House."

"Eleven is a lot at the big place. Mostly Clinton and Bush, huh?"

"The Agony and the Ecstasy," she said, "but I still haven't decided which was which."

They both laughed. She also admired the Blue Dolphin's way with a mini-croissant. "I've paid, Rick," she said. "Same way we all do, one way or another. I don't know what I've bought, but I know I've paid."

"You thinking of leaving the Service after this?"

"I'd like to be able to put in my twenty years," she said. "But I don't want to end up in a grave at Arlington at the end of this one, either. So we'll see." She paused. "Know something? Looking back, sometimes I don't know why I feel for that whole spiel about God and country. I know why people with eighth-grade educations fall for it, because it gives them something to believe in. But why did I? Who talked me into it? Must have been someone's magnetic personality, but I forget whose. I'm increasingly disillusioned."

"I think we all are," he answered. "We run around in domestic security, we chase shadows, we make the occasional small-time case and the big fear is that someone has assembled a nuclear bomb underneath Washington or New York and no one had a clue. Sobering, huh?"

"Very."

But by now Laura sensed having said too much. She changed the subject.

"When Sam arrives let me run the discussion," she said. She had Juan take away one of the two remaining chairs and left the one that would be in the sunlight.

"I know exactly how I want to handle this. Just back me up and go along with things," Laura said.

"That's what I'm here for. Count on me."

"I have plans for Sam," she said.

"That's good," Rick said. He glanced to the side and motioned. "Sam just walked in," he said. "I'll watch you work."

chapter 83

Already, the sun had risen to a point where the terrace was flooded with yellow heat. Waiters scrambled to set up awnings as Sam settled into the one empty chair at their table.

"Morning," he said. His eyes shot back and forth between Laura and Rick, coming to rest unpleasantly on Laura.

"You two gentlemen know each other?" she asked. "I believe you do."

McCarron nodded.

"We've met," Sam said. "No point wasting time. What's this about?"

"Sam," Laura began evenly. "I have some thoughts to put to you. You're going to appreciate them, but be comfortable. We're having coffee. You may want something stronger."

Juan, the young waiter, hovered uncertainly nearby.

"It's early," Sam said. He hadn't shaved. There was a stubble on his face that made him look like an old man.

"It's also a Sunday and who really cares?" Rick chimed in.

"All right," Sam finally said. "If you can get this dumb little *cholo* to come over here, I'll accept a drink. If the government's paying, supersize it."

Laura bristled at Sam, then turned politely and summoned Juan.

"Yes, ma'am?" the waiter asked, thickly accented.

Head games. No one played better than Laura. She hit Sam with both barrels.

From the young waiter, she ordered Sam's usual. *"A mi amigo le gustaría un whisky Glenmorangie. ¿Le puede traer, por favor, un doble, sin hielo, y un vaso de agua con hielo?"*

Turning to a flummoxed Sam, she added, *"Creo que eso es lo que tomas habitualmente, ¿verdad, Sam?"*

Sam, with an *oh-shit* look in his eyes, answered quietly, *"Así es."*

The waiter smiled to Laura, boyishly charmed, half falling in love. *"Un whisky Glenmorangie doble, sin hielo, y un vaso de agua con hielo. Perfecto, Señora. ¿Y a usted y al otro señor les gustaría tomar otra cosa?"* Juan asked.

"No, gracias," Laura replied in A-plus *español*. *"Quedamos con el café, nada más."*

She turned back to Sam. "I followed up and learned some Spanish since last we met, Sam," she said. "Thanks for the constructive career advice."

A long nasty take from Sam. McCarron suppressed a smirk. "If you spoke such fancy Spanish you could have told me," Sam said. "Very funny."

"You didn't ask, you rudely presumed, and no one's joking these days, Sam."

The whiskey arrived quickly. Sam sipped his first booze since breakfast.

"You're a little bitch, you know that, Laura?" Sam said.

McCarron made a brief move, as if to lunge. Laura stopped him with a hand. There would be plenty of time later, she knew already, for the boys to mix it up.

First, however, business:

"I'm torn between two notions, Sam," Laura began, "and I have to figure out which one flics back in Washington. I mean, Mitch Hamilton sold me a bill of goods on you. That's the first notion, the one I want to believe. He said Sam was the man to see in South Florida. We had a source here and an investigation that began here. And Mitch convinced me that if anything major went down here, you would be able to help us. That's what I came down here thinking."

"I do what I can," Sam said, sipping, leaning back. "You know that."

"Of course I do, Sam," Laura said, knowing no such thing. "Why, it would be downright unpatriotic if you didn't, wouldn't it?"

McCarron settled in to play bodyguard.

Sam's jauntiness was gone. In his eyes were surliness and distrust. McCarron listened as Laura proceeded slowly and let the brief pauses suggest their own accusations.

"I mean, as I said," Laura forged onward, "we have a major case before us in Washington and it's terribly important that you'd be able to help us. And your future rests upon it, also."

"I asked you once before what this was about and you wouldn't tell me. If you won't tell me, how can I help?" Sam asked irritably.

Laura opened her folio. She pulled out the photograph of Jeremy Wilder. "Ever seen this man?" she asked.

Sam looked. Carefully. "No," he said.

Laura let another moment pass. Then she said, "Okay," with a tone that suggested that Sam's response disappointed her in more ways than one.

She put away the photograph. She found shots of Bilsky and Schumann. She placed them before Sam, also. She laid the photographs on the table carefully, facing Sam, as if she were meticulously setting a dinner serving for valued company.

"What about these two?" she asked. "Anything?"

Sam looked again. *"Nada,"* he said.

"You're sure?"

"¡Claro que sí!" Sam said.

She sighed and made a small production of putting away the two Israelis. "Unfortunate," she muttered without explaining.

"Never seen any of those people in my life," Sam said. "I'd swear on a stack of Bibles."

Sam's tone told Laura she was winning. McCarron's eyes slipped back and forth between the two of them. She said nothing and fished for something else within the folio. Sam knocked back half of his late-morning Scotch.

"Is this official?" he asked belligerently. "What's going on here?"

"Official business," Laura said. "We're on assignment. Help us and it works in your favor."

"It's official from my agency, too, Sam," McCarron chipped in. "And we're not happy about what happened to a valued witness."

"Well, that's too damned bad!" Sam retorted quickly. "If I had enough money and manpower there wouldn't have been a problem."

Laura's eyes rose and hit Sam's hard. "But that *was* your problem, Sam, and it was *your* responsibility. You screwed up major on guard duty. A woman whom I rather liked personally is dead because of it."

"That slope-eyed hooker, you mean?"

Resisting the impulse to explode, Laura played Sam carefully. "You don't seem to get it, Sam. So I'll phrase it another way. Your last screw-up was your last screw-up. Unless I intervene."

"Bullshit! I'm protected!"

"Want to run a test? Get up and leave. See if you get another federal dollar in your life."

Sam went to speak, then, in a rare moment, thought better of it.

"Things have changed, Sam," Rick said. "The world is not one that you're used to. You screwed up. Agent Chapman is offering you an opportunity to stay active. Don't blow it."

"What the hell does that mean?" Sam snapped. "Nothing has changed as far as I know."

Sam looked to McCarron. Rick shrugged.

Laura threw Sam a tease. "Sometimes word takes a little while to get around," she said without elaboration. "About changes," she said.

"So true," McCarron muttered.

Laura laid the picture taken off her computer screen in front of Sam. The entry to Sam's file, the one that had self-blocked its path as soon as she had accessed it.

"Tell me everything you can about this," she said.

Sam looked at it. "If you're so damned interested, access it yourself."

"I can't and I don't have time to obtain permission. You need to tell me."

"I don't know!"

"Make a few educated guesses," she pressed.

"Reports? On our operations?"

"There are written reports? On the Nightingales?"

"I imagine so."

"Interesting. Who writes the reports?"

"I have no idea."

"How could you have no idea, Sam?" she said. "Someone has to write them."

"How would I know? Janitors. Tennis players. Goofy liberal judges."

Laura's response was—intentionally—terribly slow in arriving. Her tone suggested an inquiry made of a wayward child, from whom dishonesty was personally disappointing.

"I doubt it, Sam," she finally said. "Do *you* write them?"

"No!"

"Does the person you report to write them?" McCarron suggested.

"I don't know. Maybe."

"Who *do* you report to, Sam?" Laura asked immediately, seizing on a critical point. "Mitch told me that you were the head man down here. You mean you're not?"

Sam wanted to clam up, but couldn't. "I'm not going to be interrogated, Laura Chapman," Sam said. "I know these tricks and I'm not taking the bait."

He knocked back the rest of his drink. He looked as if he were about to bolt.

"Let's look at the words on this page," Laura said, bringing attention back to the file. "Private annex, Sam? What does that mean?"

"I have no idea."

"Give us a thoughtful guess."

Sam's dark eyes slid from one of them to the other. "Look," he said. "I have a chain of command, same as both of you. Until I hear that I'm supposed to talk about things, I don't."

A silence accused. As McCarron observed, Laura played Sam like a violin.

"*¿Quizás preferirías que habláramos de eso en español?*" Laura asked next.

Sam was apoplectic. "*¡Coño! ¡Me da igual en qué puta de idioma hablamos!*"

"There, there, Sam. Okay. We'll stay in English, since you prefer. Let's go back to the terms on this mysterious file. Private annex," she suggested again. "Give us something. Then I can work on that scholarship for your boy and maybe even keep you connected with Washington. Otherwise, you are so finished that you won't even remember what you used to do for a living. Understand me?"

It felt like a week passed. It was closer to ten seconds.

"Can I make a phone call?" Sam asked.

"Of course not," Laura said. "You have to make a decision, instead."

More silence. Laura pressed. "Even a private annex has to be located somewhere, whether it's real space or cyberspace. Which is it? Let's start there."

"It's real space," Sam said finally.

"Ah. Where?"

"A safe. A personal safe where records are kept."

"Whose safe? What records?"

"Nightingale records. And a bunch of others probably."

Sam looked like he would rather have root canal therapy than give Laura anything more.

So Laura waited.

"The DCI has a personal safe and Nightingale records are in it," Sam added. "Or, that's what I'm told. There! Are you happy?"

"Not yet. Do you have access to that safe? Or a combination to it?"

"Of course not!"

"No? I'm surprised."

From the corner of her eye, Laura felt Rick move slightly forward at the table, closer, easier to jump in between them, if necessary.

"Why the hell would I have the combination?" Sam asked.

"Well, it strikes me that your name and your deeds are all

over this operation. *Los Ruiseñores*. The Nightingales. I mean, you would appear to be the top bird, so why shouldn't you have access to the reports?"

Sam's fuse burned low. He drew his cigarette down to the final half inch.

Laura continued to twist the knife as Sam flicked away the smoldering butt.

"But now you say you don't have access, Sam. This is what doesn't add up. That, and your insistence that you have no knowledge that might help us. It makes me think that you're a much smaller player here than anyone imagined. Even after putting in so many years for your country."

McCarron edged forward again.

Another long pause. "That's very sad, Sam," Laura said. "Pathetic, really."

She began to assemble her papers. "Obviously, we're wasting our time, Sam, in the same way you're wasting yours hoping for the basketball scholarship."

"It's football, damn you, it's football!"

"Whatever," she said. "It's no scholarship at all, that's what it is. Rick, get the bill?"

"Sure, Laura," Rick said affably.

McCarron signaled the waiter, international sign language, the gesture of adding up and signing a bill. *"La cuenta, por favor,"* he asked.

"I mean, this brings me reluctantly to Thought Number Two, Sam," Laura said, everything back in her folio now. "Sam DeLuccia is a has-been. Not a never-was, but just a has-been. No juice in South Florida anymore, completely unable to help. The reason you're not forthcoming with information is because you don't have any. What a laugh. I should have known better."

Sam's eyes were burning into her. The sweat on his forehead rolled like tears. Mother Nature had intervened, also: Sam was now in direct sunlight. Twice over, he was boiling.

The check arrived. Laura laid out a display of cash, lavishly overtipping the waiter, then throwing in an extra five just because she liked him.

"*Muchas gracias, Juan. Está bien así,*" she said.

"*¡Muchas gracias, señora, usted es muy amable!*" Juan bowed low, cleared the plates, and departed.

Laura continued the torture.

"Sam isn't a player anymore, is he, Rick? Oh, he sits in South Beach and eyes fourteen-year-old girls. But Sam is more like a steer that's mistaken for a bull. He's grateful for the compliment, but he'd be happier to have his *cojones* returned. Let's go, Rick. We don't have time for losers."

Laura stood to leave, straightening her skirt.

Sam went nuclear. Even from where he sat, McCarron was not fast enough.

Sam leapt forward. His brawny hands lunged for Laura's neck. He grabbed her violently and went for a choke, cursing profanely as Laura swung a sharp elbow in her own defense.

Two chairs toppled and crashed as nearby diners bolted.

The table skidded but remained upright.

McCarron lunged and hit Sam half a second after Sam assaulted Laura.

Laura smashed an uppercut from the heel of her right hand into Sam's jaw, driving it upward and weakening his grip. She followed with a similar shot to the midpoint between Sam's eyes, breaking his glasses as both went hard to the floor.

From the tangle, amidst nearby screams, McCarron put a knee to Sam's spine. He found Sam's thick right arm and jammed it backwards into a lock against Sam's back, damned nearly breaking Sam's wrist as he did so. Laura hit Sam again, this time with a left to the right temple, knuckles extended.

It felt good: the hardest shot she had ever thrown outside the gym.

Rick pulled the burly Sam from the floor and lifted him as guests at other tables began to move away. At the same time, McCarron forcibly settled Sam back onto a chair with a thud.

From somewhere, there was a gun on the floor.

McCarron quickly gathered it up, removed the magazine, and tucked it into his belt. Initially, as Laura gathered herself, righted her own chair and stood, she thought it was McCarron's. But it was Sam's, which Rick was now safekeeping.

Laura stood.

She straightened her blouse and suit jacket as if nothing had happened.

Sam glared, wounded.

"Goddamned crazy bitch," he barked. But by this time Sam was dabbing at his right eye, near which a major gash had sprouted. The eye was partially swollen.

Laura theorized that Rick had hammered him during the altercation. Then she realized that the cut was where she had landed her left hook. Momentarily, she felt inspired. She thought back to the hours she had put in at the punching bag.

A manager appeared and wordlessly stared at them, but it was McCarron who spoke. "We're fine," he said. "My friend here is a bit edgy today. Must be the heat."

The manager scanned for a reason to throw them out but couldn't find one.

No breakage. No autopsy, no foul.

McCarron slipped the man a fifty, courtesy of the U.S. taxpayers. He mumbled an apology about the disturbance. Mollified, the manager's mood changed. He withdrew to reassure other patrons.

"Assault on a U.S. Secret Service agent in front of witnesses, Sam," Rick said. "That wasn't the smartest thing you've ever done."

"You're completely busted, Sam," Laura said. "Out of work and probably facing charges once I file a report."

Sam might have responded with more profanity, but he was busy dabbing at the corner of his mouth with a cloth napkin from the table.

"It might be a good time to give us something, Sam," McCarron insisted. "You have one last chance and that chance is now."

"Not here," Sam said. "Not here." He tried to catch his breath. "All right. You win, you bastards. Let's go to my car."

Laura glanced to Rick, who gave a nod.

They paid their bill and departed.

chapter 84

MIAMI
JUNE 28, 2009; 12:33 P.M.

They sat in a shiny Jaguar four blocks up Collins Avenue. Sam's ride.

Inexplicably, the Jag bore North Carolina license plates, the numbers and letters of which Laura noted. She figured the out-of-state thing was one more of Sam's petty scams.

Sam sat in the driver's seat. The air conditioning hummed. Laura sat in the shotgun seat, right side front. Rick took a position in the center of the back seat.

Sam was sitting straight, barely using the seat back to lean on, and he was wise enough to keep his hands on the top of the steering wheel. Without looking, Laura knew that Rick had Sam covered from behind.

For his part, Sam didn't look at either of them. He was too proud and didn't enjoy being cornered. Instead, he watched the pedestrian traffic as it passed, particularly the females. Lithe, brown, and young: Sam's type, or at least he liked to think they were.

A kind of calm had settled. It was the reassurance that Laura had been looking for.

"So what exactly are you after?" Sam asked. "What is it that I know that you're so desperate to hear about?"

"I'm not even sure, Sam," Laura said. "But it seems to me that you could write the book on official stuff that happens unofficially. Why don't we keep the discussion in that area?"

"May I open the glove compartment of the car?" Sam asked.

"Why don't we do that for you," Rick said.

"What do you need?" Laura asked.

"A new pair of glasses. I've got some tinted ones in there. For the sun. The compartment is unlocked."

Laura glanced to Rick. Rick's eyes said okay.

"Whatever makes you comfortable, Sam," Laura said.

She opened the glove compartment and easily found Sam's back-up specs. She handed them to him. He put them on.

"All right, here's something," said Sam. "But you damned well didn't hear it from me."

They waited.

"William Casey," Sam said.

"Casey died in 1983," Laura said. "That's twenty-six years ago."

"Yeah, Casey died," Sam said. "But he set up some networks that would last forever. Financed by trusts. Off-shore accounts. Annuities that exist in perpetuity. The Nightingales are just one. Sure, Washington pays me. But I don't even know who my direct commander is."

"How do you communicate?"

"Mostly secure e-mail."

"It couldn't have always been like that," Laura said.

"It was mostly dead-letter boxes to start with, messages encrypted," Sam said, cooling slightly and lowering his voice. "Casey's men still used microdots back then. Very old school, but sound security. You'd have to take them to a library to read them sometimes, the dots. You'd use one of those old microfiche machines. There was one drop at a Catholic church in Little Havana, right below the place where they light all the candles. There was a loose brick in the wall and messages would be stashed there." He paused. "The priest was a CIA guy. An old Panamanian with one dead eye. Good reliable man. Solid anti-Red."

Sam paused and worked on his temple, which was still oozing some blood.

"How did you communicate back?" Laura asked.

"I had an emergency phone number to call if I ever needed it," Sam answered, still working the napkin. "Only used it once. There was another number. I'd call and fake a misdial. Alphabetical system. 'A' for Sunday. I'd call for Mr. Andrews if I were going to do a Sunday drop. Mr. Baxter for Monday. Mr. Chester, Tuesday. And so on. Get it? The venue was always the last place used, the information to be dropped before noon. If there was a problem from watchers, the drop would take place later in the day and whoever would retrieve would come back the next morning."

"How did you get paid?"

"Same way. Cash. Fifth of the month."

"Currency in the dead drops?"

"Yeah. Wrapped in a nice little bundle, newspaper around it. Sometimes it was foreign dough. I seen a lot of pesos. Once I got a pile of German marks. Don't know what that was all about," he said in a tone of injured virtue.

"I assume the foreign money was proceeds from operations abroad," McCarron said.

"That would be a good guess."

"What did you get this month?"

"Dollars, thank God. Way this world is going, next thing you know I'll be getting some Euros."

"So it's still going on?" Laura asked.

"I'm still eating, aren't I? Christ, you can ask some dumb questions."

"Easy, Sam," McCarron said.

"Easy, yourself! Bullshit! Have I told you enough?" Sam took on the off-balance air of an abused stray mongrel, who didn't know whether he would next be kicked or fed.

"No, you haven't," Laura said firmly. "I want to go back to the terms on this mysterious file. DCIA(x)," she suggested. "That implies there's a single hard copy of your operations stashed in the director's safe. My sources tell me that means that only the director can get at it. Would that be correct?"

Sam glanced at McCarron via the rearview mirror, then his gaze came back. "It might be."

"So we all agree that the DCI has a personal safe and Nightingale records are in it?"

"We've been over that."

"And you don't have access?"

"No."

"Do you know anyone who does?"

"I imagine the president does," Sam said, making a joke of it.

"What I'm getting at is what kind of security clearance you have. And tell me the truth, Sam, because it might help come football season."

"Top stuff."

"You could walk into the CIA building?"

"Done it many times."

"Even though you're not officially listed as an employee?"

"Don't need to be. Most times, it's better if you're not."

"What about Treasury?"

"Never tried. But I'm sure I could."

"Capitol Building?"

"I have a few friends there."

"White House?"

"Easy. Done it."

Rick, jumping in: "Don't you need Secret Service clearance?"

"Whoever still runs these operations works our eye scans into White House Security," Sam said. "Been doing it for years."

"Good God!" Laura muttered. "You're telling me the retina scans are compromised?"

"I didn't tell you that. I just said *I* could get past it."

Now she felt McCarron's eyes on her.

"So how many extra folks would that be who can access all these high-security places like Treasury, the Capitol, and the White House?" McCarron asked.

"Don't know."

"Sam, we want a ballpark figure," Laura said. "You've got your Nightingales, you've got other similar groups formed by Bill Casey, you've got a brain and you've got thirty years of experience. Crunch time, Sam: Give me an educated guess, a number, and I'll see what I can do on the football side."

Sam's gaze floated away and settled on a pair of young Hispanic women passing. Then it came back.

"Maybe two hundred and fifty," Sam said.

"And is there any way of knowing who they are? I need names."

"Ask the DCI," he said. Then, with a smirk, he added, "Or find someone with the combination to that safe."

Laura drew a long breath and exhaled. "Thank you, Sam," she said. "You've been helpful."

Sam might have finished there. But he didn't.

"Two hundred fifty or maybe two forty-nine," he said. "Who the hell knows what goes down these days?"

"What are you talking about?" Laura asked.

"I'm talking about how many unauthorized people might be able to penetrate White House security. There's maybe one less than there used to be." He paused. "One of my people disappeared out west two or three weeks back."

"Disappeared how?" Laura asked.

Sam turned and looked directly at McCarron. "Maybe you can snoop a little and get back to me, Agency boy," Sam said, ignoring Laura.

McCarron in return: "Can't do anything without a name, Sam."

"Vincent Rivera," Sam said. "Miami guy. Born here. Got sent west to do something. His dad was from El Salvador. His mom was a Montefiore from Brooklyn. We used to call Vinnie our Salvitalian. He's a good man. I want to know if he's jammed some way. I can't locate him. So maybe you can give me a little same-day payback and help him. Right?"

"What exactly was he involved in?" Rick asked. "When he disappeared?"

"Something involving a U.S. Marine who went missing from the embassy in Mexico," Sam said. "That's what he told me before he left."

"So he was on official business?" Laura asked.

Sam cleared his throat. "Yeah. Like you said it yourself,

huh?" Sam answered. "It's all pretty much that same b.s. isn't it? The more *unofficial* it is the more *official* it is, right?"

Laura and Rick exchanged a glance.

"Give us a couple of days, Sam," Laura said. "We'll see what we can do. How's that?"

Sam looked them back and forth. "You two are priceless," Sam grumbled. "What a pair of extortionists. Get in touch with me after I retire, I wouldn't mind running bag for you."

McCarron reached to his belt and drew Sam's pistol. He handed it back, magazine separated. "Try to behave with this, okay?" Rick said.

Sam accepted it.

Car doors opened. Laura and Rick sidled out.

"Need a lift back to your cars?" Sam asked after them.

Laura concluded: "It's okay, Sam. We'll walk."

chapter 85

MIAMI
JUNE 28, 2009; 1:08 P.M.

Odd images of other recent nights and days drifted before Laura as McCarron drove her in the direction of the Park Central Hotel.

The paranoia of being under surveillance, the collision she had witnessed on the Key Bridge driving home. The strange configurations of shadows in the back seat of her car, the ones that had morphed and unfolded into the silhouette of a man, then vanished again very quickly.

The visit from her father three nights earlier.

The haunting dream of Walter McKiernan drowning long ago.

And how did all that tie in with the perpetual sense of a trailing shadow that she only felt, never saw, till her back and the darkness beyond the bright light of day always seemed to tingle with the intensity of an unseen watcher's gaze.

What was real? What was imagined?

"Victor Rivera's DNA was on the money from Anna," Laura said. "The bloodstains."

"I know," Rick said. "The name registered right away. You were wise not to tell Sam."

"I'll tell him eventually," Laura said. "I'm sure I'll need to trade information with him again. For now we need to know what he knows and he does not need to know what we know."

"More good thinking," he said.

"Rivera's a middle-range Miami hood," she mused. "I wonder where he works into this."

"Maybe nowhere," Rick agreed. "And maybe right at the heart of things."

Laura flipped down the passenger side sun visor in his car. She positioned the vanity mirror to allow her to scan behind the car. What eyes were on her back today, she wondered.

"Sam won't follow us," McCarron said, reading her thoughts. "He's had enough of us for one day." A Volvo with New Jersey plates cut them off and stopped. "Dumb klutz," McCarron muttered, unrelated to their conversation. "And no one else is following us, either."

She flipped the visor back up.

"Am I that obvious?" she asked.

"Yes." He smiled.

"So you read me as well as I read you sometimes?" she said.

"Don't flatter me," he said. "I'll mistake it for personal interest."

"How do you know no one's following?"

"I've been watching, too," he said.

"Thanks," she said. "That's good to know."

Her phone rang as they neared the Park Central. Charles Yee with an unexpected update.

"I worked on some new technology with that Nokia," Yee

said. "New tracking technology. It was my test case. What I did was, I imbedded the tracking three times into the entire device. There was the main tracking in the SIM card. That has ceased functioning. I'd guess it has been destroyed, as you suggested."

"But you had back-up tracking?"

"Two times," Yee said, "each with their own identifiable pattern. One device in the metal chassis. That continues to function. It's emitting a weak stationary signal on the outskirts of Dallas. My guess is that whoever had the phone pulled it apart, burned or crushed the SIM card, then threw away the chassis."

"So what's the third?"

"I embedded a micro cell in the film band that surrounded and packaged the SIM card. You see, when all three work, they support each other and we get a stronger signal. But each can function on its own. In this case, the film band has been activated to a more powerful level by release of synthetic hydrogen reactors programmed in."

"Film band?" she asked. "Hydrogen reactors? If you'll excuse me, what's that about, Charles?"

"It's like cellophane. Like the wrapper on a pack of cigarettes."

"And you're still getting a tracking signal from it?"

"Exactly," Yee said.

"Incredible. Keep talking."

"The signal is actually very clear," Yee said. "It *is* remarkable. The film band is in Dallas. It continues to move. I'd say it's on the floor of a vehicle. Or in someone's pocket. I can pinpoint it within a few dozen meters."

Laura asked Yee to transfer the coordinates to her PID, which he did. When she saw them confirmed on her PID, she placed another call to Sgt. Foster in Miami.

Why hadn't the FBI intercepted the phone and the car carrying it, she wondered. It was a call with an unhappy resolution. From Foster she learned that the FBI in New Orleans had not yet placed a surveillance team on Anna's traveling phone.

Laura disconnected from Foster. "Son of a bitch!" she said.

She slammed her phone back in her purse and sat with arms folded, staring out the passenger side window as McCarron pulled in front of the Park Central.

He let the engine idle as he stopped. The air conditioning continued to purr.

"You going to tell me what you're so happy about or keep it a secret?" Rick asked.

"No FBI follow-up on the phone. The phone may have been destroyed but the tracking signal is still out there, maybe with the man we're looking for. Essentially, we're tracking a piece of Saran Wrap."

"Can you explain that one to me slower?"

She did, then went to the bottom line: "Whoever has the last piece of Anna's phone drove to Dallas. But I have no idea who's got it or who my suspect is because I can't get follow-up."

"Been there, done that," he said.

"Doesn't make it any better," she growled.

"How well can you pinpoint where that signal is?" he asked.

"If I were on the ground in the right location, I could find it," she said. "Easily."

"I don't know what you've got planned for the rest of the day," he said, "but my plans are flexible."

"What's that mean?"

"The time difference between here and Dallas is two hours. A flight takes maybe two and a half hours. It's not yet one o'clock here. It would take thirty minutes to get to the airport. I'm sure there are flights that are open. You'd still be back in Washington tomorrow if you had to be."

"For all I know, the phone is lying in a sewer somewhere and the cellophane wrapper is in a garbage truck."

"I know."

"And you're coming with me?" Laura asked.

"Someone has to watch your back. Someone you can trust."

"You do it pretty well."

"So far," he answered as she stepped out of the car and

strode purposefully into the hotel lobby. For once, as she felt eyes on her back, they were friendly.

Or so she reasoned.

"It will take me ten minutes to check out," she said. "Wait here."

chapter 86

DALLAS
JUNE 28, 2009; AFTERNOON

The blond man was a meticulous planner. So leaving behind a witness who knew anything about him was not a notion he liked.

In the afternoon, he rented a new car while not yet turning in the one he already had. He loaded his gear into the trunk of the new vehicle and left it parked in the same covered lot where he kept his other vehicle. He paid his hotel bill through the next night.

Then he killed time in a bar, sipping beer and watching Texas Rangers baseball on a big-screen television. With monotony building, he returned in the late afternoon to his hotel and used the swimming pool. It was not till midway into the evening that he used his first car, the one that he had cleaned out, to drive the eight blocks to where Tiffany was employed at Diamond Lil's.

Murder is a crime with an alarming failure rate among amateurs, but with pros the reverse is true, and the blond man was a pro. He had several potential routes of escape this evening. He would leave his first rental, the green Nissan, a block away, wheels pointed out for quick escape. The second car would be in a favorable spot at his hotel, ready to go, but reachable on foot.

He also knew when the club closed and how long it took for the girls who worked there to dress and leave. He would be able to cruise the parking lot for a few minutes but not for very many. Timing was everything. And if he failed to connect with Tiffany here, well, he also knew where she lived.

A hot muggy afternoon collapsed into a violent North Texas thunderstorm, then unraveled into an evening that was a perfect match for the day.

chapter 87

ABOVE THE SOUTHEASTERN UNITED STATES
JUNE 28, 2009; 8:06 P.M. CDST

The flight was an hour out of Miami. Fatigue was slowly strangling Laura. Events had their own madness and she remained unable to sort through all of them. She sat on the aisle while Rick sat at the window. Her eyes hung heavily and tried to close. It was then that he finally spoke.

"You're quiet," McCarron said to her.

"I'm thinking," Laura answered. "I'm also exhausted."

More minutes frittered away. Then, trying not to be too chilly, she turned back to him.

"Thanks for rescuing me back there," she said.

"I didn't know I did."

"When Sam came at me," she said.

"Oh," he said. "That. It's already ancient history."

"That," she said. "I understand having a larynx rebuilt isn't such a pleasant experience."

"Forget it. I've wanted to thrash Sam for years," he said. "You did me a favor."

"You guys have a past history?" she asked.

"There's a bit of one. Goes back a few years."

She turned toward him. "What was her name and was she pretty?" Laura asked.

"Still in your interview mode, huh?"

"I'm rarely out of it," she said.

"Her name was Diana and yes," Rick said.

"Thought so," she said. "The meeting had that certain type of tension."

"You *are* observant," Rick said.

"I notice things."

She looked back to the window and closed her eyes.

She must have fallen asleep, because the next thing she knew, there was a flight attendant—a pretty girl who reminded Laura of the way she had looked years ago when she had worked in the dress shop in Paris—touching her shoulder gently, asking her to move her seat to the upright position.

"We're landing," Rick said.

"Oh," Laura said sleepily. "Of course."

For a moment, confusion hop-scotched across her mind. She was disoriented and pictured herself going off on a brief vacation with a man she had recently met. Then the truth crawled back from somewhere and insinuated itself.

She was visiting a distant city with a man she had just met, but there was no vacation about it. Nor would there be.

Descent began and the aircraft was smoothly on the ground seventeen minutes later.

chapter 88

TRIPOLI
JUNE 29, 2009; 1:12 A.M. GMT

And in Tripoli, Sunday turned into Monday.

Alan Savett lay on his bed, staring at the ceiling, trying to sleep but failing.

His bedroom door was open to the next room where two policemen maintained their vigil, occasionally looking in on him. Outside, below his windows, shifts of other policemen took their turns, coming and going, joking with each other, making certain Savett went nowhere.

What was keeping Langley from responding to him, Savett wondered. He had filed a dispatch of the highest urgency. So far, no response. Had the Americans bailed on him? Normally a turnaround of vital information took less than three hours, at least to receive an acknowledgment.

Savett was starting to sense disaster.

His nerves were shot to hell. Almost an entire day had passed since filing the most recent steganography. Every once in a while, Savett would break into a hot hard sweat, for no reason and for every reason. He was a wise enough man to know that this whole CIA thing that he had bought into years earlier was about to blow up in his face.

Fatigue overtook him. He started to drift to sleep, consoling himself that he had, in fact, survived another day. Perhaps if he survived a day at a time he would weather this current storm and survive for years to come.

He neared sleep. His building was quiet. In the distance he was aware of his neighbors, two units away. Somewhere in the same distance he thought he heard a woman crying, then further decided it was a child.

It made him think of the housing he had lived in as a boy in England, which reminded him of his own son, whom he had not seen in many months.

The thought further saddened him, depressed him even, and he dropped off to sleep, deeply troubled.

chapter 89

DALLAS
JUNE 28, 2009; 8:34 P.M. CDST

Upon arrival in Dallas, Rick took care of a car rental while Laura picked out lodgings that would be convenient and economical. She selected a Radisson not far from the airport, easy for arrival, easy for a getaway the next morning.

They drove to the hotel and quickly checked in. Separate rooms on the same floor.

Laura worked her cell phone constantly.

Back in Langley, Charles Yee had been tracking the coordinates of Anna's missing cell phone. The location had moved a bit during the day, but not by much.

"Chances are, the phone is in someone's possession or in a vehicle," Yee said. "Keep in mind that whoever has it may be the person you're looking for, but might not be, also."

"I'll find out when and if I find the phone," she answered.

Holding her PID in one hand, her secure cell phone in the other, Laura—following Yee's instructions over the phone—programmed in a map and tracking mode that would refine the information she could access on the location of Anna's tracking signal.

Yee would now be on active duty indefinitely, relaying information to Laura as she closed in on the phone. Chances were, she reasoned as she signed off with Yee, whoever had the phone had no idea it could be tracked or he would have ditched the device by now.

A major slip-up. But that was what criminal investigations were all about: waiting for the opposition to make a mistake, sometimes tiny.

Four minutes after ringing off with Yee, Laura met Rick in the corridor between their rooms. "Ready to rumble?" he asked.

"Ready," she answered.

"Nice to get out of the office, isn't it?"

"Yeah. Sure. A blast."

Rick seemed calm and gathered. A wave of anxiety was upon her, one she could not quite control. Never, she swore, had she ever experienced anything quite like this. Never, she hoped, would she experience anything similar again.

She thought of Anna as they entered the elevator.

"Artillery inspection?" he suggested. They were alone.

"Good idea."

They checked their weapons inside the elevator, hoping it wouldn't stop for more passengers while they had guns drawn. Then again, it was Texas. Idly, she thought of the recent days at the firing range where she felt as if she couldn't put a bullet in the ocean from the end of a pier.

Involuntarily, she let out a long sigh. It caused Rick to look at her and sense her alarm.

"Don't worry," he said. "We do this by the book. I've got your back, you've got mine."

She nodded.

"We could get local police back-up, too," he said. "What do you think?"

"They'd make things more difficult," she said. "We'll go that route only if needed."

"I agree," he said. "I'll tell you something else. Given the situation, the time of day, the background of this case, if I've got to make a split-second decision on whether to shoot or not, I'm pulling the trigger. Just so you know."

"We're on the same page," she said. "You good with a weapon?"

"Not particularly. I'll do better if I can get off the first shot."

He looked as if he were kidding. Maybe.

The elevator door opened.

They were out into the lobby and, moments later, into the car. Rick drove.

Laura brought up the screen on her PID.

"The target hasn't moved in two hours," she said. "I'm getting a reading on a street and a specific block. Ever heard of Solanger Street?"

"Not till now."

He glanced at what she had.

"Got it," he said. "It's your game. You call the moves."

chapter 90

The blond man parked his green Nissan on Solanger Street a block away from Diamond Lil's. He sat in his car, smoked, and waited. Eleven o'clock came. From where he sat, through an alley, across a parking lot, the blond man could see a few patrons starting to leave Lil's.

Perfect! The girls would be out soon. Lil's closed early on Sundays.

He had an old Colt .38 that he would use this evening. Registration number long removed. The weapon had been laundered perfectly; completely clean.

The blond man wore a dark jacket and dark suit pants that would conceal the weapon well. He now pulled latex gloves onto his hands. He loaded the weapon with five bullets from his jacket pocket. Fewer shots than five would be needed; no point to risk an accidental firing, so the chamber beneath the hammer he left empty. He screwed a small silencer in place at the end of the bore.

He left as little to chance as possible.

He tucked the gun into his right side pants pocket, drew a breath, said a small prayer, and stepped out of the Nissan. He left the doors unlocked so that he could access the vehicle quickly if he had to. Timing, along with speed and accuracy, was always crucial in a situation like this.

The blond man was buoyant and confident. There was something special about a kill for a good cause. He tucked his weapon into his belt and set out slowly on foot.

chapter 91

Rick drove slowly and cautiously down Solanger Street. It was a Sunday night in a commercial industrial area. The street was not busy, there were few cards parked. No pedestrians.

Laura watched the street alternatively with the monitor of her PID.

"Slowly, slowly," she said. "We're close. I mean *really* close."

The street lamps were sodium vapor and cast sharp shadows. Rick drove with one hand. He pulled out his weapon with the other and laid it across his lap. His hand remained upon it.

"The monitor's about to explode we're so close," Laura said. "Inch along."

Rick slowed to a crawl. There was a Chevy van parked at a hydrant. Three parking tickets on its window. Nothing more along the curb until halfway between them and the corner.

The car was fresh and clean. A green Nissan. It looked and smelled like a rental.

"Careful here," Laura said softly. She scanned the coordinates. "That might be it. Approach it carefully."

Within their car, two weapons drawn, two hearts pounding, four eyes sharp as tacks on full alert. They pulled abreast of the Nissan.

"We got it," Laura said softly. "The tracking signal is coming from this car!"

They pulled close enough to scan. No one in the car.

"I'm going to back up and park," Rick said.

She nodded. She closed the PID and set it aside.

Rick backed to a position thirty feet behind the Nissan. The moment tingled. Neither of them said anything for half a minute. It seemed much longer.

"Let's have a close look," Rick finally said. "Keep your weapon up. I'll go first. Give me a ten count before you follow."

"Rick?"

"Yeah."

"Careful."

He squeezed her free hand with his.

"Sure thing."

He stepped out of the car. He kept his right hand low, his arm downward, his gun concealed. She watched. He took five casual steps forward as she gave him his ten count.

Then he turned slightly and nodded.

Laura stepped out, her weapon downward and against the side of her leg. Textbook approach. They stalked the Nissan from the rear, Rick in the street, Laura on the sidewalk.

She stayed five feet behind him, barely breathing.

The paces were painful. Rick arrived at the car with short cautious final steps. He stopped where he could see into the back seat. When he took another step forward, she knew Rick had not seen anything to set off alarms. He took another step and was in viewing range of the front seat.

Still no traffic.

No strollers.

Nothing set to explode other than their insides and their nerves.

He gave her a final motion with his head: It was safe to advance. Laura came up on the passenger side of the car, alternating her gaze at the car and at the surroundings.

The street remained dead. Shop windows behind grates.

Car part emporiums.

Tex's Duke of Hubcaps. Sal's Sandwich Shop.

A hardware store and a religious bookshop.

R&T Paints.

An overweight red cat sat in the window of Mike's Coffee

& Pastry. The cat watched them as if they had taken leave of their sanity. Maybe the cat was right.

A little wave of relief as they stood on opposite sides of the Nissan. No danger from the storefronts. The opposite side of the street was as dead as this one. The only visible activity, through a long alley that intersected Solanger Street, was a "Men's Dining Club," according to the sign, named Diamond Lil's.

To Laura, it looked like a fancy tittie parlor.

They turned their attention back to the Nissan, eyeballed it bumper to bumper.

Absently, Laura thought of her automobile boys Vlad and Zarko back in D.C. Here was a vehicle they would have loved to rip apart.

"We should move away," Rick said. "Watch the car from a distance. See if we can finally get some surveillance put on it."

"Yeah," she said. "The FBI was so helpful the first time. And the Dallas PD has this great reputation for helping federal investigations."

"Got a better idea?"

"Maybe."

She drew a tissue out of a pocket and covered her fingers. She fiddled with the door handle.

"Bad idea," he said, waiting for hell to break loose. "Very bad idea."

"I know. I'm going to do it anyway."

He stepped back quickly.

"Gut feeling. It's okay," Laura said.

"Remind me never to assign you to a bomb squad," he said.

She almost laughed. Almost. Instead, she tried the door. The latch clicked upwards.

He stepped farther away.

The door opened slowly. A little breeze of discernibly cooler air crept out.

"Rick . . . ?" she asked.

"Could be booby trapped," he cautioned. "Come on, Laura.

Don't mess with it till we can get it sniffed, towed, and impounded."

"Wonder how long it's been sitting here," she said. "The van behind us has parking tickets. This one's got none."

She closed the door. Gently.

"Damn!" she said. "If this car could talk we'd be in business."

Then a realization smacked her in the face. "Rick! The interior was cool. Air conditioning. This car couldn't have been here that long."

"I think we should get away from it as quickly as possible," he said again.

Then he had his own epiphany. He went to the hood and touched.

Warm. Too warm.

Someone had cut the engine within the last hour.

"This thing's alive," he said.

"You're right."

"You want to call it in or shall I?"

"Neither," Laura said. "Let's eyeball it for a little while."

"Half an hour?"

"Then we'll get some Dallas PD back-up?" she asked.

"Deal," he said.

"You watch from the car, I'll take the alley," she said.

"Sure you don't want to do it the other way?"

"Who's got the car keys?" she asked.

"I do," he said.

"Then you take the car. We'll switch in fifteen minutes."

"You're too generous," he said. "I like working with you."

"Thanks. Not everyone does."

"Don't get yourself killed, Laura. I'm starting to like you."

"Just starting?"

"Just starting."

He retreated slowly to their car. She watched.

He got in, lowered the window slightly for a breeze.

Laura went to the alley and stood with her back almost to the wall, watching. On the other side of her, about fifty yards away, she could see the lights of Diamond Lil's and part of their parking lot.

She could hear music from within, and occasionally voices. Idly, as she stood sentry, she wondered what sort of man frequented a place like Lil's.

She wished she had access to a drink. Well, she'd have to do without this time. Maybe later, however.

chapter 92

DALLAS
JUNE 28, 2009; 11:54 P.M.

Tiffany was wearing a blue dress suit when she stepped from the comfort of Diamond Lil's into the muggy Dallas night. With the suit she wore a light blue blouse. She had carefully coordinated the colors.

Now she stepped quickly across the parking lot. The guards had already gone and she had run a little later than usual because the owner, Tony, had a gentleman named Mr. Goldman from New York whom he wanted her to meet and date. Tony had pointed out that she could take a week off at his expense if Mr. Goldman had a good enough time. Mr. Goldman was exactly the type of gentleman she didn't want to meet or date.

"You late on a loan payment, Tony?" she had asked.

"Just think about it," he said.

"I'll think about it a lot but the answer is no," she had answered.

The business was getting sleazier and sleazier, she told herself. How much longer could she work here and live with herself?

Now, in an angry, frustrated mood, Tiffany just wanted to get to her car and safely home. If this parking lot had been a toxic waste site—and sometimes it smelled like one thanks to the refinery down the road—it couldn't have been more unpleasant. There were mosquitoes the size of hummingbirds thanks to the drainage slew at the northern edge of the lot. Then there were the occasional loiterers.

For the former, she carried bug repellent in her purse. For the latter, she carried the small derringer she owned.

What a life, she said to herself. *What a life.*

She had this way, at this hour each working day, of walking purposefully toward her destination with her head down. The posture was perfect for not catching anyone's eye contact, but leaving her able to scan her immediate surroundings for intrusion on her space.

Now she detected just such an intrusion. Her hand went into the purse for the derringer. There was movement in a shadow just beyond her car.

"Hello, Tiffany," the voice said.

"Get away from me!" she answered. Anyone who had ever attended Diamond Lil's knew her performance name. Her grip tightened on her weapon.

The man stepped from the shadows. "Don't you recognize me?" he asked. "We spent a great night together."

Suddenly, recognition. She raised her gaze.

Could it be . . . ? *Was* it . . . ?

"Kevin?" she asked.

She looked and thought she was seeing things. It was *him!* Softly: "That's me."

Excitedly: "Oh, my God! What are you doing here?"

"Looking for you."

"I didn't see you inside tonight. Were you in for dinner and the show?"

"I just got into town," he said. "I thought I'd surprise you."

"Well, you did, honey." She moved toward him and then broke into a joyful run. "Have you got a kiss for me?"

"A kiss and more," he promised.

Her spirits soared. He opened his arms as if to invite her into his embrace.

She accepted.

She moved several feet toward him. Her mood was still high as she neared him.

Then he swung one hand toward her. She stopped short in horror. She recognized the object in his hand.

She was no more than five feet away. Her love gave way to fear and then disbelief because she thought it must be a joke—a very bad one—that he was waving his gun around.

He pulled the trigger.

The first shot felt like a kick in the chest. It staggered her and propelled her backwards. Then, in a nano-second, she knew that nothing else mattered and the final verdict was that the world was one scummy cruel place.

He was there to kill her.

Her hand gripped her derringer. He shot her a second time and she fell hard to the ground.

She was stunned and dazed, full of hurt and the trauma of impending death. She knew exactly what he was doing. There was a silencer on his weapon and no one could hear or witness what was happening.

He stood over her. He pressed the nose of his weapon to her skull.

Her hand found the trigger in her purse and she harm-lessly drew her own weapon.

She was unable to raise it.

Her body kicked and reflexed. Near death, she pulled her hand from her purse. She fired one shot from her own small .22. The bullet sailed off into the blackness of the night.

The blond man fired a third bullet, this one into her brain.

His shot had been quiet. Hers had not been. The sound of small-bore gunfire resonated through the immediate area.

chapter 93

Laura heard the shot. She felt a surge within her. She had spent enough time at the firing range to recognize it. One shot. Not much juice. Not too loud. Small caliber.

"What the hell?" Laura whispered aloud.

Instinctively, she turned toward it. She was a few feet down the alley between Solanger Street and the parking lot that led to Diamond Lil's. She could see the illumination of the parking lot, but not the entire lot.

She stepped quickly to Solanger Street and waved to Rick, still waiting in his car. He must have been looking downward. No reaction. The sound of the small caliber had not carried that far. She waved a second time and got his attention.

She indicated distress. He should follow. She saw him break from his car.

Laura turned and ran through the alley, barely avoiding twisting her ankle on fallen bricks. The alley was fifty-some feet long, garbage strewn, home to more than one rat.

She moved deftly. *Thank you Jesus for sturdy shoes*.

She was halfway there, then a few feet from the corner and then, still in shadows, she went into a cautious turn, weapon up and ready.

Footsteps oncoming. Fast. Fleeting. Danger. Maybe death.

From around the corner thundered a large man in full flight.

Tall and sturdy. Laura's heart nearly left her chest: A bulky figure turned a few feet in front of her.

Then they crashed into each other, head on.

The blond man hit her with full force, a solid shoulder to the upper torso, the midpoint of her sternum, and something hard—his head, an arm—cracked her alongside the right side of her skull. A forty-yard-line open field hit. Texas–Oklahoma.

He sent her flying, and staggered himself doing so.

She tumbled backwards, hurting.

Her weapon flew from her hand, clattered, and landed. Somewhere. Her body sprawled to the left, crashing hard against a series of trash cans and falling. It was the hardest she had been hit in her life, made worse by the sudden unexpectedness of it.

The blond man staggered but did not fall. A street light blazed behind him.

Laura's head throbbed. She gasped for breath. Her chest hurt. She wondered if a bone was broken. Her whole body ached and shook. She feared she was going into shock.

Then she wondered.

Was this the man?

Was this the moment she would be killed?

Christ! He's blond!

It's him!

Even in the severe shadows, she knew this was the man she was looking for. And as she looked up, she realized that she must have hit him hard, too, because he had his hand to his jaw.

She yelled. "Rick! I'm down!"

She groped for her weapon and found it. Clumsy grip. It slid away, eluding her.

She shielded her eyes.

His face! His face! She could see only half of it!

A voice came out of the sturdy blond silhouette that loomed before her.

"Laura? *Laura Chapman!*"

The voice was deep but silky. It was the voice she had heard on the telephone.

All she could think of: Anna hanging bled dry in a closet. This manhunt was driving her crazy.

"Go to hell," she said, half dazed.

Her skull felt as if someone were drilling it.

She fumbled again for her gun.

Rick's voice, finally. From the other end of the alley. "Hey! You! Freeze!"

The blond man whirled and raised a weapon at Rick. Aimed. His other arm to his jaw.

Laura heard her own voice. "Rick! Gun!"

Rick fired twice. Shattered bricks off the wall with the first. Missed wildly with the second. Lethal ricochets everywhere.

The assassin fired two shots. Nasty little squirts from a silencer.

She heard Rick dive or fall. She heard her own scream. She still couldn't see.

Two shots. Followed by a click. He was tapped out. She grabbed her own weapon, securely this time, tried to raise it.

The man kicked at her, got the underside of the forearm. Solid impact. The gun broke loose again, slid and hopscotched through garbage. Somewhere in the distance a siren wailed, then a second closer by.

Laura thought as she struggled: *Dallas PD, finally!*

The man chopped down at her, tried to break her neck, failed, kneed her in the ribs, jarred her badly, almost flattened her, in which case he could kill her by stomping on her head.

She rose and he missed a death kick. He was off balance. She smashed an elbow backward and kneecapped him.

Direct hit!

Fighting her way up from the ground: never a good idea, never easy. But it was a good skill and she had learned it well. She was back from the soon-to-be-dead.

She threw up the fist of the same arm, aimed for his testicles, just missed. But he grunted on impact. She had hurt him! She threw a second shot at Genital Central, missed again but scored more points. He kneed at her and missed.

She saw Anna again as she fought. Saw her dad, too.

A whole spiritual cheering section.

Then the real world returned.

Rick, screaming: "Stop! Freeze!"

Rick again, maybe wounded, but not taken out, back up on his feet, charging.

The man picked up a wino's leftover Tiger Rose. A nice cheap bottle. He hurled it. She heard impact, glass shattering.

Rick fired, missed. Fired and missed a second time, too. Laura stayed low in the filth.

Rick was as bad a shot as she was!

Absurdly, she thought: *Jesus! No one can shoot straight anymore!*

The assassin whirled, pulled down some boxes to obstruct his follower's path, and turned. She found her own weapon, leaned between a space in the trash heap, and fired twice, missing both times by half a planet.

Rick arrived, jumped the trash, kept going, fired once more and hit the Big Nothing a third time. Another frantic step. He slid hard on wet trash and bricks.

He hit the ground hard and twisted. She was afraid he had broken a leg. Her heart thundered.

Several seconds later, he got up limping, cursing violently, pant leg torn, blood running through the fabric, angry as living hell. He took a step to run in pursuit, but couldn't.

By now, she was standing, too, ribs, upper chest, and skull all throbbing.

He looked into the empty distance where the blond man had run. No one in the history of the world had disappeared so fast.

He walked back to her.

"Mother of God!" he said. "Look at you."

"That was him, Rick! That was our killer!"

She was fighting off shock. Shivers pulsed through her.

From Solanger Street there was a flashing red and white light and the noisy electric crackle of a police radio. Then a second. Then another one pulling into Lil's parking lot. Soon there would be enough for a whole Panzer division.

"That was our man," she said again. Her heartbeat slowly started to return to earth. "And he knew me. He knew my name, Rick. I mean, God damn it, *he knew me!*"

"Yeah," Rick said, badly shaken. "Yeah."

He put an arm around her. She accepted it.

A moment later, Dallas policemen arrived next to them.

To an astonished small audience, with federal government IDs out on enemy turf, Laura and Rick began their backstory of who they were and why they were there.

chapter 94

DALLAS
JUNE 29, 2009; 12:54 A.M.

For the second time in nine days, Laura stood over a murdered woman and wondered.

What in hell is this all about?

How do the dots connect?

How does the killer know me? How does he know my name?

Jesus! From within the Service. It's got to be from within Service that he knows my name.

There were enough DPD sector cars here now to start a flotilla, plus a helicopter above and another small fleet circling the local streets, looking for *el hombre rubio* and finding more *nada*. The night simmered with sodium vapor and red strobe, plus a twisted body under a blanket, blood flowing. Someone's daughter, someone's sister: a little crimson stream on warm asphalt.

Laura seethed with pure hatred for the man who wasn't there.

A final police car arrived. A big white guy stepped out in plainclothes. He had the shoulders of a bear. He hoisted a Lone Star belt on a thick belly. A hard mean gaze took inventory. He looked like something out of the JFK hit in '63, minus the white ten-gallon hat.

He dropped a captain's brass shield on his breast pocket

but didn't need to. The harness bulls knew him already. They looked scared. He was a DPD captain named Hinson and wore anger like yesterday's cologne.

"What's all this about?" he asked.

A sergeant gave a head jerk toward the body under the canvas.

"Yeah? So?"

The sergeant took a minute to pull the captain up to speed. Hinson's eyes rose to Laura and Rick as the tale was told. Then the captain lurched over to them.

"CIA and Secret Service?" he asked. "I'm hearing this right?"

Laura answered. "You're hearing it right."

"Which is which or doesn't it matter?" Hinson asked.

They had their IDs waiting. Hinson took them. "What the damned hell?" he asked. "You folks on assignment? Or vacation?"

"Assignment."

"Right. How come we didn't know you were in town?"

"No time. It's a Sunday," Laura said.

"Yeah. Mind if I run those IDs? Of course you don't."

"Don't mind at all," Rick said, after the fact.

"This ain't exactly the Secret Service's favorite city, is it?" he asked Laura.

She didn't answer.

"No offense. Every time I have to do face-to-face with Secret Service they got a burr up their asshole just being here. Now they send lady agents. You got a burr somewhere, lady?"

"There's a car you need to run," Laura answered. "Solanger Street. Green Nissan. Looks like a rental. Can't miss it."

"You trying to tell me how to do my job?"

"We're appreciative of local help."

"Nissan. A Jap car, huh? It's related to this?"

Rick spoke. "We think so."

"Do we need to do dogs? Bomb squad?"

"Your call on that one," Laura said.

"Wait here."

Captain Hinson trudged back to his car, in no hurry. Laura worked on the parts of her body that felt as if they were going to explode. Minutes ticked off everyone's life except Tiffany's.

Hinson received confirmation on the IDs.

He walked back and handed them back their identification. It was a kinder and gentler moment since the IDs had passed. "You folks need to see doctors? Hospital maybe. We can take you."

"I think we're okay. Some bruises."

"You both look banged up. You in particular, Laura Chapman of the United States Secret Service. Ought to get it checked out. We got doctors here in Dallas. They're even licensed."

"Maybe tomorrow."

"I can't force you. I can recommend. Parkland Memorial Hospital's not far from here."

"Isn't that where JFK died?" Rick asked.

"No, he died in the street," Hinson said. "But they put his head back together at Parkland. What are you, a smartass?"

It is where they took the slain president, Laura thought, but didn't say. She put her hand to her forehead and felt something wet and sticky on the surface of a nasty lump. She was starting to bleed again. Her ribs hurt just as badly, left side and lower right back. But only when she breathed.

She winced at her own touch.

"X-rays might be a good idea," Rick suggested. "So might some attention to cuts and scrapes." Rick ate some crow. "Thank you, Captain," he said.

He motioned to the torn section of his pant leg, with the crimson markings from within. "This used to be a new suit," he said. "As recently as yesterday."

Captain Hinson gave them a wry smile. "We can give you some first aid right here," he said. "And a sector car can lead you to Parkland. That's if you choose."

"I choose," Rick said.

"Okay. Both of us."

They gave a statement of what they had seen and heard.

They mentioned nothing about Washington, but cited the pursuit of the killer here as an ongoing investigation from a homicide in Florida.

The DPD checked the Nissan two ways for explosives. They had a young officer open the door, then he started the engine. Nothing boomed.

Then Laura and Rick watched the green Nissan be impounded. Captain Hinson allowed Laura to inventory and remove the film band from the cell phone when she found it under the right hand front seat. She felt Anna's karma as she grasped it. She remembered well the moment when she had placed the phone in Anna's hands.

Captain Hinson was a crude man, but not a stupid one.

What a CIA and Secret Service pairing might be doing working a homicide case gave him room to grin. He could have asked a hundred questions.

He asked none.

Maybe, Laura reckoned, he didn't much care.

chapter 95

DALLAS
JUNE 29, 2009; 2:04 A.M.

The middle of the night: Parkland for x-rays. Emergency rooms are never cozy in the hours after midnight. This wasn't, either. Sometimes the whole world is crazy past 2 A.M.

A trim young Haitian intern named Marcel-Louis dressed and treated their cuts and bruises. Laura got a course of antibiotics to fight any infection from the cuts. Laura spoke French with the young man. He liked her so much he gave her some extra painkillers, too. A narco bag of M&M's. Rick got the same party favor, plus bandages to the knee and elbow.

Negative on the x-rays. All of them.

Laura and Rick checked out of Parkland.

Laura was still thinking: *How did he know my name?*

How am I going to stop him?

How much closer do I come to being killed without being killed?

The night in Dallas was otherwise quiet. They drove in near silence, each trying to assimilate the events of the night.

"Did you get a good look at him?" Rick finally asked.

"No. You?"

"No."

Laura continued it several blocks later, crossing humid empty streets.

"I don't know which I would have wanted more. A good look or a good shot."

"Maybe next time you'll get both," he said.

"Cover my back when I do," she answered.

He patted her on the back of the hand.

"I promise," he said.

"I trust you," she said. She was surprised to hear the words pass her lips. She couldn't recall when she had last said them. "I'm sure you will."

Again a silence reclaimed the car, but they were almost back at the hotel. Then they *were* back, at 3:23 A.M. They stood together in an empty elevator that took them to their floor.

They arrived and stepped out, weary, beaten, exhausted.

"You going to be okay?" he asked.

"I'll be all right," she said.

"I'll walk you back to your room," he said.

"Mine's right next to yours," she said.

"I'll walk you, anyway."

She didn't need the escort. But she did not decline the courtesy.

The hotel corridor was quiet. There was a large picture window that gave a view of the city and a moon that hung above it. Neither said anything but each was starting to read the thoughts of the other.

They kept going past the window. They arrived at the door to Laura's room.

She swiped the room card, had her hand on the door handle, and wondered vaguely if Rick would try to kiss her.

She hoped he would. But then what? She was in a place where she hadn't been for a while. Yet she felt her old skills and desires returning to her at just the right time.

She turned toward him. "Want to come in for a few minutes?"

When she turned, however, she caught his eyes on the divide of her blouse, just above the top button. She might have feigned annoyance, but instead reacted with a silent pleasure. She liked it when a man she liked behaved like a man.

Their eyes met.

"Do you have a girlfriend somewhere?" she asked. "A wife even?"

"No."

"Should I believe you?"

"Yes."

"That's good, because I do."

"It's also good because I want you. Right now," he said.

His arms slipped around her back and his lips descended upon hers. They were firm and warm.

She responded to his kiss, mouth open.

There was no further conscious moment of decision making.

She drew back from him for a second. The door opened. She pushed the door open and motioned with her head to follow.

They stepped inside her room. Then desire overwhelmed both.

There was a flurry of hands and of clothes coming off; Laura removing his, Rick helping her out of hers. Then their bodies came together, completely naked, and suddenly the aches and discomforts of the evening's physical combat were no longer relevant. It felt good to have a man wrap his arms around her, his muscles, his hardness against her.

She led him to her bed, fell backward upon it, and he moved aggressively forward upon her. She was hardly aware who had seduced whom, nor did it matter.

chapter 96

A twenty-ounce cup of coffee sitting to the side of his monitor, Martin Thayer eased into the assignments that had been waiting for him since Saturday. Already, this looked like a bad week. Normally someone would have come in on Sunday to cover his post, but, once again, budget cuts had dictated otherwise. It made more fiduciary sense to pay him overtime and let him do his own catching up.

Thayer opened his screen.

He spent a few moments on the *Washington Post*'s online edition. Then, hearing footsteps approach that could have been the department supervisor, he opened his screen to work.

One hundred sixteen new messages. He felt a tumbling sensation. It would take two days to dig out. "Shit," he muttered to himself.

The footsteps passed him. Another steganographer. No hassle.

Thayer scanned for the codes that would suggest unusual importance. He gave a sharp eye to the messages that had ended his previous Saturday, the ones relating to the Israeli agent who had been shot in Beirut.

Nothing further on that one, thank God! Mercifully, the higher-ups had taken care of it. *What the hell, anyway?* His job was only to unzip the briefs, de-crypt them, and kick them along the proper channels. It wasn't on Thayer to enforce intelligence policy, much less understand it, much less get emotionally wrapped up in it.

Thank God, again.

The footsteps moved away from his desk. He went to

personal e-mail. A note from his brother in Montreal. Hey! What's this: A note from a former girlfriend, Lynn, whom he had dropped when he had decided she wasn't pretty enough.

Surprise.

Their break-up had been rocky; he had just spent a lonely Sunday, so he was wondering if—no, *hoping*—that she was proposing a reconciliation.

He opened her note. Guess not.

She seemed to be having the time of her life with a new boyfriend in Hawaii. She attached a photograph of the two of them. She had lost weight and was in a small red bikini. The muscular boyfriend preened impressively in his banana hammock.

Thayer felt his cheeks go crimson.

A nice cordial *Screw you, Marty!* subtext. Thayer needed this on a Monday morning.

Angrily, he closed out the message and the photo. Then he zapped it.

More footsteps. Conversation nearby. Uh oh.

A fey little prick named Ken Kellerman.

Thayer's boss, whom everyone hated working for and who didn't have a life outside these walls.

Kellerman's irritating nasal dairy state accent was like fingernails on the blackboard to anyone within fifty feet. Right now, the boss was grumbling about the air conditioning and how it was impossible to keep these offices under seventy-nine degrees on afternoons in the summer. Thayer wondered how long he could deal with this job. He was starting to hate it, and Lynn hadn't made him feel better about it this morning, either.

Thayer quickly brought work to his screen. Now, what the hell was *this?*

A coded dispatch from Chiron. Two days earlier than Chiron would next be expected to report. Thayer had no idea who Chiron was, but knew he was important.

So what was this? Trouble?

Thayer was only a conduit but his job was to move these

things along as quickly as possible. He clicked on it and opened a photograph.

Suddenly, Thayer was wide awake, opening the steganographic software.

The message was time dated.

Saturday night.

Oh, shit!

This signal must have come in right when he was leaving.

Oh, shit again!

The message had come in before he had gone home. He recalled finessing his work station in order to get out before midnight.

He calculated quickly. A message of alleged urgency had been sitting there for thirty-six hours. His sorry ass would soon be in a sling.

He found the pixel that carried the code. He worked the steganographic keys against the pixel. The message unfolded. He printed it and for the first time read it.

"Oh, Christ!" he blurted out.

He turned and started down the hall on a double step, looking for Mr. Kellerman.

A new job for Thayer? Count on it.

chapter 97

WASHINGTON, D.C.
JUNE 29, 2009; AFTERNOON

Laura sat at her desk, reconstructing events, or trying to. It had happened like this, she told herself: Anna had come to America and stumbled upon a plot to murder the president. She had gone to the FBI, partly out of a sense of civic responsibility and partly to score the big payday that would let her retire from her current life.

Meanwhile, the CIA and the Secret Service were in denial. If Laura were to tell them that their White House security was blown she would be telling them exactly what they did not want to hear. But Sam Deal was incarnate proof of faulty security and compromised cells within the government, fully paid for by taxpayers who didn't even know they existed.

Beyond a closed door, Vanessa was humming to herself. Laura could hear it, but she kept reconstructing.

Her suspect had been in the company of two men who might have been Israeli.

Or they might have been Arabic.

Or they might have been either.

Where did that snake its way into the equation?

One of Sam's peers, Vincent Rivera, had gone AWOL. Maybe he was dead, probably somewhere out west. That connected somewhere. A woman was dead in Dallas with a link to the phone that had disappeared from Anna's sex pad. That connected somewhere, too.

Then there was an AWOL marine in Mexico, who connected to the missing Rivera, and since Rivera connected some way to Anna, there was that link, also.

So what did it all mean?

The question brought her back to Dallas and the blond man. Could she say with certainty that *this* was her man? Her gut feeling told her, yes.

Great.

But could she stake her career on it?

Would she recognize him again? If she had a Secret Service graphic artist construct a picture, could she describe him?

Probably not.

She brought up Jeremy Wilder on her computer screen. *The* picture.

Was this the man she had seen in Dallas?

Well, yes.

Well, no.

Oh, hell.

Oh, damn it to hell.

If the man who had shot at her in Dallas *was* the assassin, and if he were a member of the Secret Service, she could eliminate any Service employee who was not in Dallas that day. But if such a conjecture were wrong, she was giving the actual killer, Jeremy Wilder perhaps, free rein to enter the White House.

Her head felt as if it were set to explode. Thoughts wandered, loose associations:

Dallas, Dallas, Dallas.

Dallas forty-six years ago: the epicenter of the Service's worst security meltdown of the twentieth century. According to JFK assassination lore, a prostitute had been picked up by three men on a highway leading to Dallas a few days before the assassination. They had boasted that the president was "going to get whacked in Big D."

No one ever identified the men. But the woman told her story and turned up dead a few weeks later. Laura wondered: Was some cemetery out there beckoning her at this moment?

Laura knew too much, after all. She probably knew more than she knew she knew.

Then there was Rick.

She had jumped into bed with him. Well, damn! The sex had been good.

More of this in the future or was Rick a one-time guilty pleasure?

God knew, a woman was permitted a bit of both, wasn't she?

Or, by getting involved personally with Rick, had she just screwed up her case in more ways than one?

At least Rick was the one man who was her ally these days.

He was the one man she could trust, wasn't he?

Wasn't he?

Actually, the sex had been better than good—multiple times.

She sighed. Oh, well. Maybe it was what it was, nothing more, nothing less.

Her body ached.

Connect the dots, connect the dots, connect the dots, she told herself, returning to the case before her. But she knew she did not yet even have all the dots visible.

Her doubts, her suspicions, surrounded her like a squad of soldiers, not letting her thought processes escape. She reached to her phone, called Bill Vasquez's office, and reconfirmed her meeting for that afternoon. Outside, beneath a summer sky, Washington cooked. Triple digit temperatures again. Global warming was no longer a theory. Thunderstorms predicted for later.

She made some calls again about the missing marine in Mexico, but could not connect with the people she wanted. Then she received bad news from Dallas.

The green Nissan was clean. Rented on a fraudulent credit card, bad name, bad address. In the credit card business the card was known as a one-hit wonder. It mocked the computer system and morphed into a live number, but was only good for one authorization. The card led nowhere and so far, fingerprints in the car led just as fast to the same place.

Nor, as she had already known when she left Dallas, was any arrest imminent for the murder of the waitress at Diamond Lil's.

She put down the phone. Where would this end?

She felt for the girl who had lain dead in the parking lot, and she felt for the family that had been notified back in Michigan. What a deplorable world it could be. Moral triumphs and goodness were often rare and ephemeral.

She ached badly from her bruises. The cuts itched. She had a headache and neck ache that would not quit.

She found the young Haitian doc's prescription pain zapper and treated herself to two tablets. It gave her a good rush. She wished for some Barbancourt rum to wash it down.

For that matter, she thought to herself, a little bit of reefer in the near future might soothe some nerves.

Okay, back to work.

She spent the rest of the day taking stock of what she had,

trying to assemble some sense where none wished to be assembled. She wondered what sort of spin to put on things for Director Vasquez.

And outside, in more ways than one, the American capital continued to broil.

chapter 98

NASHVILLE, TENNESSEE
JUNE 29, 2009; 2:53 P.M. CST

The blond man had been on the move since Dallas.

That episode surrounding Tiffany's elimination had been too close for comfort. The Godless opposition had picked up his scent. Unless he had been mistaken, he had even recognized the Secret Service agent, Laura Chapman, whom he had so narrowly slipped past.

He had abandoned his original car in Memphis. He also had sorted through his clothing and various belongings and had thrown away many of them. He had packed everything he still owned into two suitcases and taken a bus to Nashville.

There was no way, though, he reasoned as the Nashville skyline rose on the highway in front of him, that they could possibly know who they were looking for.

Was there?

His identity had been cleansed and renewed several times. He would be able to access the White House easily. He would be able to accomplish his mission without further complications.

But nagging fears were starting to follow him. Well, fears will follow any man all the way to the grave, he told himself. It was only the glory of the next life that mattered, was it not? A paradise in God's kingdom, purged of all infidels and non-believers.

Now he enjoyed a lunch of Nashville barbecue at Rippy's at Fourth Avenue and Broadway. He sat alone and admired the wall of country music legends. An eerie wave of nostalgia overtook him as he gazed at black-and-white photos of Ernest Tubb recording. Hank Williams in a white suit, scarf, and Texas-style white hat. Cowboy Copas. Patsy Cline.

What a great world that had been, speaking of black and white. One time, when the blond man had been a small boy in rural Texas, his grandfather had gone on a rant about the "decline of America."

Granddaddy, over chicken, biscuits, and pitchers of iced tea at a Sunday picnic, had gone on and on that the decline began when "Presley started singing nigger music. Nothing ain't been the same since."

Well, the old man had known a thing or two. Blame it on Elvis. Blame it on Franklin D. Rosenfeld and Dwight Star of David Eisenhower, who were beholden to the Elders of Zion. Later on, blame it on the Holy Roman Kennedys and the Internationalists on the Trilateral Commission.

No one ever asked exactly what "it" was but there were plenty of American traitors to blame "it" on.

He glanced around. His waitress today was a cute teenager in jeans and a trim T-shirt. But she was Asian of some sort. A mud person. Maybe Vietnamese or Cambodian or Korean or something.

Lord Almighty! Even the American South was being polluted with an ethnic mix. The coming inevitable race war would be a wonderful thing, he reasoned. Hopefully, murdering the president would be a small but significant part in fanning the flames of the coming conflagration.

After lunch, he walked up Fifth Avenue and found himself standing next to the old temple that had long ago been converted into the Ryman Auditorium. The Grand Ole Opry.

Rambling thoughts on the modern world: If Jesus and Paul and some of the prophets were living today, he reasoned, they would be put on Ritalin or tranquilizers.

"It's a good thing those drugs weren't available in those days," he thought. "We wouldn't have a Bible. 'Paul, go take your Ativan. Settle down. Don't talk like that and don't write those things.' "

The blond man sat down on a bench across from the Ryman. He looked to the sky. He wondered if God would bring him straight up to Heaven right there.

Apparently, God was busy with something else.

The blond man started to speak aloud.

"Jesus, you must be a schizophrenic, saying you came down from heaven and that you're God. We know who you are. We know you are Jesus. Let's keep things predictable! We want to come here, go through the ritual, and go home. Here you are, saying things that are not consistent with what we have been taught in the past."

A police car passed him. Uh oh.

The blond man waved to the sector car. "Praise Jesus," he said aloud. He made the sign of the cross to the police car.

A Nashville cop nodded and kept going.

Back to reality.

There was a job to do in Washington. Time to move along. If he could kill the Chapman woman on his way to murder the president, so much the better.

She deserved it. Women shouldn't be working in presidential protection, anyway.

chapter 99

WORLD WAR II MEMORIAL
JUNE 29, 2009; 5:34 P.M.

Deep gray thunder clouds rolled into Washington from western Maryland in the late afternoon, turning the city into a barometric pressure cooker. The clouds were low, dark, and eerie. The statue of Freedom on the dome of the Capitol disappeared into a black haze. A midsummer storm was imminent. The only questions: How soon and how violent?

The first lightning flashed at a few minutes past six while Laura was still in her office. Rolling thunderclaps resounded thereafter, one following another, relentless to the point of almost being unearthly. A steady rain followed. It gathered intensity and was followed by a cloudburst to end all cloudbursts, drenching the back end of rush hour traffic.

Drivers pulled to the side of the road to wait it out. Government workers on overtime stopped what they were doing and went to windows to marvel. A few tourists who were crazy enough jumped into the tidal basin fountains and danced.

The storm brought the angriest weather in recent memory. Lightning hit the Washington Monument and the spire of the National Cathedral. No damage followed either hit, both edifices had long ago been properly wired. At the Lincoln Memorial, a combination of wind and lightning shattered and uprooted a stand of cherry trees.

The core impact of the storm lasted less than half an hour. Then slowly the rain withdrew and the clouds overhead passed down the Potomac to the ocean.

The temperature plummeted: one hundred one degrees to seventy-one. There was a bit of breezy steaminess but still some daylight as Laura emerged from the Longworth Building for her meeting with William Vasquez, and enough stray raindrops for her to carry an umbrella.

Laura arrived first. She took a seat on the same granite bench where six days ago she had met Mitchell Hamilton. Her eyes drifted thoughtfully out over the Rainbow Pool.

She looked again at the low wall separating the memorial from the reflecting pool that led to the Lincoln Memorial in the distance. The wall was covered in gold stars, representing people who had been a long time dead. But as she looked at them, Laura wondered—as she increasingly had recently—about life and death and how long she herself would live, and about what sacrifice meant, and whether it was worth anything in the end.

The humidity assaulted her. She would have removed her jacket, but didn't wish to advertise her weapon. So she silently suffered. A few moments later, she cast her eyes to Eighteenth Street. A black government Humvee arrived. Director William Vasquez stepped out of the vehicle. He approached her, walking down the steps that led to the center of the monument.

Vasquez was in a white shirt and tie. In Washington male government employees and K Street lobbyists were the only people left who wore suits and ties.

Arriving next to her, he looked at her bandaged forehead. "Too much time in the gym?"

"*Not enough* time in an alley in Dallas," she replied. "That's what I'm here to talk about."

"If I remember properly, Laura," he said, sitting. "*Vous parlez français.*"

"Fluent," she answered, surprised. "*Couramment, comme vous devez vous en souvenir.*"

"*Parlons français,*" he said, switching into French. "*On ne sais jamais qui écoute.*"

"*D'accord,*" she said. "*Je comprends.*"

"What have you got, Laura? *Allez-y. Parlez.*"

"It's no rumor: There's going to be an attempt on the president's life within the next week," she began in French. "It will take place within the White House, maybe on the morning of July Fourth. The access codes in the White House are not secure. They haven't been for years."

"*Expliquez, s'il vous plaît,*" he answered.

"There are several cells of right-wing activists, financed by William Casey's old networks, who have been funded for twenty-five years. There's a file in the safe of the director of Central Intelligence attesting to this. Or I think there is. We need to access it."

"I've heard stories like that, too. Haven't seen one proven yet. Can you prove yours?"

"Prove, no. Make a credible case, yes."

"You want me to go to the DCI and insist there's a file there that he won't let me see?"

"Yes."

"Who's going to do the shooting?"

"I don't know. If we can learn more about these cells, it might help us."

"Originally you were focused on this Wilder fellow. Still looking for him?"

"Yes," Laura said, "but I was never convinced on Wilder. He was my only suspect."

"Who's your suspect now?"

Still in French: "*Un homme blond.* I caught a glimpse in Dallas yesterday, but not a good look. He may be Wilder and he might not."

"You were in Dallas yesterday?"

"Yes. With Rick McCarron. CIA, Miami."

"Did Rick see your blond suspect?"

"Not enough to recognize him."

"But *you'd* recognize him?"

"I don't know."

"Tell me what happened in Dallas," Vasquez said.

She did, continuing in French. Even to Laura, the story sounded particularly absurd, even more so as she recounted it *en français*.

Vasquez rolled his sleeves and loosened his necktie. "*Hablamos español*," he said, switching languages quickly to scramble any listeners.

"*Si le gusta.* I can also link this to a Miami mob guy named Victor Rivera," Laura said.

"Who?"

She explained.

"Where's Rivera now?" Vasquez asked.

"Probably dead."

"Convenient. And I suppose your blond phantom killed him, too?"

"I don't know. Maybe." She explained several minutes more, getting nowhere.

Vasquez leaned back. "You expect me to go to the DCI and ask to look in his safe over your gut feelings?"

"It would be good if you could."

"Well, I can't do that."

"Can't or won't?"

He glared at her. *"Los dos,"* he said. Both.

"What's lateralism about? Do agencies share information these days or not?"

"Lateralism has its limits," Vasquez answered. "What's your killer's motivation? Money? Glory? Give me something I can latch onto, Laura. Is your spook sane or wacko?"

"I don't know."

"And he's going to act alone?"

"I'm not sure."

"How does he plan to escape?"

"He might not plan to escape."

"And he's one of *our* people? He's American?"

"I think so."

"And again, you have no proof." He gave her a long final dismissive look. "Look, Laura. What goes on here? How does a foreign government get to a member of the Secret Service?"

"Maybe they walked up to him and showed a big bag of money," said Laura, her anger building to outright intemperance. "How else?"

"How did they know who to approach?" Vasquez said.

"Intelligence work, same as we do. Most of the time, ours is better than theirs. This time it might not have been. Maybe they found the one person in our whole service disaffected enough to do something like this."

"No sale," Vasquez said. "I still don't buy it."

"Consider also the unthinkable," she suggested. "Maybe one of *our* disgruntled employees approached *them*."

"Every one of our agents has been vetted since the day of birth."

"Sure. And among them, are you telling me that there is *not one* who could potentially be disgruntled? *Not one* who might have turned against the Service? Someone took five million dollars in the bank transfer, and everything Anna Muang said works into this picture."

Vasquez was silent. Then, still in Spanish, "You have another minute to convince me."

Laura went for broke. "Look," she said. "What we're

facing is not far-fetched. In 1998, the head of the Swiss guards at the Vatican was murdered by one of his own soldiers. The same man could have killed the pope. The killer had access. Anwar Sadat was murdered by his own soldiers, so was Indira Gandhi, so was Rajiv Gandhi. Charles de Gaulle spent most of his latter years ducking bullets from former officers of his own army. We're both educated. Do I need to remind you about Julius Caesar? We were both raised as Christians. Need I remind you about Jesus?"

Laura's voice was unemotional, flat, and final. She continued.

"The enemy within the Service," she said, "is the most dangerous of all assassins. He reduces all our security systems to absolute impotence since the threat is from *within* rather than without. Add into the equation the fact that our suspect is not only a traitor and a skilled gunman but also thoroughly versed in our own security systems and seems to have a way of beating them. An assassination threat to the president from *within* the Secret Service is the single most dangerous concept I could imagine."

She paused and watched his expression, which was unyielding.

"Without heroic, elaborate, and unprecedented efforts on our part, I—if I were a betting woman, which I'm not—would give this killer an excellent chance of succeeding."

For a moment, the words hung in the memorial like extra black crepe.

"For the sake of discussion," Vasquez said, "hypothetically, what do you suggest?"

"This inquiry has to take two paths," Laura said. "Prevention and detection. First, we need to secure the president even within our own lapsed security system. Something beyond previous penetration. My suggestion, in addition to what I've already stated," she said as she looked toward Vasquez, "is to change the entire forthcoming assignment of White House guards."

"They're being changed July 1, anyway. Wednesday."

"Change them again. Pull in agents from remote bureaus

like Kansas and Nevada and the Dakotas who never expected to be at the White House. At least temporarily."

"Impractical," Vasquez scoffed. "Shake up the White House security detail, we show our hand. It would alert the opposition, if there is one, that we're on to something."

"Which might accomplish prevention," Laura argued.

"Or," said Vasquez, "it pushes the assassin to act immediately."

"I don't think he's close enough yet to strike," she said. "But if we wait, he will be. My guess is he's on the way to Washington right now."

She paused. Vasquez grimaced.

"The agents being rotated in: Were any in Texas in the last few days?"

"I'd have to check. Why?"

Laura again mentioned the incident in the alley. If the blond man there had been her suspect, no point to rotate him into the PPD.

"That much I will check," Vasquez conceded. "I'll have my office advise you."

"Good. You will also need to tell the president that the Secret Service's security has been penetrated," Laura said. "Then, after the president hits the roof, pull in our best defenses as tightly as possible until we find the traitor. Somewhere we missed something. Additionally, the president should not travel or appear in public."

"This president will never buy that. He won't hide in the White House the way Richard Nixon used to, pumped up on Thorazine. What else?" Vasquez asked.

"We could also have the president and his family move to Camp David immediately," Laura said. "Until the threat has passed."

Vasquez thought for a moment. Then he switched back into English and shook his head. "White House security is impenetrable," he said. "And there have been stories for years about cells organized by William Casey. I can't rip apart the present security without more."

He stood.

She began again. "But if—?"

"That's all the time I have for this, Laura. I'm sorry. Stay with it through the holiday. We'll see what we can do for you thereafter. Thank you. You did the best you could do."

He turned to walk back toward his Humvee. Laura followed and, completely out of order, grabbed him, wet hand on the wet wrist, and stopped him.

"I'm not nuts," she said in Spanish, face to face. "Someone's out there. Someone's going to walk into the White House undetected and shoot the president!"

Eye to eye. "Of course, Laura," he answered, in a quiet distant way. "Of course. So if you see him, you shoot him first, okay?"

"May I quote you?"

"Of course not."

Vasquez walked back to his Humvee.

He gave Laura a look before he entered. Their meeting was over. Again, more than ever, she wondered if her career was also.

PART FOUR

chapter 100

For the past three days, Alan Savett had spent his life in limbo. He was unable to sleep, but rose late. He padded around his apartment in his dressing gown, dusting things, cooking food that he didn't eat, giving attention to small details in his home that were meaningless.

When the telephone rang, he went to it quickly, only to be disappointed. His life was in a stall. Langley, Virginia, had not responded to him and he did not know why.

Four guards from the National Police were posted at the only door of his apartment, two inside and two outside. When Savett spoke to them, he gained the impression that they had been instructed not to fraternize. He was unable to initiate any conversation, or even lure them into a game of cards. The soldiers tended to look at him as a lunatic, or worse, a condemned man.

For many idle hours, Savett studied the view from his bedroom window. The bedroom and bathroom offered him some privacy, but his captors had removed the doors to both, so both rooms were compromised. When he watched the street, he saw few passersby, and usually the same ones, neighbors who lived nearby. There was no vehicle traffic. Obviously, the police had sealed off this section of street and had prohibited anyone from the outside from traveling upon it.

His observations about his own block ruled out any escape from the bedroom window. If he jumped—and he worked the scenario in his head a few times before he abandoned it as futile—he would surely break a leg, an ankle, or a wrist. He would be apprehended within a few meters. So there was nothing to gain, other than pain, injury, a possibly severe punishment.

On the second morning of house arrest, the major had reconnected him with the Internet. Savett was allowed to send out another urgent plea to Langley for some sort of response. Savett had no idea what was delaying Washington. He cursed the day that he had ever decided to work with them. If he were ever lucky enough to escape this current predicament, he swore to himself, he would get back to England and extricate himself from this messy business of espionage.

He didn't have the stomach for it anymore. He wondered how anyone did.

But where was the response that he was waiting for? Normally, messages of urgency were turned around within six hours by the Central Intelligence Agency. What was happening in Langley? What was wrong? For that matter, what was happening in Tripoli?

Never had he felt this isolated.

On Monday morning, the policemen gave Savett Internet access again. Again he checked for a response from America. And again he was disappointed.

Toward 10 A.M., he heard footsteps on the stairs beyond his entryway. His guards came quickly alert. There were agitated voices in Arabic beyond his front door. Then the door flew open and Major Housahodi appeared again. The policemen within the apartment bolted to attention immediately. Savett appeared at his bedroom doorway and greeted the major.

"Mr. Savett," the major began, "have we received a response yet from the Americans?"

"I'm sorry, sir. We have not."

"And why not?"

"I have no idea, sir."

"Who is Chiron, Mr. Savett?"

"I am, sir."

"Then why do they not respond to you?"

"I cannot explain that, Major."

The major looked troubled. He must have given some

faint signal that Savett did not detect, because his policemen quickly followed a command. They came to the journalist and marched him forward, one policeman on each arm.

"Time is very short, sir," the major continued. "The National Police must make their move at a specific time. We must have U.S. support. Why is your message not getting through?"

Savett began, "I . . ." But he did not finish.

"I sincerely hope," Major Housahodi continued, "that you do not mistake my education and sense of culture as softness," he said. "That would be a tremendous error to have made."

The policemen held Savett's arms tighter now. Savett's heart raced in his chest. Major Housahodi drew his sidearm and pointed its nose downward against Savett's left kneecap.

"I see you as a man of tremendous conviction, Major," Savett answered. "I would not mistake your character."

"If you have told me lies," continued the major, "you will wish that you had been executed in the desert. Such will be your misfortune here. Do you understand me?"

"Perfectly. Sir," said Savett.

The nose of the pistol pressed firmly against the kneecap. The men were eye to eye from less than a foot away.

"I hope so," said the major.

He moved his pistol backward a few inches. Then he flicked it hard upward, catching Savett—still throbbing from the squeeze in the van two days earlier—directly across the gonads.

Savett bellowed and lurched forward. His captors let him fall. He hit the ground hard, wanting to throw up, surrounded by the shoes of his tormentors.

"Your Internet is reconnected for the next thirty minutes," said the major. "Send one final message. Make sure this one is successful. Allah have mercy on you if it is not."

In agony, Savett climbed to his feet, the lower part of his body feeling as if it were set to explode. He stumbled back to his workstation as the major followed, and slid into a chair, gasping for breath.

chapter 101

Four hours of fitful sleep, then a phone rang like a fire alarm in the middle of the night.

Laura tumbled out of a dream, back into on-duty reality.

The phone. That damned phone.

Outside, darkness. In her room, darkness.

Groggily, she mumbled, "What the—?"

A quick glance at the clock radio. Ouch. Four hours eighteen minutes into the new day. No one ever called at this hour with anything good.

She reached for the phone. She answered.

Vasquez's voice, as if she hadn't recently had enough of it. "You awake?" he asked.

Laura, coming to: "I am now."

"We got him," Vasquez said.

Sitting upright in bed: *"What?"*

"We've got an incoming flight to Kennedy in New York," he said. "American 956, arrival 7:03 A.M. Jeremy Wilder is on the flight list. We're going to detain him on arrival."

"All right. All right. Good," said Laura. "Where's the flight coming from?" she asked.

"Buenos Aires," Vasquez said.

A couple of seconds as her mind untangled, weighing travel time from Texas to Argentina back to New York. "What?" she asked.

"Jeremy Wilder flew out of Buenos Aires last night," Vasquez said. "It's a non-stop. When it lands we take him into custody."

Two more beats, then, "How do you know it's the same Jeremy Wilder?"

"Passport number. Airport retina scans. Boarding surveillance photography in Buenos Aires. It all checks."

"Great. But it doesn't make much sense."

"It doesn't have to. I'm going to New York. Terminal Five security area. Meet me there if you're still working this case."

She put the phone down, shook the lingering cobwebs from her head, "Christ," she muttered.

If you're still working this case? Who the hell was he kidding?

On her feet, she started moving.

Living room. Kitchen. She threw off her night clothes.

Naked, she flicked on the kitchen coffee maker.

She showered and dressed, grabbed her Secret Service ID and weapon.

She came back to the kitchen, poured coffee, mixed in some milk, grabbed a pastry from the freezer, and took breakfast with her.

She headed for National Airport, arriving in time for the 5:50 A.M. flight to New York.

chapter 102

JOHN F. KENNEDY INTERNATIONAL AIRPORT, NEW YORK
JUNE 30, 2009; 7:16 A.M.

At the airport Laura used her Secret Service ID to go to the police holding pen in Terminal Five. Security was maxed; she was delayed another ten minutes as New York City police checked her federal credentials. Then, passing two more internal security checkpoints, a female FBI agent named Martha Henderson finally ushered her toward Interrogation Room 7.

"Your timing's good," Special Agent Henderson said. "The suspect was taken into custody less than fifteen minutes ago."

Outside of the door to Room 7, across the hall, sat a

strikingly pretty Latino woman, very light brown skin and a delicate face. The woman wore a short blue summer dress and matching designer espadrilles with lace-up straps. Two security men flanked her. She sat with a purse on her lap, her legs crossed. She clutched a pack of Marlboros. She spoke angrily in Spanish with one of the security men.

Laura tuned in. She was complaining about a friend being detained.

On the woman's hand, a ring with expensive sparkle. Laura processed: The stone must have been two carats. The woman looked as if she were awaiting the outcome of the Room 7 interview.

Laura entered. She closed the door quietly behind her.

The room was small, cramped, and overheated. Faded green walls the color of rotting celery. The room's centerpiece was a gray steel table, bolted to the floor.

There were five men present, four sitting, one standing.

Jeremy Wilder was one of them.

Two FBI agents and the director of the Secret Service, William Vasquez, sat at the table. Their focus was Wilder, a handsome blond man. They had him surrounded. Laura was jolted: She stared at the man whose photograph had been her companion for these last few days.

Laura looked at him hard, thought back to Dallas, ran through everything in her head, and thought of poor Anna hanging in a closet bleeding to death. She oozed hatred for the man who had done that to Anna and right here felt a sick sinking feeling in her gut.

She thought it, but didn't say it: *Dead end!*

Wilder was at the end of the table. His hands were in his lap, cuffed. He looked tired from a long flight and more than routinely agitated.

Vasquez sat across from Wilder. The FBI men sat at the table, one very close to Jeremy Wilder in case he made a move. The fourth man was Secret Service, Laura could tell by the lapel pin. She did not know him and figured he had accompanied the director from Washington. But he could have come out of the New York office.

He looked more New York than D.C. Not that it mattered.

Laura stood by the door and let her attention descend on the scene before her. She folded her arms and tuned further in to the conversation. Wilder, with considerable irritation, was indignantly recounting his movements over the last month.

"How long have you been in Argentina?" one of the Feds asked.

"Since June eighth. Check my passport."

"Why did you make a trip to Havana first?"

"Who says I did?"

No one answered, so Wilder provided his own response.

"I connected to Buenos Aires from Havana the day after arrival," he said.

"But why *Havana?*" asked Vasquez.

"It's a nice city again and it's legal," Wilder answered churlishly. "You should burn a weekend there sometime." He waited and further offered, "That's also the route my employer paid for. Harder to be followed, understand? Everything was in keeping with U.S. laws."

"You made a side excursion within Mexico for a day, also," Vasquez said. "Ixtapa. Pacific coast. What was that all about?"

"I never set foot in Ixtapa. I was twelve miles south in Zihuatanejo."

"What for?"

Wilder looked especially peeved. "I have a friend who sings blues. She was performing at a couple of clubs. Rick's Bar and the Blue Mamou."

One of the Feds was making detailed notes. Fat chance of any of that being confirmed, Laura thought. "Is that something you wouldn't want us to mention to that Latino broad outside?" the other one asked.

Wilder held his tongue. "What are you guys fishing for?" he finally asked. As he spoke, his gaze traveled the room. It settled on Laura. Then, failing any recognition, his gaze moved back to his tormentors at the steel table. "Why don't you ask me the direct questions so I can set you straight?" he asked.

"Where were you five days ago? The twenty-fifth?" asked Vasquez, as Laura watched.

"At my office."

"On Long Island?" asked one of the FBI men.

"In Rio Gallegos, for Christ's sake!" Wilder snapped, raising his voice and turning toward him. "You think I commute seven thousand miles back and forth?"

"Is Rio Gallegos the same as Rio de Janeiro?" one of the Feds asked.

"Rio de Janeiro is a different city and it's in Brazil, okay?" Wilder asked. "How dumb is the FBI hiring these days? Never mind. Ignore my question. I think I know."

"An attitude isn't going to help, Jeremy," Vasquez said quietly. "We have important things to clear up."

"Damned right," Wilder said. "You've got a lot of explaining to do for this. All of you," he insisted, looking the director, his former boss, squarely in the eye.

But predictably, it was Jeremy Wilder who ended up doing the explaining.

He worked in industrial security, he said, for Yacimientos Petrolíferos del Sur, a private Argentinean oil-producing consortium based in Patagonia. YPS had hired him two months earlier to head their private police force. His assignment was to reestablish and maintain a secure perimeter around certain holdings of the company in the Austral Basin. There were narco-guerillas in Argentina, *peligrosos* ones, just like in all other countries in South America.

Wilder's additional mission was to ensure a continuous disincentive to bandits who might sabotage the oil drilling conglomerate. Argentina being Argentina, no inconvenient questions were asked by local authorities about the methods Wilder used. Wilder was, from his own account, running his own private militia, enjoying it, and doing a pretty good job at it.

"Interesting," Director Vasquez said. "Why are you back so soon?"

"To pick up my fiancée."

"What do they pay you for this?"

"None of your goddamned business," Wilder answered. "But annually? Think of what you make, then multiply it by three. Maybe four. How's that?"

"Normally former Secret Service employees register their new assignments with Washington," one of the Feds pressed. "Why didn't you do that?"

"I'm not legally obligated."

"Maybe not," Vasquez said, "but there's protocol."

"Sure, there's protocol. And there's damned well the issue of my personal safety, too," Wilder complained. "If I had any faith in your agency's ability to maintain secure personal records *maybe* I *might have* shared the news of my new employment."

Vasquez asked, "You didn't come into five million dollars recently, did you?"

Wilder's indignation rebuilt. "Would I be sitting here with you dimwits if I had?"

"Who's the woman who's waiting for you?" the other Fed asked.

"That's my fiancée, damn it! And what have you done with her?"

Immediately, Laura realized that he was speaking of the woman in the next room, accompanied by two agents.

"Fancy jewelry," said the first Fed.

"Maybe someday you'll be able to afford something nice yourself," Wilder said. He was seething. To Laura's mind they had run this interview all wrong. Even if there were anything to get out of Wilder, they wouldn't get it now. "Both a woman and a ring," Wilder said.

"She doesn't have identification and she says you're a business contact," one of the Feds tried. "We're probably going to arrest her."

Wilder wasn't buying it. "Bullshit!" he shouted. "Bull-*shit!*"

Laura now saw that not only were the hands manacled under the table, but one of the wrists was cuffed to the table leg, which was bolted to the floor.

"We'll be checking everything," said one of the FBI men.

"See that you do. And do it accurately for a change," Wilder shot back.

"What's your fiancée's name?"

After an unsettled pause, "Rosalinda."

"Puerto Rican? Mexican?"

With a sneer: "American. Same as yourself. You people *are* morons, aren't you?"

Laura studied the floor. It was dirty.

"Does she have a last name?" The agent waited with a pad and pen.

"No. I don't think so. Fact is, I never asked."

"This is a bad attitude to take, Jeremy," Vasquez said, leaning back. "We can hold you indefinitely if we wish, and that woman outside, also. You're just prolonging things."

Wilder responded with a furious look but held his tongue. Vasquez looked up to Laura.

"Does this gentleman look familiar to you, Agent Chapman?" Vasquez asked.

"Only from his photograph," Laura said softly.

"*What* photograph?" Wilder asked. "Look! What the hell is this? I'm going to lawyer up in sixty seconds if I don't get some answers."

"Why don't *you* ask him a question, Laura?" Vasquez asked.

"I don't want to repeat territory you've already covered," she answered.

"Ask him one anyway."

She looked at Wilder. "*¿Cuándo estuvo usted en Tejas la última vez?*" she asked.

"*Estuve allí en 2004, durante la segunda campaña electoral del Presidente Bush.*"

"*¿Y no después?*" she pressed.

"*No. Si hubiera estado allí después, me acordaría perfectamente de eso, y no tengo tal recuerdo al más mínimo grado.*"

"*Gracias, Señor.*"

"*De nada, Señora Wonder Woman.* Now why don't you fly out of here on your invisible jet?"

The other agents looked lost because they were.

Laura turned to her boss. "Sir, could we speak outside?" Laura asked.

A moment's grudging reluctant thought. Then, quietly seething, "Of course, Laura."

Vasquez pushed back from the steel table and stood. "Keep taking his statement," he said to one of his assistants.

Laura opened the door. Vasquez followed her outside. An FBI agent began to drone on about the company Wilder worked for, asking for a spelling of the company's name.

To irritate further, Wilder started spelling in Spanish. The door closed.

Laura and Vasquez moved down the corridor away from Rosalinda in blue.

They stopped in a quiet stretch of corridor.

"That's not him," Laura said.

chapter 103

JOHN F. KENNEDY INTERNATIONAL AIRPORT, NEW YORK
JUNE 30, 2009; 7:53 A.M.

Down the hall, one of Rosalinda's guards had just noticed she had a cell phone and had taken it away. The other one was crudely going through her makeup case. As she sat before them, arms folded and indignant, she was no less angry than Jeremy Wilder in Room 7.

Vasquez stood, arms folded, no happier than either of the morning's two captives.

"It's Jeremy Wilder and he fits the profile," Vasquez said.

Laura said, "I'm sure he is, I'm sure he does, and you heard him as well as I did: He claims he hasn't been in Texas since the Bush campaign of '04."

Vasquez replied, "The computer spit him out. He was the only name you came up with."

"I know that."

"We have to vet every goddamned second of his life now for the last several years."

"I'm telling you straight off: He's not the man I ran into in Texas."

A pained silence. "You said you didn't get a perfect look."

"I got a good enough one to know that's not the man."

More aggrieved silence.

"So you're telling me we made this trip for nothing?" Vasquez asked.

"I would have made the trip myself," she said, "and you wouldn't have had to if you had flagged me that he was on that flight. And I told you when we met last that the *computer* focused on Wilder, not me. He was worth eliminating as a suspect, but he was never prime. And once again, I ran dead into that man in Texas; I'll know him when I see him again."

"Uh huh," Vasquez answered.

"And where did you get that Mexicana Airline information? I don't remember passing it along."

"You didn't."

"Did Rick?"

"No. We have other means."

"You have another investigation going?"

"Information is an expensive whore," he said. "It gets around faster than you'd think."

She didn't like the tone, much less the possible allusion.

"That's just great!" she said. Furious, she might have continued, but Vasquez spoke first.

"So this is Tuesday morning and it's still your conjecture that your phantom is going to try something this Saturday?"

"It is," Laura answered.

"And this is the wrong phantom? The one we got manacled to the table in there?"

"That's my feeling. Nor do I see how he could be in Texas and an oil drilling site in Patagonia at the same time."

The director prickled further. "We can't let Wilder go just because you say so."

"Vet him, vet his story and all, but I'd say he's completely clean."

"Then why did you come to New York?"

"Same reason you did. Just in case."

Vasquez made a pained expression. "This was the *one god-damned name* the computer gave us. And it's the one name you gave me."

"I'm aware of that."

"I don't know whether to promote you or demand your resignation."

Angering even more, she said, "Then flip a coin!"

"Excuse me?"

"I'm as tired and frustrated as you are, sir. Maybe more. In terms of whether to promote me or fire me, we'll both know by the weekend."

"I think I know already."

"I'll save you the trouble," she said. "If I don't have a suspect by the weekend, I'll resign as of Monday morning. Does that work?"

Vasquez gave her a long hard look. "Perfectly," he answered.

There was a frigid pause. Finally, "Do you want to talk to Wilder again, yourself?" Vasquez asked. "It will be your final chance."

"No. It's a waste of time. Let the FBI people interrogate him. I'd prefer to go back to Washington."

"Have a good trip," the director said.

He turned and walked back toward Room 7, outside of which Rosalinda was barefoot with tears on her cheeks.

Her two mulish guards were now running a handheld metal detector over her espadrilles.

chapter 104

The blond man, freshly arrived in Washington, eased his car into a temporary parking place in front of the Mayflower Hotel on lower Connecticut Avenue, just up from K Street. He was now six short blocks from the White House. He stepped out and asked the valet to park the car for him in the hotel garage. Then he strode into the crowded, ornate lobby.

The Mayflower had been built as a luxury hotel back in the 1920s. It offered a welcome contrast with the character-less egg-crate office buildings that had sprung up around it since the 1960s. Its lobby was a riot of marble and brass, but without any of the vulgarity that accompanied attempts by today's architects to use a "rich" style for hotels. Off of the lobby was the wood-paneled bar famous for being the place where the corrupt gay basher J. Edgar Hoover came every day for lunch with his deputy and—in more ways than one—"bosom buddy" Clyde Tolson.

Why not the best? the blond man thought with a smile.

After all, he was here on business: nothing short of God's business at that, but why not the best? It was like that girl at that strip joint he had picked up in Texas: She was the classiest one there, if a devout man could talk about class concerning someone in her trade.

Of course, he had had to kill her. Hopefully, he wouldn't have to blow up the hotel, or kill anyone in it, though he wouldn't hesitate to do so if that was what was required to carry out God's orders to him, those orders that he heard so insistently, as if God were actually standing next to him.

For all its '20s elegance the Mayflower had fully modern computers at its front desk. Not that they caused a problem.

He produced another one-hit-wonder credit card that stole an authorization amount from another active account. The computer accepted it without question.

He was given a room on the top floor. He went up in the elevator by himself, instinctively scanning to see if the elevator had a security camera. He couldn't find one.

He opened the door to his room. He was pleased with it. The room was comfortable to the point of being luxurious.

While waiting for a porter to bring him his bags he went to the window. The Mayflower had air conditioning, but the remodeled windows still opened. He shoved up a sash and leaned out, looking down Connecticut Avenue and across K Street—the street of sinful lobbyists and lawyers who were part of the whole system that was so hateful to God— in the direction of the White House.

It comforted him to know that he had come this far and was now this close. He smiled and savored the view for several minutes, until he heard a knock on the door.

It was the porter with his bags. He gave a generous tip, and then when he was alone again he opened them. He unpacked his weapon and placed it in a holster on his hip. He examined the Secret Service identification that he had not touched in weeks.

Then, still savoring his mission and how close he had come so far to successfully completing it, he knelt to the floor to spend some time in meditation and prayer.

He spoke to his God again and was more certain than ever that he was embarked on a mission that could not fail and equally could not be anything except the holiest.

chapter 105

The president was increasingly angry as he read the CIA document in front of him.

He had already decided on a course of action against the Libyans, and now the policy wonks over at Langley were complicating things.

He read the report with great displeasure. If there were a coup brewing in Tripoli, why was this the first he had heard of it? If Col. Gerald Straightorn had survived the crash of his Warhawk, who in hell had they buried in the desert?

And what was this nonsense about a spy with a code name of Chiron?

This was the real world, the president scoffed. Not something out of Tom Clancy.

He finished the report and then, with growing cynicism, read it a second time. The president was sure the Libyans had "fed" this information to U.S. intelligence. Their motives were, to the president, even more transparent a second time through. Everyone on the planet knew he was about to hit the Libyans good and hard, courtesy of the United States Air Force. What was the point of letting them get ready? Give them another few days to plan and prepare and the United States would lose more personnel and aircraft than with a quick strike.

What was happening on the ground over there, he asked himself. The bigshots in the government: the ones who had participated in the shoot-down of the American jet? Were they scrambling to fortify their personal bunkers as Qaddafi had in 1986? Or were they heading for some remote oases outside of town?

He would keep that thought in mind.

And why, the president wondered further, should he give any credibility to a contrarian CIA report anyway? He knew some good people who worked over at the Agency, but, by God, their analysts hadn't just muffed most of the big events of the last decades. In most cases, they had gotten their research exactly bass-ackward.

The Shah can hang on indefinitely.

The Soviet Union is in no danger of collapse.

The Iraqis have weapons of mass destruction and ties to al Qaeda.

The Chinese have no intentions of grabbing Taiwan, Quemoy, and Matsu.

The president reached for the fountain pen at the far center of his desk. He angrily wrote a note across the top of the report. Big bold assertive handwriting:

Get me something to substantiate this "Chiron" bullshit within twenty-four hours, or as far as I'm concerned, it doesn't exist!

He called in his secretary, Mary Corliss.

"Put this in a sealed envelope and have someone from the Secret Service drive it over to Langley," the president said. "It goes directly to the DCI."

"You mean a White House courier, sir?" she asked.

"No. Secret Service. Let them do something useful for a change other than keeping me locked up here."

"Certainly, sir," Mary Corliss answered.

She took the envelope from the Oval Office, made a call, and sent the president's instructions on their way.

On the flight back to Washington, Laura had slept. She retrieved her car at National Airport and returned to her office. Once again, she reexamined what she knew and didn't know.

She phoned the police in Dallas. They had retrieved parts of Anna's phone from the Dallas sewer system and the plastic film from the encryption card from the abandoned Nissan. But no fingerprints on the car matched anything of significance. And as for the murder of Tiffany, it was one of those things that happened to girls in her line of work, the police said. There were no surveillance tapes at Diamond Lil's and no leads beyond what Laura and Rick had given them.

She had asked for someone from the FBI to go over and do a DNA inquiry on the car, but so far the Dallas police hadn't released the car to the FBI. Anna's telephone was already at the Secret Service's Forensics Services for a DNA examination. But nothing was yet forthcoming.

A call to Sgt. Foster in Miami turned up no leads there. Laura gave Foster the information that she had on the homicide in Dallas and suggested a link. Foster listened with interest. Laura recommended a ballistics evaluation of the shots fired in Anna's home that killed her dog with the weapon used in Dallas on Carol Susan Mackowiack, a.k.a. Tiffany.

Laura knew she was grasping at straws. What else was there to do?

Her eyes drifted to the calendar. The time remaining between the present and the Fourth of July would soon be measured in hours, not days. So much for eleven days in purgatory.

She picked up the phone again.

A call to Rick in Miami gave Laura the opportunity not only to bring McCarron current on the detainment of Jeremy Wilder in New York, but also Wilder's elimination as a suspect. The call had further elicited a good conversation and much sympathy, but nothing that helped.

Rick offered to come to D.C. if and when he was needed there.

"I'll put the offer on hold," she said.

"It's not if, it's when," he said. "I know how these things play out."

"Are you always right?" she asked.

"No, but I usually think I am," he said.

She felt like pursuing his remark on a personal level, but didn't. Instead, "Welcome to the club," she said.

She set down the phone, reassured that she had one firm ally. She spent the rest of the workday relentlessly poring over information she had already gathered, hoping, as time began to run down on her investigation, that she could nail one small lie, one small warp in the logic of what was before her. She wanted some tiny something that might expand into a key that would unlock the rest of the mystery before her.

Over and over, she re-considered what she knew about Sam, what she knew about William Casey's operations from the 1980s, and what she could learn anew. She requested a set of new files from Rick in Miami, who fed her fresh but sketchy information on Casey operations in secure attachments from Agency records. And she wasn't so foolish as to think that the files had been closely annotated for future generations of readers.

Rick phoned back late in the afternoon. More banking records from the Caymans. An Agency financial encryption specialist thought he had untangled a pair of transfers that could have been related to the original $5,000,000 transfer. A million dollars had been forwarded to something called The Army of God in Switzerland. Another 1.4 million had gone to the Soldiers of the Almighty in the Philippines.

"But who the *hell* are all *those* people?" Laura demanded.

"Sounds like religious crazies of some sort."

"Obviously. Christian? Islamic?"

"We're working on that angle but it could take weeks," Rick said. "And I hasten to add that the link is speculative. We're analyzing large transfers of money to sources we can't track. We don't even know if it's the same funds moving."

"Keep me updated," she said. "Thanks."

And so, still, in the larger picture, nothing coalesced.

Toward seven in the evening, as an air of final exasperation washed over her, William Vasquez phoned from New York.

The home offices of Yacimientos Petrolíferos del Sur in Buenos Aires had confirmed Jeremy Wilder in Argentina since June 8. The local YPS office in Río Gallegos had confirmed the same and had worked with him on a daily basis since then. They were looking forward to meeting Rosalinda, his fiancée, with whom they expected him to return.

Similarly, a cooperative Aerolíneas Argentinàs had that afternoon compared retina scans for Wilder on all legs of his trip and confirmed that the Wilder in New York and on their aircrafts matched the Wilder who owned the passport.

Accordingly, Wilder had been released by airport security in New York and eliminated as a suspect in the manhunt initiated by Anna Muang's story in Miami earlier that month.

The official inquiry, in other words, had caught up to what Laura had already known.

She was once again at square one, but now it was official. She leaned back at her desk.

The black dog was jumping all over her. Spiritually exhausted, she could see the writing on the wall in terms of her employment at the Secret Service. The remaining days were few.

All she could do now was get out on the street and try to make her own luck, try to keep her head unscrambled, try to find inspiration and truth where none was immediately forthcoming.

She reached to her purse and sifted through business cards she had recently collected. Then she found the one she wanted, one with a big oily thumbprint next to a local number.

All right. I'll give it a shot.

She found her cell phone and dialed the number.

A husky male voice answered and seemed to come up from the ground.

"Yes?" Loud rock music in the background. She hadn't heard Dexy's Midnight Runners for years and frankly, poor old Johnnie Ray notwithstanding, didn't need to now.

"This is Laura Chapman," Laura said pleasantly, "I believe you know me."

"You talk," said the man. Magically, the music went lower. *Come on, Eileen,* over and out.

"I'm going out tonight to have a bit of a look around town. I wouldn't mind having a couple of gentlemen watch my back. I wonder if that would be possible."

"What time?"

"Ten o'clock?"

A hand smothered the mouthpiece on the other end. She heard voices in a language she could never comprehend. Several seconds' worth.

"Good. You come, Miss Laura. You know where to meet, sure, yes?"

"Yes," she said. "Of course."

The voice on the other end clicked off. Laura clicked off in return.

She spent another hour in her office, going over useless files for a final time. Then she checked her weapon, made certain that it was loaded and ready, a bullet in the chamber. She reholstered it on her belt. She wondered if she would be as bad a shot next time—if there were a next time—as she had been in Dallas.

She changed into a snug pair of jeans and more comfortable shoes. She kept her jacket: easier to carry the weapon. She went out for a quick light dinner, then headed a few blocks away to her rendezvous.

chapter 107

Incredibly, Scott Thayer thought to himself, he had not yet been fired.

Well, maybe he was a more valuable employee than even he had thought. After all, they were entrusting him to enmesh their newly encoded steganographic message in a photograph of tourists in New York and send it back to this Chiron source in North Africa.

Thayer worked carefully at his desk. Part of him didn't want anyone to know that he had figured the codes out himself by tinkering with the computer in front of him. He knew damned well that the message going back was from a fairly high level in Washington, possibly even someone at the White House.

He had figured that much out because the coded message was a standard signal for a further clarification of his earlier message. He wrapped it, and nestled it into the usual array of pixels.

Chiron, wherever he was out there in cyberspace, would be an unhappy centaur when he received this baby. The coded signal would call upon him to clarify, confirm, and amplify his previous message.

Thayer saw this type of crap all the time.

If there was one thing that the higher-ups in the Agency did not like to receive it was a message that they did not wish to receive. If they didn't like the contents of a dispatch, they were always sending clarification requests back through the same channels.

"Yo-yo espionage" was how Thayer thought of it. He had a particularly low esteem for those who gave him the orders. But there wasn't a damned thing he could do or say about it.

He sealed the message and sent it.

He reported to his boss, Mr. Ken Kellerman, that the message was sent.

Kellerman seemed pleased, or at least not as churlish as usual.

"Do you have any plans for the next twenty-four hours?" Kellerman asked.

"Nothing specific," Thayer answered, "aside from what I do here."

"Use the cot in the blue room. Don't go home. Check for a response on this at least once every fifteen minutes and let me know when we receive one."

"I'm getting overtime for this, right?"

A grimace crossed Kellerman's face. "The deficit's at eight hundred fifty trillion and you're asking for seventy-one dollars an hour instead of your usual fifty-four. Is that it?"

"Pretty much. Why shouldn't I? I got to live, don't I?"

"Don't worry. You'll get it."

"You'll okay my time sheet if I sleep in?"

"If Uncle Sucker's gonna print the money, I'm gonna help spend it," Kellerman said.

Thayer smiled. Sometimes a guy could really land on his feet in this crazy place. He had screwed up big time and possibly endangered someone's life on the black arts end. Yet he was going to come out with some butt-kicking overtime on top of his normal salary. It even looked as if his original screw-up had already been lost in the shuffle, lessened by its comparison with more important things.

Perhaps the job didn't suck as badly as he thought. An international crisis was a terrible thing to waste, especially if one could sleep overnight at the office and score seventy-two bucks per slumbering hour.

chapter 108

Laura arrived at North Capitol Street in her Lexus at 10 P.M. precisely. Kalpurna was turning out the lights in the Exxon station. The pumps were already off.

Laura saw Vlad and Zarko sitting in a massive SUV, a new Chevrolet Goliath, to the far left of the parking area, adjacent to the air pump. Vlad spotted her immediately and held up a hand, palm out, indicating that Laura should wait.

She parked and cut her lights, but not the ignition. She kept the air conditioning purring. Kalpurna was locking up and setting the alarms. Obviously, the Serbs wanted the Indian woman to go home before any extracurricular activity took place. Laura was used to such machinations.

She sat quietly, her radio playing softly. The fingers of her left hand tapped her steering wheel. Inside, she was as jittery as a dozen spooked cats.

Kalpurna went home. Or somewhere.

Laura drove her car over to the Chevrolet, lights off. She stepped out and approached the car. They watched her like a pair of bull terriers.

Vlad was in the driver's seat. His window glided down. His eyes quickly ran up and down her figure. The Serbs were surprised to see her in jeans. Vlad was a letch. Zarko, given the chance, would probably be worse. They knew they had to stay to business tonight, however.

She went to the driver's side window and leaned up to it. Vlad wore a gray zippered sweatshirt over a mat of chest hair. Zarko wore a black T-shirt and had an oil-stained Budweiser beach blanket across his lap, his hands under it.

Vlad spoke: the rumbling up-from-Hades voice. "Hello, Miss Laura."

Behind him, Zarko gave a polite nod.

"Nice night, huh, guys?"

"Yes. Is," said Vlad. "Sure."

Zarko was already talked out. Temporarily.

A huge cluster of moths swarmed around an overhead sodium lamp. A few fluttered to earth and began a messy dance of death.

"I'm looking for a suspect," Laura said. "A blond man. I might recognize him if I see him, but, I mean, I'm not sure, okay? I'm going to places where he might turn up. I'm going to follow my instincts, maybe make some luck. I need my back covered. That make any sense?"

Vlad again: "Some."

"I'm guessing you fellas are up for it?"

Vlad, by way of answering, tugged down the zipper on his sweatshirt. Laura's eyes followed. His skin glistened with sweat. On his left rib cage, however, he wore a massive .45 semiautomatic, gleaming silver, positioned for a reverse draw.

"Sure," he said.

At the same time, Zarko lifted the beach blanket. There was a sawed-off shotgun across his lap. Zarko grinned. Top left: a missing incisor.

"Holy shit," mumbled Laura.

"Holy shit," nodded Vlad. The boys laughed.

Laura reached to a billfold in her blazer pocket. She withdrew six one-hundred-dollar bills. She passed them to Vlad. He picked off the top three and moved the others along.

"Will that keep you happy for a couple of hours?"

They said it would keep them very happy.

"You have your cell phones, right?" Laura asked.

"Got," said Vlad.

"You know my number?"

Vlad flipped open his phone and glanced down. "Got," he reiterated.

"Use your judgment," Laura said. "If I disappear for more

than a few minutes, call me or come get me. If I call and say I need help, come in ready for war. Follow?"

Vlad nodded, turned, and brought Zarko up to speed in Balkan.

Zarko smiled. "Got it," he said, too. He folded away his money.

"Let's go," Laura said.

She turned and went back to her car.

And so began a long night.

chapter 109

WASHINGTON, D.C.
JUNE 30, 2009; 10:26 P.M.

By car, Laura led the Serbs back to the Longworth Building. She ditched her car in a government lot, then set out by foot, carefully staying in view of the Chevrolet SUV that followed her.

She turned right along Independence Avenue, and then followed Pennsylvania Avenue toward the Capitol. The great white wedding-cake dome loomed in front of her. The light in the "lantern," the pimple-shaped protrusion above the dome on which the statue of Freedom stood, was turned on. Congress was in session.

Laura walked through the Capitol grounds, showing her ID to no fewer than three cops who stopped her. Anti-terrorism paranoia, ever accelerating, now completing its first full decade. It was because of her ID that she was able to get onto the terrace behind the Capitol, once a favorite spot for tourists, now barred to the general public.

The view remained superb: the floodlit Washington Monument in the distance, two red aircraft warning lights blinking in turn on the top. Pennsylvania Avenue, with the trademark clock tower of the Old Post Office, angled away to her right, while Constitution Avenue ran almost straight ahead.

And where is my blond assassin? she mused. *Where is the bastard who butchered Anna and nearly killed me in Dallas? Come on out of hiding, you son of a bitch! Give me one good shot. It's personal now. I promise to do better than I might do at the pistol range!*

She thought of her stash of maryjane back home. She wished she had brought a joint, felt like one in fact, but never would have done one in public.

What's slipping away faster? she wondered. *My remaining energy or my sanity?*

Laura headed down the steps on the slope of Capitol Hill, then walked past the reflecting pool, with its impressive bronze statue of General Grant on horseback.

Solid military man, rotten president, she thought.

Grant wore a heavy cape and looked tired and discouraged, as he must have often felt.

As Laura felt now, for that matter.

She wondered what Rick, her most recent lover, was doing this night. She wondered if he was with another woman.

With depression and frustration surging inside her, she continued on.

chapter 110

WASHINGTON, D.C.
JUNE 30, 2009; 11:22 P.M.

Across the city, less than a mile away, the blond man whom Laura sought was equally restless. He packed his weapon, dressed in a sports jacket and slacks, and went out. His final night on the town before the Almighty's work was to be completed.

His car crawled along K Street under the elevated Whitehurst Freeway, halting at the stop signs that barred its progress
at every intersection. He cursed the fact that there was no
Metro stop in Georgetown. Not that there couldn't have been,
the line ran under the Potomac a few hundred yards away.

But when the Metro was planned in the 1970s, the rich
residents of Georgetown had prevented construction of a station. The residents had alleged one spurious reason after another, but the real reason was that they had feared an influx of
tourists. Being well connected, they had gotten their way,
and the proposed station had been dropped. Then they had
gotten the tourists anyway.

He pulled his car up to Harbor Place and stepped out. He
eyed the surroundings: a curious development, with a hotel
and apartments and various shops and restaurants around a
sunken plaza with a big fountain. It bordered on the Potomac,
which curved in front of it. To his left, the Kennedy Center for
the Performing Arts. To his right were the arches of the Key
Bridge, named after Francis Scott Key, who had been a
Georgetown resident.

He walked along the promenade and then through the
park adjacent to Harbor Place to the intersection of K and
Wisconsin. Increasingly agitated, he glanced along K to
where the freeway disappeared, turning onto the Key
Bridge, and a mass of foliage could be seen: the Crescent
Trail, a favorite of joggers, as he recalled from his own
time in this city.

He strolled up Wisconsin Avenue, glancing down at the
C&O Canal as he crossed it.

At the intersection of Wisconsin and M, the blond man
headed into Nathan's for a Bloody Mary. It was a pleasant
place: pictures of America's Cup boats on the walls of the
barroom. He sat at the bar in full view of everyone and lingered over his drink, surrounded by young corrupted people
enjoying themselves.

He hated all of them. Would have liked to chain the doors
and torch the place.

Out of instinct, he glanced at his watch. He knew where

the sleazier sections of Washington were located, the strip
clubs and the flash parlors for which he had an abiding love-
hate relationship.

He would head over there and then call it a night.

It was 11:56 P.M. Almost July first.

chapter 111

WASHINGTON, D.C.
JULY 1, 2009; 12:17 A.M.

Georgetown's M Street was packed. Laura walked past The
Guards without any temptation to go in. It was just another
bar with more people enjoying life. Or maybe they weren't.
Who knew?

Laura crossed Rock Creek on M Street and walked in the
direction of downtown past a string of upper-middle-class hotels. As she approached Connecticut Avenue she arrived at the
pathetic remnant of Washington's "hot" district. Long ago, the
city had had numerous strip joints and porno stores in various
locations. But development had replaced almost all of them
with colorless office buildings, and zoning had prohibited the
opening of new establishments.

Here on M Street there were a handful of grandfathered
establishments hanging on. Richie C's Lounge. The Enchanted Zebra. Elle's. Ray and Ronny's Playpen.

She started with the first. Richie C's Lounge.

From the vehicle that passed behind her, Vlad and Zarko
gave her big smiles.

Richie C's Lounge was small, with tables jammed close
together, and a little stage on which a girl without any clothes
was gyrating in a rhythmical fashion.

The hostess did not seem surprised to see a woman enter,
and there were a few other women seated at tables, including some holding hands. Most of the customers were men.

Laura settled in to watch. The dancer's name was announced as Jeannette. She was a pretty girl with dark hair and a trim body. Laura judged she was about nineteen, with a deep uniform tan everywhere except across a lower area where a tiny bikini bottom had covered her during sunbathing, front and back.

Every few minutes one of the men in the audience would go up to the dancer and stick a dollar bill in a frilly red garter on her left leg, the only clothing she had on.

Despite the nakedness of the dancer the atmosphere was surprisingly respectable. The prices on the menu were reasonable.

Laura scanned the crowd. One blond man, but not *the* blond man.

Laura ordered an Amstel. She looked at the girl on stage and wondered if she was happy.

On impulse, Laura walked to the stage. She had to wait her turn behind a man—like all the customers, middle class—and then inserted a five-dollar bill in the garter as the girl stopped her gyrations long enough to accept the money. She gave Laura the same meaningless-sweet smile she did all the other donors, and said "thank you" in the same meaningless-sweet tone.

A final vain scan of the patrons and Laura walked back out onto the street and waited for a moment. Two men passing by brushed past her and she wondered if it had been intentional. She stepped away, her hand instinctively moving to her weapon.

The men continued on, not looking back, saying nothing.

Laura's gaze worked the street. She saw Vlad's car parked in a loading zone down the block. She gave him a slight nod. He responded with a quick single flash of his headlamps.

He had her in view.

She looked at the next establishments on the block. Three more.

Might as well check them all. This was the type of place her blond assassin might turn up. He had killed a woman from such a place in Dallas, he had spent time at a more upscale club in Miami. Presumably he had a taste for establishments of this kind. It depressed her that this was almost all she knew about him.

She gave another nod of her head to the next closest bar and gave Vlad and Zarko a quick show of three fingers, suggesting that she was going to check all three.

Vlad flashed his lights again. He understood, or at least thought he did.

She turned and entered the Enchanted Zebra. She spent ten minutes there, working the crowd, not spotting the shadow she kept searching for. Tiring, she used her Secret Service credentials to gain admission to the final two places, taking quick scans and looks around.

Still nothing.

She emerged, a sense of disconsolation descending on her now in addition to the fatigue.

She wondered what to do next. She decided to head to Union Station. Why not? It was a whim but something told her to go there. Some inner pulse.

She started walking, clicking on her cell phone as she proceeded.

She phoned her pursuit car and advised Vlad where she was going.

Then she rang off.

Exhausted, she walked down an increasingly deserted Connecticut Avenue.

She then turned left onto K Street at the same time that the feeling began to emerge within her that somewhere in the shadows, somewhere in a realm that she did not understand, a presence was again emerging and following her.

My own people. Or the opposition? she wondered.

This whole case was starting to acquire a certain geometry, returning as it was to where it began, with a certain professional paranoia and the notion of unexplained surveillance. At least this time, she reasoned further, her Serb brothers were watching her back.

Occasionally, a D.C. cab raced past, rattling and leaving a greater emptiness behind it.

Also behind her, several minutes behind, yet close enough to be relevant, the blond man she sought entered Richie C's Lounge, and sat a few seats away from where Laura had sat.

He lasciviously eyed the nearly naked Jeannette, who was just finishing her final show of the evening, and who was more anxious now than ever to return to the safety of her home.

The evening had already been strange enough.

chapter 112

WASHINGTON, D.C.
JULY 1, 2009; 1:12 A.M.

In addition to its trains, which it still had in abundance, Union Station had been partially converted into a mall. But with its massive bulk, with its three great arches and the matching three towering flagpoles in front of them, it still projected all the belief in the future that characterized the time it was built, almost a hundred years before.

Laura walked through the center arch into the main hall of the station with its soaring vaulted ceiling. The great hall had been the waiting room back when the station was built, but now the train passengers waited in another space right next to the tracks. At this hour, the main rooms of the station were unnervingly quiet. But Laura continued to scan for her blond man, though her hopes of spotting him were now down to almost nothing.

Suddenly her fatigue began to overcome her. She had traveled every mile she could, and almost felt dizzy. She found her way to a deserted bench and sat down. She reached to her cell phone and meant to call Vlad. Instead, she turned the phone off.

The station was quiet now. It wouldn't be so bad, she told

herself, to close her eyes for a moment. A minute or two of rest might get her through the rest of the evening.

She leaned back and relaxed slightly.

She moved her right hand within her jacket and let it settle upon the handle of her gun.

She felt herself drifting. Relaxing.

A few moments later, she had the sense of another weight arriving on the bench, as if someone were sitting down. Then she heard the voice.

"Don't open your eyes," he said.

She smiled slightly. "And why not?" she asked.

"It's easier if you don't see me," her father answered. "Easier if no one sees me."

She kept her eyes closed and breathed evenly. "I knew you'd come," she said.

"What's the difficulty?" he asked. "Be specific."

"I know he's out there," she said, mouthing the words softly. "The blond man. I just can't put it together."

"What do you think? What does your gut tell you?"

"I think he's in D.C.," she mouthed sleepily. "He must be by now. Must be."

She opened her eyes a sliver, then closed them again.

"Then why wait?" her father asked.

"I can't find him," she said. "It's not a matter of waiting."

"No. I mean, why would he wait?" he asked. "If he's here now, why would *he* wait?"

"What?" she asked.

"If he's here now, do what your boss suggested. Shoot him on sight."

"Huh? What?"

She reached her left hand to her side and tried to find him. Nothing.

A male hand landed on her shoulder instead.

"Shoot *who* on sight?" she asked again, louder.

"Laura?"

"Yes?"

"Sure. *Hey!* Who you going to shoot?"

The hand released. She felt a tumbling sensation, as if she

had finally gone from sanity back into madness. She felt herself shudder.

Weird accents! *Arabs? Israelis?*

She felt her right hand move on the butt of her weapon. Felt her fingers grow tight. Felt herself try to draw. "Hey! Laura! Dead zone, you in now!"

Near panic! So tired, she was unable to open her eyes.

"Hey. Hey, hey, Laura!" The hand was back, shaking her hard. Then it grabbed her right hand and stopped her grasping for the weapon.

Her eyes came wide open.

Dead zone!

"Hey! No good fall asleep on duty." Big gruff accent. A man to match. Vlad. Her new best friend and bodyguard. "Dead zone with phone, too. I call. No answer, so come looking."

"Oh. Oh, Jesus!" she said, coming awake.

"I think you too tired, Miss Laura."

She looked at the clock in the station. Two twenty-seven A.M.

"Yeah," she said. "Much too tired."

"I drive you home safe, huh? We go back to your car, Zarko follow. Right?" he asked.

"Yeah," she said. "Yeah, thank you."

The night was over. As expected, she had come up empty. Then, answering in terms he would understand, "Sure," she said. "Sure."

She rose and walked with Vlad back to the station entrance and her car across the street.

She arrived home shortly after 3 A.M. By that time the blond man was back at his own hotel, sleeping soundly.

Jeannette was at her home, too. Fortunately, her boyfriend picked her up after her final shift. There had been a stalker hanging out on the sidewalk right when she was leaving and she didn't wait around to find out if he was after her or one of the other girls. All she knew was that he had been big and fair-haired. She thought she recognized him from the audience earlier and he had given her the creeps.

chapter 113

Alan Savett was livid!

He had put everything of importance into his previous signal to the Central Intelligence Agency. And now, after too long a wait at a critical time, they were asking for supporting documentation. This was a worst case scenario of what Savett had always referred to as ISP: intelligence service paralysis, a situation in which, faced with unwelcome or surprising information, an intelligence service rejected the receipt of it until it was too late to act upon it.

Unhappily, the Americans had elevated this to an art form in the first decade of the twenty-first century and had frequently suffered the consequences thereof.

Documentation! What did they want? An engraved message from Colonel Mesdoua stating that he was about to be deposed?

"What sort of clarification or documentation?" asked Major Housahodi, as he stood over Savett. The sweat was pouring off the journalist's brow by now. He was a sage enough man to recognize a situation that was slipping away from him when he saw it.

"Anything we can give them," Savett answered. "It's vitally important at this stage."

"Don't they trust your previous message?" the major asked.

Savett made an attempt at diplomacy. "They wish to be sure," he said.

"They're endangering the life of their own airman," the major said. "As well as our lives."

"I know that."

The major's voice was laced with disappointment and

growing anger. His expression matched. "We could transmit to them a photograph of their air force officer," the major began. "But if the photograph escaped security and were published, I—and you—would be arrested by the army and executed immediately. And I don't trust the Western press not to publish the picture if it is available."

The major spent another long moment in thought.

"You would think they would *desire* a change in governments here. Chiron has been their source here for years. You would think the source would be trusted."

"You would think," Savett agreed.

"We cannot go forward with a change of government here without American support. And I cannot go backwards without taking extreme safeguards."

"Meaning?"

"I would have to execute the two key witnesses to my plans."

"And that would be Colonel Straighthorn and myself?"

"Unfortunately, sir. Yes. Though I would deeply regret it, you understand."

Several lines of profanity came together in Arabic in Savett's mind. He didn't know, however, whether to aim them at the major or the recalcitrant Americans.

He held his tongue.

"Make another transmission," the major instructed. "Advise them that the situation is in its eleventh hour and we must know of American support for a change in government here. Advise them that without their promise of support there will be no further transmissions from this location and no change in government in Tripoli will be possible. And tell them that we must have their response within twenty-four hours."

"Major, sir, I would caution you that—"

"There is nothing further to discuss," the major said.

Savett turned back to his Internet access. He formulated a message which the major oversaw and approved. Savett merged it into a pixel and incorporated it into a transmission to Reuters.

Savett launched the message.

"Now, sir," the major said, "we will await. You will need to come back to police headquarters. I regret deeply, Monsieur Chiron. But you did accept the perils of your position when you first engaged in espionage."

"Major, I—"

"Hopefully, the Americans will respond with wisdom."

"Major, I—" Savett tried again.

"There is no need for further discussion," the police chief said. "And it is my understanding that the centaur Chiron was of a noble soul, unlike the other centaurs, who were a brutal, unruly lot. And so he accepted his fate and understood his subservience to the gods. I am saddened by having a present-day parallel for you. But please bring whatever personal effects you desire."

Savett gathered a few changes of clothes, several books on the ancient world, and the photograph of his son from his living area. He packed a small bag as the police silently watched. Police officers led him back to a Land Rover that waited on the street.

As the vehicle turned in the street and began its return trip to the desert police outpost, Savett looked wistfully at the window to his flat where he had spent eight entertaining years in the Libyan capital.

chapter 114

WASHINGTON, D.C.
JULY 1, 2009; 8:02 A.M.

The blond man rose from sleep, showered, shaved, and dressed, and then raised the window of his hotel room, so that he could look at the White House a few blocks away. Tourists never tired of looking at the White House. Nor did he, though for different reasons. It was quite something, after all, to answer only to God.

A scary feeling because of the responsibility.

But also a euphoric feeling.

The blond man went down to the breakfast room of the Mayflower. He wasn't really hungry, but the idea of having breakfast in the same room where J. Edgar Hoover and Clyde Tolson did so regularly appealed to him. The FBI! Wasn't that one of the main pillars of the system that God so hated?

The Mayflower being the Mayflower, there was a linen tablecloth and a linen napkin. The blond man appreciated the touches all the more because he knew that soon God would sweep all this away.

He looked at the other diners. Men and women in suits on expense accounts, ready to further the corruption of the American system. How he hated them and their system. He felt increasingly anxious and agitated as he drew nearer to his target. The urge was on him to stand and spray this room with bullets. But he didn't, in deference to his larger target.

He finished breakfast. He went back upstairs.

He opened his computer and, recalling a series of codes by memory, he accessed the bank accounts he had opened in the Cayman Islands. Using a series of macro commands, with the flick of a few more command strokes, he dispersed what remained of his money all over the world. Every cent of it went to religious or paramilitary organizations around the planet that shared his ideology. He felt a surge of joy, having enriched many forces that would continue his fight after his death.

He waited to see if he would be called up to Heaven on the spot. He wasn't.

So he then gathered all of his belongings in his room, other than the clothes he would wear today, his weapon, and his computer. He packed them into three medium-sized garbage bags.

He placed the DO NOT DISTURB sign on his door.

He carried the bags of his final belongings down to the street, cut through a few alleys, and discarded everything in a pattern that no one would ever be able to understand or re-create.

He returned to the Mayflower and summoned his car. He drove it three blocks away and turned it in to the rental company. He glanced at his watch. It was past 9 A.M. now. He walked back to the hotel, located the service shaft for trash within the hotel, and returned to his room.

He knelt on the floor and said a long, thoughtful, deeply meditative prayer.

Then he withdrew his weapon from the holster on his belt.

He held it in his hand by the barrel. He opened his computer. He took the hard drive to low level format, wiping it clear of all information.

Then, holding the weapon like a hammer, he smashed his laptop, destroying the screen and the circuits within, taking special care to smash the hard drive and all memory chips.

He felt good.

He found the plastic bag for laundry that hung in his hotel room.

He placed the remains of his computer in the bag, walked it to the trash shaft, and dumped it. He walked back to his room and closed the door.

Finally, he was ready.

chapter 115

WASHINGTON, D.C.
JULY 1, 2009; 9:16 A.M.

The president was used to making the big decisions by himself. He had always done it that way and would continue to do so now. Hence it was not surprising that he sat in the Oval Office much as he had when this crisis had broken several days earlier—alone and in a surly, contentious mood, determined not to be pushed around by anyone, whether it was a domestic adversary or a foreign one.

He studied for a final time the schedule of air attacks to be carried out against Libya. Well, they had brought these attacks upon themselves, he mused, barely giving a second thought to the loss of life on the ground. Because the targets were close to the Mediterranean, American firepower was so superior in the area that many of the strikes could be made by the navy from the Carrier USS *Abraham Lincoln,* which was currently stationed with the Sixth Fleet.

Or, he mused, he could reprise Ronald Reagan's strikes against Libya in 1986 by sending aircraft from England.

He paged through the targets.

Nothing against Colonel Mesdoua, himself. The president figured that Mesdoua was bunkered up somewhere. The Libyan army and navy would take the bulk of the hits. Their new radar installations, their underwater missile sites that had brought down the United States reconnaissance aircraft, a couple of army bases scattered around their sandy North African dictatorship. Target practice for the U.S. Navy.

He also threw a bone to his old friend Colonel Small in Sardinia. Since the boys at the Sardine Can had lost a pair of men from their unit, they could have the pleasure of destroying many of the newly constructed military and police installations in Libya. The National Police seemed to be gaining power in the country, if some of the previous intelligence reports could be believed. So why not put a little dent in their armor, too?

As for that recent CIA report that some sort of discontent was brewing within the ranks of the National Police, well, this president was not planning to wait around for more hearsay from his spook agency. If the CIA wasn't going to get back to him in a timely manner, he wasn't going to be their wet nurse and wait for them. And in terms of the National Police in Libya, who cared, anyway? Might as well keep them in disarray.

The president reached for his pen again. He particularly liked the USAF's notion of destroying anything new that the Libyans had constructed within the last few years. That was an excellent plan.

He wrote,

If it's new, destroy it. That'll teach the bastards a lesson!

He then closed the briefing book and sent it back to the Pentagon for execution. Americans liked fireworks for the Fourth of July? Fine. This president would give his country and the world a show to start the holiday.

"Thank you, Colonel Mesdoua," he thought with a smile as he closed the book, "for making this possible."

chapter 116

ALEXANDRIA, VIRGINIA
JULY 1, 2009; 9:22 A.M.

Distantly, Laura Chapman thought she heard something that sabotaged her deep sleep.

It was like the sound of metal hitting metal, sharp, hard hits with some broken glass tossed in, followed by some smaller hits.

What the . . . ?

She opened her eyes. She awakened with a horrible feeling, a throwback to what she had been feeling three weeks earlier when that horrible notion had been upon her, the one of paranoia and conspiracy.

Of being watched.

Of something horrible about to happen.

Of a day of reckoning.

Holy Jesus!

The day was here!

She knew it!

Oh, Christ!

She looked at her clock. It was past 9 A.M. She never overslept, but had badly overslept this morning. Where was the excuse for that? She had an explanation, sure, but not an excuse.

She was physically exhausted. Beyond exhaustion, actually.

She had been up till 3:30 A.M. the night before, chasing shadows in train stations and along dark streets, following figments of wonderment and fantasy as they dipped in and out of reality, before her eyes and within her mind.

She sprang to her feet, grabbing yesterday's clothes, a rumpled suit from a knapsack, her jeans on the floor, her weapon unsafeguarded on a coffee table in the kitchen.

Good thing there had been no intruder the previous night.

She went into the shower and blasted herself awake. First water that was too cold, then water that was too hot.

The previous night. The Serbs. Oh, yeah. They had brought her home. Had she slept with anyone? No. Of course not.

The notion made her think of Rick.

She turned off the water. Grabbed coffee. Threw on the rumpled clothes.

"Oh, shit. What a life!"

Well, so what? The end of her career beckoned.

End of your life, too, Laura?

Where the hell did that thought come from?

She was dressed. Went downstairs. Found her car. Got in.

This is not a dream. This is a nightmare.

Paranoia again as the engine turned over: Was there a bomb linked to the ignition?

She waited. Guess not. Or if so, it hadn't gone off.

Yet.

Now what?

She put the car into gear and headed for her office.

chapter 117

The blond man walked through the neo-baroque lobby of the Mayflower with its colored marble and gold leaf and brass. He started toward the White House.

The people who built this thought they were building for all time, he thought, but of course what was "all time" compared to God's eternity? This too would pass, and he would help it pass. His was the first step that the world would take to the fulfillment of God's plan.

He stepped onto the street. It was still morning. The summer heat was still moderate, but one wouldn't know it from the humidity. In a jacket and tie, he was already too warmly dressed, but he had to be in uniform.

He turned left and walked down Connecticut Avenue to K Street. There were plenty of people about, heading for work. Work that was almost certainly offensive to God. Well, that could be fixed, and *would* be fixed. He was just one of the advance troops.

At the corner of Connecticut and K he waited for the light before he could cross.

He stared in the window of a store called The Dress Barn. Despite its pseudo-modest name the female dummies in the window were wearing clothes that were an offense to God.

The light changed and the blond man crossed.

K was a broad street with a subordinate service road on either side, separated from the main thoroughfare by a line of trees. As he crossed, the blond man looked west along K at the ugly modern office buildings that lined it. Within them worked lobbyists and lawyers who toiled hand in hand with members of Congress and the executive branch to flaunt God's will. That was, after all, what they lived for, if that could be called living. They enjoyed the money and the power, but spitting in God's eye was what they really got off on.

Not that anyone could really harm God. But it was possible to work against his Plan, as they were doing.

He was called out of his reverie by a honking of horns. He had paused in his ecstasy in the middle of K Street and the light had changed. He hurried over to the other side. When he had gained it he looked back again at the ugly buildings with their God-haters. He imagined how God would deal with them one day, the fire and brimstone pouring down and rolling along the street in a great tidal wave. People would seek refuge in the Metro. The Farragut North station was just behind him. Of course the hot seething lava of God's wrath would follow them, pouring down the escalators—which would be broken, they always were—and filling the station, drowning the unbelievers in liquid fire.

The fantasy was so powerful that for a moment he was entranced. Then he managed to snap out of it, as he always did. It was so wonderful to imagine God's Plan that he could get lost in it, but he always pulled back. He had to focus on doing his own part in the here and now on toward the fulfillment of God's will.

The quickest route would have been down Eighteenth Street, but he could not resist getting a better look at the Beast. So he walked diagonally across Farragut Square, and then into Lafayette Park. And then, there it was: the White House. Pennsylvania Avenue in front of it had once been one of Washington's busiest streets. Now it was just a pedestrian walkway. A security measure established a decade ago, even before 9/11.

A fat lot of good that will do, he thought, and turned right toward Eighteenth. As he waited to cross Pennsylvania as he looked at the Old Executive Office Building on the other side of Pennsylvania, with its extravagant Victorian façade done in gloomy gray granite.

The blond man crossed and walked down Eighteenth, then

turned left toward the employee entrance for the National Security Council Staff.

He encountered a stranger at the security gate. He didn't speak. Instead, he showed his Secret Service credentials. They were scanned and passed.

Then he did the eye scan. He passed that, too. His insides surged. He was almost in. He took four steps forward.

The guard turned abruptly. Shouted: "Hey! Hold it! What's the matter with you?"

The blond man turned back, coiled and ready.

Eye to eye.

Suspicion. The guard approached.

Something out of order! *Something wrong!*

The blond man wondered: Would it all end here?

Would he have to shoot the first security person, then make a run for the president? If so, he knew he would never make it. The distance was too great. He stayed perfectly calm.

"Sorry. What?" he asked.

The guard pointed to a small box on the wall. Thumb scan.

"Oh," the blond man said.

"New since you were here last?" the guard asked.

"Yeah. It is."

"It's been in for eighteen months," the guard said.

"I've been assigned to currency and counterfeit. West Coast."

"Bring me some samples next time you come by," the guard said with a smile.

"Yeah. Sure."

The blond man placed his thumb in the small electronic box. He felt a gentle buzz.

"You're good to go," the guard said, reading a computer screen a few seconds later. "Go on in, Mr. Wilder."

"Thanks," the blond man said.

He continued quietly on toward his destination.

chapter 118

Laura came across the Key Bridge and turned off onto the Whitehurst Freeway heading toward downtown. The traffic was heavy. The radio was filled with speculation about Libya.

Then it was upon her again, another gut feeling: Don't go to the office.

Go to the White House instead.

July first! New staff!

Again: She was seeing things no one else saw.

The president would die today if she didn't do something.

She cursed the traffic. She grabbed her cell phone. She punched in Rick's number in Miami. By good fortune, he answered directly.

"Do you ever do anything solely by instinct?" she asked.

"All the time."

"I'm on my way to the White House," she said. "I had a dream. A hunch. A gut feeling."

"And you're following it?"

"I'm following it," she said. She took the E Street exit from the freeway and headed for Eighteenth Street.

"Good luck."

"Look, Rick. You know all the ground I've been over in the last two weeks. You know the places, the names. The people. You know what this is about. If something strange happens, if you don't hear from me in twenty-four hours, will you follow up?"

"I'll follow up."

"Is that a promise?"

"That's a promise."

The White House was now within her sight as she headed

up Eighteenth. She weaved in and out of traffic, miraculously not being stopped by city police.

"Think I'm crazy?" she asked.

His response was swift. "No."

"Thanks."

There was a pause between them.

"Laura?"

"Yes."

"Don't get yourself killed. Or worse," he said.

"I'll try not to. Thanks," she said again.

Whatever else was to be said between them remained unspoken.

Laura turned her car into the first checkpoint at the White House parking lot behind the Old Executive Office Building and signed off.

chapter 119

WASHINGTON, D.C.
JULY 1, 2009; 10:17 A.M.

For the blond man, entry to the White House was almost as easy as entry to the hotel had been. The old principles remained valid: When one can't pass security, one goes around it. It was laughable.

The blond man showed his fraudulent credentials as he approached the first metal detector on the east corridor. Two young Secret Service men were on duty.

He handed them his Secret Service pass. "Take your time. Make sure it's good," he said to them.

They swiped it. He pulled out his semiautomatic, handed it to them, and passed through the metal detector. They handed his weapon back to him.

"New to the job here?" the blond man asked.

"Just started today, sir," one answered on behalf of both.

"Enjoy," he said. "I'm okay to proceed?"

"Everything perfect, sir."

"No surprise here," he said.

The blond man reholstered his weapon and proceeded into the lowest level of the White House.

Once, when the United States of America was much smaller, much younger, and much more innocent, these corridors and offices had served as the home of the Army, Navy, and State departments. Now the area housed the staff of the National Security Council. The fact that the staff of the president's security advisor now took up as much room as was once taken up by the country's military and diplomacy said much about the bloat of modern bureaucracy.

The blond man walked along one of the corridors, then past one of the circular stairs, which were in each corridor of the building, and out a door on the other side. There in front of him was the low profile of the White House West Wing, where the president had his office.

Originally, in a less bureaucratic time, the president had had his office in the White House itself, and indeed the Oval Office had been in the second-floor room behind the curved South Portico where tourists still imagined it to be. But growth of staff had meant that two wings had been added, East and West, in the same classical style as the White House itself, but just one story high, with a hilly rise on the adjacent lawn that came up half a story on the north side. The landscaping had been neatly done: from Pennsylvania Avenue the wings were hardly noticeable.

It was the West Wing that counted for the blond man, for it was there that the Oval Office—the real one, built to the dimensions of its predecessor in the main building—looked out on the Rose Garden. Here was where the president would be found.

The blond man showed his credentials again. He was taken aback for a second when a young uniformed Secret Service agent named David Porter looked up and studied his face.

"I know you, don't I?" Porter said.

"Don't know. Do you?"

"I know your name. You used to work here, right?"

A pause, then, "Several years back."

The uniformed man shook his head. "Sorry. Didn't recognize you. Must have been around the time I started."

"When was that?"

"About five years ago."

The blond man went silent. By computer, Porter logged the blond man in.

"It's been a long time, I guess," Porter mused, waiting for further computer approval. "Back on duty in the Head Shed, huh?"

"You could say that," the blond man said. "One last job."

"Lucky you. I've still got fifteen years to retirement."

"It'll go quickly."

"Yeah, right," Porter said. "Some *days* seem like fifteen years."

Porter studied his computer. The blond man took an impatient step to pass, but Porter put an arm out to delay him. Then Porter frowned.

"Shouldn't you have a day pass here if you're not on the White House rolls for the day?" Porter asked.

The blond man looked sternly at Porter. "I don't know about any day pass. But I do know that the president is waiting to see me on a special assignment. And if you don't like this job, and you're already talking about retirement, maybe I can make arrangements and have you start looking for another."

For a moment, Porter thought it was a joke. Then he realized it wasn't.

"No offense, sir," Porter said.

A contentious moment passed between them.

"Then stop bitching," the blond man said. "You're lucky to be able to serve your country."

"Yes, sir. And I need to see your weapon," Porter said. "Sir."

"What for?"

"Standard directive, Mr. Wilder. I'm just following regulations than went into effect December 2008."

The blond man seethed. "A lot of leftwing liberal socialist bullshit, if you ask me."

"Maybe. But I still need to inspect your firearm."

The blond man reached briskly for his loaded weapon.

He pulled it out by the handle, held the nose upright for a moment, and eyed Porter. He saw a flash of fear and indecision in Porter's eyes.

Then the blond man lowered the weapon. He removed the clip, and handed both weapon and magazine to Porter.

"Standard direction, standard-issue weapon," the blond man said. "Loaded. Twelve rounds."

Porter inspected the weapon and the clip. Then he handed them back to the blond man.

"Thank you, sir," Porter said.

"May I finally keep my appointment?"

"I regret the delay, sir."

"I'll tell the president you caused it."

"Whatever you wish, sir."

The blond man returned his weapon to his holster and continued onward.

chapter 120

WASHINGTON, D.C.
JULY 1, 2009; 10:34 A.M.

Laura raced from the parking lot to the east corridor.

Departing Secret Service staff were still carried on the computer databanks of those authorized to enter the White House. She had no problem at the first checkpoint.

Seconds later, closing her distance on the blond man, on the identical path he had walked minutes earlier, she came to Special Agent David Porter.

"Hey, Laura. How you doing?" he said. "Are you back?"

She set down her weapon and ammunition clip for inspection.

She answered almost breathlessly. "I'm okay. How are things here today?"

"Busy. Something big's probably going to happen on the Libyan situation. That always gives the place a buzz."

"Right," she said.

"Nothing like bombing a bunch of towel-heads to rally the American public and give the capital some excitement, huh?"

"Yeah," she said, looking around with extra vigilance. "Right."

Porter handed her weapon and ammunition back to her.

"How about you personally?" she asked. "See anything strange?"

"Aside from the big blond guy who just came through in front of you?"

"What big blond guy?"

"Wilder, I think his name was. Used to work here. Somehow I remember the name, but not the face. It doesn't figure. He claimed he worked here when I was here, but he left a year before I began. Presidential Protection, maybe. I don't know. What do you think—?"

The words cut off as a surge of fear squeezed her.

"Where did he go?"

"West Wing. Appointment with the Chief. Or so he said."

But Laura was no longer listening.

She slammed together her weapon and was on the full run in another second.

chapter 121

The blond man penetrated deeper into the White House.

The West Wing was surprisingly modest. On the right was the cafeteria, with its food served by navy stewards. It was a curious little bureaucratic triumph of the navy that it had managed to get responsibility for the White House's restaurant. The tables were full, mostly of nobodies, at least in terms of governmental importance.

Another credential check: an easy one this time.

Then he was in the part of the West Wing that was dedicated to the press.

He had no trouble getting through another check into the real working space where the National Security Advisor and other senior members of the president's entourage worked in proximity of their boss.

Just think, if you could only get a truck bomb close enough you could bag the lot! the blond man thought. But that was not possible. Even though the White House and the West Wing had been built long before the existence of truck bombs, they were set back too far from Pennsylvania Avenue, which was now closed to traffic, and had been for twenty years. And the hilly landscaping outside provided an extra level of protection.

He paused for a moment and took stock of his situation.

All right, he would get the job done. He would die at its conclusion.

But then, that was what God had chosen him for, and that election, that divine martyrdom, was the most important thing that could happen to any human being.

Here he was in the president's outer office. It was astonishing how once one was inside a perimeter, one could move around easily. But the reason was not hard to fathom: Even a fortress has to allow the free movement of people—as long as they have the right identification—in order to function.

He walked up to the president's secretary and receptionist, Mary Corliss.

"Is the Chief in?" he asked. He didn't need to show his credentials. Not anymore.

"No, he's still at a meeting with some of the military people," Mary answered.

"When will he be back?"

"Any time now."

At that moment, Secretary of Defense Robert Lynch came by to ask her a question. Secretary Lynch gave a vague nod in the blond man's direction, but otherwise ignored him.

That's it, huh? the blond man thought to himself. *I'm not worth thinking about!*

Secretary Lynch departed. Mary Corliss looked down at her appointment book, mildly confused. "Was your visit scheduled?" she asked, shifting her attention back to the blond man. "I don't see any appointment now."

"Not scheduled. But I need to check out some digital programming to the window alarm systems."

"Digital what?"

He showed his ID. "Secret Service. I need access to the office for two minutes."

Corliss shrugged.

Behind her, Special Agents Larsen and Reilley flanked the door to the president's office, their weight positioned on the balls of their feet, their interest in the visitor growing.

"Software check," the blond man explained more soothingly. "Window security system."

"Go on ahead," she said. "But someone needs to accompany you."

"Not a problem."

The blond man nodded to Larsen and Reilley and again held up his Secret Service ID.

They looked at it carefully.

"Which office you working out of?" Reilley asked.

"Chicago. Counter-terrorism."

"You'd think they'd tell us, wouldn't you?" Reilley asked.

"Sorry, guys," the blond man said. "You're right. They *should* have notified you."

They did not look happy, but allowed him to pass into the Oval Office, Larsen following.

The blond man glanced at the massive desk, then the view out the curved window to the Rose Garden. He eyed the marble fireplace with the Ionic columns on either side of the opening where foreign leaders and the president were always photographed. He felt a thrill in the mission God had given him—and how close he was to fulfilling it.

He tingled with excitement and anxiety. His hand twitched slightly, the one that would hold the weapon, the one that would pull the trigger. He busied himself around the window, finding the location of several parts of the computerized alarm system that functioned with the windows.

He stalled. He delayed, waiting for the Chief to return.

He had no idea what these electronic boxes did.

He only hoped that Larsen would quickly grow bored watching him or that the president would reappear so he could turn and shoot.

A minute passed. He delayed longer. Larsen was watching him carefully, maybe even growing suspicious. "You sure you know what you're doing?" Larsen asked.

Reilley stepped into the office next.

The blond man started to get cold feet. With good luck, the shooting could have been accomplished by now. This was bad luck.

"I need to go get some more equipment," the blond man said.

Larsen said, "Uh huh."

Reilley was staring, glaring. His hands near his own weapon.

"Sure," Larsen said. "Let's just close the office again and we'll work you back in later."

"Know what?" the blond man said. "I'm going to phone

the director, Bill Vasquez, and let you guys see the right paperwork so you don't seem so nervous."

A little wave of relief rolled across the encounter.

"That would be a good idea," Larsen said.

"I'll get to it right away," the blond man said.

Larsen exchanged an approving glance with his partner. He led the way back to the door.

When he arrived there, and before the door could close, they all heard a woman's voice, raised in alarm.

With some sixth sense working within him, the blond man recognized it from Dallas. He knew it was Laura.

Instinctively, his hand disappeared within his jacket.

chapter 122

WASHINGTON, D.C.
JULY 1, 2009; 10:46 A.M.

Laura arrived, breathing hard, at the entrance to the Oval Office.

She thought her heart was going to burst from her chest. She saw Reilley, she saw Larsen, she saw Mary Corliss at her desk. Then her eyes found the blond man between the two other Secret Service agents.

There was a palpable moment when their eyes landed upon each other, Laura's on the blond man and the blond man's gaze on her. Then there was another moment, one of inevitability combined with utter disbelief, as her mind processed what was before her.

This was the same blond man whom she had seen in Dallas, the man who had fired two shots at her, and one at Rick.

The same man she had spoken to on Anna's phone.

The man who had murdered Anna.

Laura couldn't prove it, nor did she have time to, but she

was certain. She had been in the game long enough to know. Moments that shatter lives or take lives transpire with blinding speed, yet afterward feel as if they happened in slow motion. So it was here.

The blond man asked calmly, "What's the problem?"

The man's hand was moving.

Laura's moved also.

Laura shouted, not calmly, "Freeze! Gun!" at the same time.

Larsen and Reilley ducked away.

Laura came up fast with a weapon and pointed it. When the blond man's hand emerged from his jacket, she fired quickly, once, then twice. Something dark flew from his hand——his Secret Service identification as it turned out—— and went to the floor, followed by his weapon.

She knew she had hit him and hit him squarely, once for her and maybe once for Anna, last seen hanging in a bloody closet in Miami. The blond man fell backwards and hit the door frame to the Oval Office.

Laura fired a third time.

The force of the bullets picked the blond man up, half-turned him in the air, and sent him sprawling backwards into the president's office.

Then all Laura could remember was screaming and shouting; hysterical voices coming from everywhere, and someone yelling *"Gun!"* someone yelling, *"Laura, no!"* and someone else yelling, *"Crazy bitch!"*

Then someone huge violently hit her from behind. She fell forward. Part of the carpet charged upward and whacked her on the side of the face, except that it was actually she who was now pinned to the floor, protesting, screaming something about an assassin and Miami and Mexico and acting just as psycho as everyone thought she was.

A powerful male torso was on top of her, arms like iron wrapped around her, nearly crushing her. Other agents were racing in from everywhere.

At the same time, five or six powerful male hands wrestled her weapon away. Special Agent Larsen helped chicken-wing her arms behind her back, and, pinned, she felt the handcuffs go on, first on the left wrist with a hard snap, then on the right.

There were more voices and shouts everywhere and the room was set to explode.

Her right side felt as if she had cracked a whole side of ribs, but she was rudely hauled up to her feet as the pain still pulsated.

She kept hearing the same phrases.

"... *shot a fellow agent....*"

"... *ohmigod, the loony bitch shot another agent....*"

And they steadied her, roughed her up some more, and groped inside her blouse, under her skirt, looking for another weapon. Then they marched her away to a cell within the White House, and for some reason, as she tried to explain to anyone who would listen, all she could think of was Squeaky Fromme and Sara Jane Moore.

They threw her in the White House cell and two male agents followed.

They ripped the belt from her skirt, opened her blouse completely and took her bra so she couldn't hang herself. They cursed her profanely, their voices over hers, and slammed the door.

She knew she would stay there until inquisitors came and people could sort out what had happened.

She collapsed onto the hard wooden slab that was the only seat in the cell.

Then she realized.

It had all happened so quickly, she never even got a really good look at the man she had shot. But she knew what she had done, even if no one else would ever believe it.

chapter 123

Minutes after sundown that same day, a squadron of twenty-four two-seater khaki and brown F-111 attack bombers streaked off runways at Lakenheath, England. They were joined by fifteen EF-111 electronic jamming planes whose mission was to disable Libyan radar. Flying at thirty thousand feet, the force rendezvoused over southern England and refueled four times during its seven-hour flight. After the first refueling, seven planes, brought along as a reserve in case of airborne malfunctions in the others, broke out of formation and returned to base.

Meanwhile, the carriers *Coral Sea* and *America*, stationed in the mid-Mediterranean, were steaming toward the coast of Libya. Between 5:20 and 6:20 P.M., close to one hundred aircraft catapulted off their decks—eighteen A-6 and A-7 strike and strike-support craft, six F/A-18 fighters, fourteen EA-6B electronic jamming planes, and a variety of support craft. As the air force's F-111 squadron rounded the tip of Tunisia, it was skillfully integrated into the navy's airborne armada by a single U.S. Navy officer providing coordination from an airborne tanker.

With one squadron heading for Tripoli and the other for Benghazi, pilots dropped to altitudes under five hundred feet to avoid radar detection. The low-level approaches were a traditional technique for the U.S. military. Low-level attacks can beat any defense when done properly.

Aircraft carrying radar-jamming devices, as well as HARM missiles to take out radar sites, were the first to reach the target cities, approaching at 4:54 A.M.

Precisely at 5 P.M., the squadron of A-6 fighters roared

over Benghazi from the Gulf of Sidra and began bombing
the airfield. In Tripoli, part of the F-111 squadron had circled around inland and approached from the south. The city
was coming awake. No air-raid alarm sounded.

Several minutes into the attacks, one of the Warhawks
dropped its bombs in a residential area a mile south of the
harbor, killing several civilians, destroying homes, and dam-
aging other buildings, including the Italian embassy and the
German ambassador's residence.

Some Pentagon officials later theorized that the bomb
may have been dropped by an attacker that was out of control. Three navy pilots reported seeing one aircraft turn into
a "fireball" and disappear into the ocean about ten miles off-
shore.

Over their targets, U.S. pilots were confronted with an
astonishing barrage of Libyan defensive fire. The sky over
Tripoli was stitched with orange streaks as tracers and missiles arced up toward the attackers.

"They fired everything they had," said a senior Pentagon
official, including an array of creaking old Soviet-built SAM-
2, -3, -6, and -8 missiles and ZSU-23-4 antiaircraft guns.

But what prevented the Libyan missiles from inflicting
real damage was that most were fired without radar guidance. The Americans had forced the Libyans to turn off their
radar. If they turned them on to guide their missiles, they
would get a HARM down their throats. Nor was any defense
mounted by the Libyan air force. Meanwhile, American
bombers destroyed the underwater missile defenses that had
taken out an American fighter several days earlier.

The planning for the air strikes required U.S. airmen to fly
through heavy flak in the dead of night and strike with precision. The primary target: Colonel Mesdoua's headquarters.
The unstated hope: that Mesdoua would be asleep there
when the bombs fell. The president's guidelines for retalia-
tion had been to hit precisely defined targets and to mini-
mize the chance of injuring civilians. Both concerns dictated
a low-level attack with precision bombing.

First on the list was the Bab al Azizia army compound,

which served as Colonel Mesdoua's command center and residence. Azizia was also targeted in the hope that the colonel would be killed or injured in the attack. No fewer than fifteen Warhawks were assigned to hit Mesdoua's compound. The hope was to "turn the barracks into dust."

Next on the hit list was the military section of the Tripoli International Airport, base of Libya's small fleet of longer range military aircraft. A third target was the Benghazi army barracks, which Mesdoua used as an alternative command post. Then came barracks at the naval port of Sidi Bilal, near Tripoli, a commando training facility, and a strike at the Benina airfield, where Libya's MiG-23 interceptors are based, as a precaution against counterattack.

The final strikes were aimed against several newly constructed installations of the Libyan National Security Brigade, the National Police. Included was battalion headquarters, based at a desert enclave twenty miles south of Benghazi.

It was there, just past 6 P.M., that Major Gerald Straighthorn, Alan Savett, and Major Housahodi all looked skyward at the oncoming sound of heavy aircraft. It was only in the final seconds, as the aircraft roared low overhead, that they came to the stunning realization that they were— for reasons they could not understand—under attack.

Then, as quickly as they had come, the warplanes wheeled out to sea, vanishing back into the gloom, all safe but one, many Libyan targets completely destroyed, including the new police barracks located out in the desert.

chapter 124

On the morning of the day after the Libyan bombing, the day after the disturbance at the White House, a new set of inquisitors sat in a locked room with Laura and led her through the same story that she had gone over relentlessly the previous day.

They were in a locked windowless room at an undisclosed location, but from the direction the van that removed Laura from the White House took, she had an inkling that they were buried somewhere in the Old Executive Office Building, adjacent to the White House. The room had a certain stink to it, an unpleasant blend of fluorescent lights and overacting pituitary glands. It was strangely reminiscent of the one at Kennedy International where one of the two Jeremy Wilders of recent memory had starred in his own pointless interrogation.

Laura was in federal-prisoner orange now, the latest tunic style for women, and was held in solitary. She had not yet seen an attorney. Under the Homeland Security Amendment of 2007, as an accused of a felonious act on federal property, she had no right to expect one.

The lead interrogator now was a stern-jawed man in his mid-forties, Special Agent Frederick O'Connor, out of the Washington bureau. He was joined by a young man named Special Agent Mike Kenitsu, fresh cheeked, ambitious, and very FBI. He sat, took notes, and never changed his expression. The note-taking perplexed Laura, as it was common ground among everyone that the camera high up on the wall behind plate glass was fully operational and in use.

Inevitably, one other female was present, Special Agent

Carol Richards, also from the Washington office of the Secret Service. She was doughy faced and ginger haired, with circles under the eyes and no makeup, matronly, in her late thirties.

She struck Laura as one of those career spinsters in which Washington sometimes specialized. *Too much like myself?* Laura wondered bitterly.

Like Special Agent Kenitsu, Richards was there to observe and not speak.

The beginning of the day's conversation was halting and banal, with O'Connor pounding along over ground covered the previous day. Finally, O'Connor made a move for his new target.

"Laura, the man you shot died. Do you understand that?"

"I understand that," Laura answered. "But he was there to murder the president."

"He had Secret Service credentials, Laura. He was there on official business."

"The whole security system at the White House has been compromised," she insisted again. "Doesn't anyone understand that? There are cells set in motion years ago by William Casey. They have access to White House codes. They can come and go as they please. Finally the inevitable happened. They created their own traitor."

"That's not what happened," O'Connor said.

"They've reprogrammed themselves into the White House security system," Laura insisted. "At least some of them have. Someone stole the DNA and identity from a former agent named Jeremy Wilder and a fake agent entered the White House in his place. Over the course of years, he had been in and out of here many times."

"Do tell," O'Connor said, disgusted.

"You don't understand what happened at all, do you?" Laura asked.

"Do you feel that you're smarter than your superiors, Laura?"

"That's not what I'm saying."

"Do you feel you're smarter than the rest of us in this room here this morning?"

Laura let a silence answer the question. She folded her arms.

"The man you shot had Secret Service credentials," O'Connor said. "It begins and ends there."

"Forged credentials."

"Real credentials until proven otherwise, Laura. You shot a fellow agent. He was in the system and on a special assignment."

"Can you prove that?" she countered.

"It's not us who have to prove things right now. It's you."

"His credentials are forgeries. Always were."

"He's listed properly on government records."

"Check it with Mitchell Hamilton," she said.

"Who's that?"

"I went over all this yesterday."

"Let's do it again."

"Mitch Hamilton is in the Office of Protective Intelligence. He recruited me to do a job."

She ran through it again, from the beginning.

The inquisitor sighed. "There's a man named that in the OPI. You told us that before. We checked his log books for the last month and we can't find your name anywhere on them."

"Have you *talked* to him?"

"We will eventually."

"When? A year from now?"

"Right now, it's *you* who needs to talk, Laura. Seems to me, you're the one who needs to access the truth here. Make it easier on yourself."

"I've been telling you the truth."

The argument was circular. "I don't think so, Laura. Try again."

O'Connor pushed back from the table. "You know what we did yesterday?" he asked.

"What?"

"We took your car apart. You left it in the south parking

lot. Bomb squad impounded it first, then we undid it piece by piece."

She felt violated. "And what did you find?" she asked.

"Nothing. Know what we're doing now? As we speak?"

She thought about it and felt a sinking feeling.

"That's right," he said. "Your apartment is being searched. Every inch of it. More than every inch. We have sixteen people over there in Alexandria, going through books. Computers. Refrigerator. Medicine cabinet. Clothing. Correspondence. Particularly correspondence. We'll be reading everything, examining everything. If you've got old love letters from high school and college, we'll be inventorying them. Looking for false panels, taking up floorboards where necessary. They'll even be going though with a dog, sniffing for drugs and explosives."

She leaned back in her chair and felt more screwed than at any other time in her life.

"We already found a gun under the closet floorboards," O'Connor said.

"That's my alternative service weapon. For undercover. Completely legal."

"How about the marijuana that was sealed in your mattress? Took the dog less than a minute to find that."

Plump ginger-haired Agent Carol Richards finally felt obliged to contribute, girl-to-girl. "Are you a habitual smoker, Laura?" she asked. "There's no room in the Service for drug abusers, you know that."

She might have screamed, might have lied, but didn't do either.

Instead, she said nothing.

"Marijuana is enough to get you jailed, Laura," O'Connor said. "Five to eight years. But that's the least of your problems right now. Now, talk to us. Make it easier on yourself."

"I have nothing further to say."

O'Connor held her in his gaze.

"I take that as a good first step, Laura. A partial admission of guilt."

"It was no such thing."

"So what else do you want to tell us?" he finally asked.

The other woman in the room, Agent Richards, chimed in again. "There must have been a reason you did what you did, Laura," she said. "You need to tell us."

"I *have* told you!" Laura snapped.

Agent Richards leaned back in her chair. "You need to do better than the fantasy you've been trying to spin for us," she scolded. "Do you see a lot of men friends on your evenings off, also? Are those your smoking partners, the various men you sleep with?"

"This isn't an investigation, it's an inquisition," Laura said.

More Go-Ask-Alice circular logic.

"You shot a Secret Service agent," O'Connor repeated.

"Have you been to my office in the Longworth Building?" Laura tried. "Did you talk to my assistant?"

"And the assistant's name was?"

"My story isn't changing. My assistant was Vanessa Stone. The office was Room 476-S."

O'Connor looked down.

"That's what you told us yesterday, Laura. There is no federal clerical employee named Vanessa Stone. The office you mentioned is vacant and has been vacant for months."

"Download the computer!"

"There was no computer in the office."

She looked from one of them to the other, her fear, her paranoia sharpening. "What are you trying to do to me? All of you? Check everything with Agent Rick McCarron in the Miami CIA office," she insisted. "Then get Bill Vasquez over here."

"The director of the Secret Service?" O'Connor sounded bored.

"Yes."

"Laura, we've gone all over this several times yesterday and once already today."

"And?"

"There's no Rick McCarron in the Miami office, Laura.

None now and never was. Director Vasquez says he knows of no operation that currently involves you."

"Those are goddamned lies!" she insisted.

"It's the truth," O'Connor answered. "Personally, I don't know whether you're consciously creating myths or are just delusional. But we'll have years to find out, won't we?"

"You need to bring Bill Vasquez in here."

"This might surprise you, Laura, but Director Vasquez is not pleased by yesterday's events. Feels it will give the Service the blackest eye that it's had since 1963 if the story gets out. Bill is a friend of mine. He wants nothing to do with you, much less to come in here."

"What do you mean, if the story gets out? No one knows what happened?"

"Complete news blackout. Thank God."

O'Connor gave a head signal to his associates. "I hope you are crazy, Laura. Otherwise, you might get executed."

They rose and left.

Laura looked at the corner of her room and for a fleeting moment, thought she saw a man standing there, shaking his head in disapproval. Then she knew he wasn't there. Much like the night in her home, the night at the station, deep down she knew he wasn't there.

She sat alone, the camera peering at her.

Five hours later, amidst great secrecy, she was transported in a van to a federal guardhouse at Fort Meade, Maryland. There she took occupancy in a new cell, even more deeply in solitary confinement. There she would await the government's next move.

The black dog was finally in full possession of her spirit.

The suicidal impulses were all in place. It occurred to her that a nice cozy cemetery would be a pleasant place to be.

And she was alone.

chapter 125

Outside, the weather in the Mid-Atlantic United States continued to be hot and oppressive. The political climate in Washington was similar, but the new president was widely lauded for his tough stand against the Libyans. Colonel Mesdoua, of course, remained firmly in power and even tightened his grip on the National Police, given the unexplained absence of Major Housahodi, who otherwise might have overthrown him.

The body of Captain Straighthorn was never returned.

Straighthorn's name quickly disappeared from the news after a memorial service in California, attended by the vice president. Also disappearing quickly from the news were the names of five American hostages who had previously been seized in Libya. Their mutilated corpses were dumped on a highway outside Benghazi two days after the raid, so the book could be closed on them, too.

And farther south, in Miami, the man Laura had known as Richard McCarron pondered her silence over the last few hours and reflected upon his own his next move, also. He was catching rumors from Washington and did not like the sound of them.

His position was not an easy one, but by evening, he had arrived at what he felt to be the solution.

He put a few things in a travel bag and headed for the airport.

chapter 126

Alan Ahmed Savett, 53, Reuters Correspondent, Dies

By THE ASSOCIATED PRESS
Published: July 3, 2009

TRIPOLI, July 1 (AP)—Alan Ahmed Savett, the writer and journalist who was the author of an influential column from North
Africa, died on July 2 at a hospital in Tripoli. He was 53.

The cause of his death was undisclosed, a spokeswoman for
Reuters announced in London.

Born in Exeter, in southwest England, to an Egyptian father
and an English mother, Mr. Savett explored his roots during
childhood vacations in the Middle East. There, uncles introduced him to the Koran, the Sunna and the Ijma, the three
foundations of Islam. At university at Cambridge, where he
read history and philosophy at Churchill College, he developed a lifelong affinity for classical Greek mythology, as well
as ancient Egyptian religion. He found the latter remarkable
for its reconciliation and union of conflicting beliefs. It was
there also that Mr. Savett developed a yen to both pursue his
cultural roots and write for a mass audience after reading
the entire works of James Joyce, F. Scott Fitzgerald, Salman
Rushdie and Mario Puzo.

He was in his 30s before he achieved his goal, being granted
a reporting job and then a column with *The Sun* in London in
1992. Later, he would resign his post on Fleet Street to become
for many years the Tripoli correspondent for Reuters. His

twice-weekly column, which focused on the tenuous relationship of European and American interests in Islamic North Africa, was published around the world in both English and Arabic. His works were read by millions of readers around the world and garnered a crop of writing and correspondents' awards.

While a student, Mr. Savett had traveled widely. He spent a year after leaving university hitchhiking around Canada, Mexico and the United States, for which he developed a keen affection despite frequent later scathing criticisms of American foreign policy in his columns. He is survived by his parents, who reside in London, and a son who is a reggae musician in New York.

---

chapter 127

WASHINGTON, D.C.
JULY 3, 2009; 10:34 A.M.

The morning of the third day, Laura's cell was quiet in the early morning.

Then the same inquisitors returned. They moved her to another interrogation room, but their hearts did not appear to be in their work. They labored over the same series of questions, almost as if they were seeking to summarize her story point by point.

They left after two hours.

Laura had the feeling that she was about to be moved again. After a distasteful noontime meal, her hunch was again proven correct. She remained in the same facility, but at 2 P.M. was taken by two burly female guards to a room that more resembled a conference room than an interrogation chamber.

Searching for good omens, she hoped that she would at least be allowed to have access to an attorney, which would give her the first contact with the outside world since the July 1 incident at the White House.

The glimmer of hope put her suicidal instincts at bay, at least for a while.

Half an hour after her transfer, she heard the approach of footsteps. Then the door opened. Two men entered. Director Vasquez and the man she knew as Rick McCarron.

After nearly forty-eight hours of incarceration, she didn't know whether her spirits should soar or sink. The door closed heavily behind them and the three were alone in the room.

McCarron carried something resembling a gym bag. It was closed. Vasquez had a leather attaché case.

"Hello, Laura," Vasquez said, sitting at the table.

"Hello." She turned to the other man. "Rick?" she asked.

"Hello, Laura," he said.

She wanted to put out a hand to him, to touch flesh, but something held her back.

"You are Rick McCarron," she asked. "That's your name, right?"

"That's who I am."

"What's going on?" she asked.

"The director will tell you."

"I've been here two days, Rick," she said with accelerating urgency. "I—"

"You're leaving soon," he answered.

"For where?"

McCarron didn't answer. He looked to Director Vasquez.

"It would be best if we all sat down, Laura," Vasquez said. "We need to walk through this carefully. Just sit, okay?" the director pressed.

She looked to the second man at the table. "Rick?" she asked. "Just tell me this. Are you on my side? Can I depend on you?"

"I've said everything I need to say, Laura," Rick said.

She eyed the bag.

"Can I get a lawyer?" she asked.

"That's off in the future," Rick said.

"Look, I—"

"I think you should hear what Director Vasquez has to say," Rick said. "Then we can discuss everything else."

They sat. Laura turned back to Vasquez and waited for the remainder of her life—or at least the blueprint for it—to unfold in front of her.

A few seconds hung in the room like a year and a half.

"I've read your interrogation transcripts, Laura," Vasquez began. "Interesting. I can't say they're pleasant reading, I can't say I'm amused. But I find them fascinating."

She waited.

"I read your explanation of what happened. Sounds like Looney Tunes stuff, doesn't it? Doesn't really have a ring of official Washington or logical events, does it? Phantom cells. Bill Casey, who's been dead twenty-five years. DNA scans. Computer penetration and corruption."

"It's what happened," she said.

He looked down and pondered something. Five more seconds that felt like the ice age.

"Barely believable," he said. "The government spent tens of millions of dollars implementing a security system which, if we're to believe you, is worthless." He paused again. "Imagine how Congress will react if they learn how much money had been pissed away on this."

"It's what happened," she said again. "And it wouldn't be the first time the government had frittered away tens of millions of dollars on something that didn't work." A quick glance to Rick, whose gaze was downward, and then back again to the director.

Another passive-aggressive pause from Vasquez.

Then, "Oh, I know it is," Vasquez said. "What happened, I mean. Your cohort Rick here got on a plane last night when he didn't hear from you. Came over to my own house with fire in his eyes. Talked to me. Brought me the evidence to support everything you said."

"You mean you wouldn't have believed it without him?"

"Eventually, maybe. In a year or two."

"So now what?" she asked.

"You have to understand, we managed a news blackout on what happened the morning of July 2 in the White House. Three reporters heard what they thought was a shot. Fortunately, they're from friendly news organizations. That's all they let in the White House, anyway. So no one asked questions."

"Uh huh," Laura said.

"The only three people who know the full story are the three people in this room right now," McCarron said.

Vasquez glanced to the camera, high up on the wall.

"Even that little sucker's been shut down right now. There will be no record of our conversation here, other than our memories," the director said.

"What about the people who took my testimony?" she asked.

"They know what you've been insisting. They just don't know that what you're saying is actually true."

She studied them. "So now what?" she asked again.

"There's a reason we call it the *Secret* Service, Laura," Vasquez said.

He opened a manila envelope from his attaché case. He pushed a confidentiality agreement in front of her.

"Didn't I sign one of these already?" she asked.

"You did."

"Isn't strict confidentiality included in my terms of employment?"

"It is."

"Then what's the point of this?"

"One more document for good measure," Vasquez said.

She let it sit before her, without signing.

"If I sign this, how do I know you'll let me out of here?" Laura asked.

"Why wouldn't we let you out of here?" Vasquez answered.

"I don't know. I only know you might not."

Vasquez made a strange expression, then answered.

"There are some things you need to understand, Laura," Vasquez said.

"Like?"

"First of all, it has been established that the man who was killed by gunfire within the White House was *not* a member of the United States Secret Service. For a while a member of the Secret Service came under suspicion, Jeremy Wilder, but retired agent Wilder has been cleared."

"I know that as well as you do," she said. "We cleared the real Jeremy Wilder in New York last week."

"That's correct."

"So who was the man I shot?"

"He was American. He had contacts within the intelligence services but exactly who he was and where he came from aren't known. His DNA matches no known records. Somehow he, or someone employing him, broke into the government databases and hijacked the identity of agent Wilder and probably many others, also. In terms of this man's identity, they probably focused on Wilder for the same reasons you did. Build, general appearance, and background."

"And you don't know who he was?"

"No."

"Not yet, anyway," McCarron added.

"But what about the cell that employed him?"

Vasquez said, "No one recognizes him."

"Meaning, you talked to Sam, and whoever employs Sam."

Vasquez was silent.

"We did," said Rick.

"Nor would anyone admit it if they did recognize the dead man," Vasquez said.

"Of course."

"The larger issue remains," Vasquez said. "Our entire computer-security system is corrupt and compromised. If one person can beat it, dozens more could, also."

"I would think you should be able to fix the breach with a few keystrokes," she said.

"Maybe," Vasquez answered. "One can invalidate every existing pass with a keystroke. But building a new system? That's what we're talking about, isn't it?"

"Maybe," she said.

"We'll probably have to take several steps backwards on presidential security. Fewer computers, fewer scans, more human intelligence."

"Makes sense," Laura said.

"In this day and age," Vasquez said, "it will be a nightmare."

"It already is," she said. She had a point.

"I should add," the director said, "there's a dig going on at a site in northern Mexico. Impromptu graveyard south of El Paso, Texas. Looking for the body of a marine missing from the U.S. Embassy in Mexico. If you recall, one of our air force recon planes was shot down off North Africa while you were busy tracking down your phantom Secret Service agent."

"What does that have to do with anything?"

Rick pitched in. "The Agency thinks that the technology for underwater missile sites leaked from Mexico. A marine guard was selling the encryption codes. The technology wasn't in Mexico. But, apparently, it may have been accessed from the computers there." McCarron paused. "The marine was about to be found out but went missing. Looking for asylum in some other country. We suspect the people who financed him also had him killed."

"Good God," she said. "Where the hell is that going to lead?"

"I doubt if we'll even know for sure."

"The Agency's working on it, Laura," Rick said. "That's as much as I know."

"Reminds me of what my father used to tell me about Vietnam," Vasquez said. "He was with the Marine Corps. We'd send in our best two-million-dollar helicopters and Victor Charley would bring them down with a bow and arrow. Any security is no better than the weakest link."

McCarron nodded in agreement.

"So now the question is," Vasquez said, "what to do with Special Agent Chapman."

Laura waited.

"Maybe you could sign the confidentiality forms," Vasquez suggested.

"Maybe I could, maybe I couldn't," Laura said.

"Why is it a problem?" Vasquez asked.

"If I sign this form, and if I went to trial for something, the government could suppress anything herein in the so-called interests of national security."

"Laura, I'm offering the deal here. You're not."

She looked back to Rick.

"Laura, did you trust me with your life in Texas?"

"I did."

"Did you trust me as your back-up if things went wrong at the White House?"

"I did. What about a lawyer?" Laura asked.

Vasquez answered, "No lawyers."

"Trust me one more time," Rick said. "Sign the form."

She looked him in the eye. His return gaze was unwavering. He nodded very slightly. "If you don't trust me, trust your instinct," he said. "Trust your gut feeling."

"And if I'm wrong, I'll be cursing you from a cell for the rest of my days," she said.

"That's correct. So sign it, Laura," Rick said.

She picked up the pen, wavered for a moment, then signed.

"There," Vasquez said. "Excellent."

He picked up the paper quickly. He folded it away. "That wasn't so difficult, was it?"

"When am I getting out of here?" she asked.

"Soon. There are just a few more things. We know, for example, from tearing up the mattress in your home, that you smoke a little pot now and then."

"So I'm dismissed?"

Vasquez again, with a change of tone: "No, the stash of marijuana got lost. Or put back. Or it didn't happen. In fact, nothing happened here, did it?"

"I do not," Laura said, "have even the remotest idea what you're talking about."

"When Mitch brought you to the White House," Vasquez said, "he was acting as a liaison between the CIA and the Secret Service. It was under financing from the Office of Protective Intelligence. Recall?"

"Yes. So?"

"Mitch is retiring in a month," Vasquez said. "Would you like his job?"

"What?"

"I think you heard me."

A long hesitant moment passed.

"Let me get this straight," Laura said. "After putting me through hell for thirty-six hours, you're offering me a job?"

"That's accurate. A pretty good job, too. You hung together remarkably under extreme stress. You'd have an office in the White House, coordinated with Secret Service and Central Intelligence. Some of it would be administrative, but a lot of it would be field work."

"Much like what you've just completed," Rick said.

"The government moves in some strange ways."

"That's accurate, too."

"The way things are going, there'll be no shortage of assignments," Vasquez said. "Eventually, you'll have a larger team of agents working for you."

Another long moment passed.

Then, "I'll have to think about it," Laura said. "And there are two details of this Wilder mess that need to be mopped up, too. By me. In person."

"Which two?" Vasquez asked.

"Sam Deal and Anna Muang," Laura said.

Vasquez was quiet. Rick broke the silence.

"I'm sure the director, as a token of what you've gone through, will allow you carte blanche for that," Rick said. "I can make sure you get what you need from our agency."

Vasquez thought further about it.

"I've arranged for you to have a month of paid leave. Do what you want with it. Put your life in order, as you wish, for whichever you choose. Then let us know what you want to do. Oh, and by the way. On this Wilder thing?"

She waited.

"Very good job," he said. "Well done. There'll be some mopping up to do in the next few weeks, but you're free to go."

Rick handed Laura the duffle bag. "What's this?" she asked.

"It's your civilian clothes," Rick said. "Come on. We're getting you the hell out of here."

"About the job," Vasquez said. "There's no rush. But if you could give me your answer within two weeks, it would be helpful. Otherwise, I'm going to offer it to Rick. He tells me he's looking to move to Washington."

Laura took Rick's hand, steadied her wobbly legs, and was through the door.

"Oh, and by the way," Vasquez said as they emerged from the room. "It is my official duty to thank you on behalf of the president. The commander in chief expresses his gratitude."

"Does he even know what happened?" Laura asked.

"I doubt it," Vasquez said. "Why would he?"

"Come on, Laura," Rick repeated. "Let's get you out of here."

chapter 128

ALEXANDRIA, VIRGINIA
JULY 2009

For the ensuing several days, Laura lived between two worlds.

She rose late each day for the first time in many years. She spent much of her time putting her home back in order. Those who had ripped through it had not been men of subtle hands. Her clothes were badly disarranged and many personal items remained "missing," taken away as "evidence," though no one could quite explain just what it was evidence against since she had not been accused of anything. No one, in fact, was able to explain much at all.

She finally retained a good attorney from a powerful D.C. firm, who assured her he was "talking to the right people" and would have some news soon. But she would just have to keep a low profile and be patient. A comfortable severance package was one of the things under discussion if she chose not to take the position with the Office of Protective Intelligence, which she was leaning against.

Her exhaustion was as much emotional as physical. She had no idea whether she wanted to go back to work or not. A long vacation to a tropical island had a certain appeal. She began pricing new scuba gear.

First things first, however, and a few sessions with Dr. Sam Feldman, her psychiatrist, friend, and advisor were in order. There were general issues of overall stress, as well as dealing with the emotional repercussions of having shot a man to death. And then there were the hallucinatory visitations from Laura's late father, a recurring issue that had contributed to her previous mental imbalance many months earlier.

Laura responded to renewed therapy. And as the shadow of the events at the White House withdrew, so did those visions of her late father.

"A very visual internal dialogue," the doctor called it. "A device you needed to use to work things out for yourself. Issues. Strategies. Benevolent spirits and ghosts."

"It seemed so real," Laura said. "One night at my home. Another in Union Station."

They were, Dr. Samantha Feldman said, a perfectly rational way of trying to reason through things. When Laura came to this understanding, with the blessing of Dr. Feldman, she was ready to take another step back toward the real world.

Rick McCarron was a source of strength at this time, though mostly by phone, as he had returned to Miami. There, he overheard some furious Agency shop talk deploring "Pentagon stupidity and Pentagon pigheadedness," and bitterly profane denunciations about their best source in

Libya, a journalist, having been "bombed to bits" by so-called friendly fire.

A dozen years' worth of intelligence nurturing gone in a heartbeat, and not for the first time in Agency annals. No one said much that was more specific and it was not Rick's place to inquire further.

So he didn't.

Sometimes Laura would go on long runs in the afternoon, five to seven miles. She chose plain shorts now or neutral colors—no Secret Service IDs on anything, please—and logoed T-shirts of sports teams, bands, or radio stations. Her runs were the most relaxing parts of the day. She regained some old speed and quickness as she persisted with the runs.

She also took out a trial membership at a private gym near her home. She bought a new set of eight-ounce boxing gloves and worked out relentlessly on the big bag. One of the trainers, a local Golden Gloves guy named Emilio, liked the way she could speak Spanish, liked the way she hit a speed bag, and really liked the way she looked. In turn, she liked the way he watched her. A bit of male admiration never hurt a woman's confidence. But when he asked her out, she declined, citing an attachment.

Meanwhile, she consciously avoided any of the training sites in D.C. where she might run into someone she knew. She had no stomach at all for the firing range, though strangely enough, her Secret Service weapon had been returned to her immediately after July Fourth. So had her ID.

Her pay continued, also.

It was a half-world in many ways, filled with half-lives and half-truths.

Often at home, Laura's phone would ring, and almost just as often, she would screen the call, letting it go to her machine and then deciding whether to pick up or not.

After a dozen days, however, her life found a brighter tone. From home, on a whim, she tried her old phone line at work to see if it was still connected. It was.

She accessed into voicemail messages and found several, mostly from well-wishers.

One was Bernard Ashkenazy over at the Ralph Edwards Room. Bernard said he had something that would interest her greatly, some information that she had requested.

He was personally holding it for Laura and said he would continue to until she felt able to come in. His tone, however, sounded confused. Not many people knew where Laura was these days, they had heard only that something bad had happened. But Bernard said he would guard the information personally and hoped she received his message in good health, wherever she was.

Laura did not return the call. But she knew she was ready. Those two messy bits of past business remained from the case recently concluded: Anna and Sam.

She began to steel herself for a return to the capital.

chapter 129

WASHINGTON, D.C.
JULY 17, 2009; 2:00 P.M.

Bernard Ashkenazy did a double take when he looked up from his desk and saw Laura. His voice was kindly, surprised, and a little fervent.

"Hello, Bernard," she said.

He stood. "I didn't know whether I'd see you or not," he said. "I've been hearing stories, you know," he said. "Deplorable ones. Are you all right?"

"Don't you know how it is when you work in government, Bernard?" she asked. "You believe nothing that you hear and only half of what you see."

"Yes, yes, very good," he said, "but *are you all right?*"

"I'm getting by," she said.

Laura arrived at Bernard's desk. He stood and embraced her. She did not resist.

"And the *stories?*" he asked. "The rumors? Gunfire in the

White House and all? The stuff we're not supposed to talk about?"

"Maybe in this case, 'half of what you hear and nothing that you see.' Can we let it go with that?"

"Most certainly, if that's your wish. I'll take it to heart," he said.

"Thank you."

"Listen," he said, shifting gears. "I have something for you. It might be a little after the fact now, but you did ask for it. So I kept it."

He reached to a business-sized envelope on his desk, one with her initials across the front in Bernard's bold clear penmanship. With a strange bit of flashback association, it occurred to her that this whole intrigue had started a little less than a month earlier with a similar envelope bearing her name.

"Open it," he said.

She did.

"Air Force Sergeant James Pearce," Bernard said as simultaneously she read the contents. "The only Jimmy Pearce to be found."

Beneath his name was a location. It looked like small-town America.

"The address is current," Bernard said. "I checked."

"What do you know about him?" Laura asked. "Anything?"

"I took the liberty of reading his service records," Ashkenazy said.

"I figured."

"He lives on veteran's benefits, social security, and receives medical disability. Was an aircraft mechanic. Was in the field one day and stumbled across a booby trap. Spent the next four months in a hospital in Guam. Honorably discharged. That make any sense?"

Laura closed the envelope and looked up.

"Too much sense," she said. "Thank you, Bernard."

chapter 130

Sam Deal, who had arrived in D.C. that afternoon in response to Laura's call, sat in his usual manner, back to the
wall. They were on the terrace of a small elegant Japanese
restaurant, the Saki Club on Connecticut Avenue opposite
the Woodley Park Metro station.

"So?" Sam asked. "What's the pitch? Or are you going to
say that there isn't one again?"

Sam lit another Lucky Strike, inhaled, held the breath,
and blew the smoke slowly out of his nose. If Sam were trying to die of lung cancer, he could not have been doing a better job.

Laura's thoughts hovered and then set down at the table she
shared with the top Nightingale. "No," she said, "there *is* a
pitch, Sam. And I'll be clear about what it is."

A great cloud of LS/MFT rolled out over the table. *What
was that ancient slogan,* Laura wondered: *"Lucky Strike
Means Fine Tobacco," and had it finally been updated to
"Lucky Strike Means Frequent Tracheotomies"?*

Sam glared at her. "Well, then? Shoot," he said. "What
have you got for me other than a sexy figure, Laura?"

She reached into her folio. "Football, Sam. I got your boy
a scholarship."

"*¿¡No me digas!?* Yeah?"

"Yeah."

"One of the colleges I mentioned?"

"Absolutely, Sam."

"Hot friggin' dog," Sam said. "What're the details?"

From the folio she pulled Ronnie Deal's scholarship

contract. She slapped it on the table, facedown. "Think Southeast Conference, Sam. SEC."

"Hey! Good work!" Sam said pleasantly.

Sam reached. Laura put her hand on Sam's wrist and stopped him.

Sam glared.

"I figure every man has his price, Sam," she said. "And this is yours."

"What's that mean?

"There's a story going around, Sam," Laura said. "You need to confirm it for me."

"Suppose I don't know anything about it."

"You won't make the mistake of not knowing when a scholarship hangs in the balance."

"So how does the story go?"

"It's about a U.S. Marine missing from the embassy in Mexico City. Young Latino kid. The story has it that he was involved in smuggling some military secrets out of the embassy to some Islamic interests. The irony is that the secrets had nothing to do with Mexico. They were pulled off a leaky computer storage system at the embassy."

"Where did you hear that one?"

"I'll continue," she said. "Part of the technology he sold had to do with the installation of underwater surface to air missiles. That's exactly what that plane was shot down with in Libya."

"The secrets were sold from Mexico City?"

"Not entirely. The young marine was assigned to the Pentagon before that. He stole secrets there, too. Figured he'd put them in the bank and cash them in someday. In Mexico, he had a security access that allowed him to break the computer codes."

"So?" Sam said.

"Rumor has it that his contact was a blond man. Not much is known about him. American born. Religious fanatic of some sort. Maybe raised in some strange cell or religious community where records were kept secret."

"I'm waiting for this to make some sort of sense," Sam said.

"It took me a while, too," she said. "All I have are still theories. But you might have the final piece."

"Where? Up my ass?"

"I'll put a thesis to you. The marine was supposed to get a payoff for the sale of the technology. He did. But not the one he expected. Then he went missing from the embassy when it was time to collect. He was murdered. Some local people did the job and got rid of the body."

She paused.

"My guess is that Vincent Rivera was sent to arrange for the young marine to be killed. The sale of the technology was so sensitive that no one wanted the story to get out. There are stories like that all the time, aren't there, Sam?"

"Count on it."

"Rivera would have known where the body was buried. And he might have arranged it."

Sam was looking her dead in the eye.

"If you think I'm going to confirm something like that, you're one crazy bitch," Sam said. "If you're so curious, though, why don't you find Vincent Rivera and talk to him?"

Laura eyed the scholarship. So did Sam.

"My guess is he's dead," Laura said.

Sam reacted with legitimate surprise: "Vincent dead?"

"I have a series of fifty-dollar bills that were in the possession of the blond man," Laura said. "That's according to a woman named Anna Muang, whose story I believe, and who you allowed to be killed by what I'm hoping was negligence. The bank notes have blood on them. The blood matches Vincent Rivera's. So what I need to know is, was Vincent definitely one of your people? ¿Un Ruiseñor? A Nightingale?"

A long pause, then, "You already know that," Sam said sullenly.

"True, I do. So the next thing I want to know is, does this story I'm telling have any resonance? Did you hear a story about a security lapse in Texas or Mexico City? Did Vincent travel down there to try to put a lid on some trouble?"

Sam sat perfectly still.

"Went down there and never came back?" Laura suggested.

"Suppose I said I'd answer you if you slept with me?"

"Then your boy wouldn't get his scholarship, would he, Sam? Which do you prefer? A night with me or the scholarship?"

"I have my choice?"

"In your dreams. The only thing on the table is the scholarship."

Quietly, Sam factored it all in.

"Connect it for me, Sam. Last time I ask."

"I'm not saying yes or no," Sam said, standing firm.

"You don't have to. See that ashtray there?" She indicated the one in the middle of the table. "You've got a half-smoked Lucky in your hands. I've noticed a lot about you, Sam. You smoke your Luckies right down to the butt. So here's what you do. If my story makes sense, if you know Vincent was on his way down to *tener una cita,* to keep an appointment, much like I described, just snuff out the butt right now. The scholarship will be yours and I won't ask another question."

For a long moment, Sam didn't move. Then he hesitated more. Then he snuffed the butt.

"Vincent fue un buen hombre," Sam said softly and sadly. *"¿Está muerto de verdad?* You really think he's dead?"

"I'm afraid so," Laura answered. "Out of courtesy, when and if I get the confirmation, I'll let you know."

"Christ," Sam said. "The man had a family." He shook his head slowly. "God damned Libyans," he muttered.

"What?"

"Vincent was dealing with some psycho religious gunman out West," Sam said. "And the psycho was bragging that he'd taken some major money off the Libyan government to get a job done. Hell, it was all rumors and that's all I heard about it. One sentence from Vincent. Then he fell into a stinking black hole."

"Anyone else know about that?"

"Not that I know of."

"Do yourself another favor, Sam. Keep it that way."

"Yeah," Sam said. "Right. That or I write a book about it, huh, and make a million bucks myself?"

Laura pushed the envelope forward to Sam.

"The scholarship contracts are made out blank from the university. You fill in your part, your son's part. Mail them back to me. Here's an envelope. I'll see that it happens for this fall."

Sam gave a neat nod. "Damn," he said.

Then he opened it. One Ronald Reagan Deal was the recipient of a free four years' tuition. There was a handwritten note from the football coach welcoming the boy to try out for the big squad. It almost brought tears to Sam's hardened eyes.

"Jesus," Sam said. "This is great!"

Then he flipped through to the end, presumably looking for the catches.

Sam's eyes shot up.

"What the hell is this?" he demanded.

"Great opportunity, University of Mississippi," Laura mused helpfully.

"That's not a college I mentioned!"

"Quite to the contrary. You mentioned Mississippi several times."

"God damn!" Sam said. "As *opponents!* I told you I *hated* Ole Miss."

"Good gridiron career at Ole Miss and who knows? Maybe Ron could make an NFL squad for a year or two," Laura suggested.

"God damn!" he said again. "Ole Miss! You think I'm going to be sitting in the fucking stands at Oxford, Mississfuck-ingsippi watching home games?"

"Sam, not too long ago we had a conversation about boxing. Remember it?"

Still angry, "Of course, I remember," he said.

"Well, I have one boxing story for you. Remember a fighter named Archie Moore?"

"One of the great light heavyweights. Held the title for ten, eleven years."

"Well, I know a little more about *el boxeo* than you think I do. Same as Spanish. Archie was a hobo early in his life, hopping on and off trains when he didn't have money for a ticket. Archie always said there was a skill to being a hobo."

Sam waited to see where this was going, but already did not like it.

"The skill was knowing exactly when to climb on a train and when to jump off. It was all about timing, making your move as to when to jump off without getting hurt." She paused. "See where this applies to you?"

"No."

"You're getting a severance package from the Agency. Christ knows, I don't like what you've been doing, but your country asked you to do it. So you get something and Ronny gets his scholarship. But it's time for you to jump off the train. See what I mean?"

Sam took a long hard drag on his smoke and cursed profanely.

"Christ," he said. "Ole Miss."

"Enjoy the games," Laura said.

She stood, straightened herself, and left.

chapter 131

NORTH CENTRAL PENNSYLVANIA
JULY 18, 2009

Early morning, Laura set out northward by car from Washington. By noon, she was driving westward through central Pennsylvania. The towns were sometimes isolated, and often far apart. She appreciated the solitude of her car, allowing the blue mountains and a long stretch of Interstate blacktops to roll by and set the tone of her day.

Trucks and truckstops. Billboards for home-style restaurants. Motels charging a cheap-o $59.95 with a pool that no one would use and HBO that many people would.

Towns cruised by. Kutztown. Schwenksville. Centralia. Sheiersboro.

At a fuel stop in St. Clair, a graying pot-bellied trucker in overalls took a liking to her. She watched him through her side mirror as she gassed her car. She was wearing a knee-length skirt and he kept staring at the back of her calves.

When she turned, he struck up a conversation.

She gave him a smile, but made short work of the dialogue. Then she paid at the pump by cash card and kept going.

The drive was liberating. It offered her a chance to be alone and to think. She blasted Queen on the car sound system and felt like a graduate student going home for semester break. For several minutes, as she played mental tricks with herself, she was free falling back in time, back in college at Amherst, playing field hockey against Harvard on a sunny afternoon in October; then in another flight of fancy, it was the winter of 1990–91 and she was back in Paris dressed in a wool skirt and leather boots against the chill, hanging out with other students along the Boulevard Raspail, listening to Zucchero or Patrick Bruel in a late-night café, flirting with a young Italian pre-med student who would be her lover over the following weeks.

It was so rare in life that one could travel back in time, and gently touch one's memories. But here she could.

Then she blinked again and the present lumbered back.

She was in her car again and her car drove through central Pennsylvania. This time, the recent past intruded, the horrible vision recurred of raising her weapon at the White House and firing the shots that changed her life and took another.

She shuddered. She knew the image would haunt her for a lifetime.

The more she puzzled over the case that had concluded at the White House, the more she was aware of its contradictions. The press releases that had accompanied the "reported gunfire" had simplified the matter for the public. Reporters kept asking questions, but no answers were forthcoming, not for the public and not so much for Laura, either.

This she knew: Treason was very much a matter of habit and higher calling.

Once the assassin had set on his course, his religion, his inner compass, had kept him there. The higher God that he had served had kept him moving forward, whatever that had been, whatever God existed or didn't.

Crazy? It was another form of hearing voices, seeing things, that weren't there. Or were there for those who chose to see?

To some degree, on her drive through the rusting rural American countryside, Laura tried to shrug it all aside. She was terminally distrustful of the standard patterns of human misbehavior and motives.

She wrestled with it.

The man she had killed: From where had come his fanaticism, from what incubator of bad, obsessive ideas? And for each –ism there were a dozen more, waiting to spread like kudzu across the landscape.

Who was more terrifying?

The McVeighs of the world or the bin Ladens?

A growing American Taliban or the foreign one?

She had no all-encompassing answers.

The highway cut through the northern fringe of the Appalachian Mountains.

Laura tired of music on her CD player and switched to the radio. A 24/7 Jesus station wanted to talk to her about the Holy Ghost and salvation, this in the middle of the afternoon. But she could have told the radio windbags a thing or two about salvation herself and maybe a thing or two about spirits and seeing things that no one else saw. And who was really going to lead the believers out of darkness into the Light of Divine Goodness? False prophets were everywhere and truth was an elusive quarry.

Through farm country on the other side of the mountain range, two events happened almost simultaneously. She looked down at her speedometer on the empty highway and saw that she was cruising at a lean and comfortable ninety. Ninety flat.

This was accompanied with the realization that the Pennsylvania State Police car in her rearview mirror had illuminated the Christmas tree on its roof.

She pulled over, careful to keep her hands on the wheel and in sight. There was a pause while the state trooper completed his radio work behind her. As he stepped out of his car, a second car arrived.

A trooper in his mid-thirties approached her window. Crew cut blond. Very Wehrmacht. She rolled down her window. Incredibly, he looked remotely like Jeremy Wilder.

The other cop was in his twenties, a rugged black guy. He stood on the other side of the car with his hand on his weapon. She longed for the Miami *chicos* whom she could have chatted up in Spanish.

She gave the man at her car window a smile. "Hi," she said.

"In a hurry?" the cop asked.

"Too much of one, I guess," she said.

"You got that right, lady," he said.

Lady? Ouch.

He eyed her.

"I've been behind you for a mile and a half. Ever look in your rearview mirror?"

"Not that much anymore."

"What?"

"Never mind."

"License and registration."

"Mind if I open my purse?"

"Do it slowly."

She obeyed.

She handed him her United States Secret Service ID first, then her license, then her registration. She was happy to be Laura again and not Linda Cochrane.

"This better be real," he said.

"Call it in. Check it." More Miami memories acid-flashed.

"I will."

"Official business?"

"What other kind is there?"

"Mind stepping out of the car?"

"Not at all."

She stood a few feet from her car in a pale yellow blouse and a navy skirt, accompanied by one officer, arms folded, waiting politely and patiently, while the other trooper phoned it in. One is never too grown up, she figured, to be hassled by the cops.

Two minutes later, the older cop strolled back to her, his attitude changed. He handed back her license.

"I don't know what you're doing out here in the middle of nowhere, but would you mind driving slower?"

"I'll do that," she said. "You writing me up?"

"Drive slower, okay?"

"Thank you both."

Like a college girl again, freshly let off the hook, she sighed in relief when the officers departed.

Toward three in the afternoon, she exited the highway in Appleton, Pennsylvania. The town was small and failing. Few people were on the streets in the middle of a sticky sultry afternoon. Empty storefronts on Main Street. A pharmacy, a movie theater, and a bank were all boarded up.

She consulted her directions.

Two minutes later, she found herself in front of a tidy tract house that was baking in the July sunlight. There were two vehicles in the driveway, a pickup truck and a ten-year-old Nissan. On a high flagpole in the front yard, Old Glory, waving proudly.

On the mailbox there was no name. Laura checked the address again and made certain she was at 4534 Shenandoah Turnpike.

She went to the front door and knocked. No answer.

When she cocked her head, she thought she heard some sort of noise or activity from the rear of the house. She had come this far, so what difference did another twenty yards make?

She circled to the rear of the house.

There she saw a stout man at an outdoor bench. He wore baggy tan shorts, safety goggles, and no shirt. His stomach overlapped the front of his shorts. He was covered in sweat and was working with a drill on some piece of machinery. There was what appeared to be a brace on his right knee, but when Laura looked closer—after she watched him take a wobbly step or two—she realized that from his knee downward his leg was a prosthesis.

Standard issue fake leg; very Veterans Administration.

Right then, Laura knew she had her man.

As Laura drew closer, he appeared to be repairing a vacuum cleaner. She stopped ten feet away and saw ever so distantly a genetic resemblance with someone she had briefly known.

She waited for the drilling to stop. It did.

"Hello," she said.

Her voice startled him. The man looked up and turned, coming quickly to attention.

Then he was startled again to see an attractive, well-dressed woman in his backyard. He stared at her for a moment, then ran his hand through his untidy hair, attempting to spruce up.

"Sorry," he said. "Didn't hear you."

"Not a problem."

He looked at her as if she might be a policewoman or a tax collector. Whatever, he had the sense of a man confronted by a social superior. He reached for his shirt.

"Can I help you with something, ma'am?" he asked.

"I think you can," she said. "Jimmy Pearce, right?" she asked.

"Uh huh."

"United States Air Force. Sergeant. From 1982 to 1985 you were stationed in Thailand."

He grinned. "Yeah. I'm a vet. Why? I done something wrong?"

"No," she said. "You're okay." She reached into her purse and pulled from it the dog tags that Anna had treasured. "But I brought these back to you."

He looked at her as if he were seeing a ghost. She understood the look and the feeling.

Or, more accurately, right now he was seeing the ghost of his own past.

"Oh, my good Lord!" he said quietly.

"I'm doing a favor for a friend who can't be here," Laura said. "These are yours?"

"Yeah," he said, limping close enough to see the imprinting upon them. "Damned right." He scrutinized them. "I can't believe this. These are a set I lost."

His hand stopped as he reached for them. On the back of his hand she saw the tattoo: the cobra and the American flag.

"Can I? I mean, may I?" he asked.

"Sure," she said. "They're yours. I'm returning them to you."

He hefted them in his hands and almost seemed to break emotionally. "I'll be damned," he said. "I'll be damned. Sheesh. These were *mine*."

He looked. "But what the—? And who are—?"

She showed him her shield. "Laura Chapman. United States Secret Service."

His face went white at the mention of the government.

"Am I in some sorta trouble?" he asked.

Laura shook her head. "None at all. Did you know you had a daughter, Mr. Pearce?"

"No, I don't," he said. "I had a son who was killed in Iraq five years back. But no daughter. You got the wrong guy."

"I'm sorry," she said. "Thailand."

There was another long moment that passed. "Oh, my good Lord," he said again. "I had a little girl somewhere?"

"If you have time," Laura said, "I have a story to tell you."

Today, Jimmy Pearce had time, plenty of it, and so did Laura.

chapter 132

Laura sat with Rick at a table for two about fifty feet from the bar. At times, she had difficulty making herself heard above the music. But it was the first time she had been in Georgetown since what she thought of as her "Bloomsday Walk" through the city. And the first time she had been out for dinner and a few drinks with Rick.

Then, from the corner of her eye, Laura saw a female shape take form out of a flurry of young women at the end of the bar. Laura immediately had the sense of being spotted.

Laura stopped talking and turned toward the woman who approached. The woman was in her early twenties, and pretty with a nice figure. She had dark hair, shoulder length. She wore a denim skirt that came to the knee. When she was within a few feet of the table, she spoke.

"Linda Cochrane?" she said.

Rick's hand moved to his own weapon. One could never be too careful.

"Don't recognize me, do you?" the young woman said with a slight laugh. "I'm with some girlfriends and we're just leaving. I thought I recognized you."

Laura looked at her another second. Then recognition kicked in for her in return.

"Rose!" Laura said. "You dyed your hair."

"Uh huh."

"Want to sit?"

Laura made an all-safe signal to Rick.

Rick relaxed. His hand came back to the tabletop.

"No. No, that's okay," Vanilla-and-Strawberry said. "And

this is my natural hair color, anyways. I been dyeing it since junior high. I figured it was time to let it grow out."

"Good for you," Laura said. "This is my friend Rick. We work together sometimes."

Rick extended his hand. "My pleasure," he said.

"Mine, too," Rose said. She looked back to Laura. "And I'm glad I ran into you," she continued. "I was meaning to get in touch. If you needed me. You know?"

"I won't be needing you," said Laura. "You're fine."

"Oh. Oh, that's good." There was a pregnant silence and Laura knew what was coming next. "What ever happened about—?"

"We found the man who murdered Anna," Laura said. "The case is closed."

"Oh. Will there be a trial?"

"No."

"Oh. So he—?"

"We know who murdered Anna," Rick said, easing into the dialogue. "He resisted arrest in the course of another crime. Lethal force was used. He's dead."

"Oh. Oh, that's horrible," Rose said. "Well, actually, no. It's good, isn't it? He deserved it if you're sure it was the right man."

"We're certain," Laura said.

"Certain," Rick agreed.

Rose looked as if a tremendous weight had been lifted from her shoulders. Her mood shifted for the better.

"I have some news, too," Rose said.

"Share it, if you like."

Rose extended her left hand. There was a prodigious diamond on the third finger. "I'm getting married," she said.

"You're *what?* Congratulations!"

"My state department guy. He's . . . You know, well, he *knows* what I used to do. That's how we met, in Miami, remember? But he doesn't care much. Says he'll make an honest woman out of me."

Her "guy" was a recent retiree, she explained further, a former client who had decided he wanted Rose all to himself. A lifetime bachelor who had met his match with Rose, in more ways than one. The man who had invited her on a cruise.

"He's a darling," she said. "He treats me really good. Buys me things, takes me places, shows me off to his friends." She hunched her shoulders and giggled. "Sometimes a girl gets lucky. He's financially secure and he wears these beautiful suits and smokes expensive cigars. And he's really smart. Speaks six languages." She paused. "He's a couple of years older than me, but he's *really really* sweet."

"How much is a couple of years older, Rose?" Rick asked. "If you don't mind an envious male asking."

"Thirty-three years," Rose said.

"Nice work," Rick said. "Both of you."

"Thanks." The former Vanilla-and-Strawberry giggled again.

"I'm happy for you, Rose," Laura added.

"These days, thirty-three years is absolutely nothing," Rick agreed.

"Anyway, look," Rose said, leaning forward. "Do you have a pen and paper? I want to send you an invitation to the wedding. It's in September. In a church here in Washington. Roman Catholic 'cause it's the first for both of us. I'd love it if you could come."

Rose took a mailing address. It was care of Laura Chapman.

"If I'm in town, I'll be there," Laura said. "Maybe my friend Mr. McCarron would like to come with me."

"Wouldn't miss it," Rick said.

"That would be awesome if you could come," Rose concluded. "Both of you."

"Consider it a date," Laura said. She stood and exchanged a long hug with Rose. In the middle of the embrace, Laura felt a slight tremble from the younger woman.

They broke apart. Rose's voice caught.

"I mean, Linda," Rose said. "I'd be lying in a ditch somewhere if it wasn't for you, you know? Instead, I got a new life and the man of my dreams."

"I'm glad I could help."

"You put my life back on track."

"I only did what I could."

Rose nodded and mentioned the wedding again.

Then, "Bye, y'all," Rose said.

Laura watched her walk back to her friends, who were waiting. A moment later, the group was out the door.

"Well?" Rick said. "Who said there are no happy endings?"

"You have a point," she said.

Laura spent a long time in thought after watching Rose leave. Rick broke the silence.

"I did some extra digging about that hotel in Miami where our blond friend stayed," Rick said. "Seems the Agency missed a few details the first time we checked who had been registered there at the same time."

"I'm listening," she said.

"There were also two men traveling on French passports," he said. "Turns out the passports were forgeries. The forgeries are similar to ones we've seen from some Libyan operatives in the United States."

"Similar to, eh?" she said.

"Right. And I should also point out that there were two Swiss arms dealers at the hotel, five Hollywood people, the chairman of Wells Fargo, and three members of the Florida Marlins. So make of it what you will."

"Libyans. Coincidence, huh?" Laura mused. "That ties in a bit with a tune Sam was humming." She connected a final hypothetical dot. "So they financed a fanatic who may have been a religious nut of another sort. With collusion somewhere within our own intelligence operations, he sidestepped millions of dollars of high-tech security. And we don't even know who he was."

"Welcome to the modern world."

She turned it over in her mind for a long half minute, her eyes still poised on the door that had led Rose out to a new life. She finally turned to Rick and spoke.

"That job that Vasquez offered me?" she said. "Office at the

White House. Part administrative, part investigative. Already in the federal budget."

"I know," he said. "You're going to take it, after all."

"How did you know? I haven't told anyone."

"I know you very well."

She sipped her drink. "Want to help? I need to hire a Number Two."

"I've been waiting for you to ask."

She nodded. "I'll call Bill Vasquez tomorrow."

"Good decision," Rick said. "He was certain you'd accept, too. Your name is already on the door."

"Bastards," she said.

chapter 133

Top Stories–Fox News Network

White House Again Denies Shooting Story

2 hours, 19 minutes ago

By E. L. Cohen

Washington, D.C. (FOX News)–July 30, 2009. A White House spokesperson again denied persistent rumors that one or more gunshots were fired in the White House near the president's office on the morning of July 1. The president was at a meeting of the National Security Counsel at the time, putting final touches on the successful raids on Libya.

The U.S. Secret Service, which protects the president, said it "does not comment or release information regarding our protective intelligence and protective methods."

"We do not discuss any alleged threats to our protectees," said Jonathan Myers, a Secret Service spokesman.

The White House had no immediate comment on how the rumors may have started and will not address inquiries on the subject in the future.

chapter 134

ARLINGTON, VIRGINIA
DECEMBER 20, 2009; 8:47 A.M.

The graveside ceremony complete, Chaplain Sullivan handed a folded American flag to the father of the deceased. Jimmy Pearce's eyes were moist, but not from the falling snow that melted against his face.

He nodded to the chaplain and turned away. The body of Anna Muang would be lowered later in the day. "Come on," Laura said to Anna's father. "It's over."

They walked a hundred yards together to where their cars waited in the snow. Laura slowed her pace and Jimmy Pearce struggled along, on one leg of his own and one from the VA.

They walked in silence. There had been much to say about Anna after her death. It had taken no small effort by Laura these past six months to have Anna's remains gathered from a pauper's grave in Miami and re-interred at Arlington. The red tape had been merciless. If moving around during one's lifetime could be a maze of bureaucracies, it was worse after death.

They looked at each other for a moment, then Laura opened her arms, amidst the persistent snowfall, and ex-Sgt. Pearce's composure finally collapsed.

Then, moments later, the embrace was over and they pulled apart.

"I never knew about her," Pearce said, one of countless times he had repeated the phrase in the months since Laura had found him in upstate Pennsylvania. "Never had any idea. None."

"I know," Laura said.

"When I lost my leg, they Med-Evacked me out of the country the next day. I wrote to Anna's mother but never heard nothing."

Jimmy's look went far away then came back again. "Always wanted a daughter," he said. "Never knew I had one until I didn't anymore."

"It's all over and done, Jimmy," Laura said. "I'm sorry. Nothing either of us can do about it now. I wish it could have turned out better."

"One of those shitty things in life, huh?" he said.

"Yeah," she agreed.

"And you still can't tell me nothing about how you got to know her?" he asked.

"She had some important information and she gave it to us," Laura said. "That's still all I can tell you and it's all I'll ever be able to say. She helped us a lot. That's all that matters."

Jimmy thought about it, leaning on his vehicle, a huge Ford SUV.

"Maybe I can take the money Anna left and adopt," he finally said. "You know. Foster kids, or something. I'm gonna look into it."

"I think that would have made Anna happy," Laura said. "Let me know if it works out."

A final awkward moment, "Yeah," he said. "And you take care of yourself, Miss Laura. You do dangerous work."

She nodded and said she would. Jimmy climbed into his vehicle, gave a final wave, and drove away. The soldiers and the minister were long gone.

Laura used a gloved hand to sweep the windshield of her car. The snow was thick and white and when she encountered snow like this, her thoughts ran in so many directions.

Her personal experiences . . .

. . . flying into cities like Detroit, Chicago, Milwaukee in the presidential jet in the winter. God bless the radar and the air traffic controllers because the pilots sure as hell could not see anything until they were on the ground. . . .

. . . further back into the past, growing up in Massachusetts, where the blizzards of the Northeast regularly inundated the northern part of the state beyond Springfield. The hockey games on frozen ponds. . . .

. . . the time in France . . . the time in Honduras, the formative experiences of her youth that had made her tri-lingual. . . .

And then there were the intellectual experiences.

Snow like this often reminded her of reading James Joyce at university. The final pages of *Dubliners,* with the snow across Ireland, and falling upon the little white crosses in country churchyards. The passages made life and death seem so snug and finite to her, just as it seemed now. The images of distant, peaceful antiseptic death brought to her mind a sad wistful vision of her own parents in their graves back in New England, and it put forth the feeling that once death had settled upon a man or woman, there was much to remember but little more to say or do.

She started her car's engine.

She glanced at the clock on the dashboard. She had things to do this morning. Laura's department had already expanded within the White House. She and Rick needed to select a staff of six agents who would work with them on special assignments, plus three clerical back-ups. She already had upwards of fifty applications to examine.

The good news was that the work was challenging and exciting.

The bad news was that it was unending.

She guided her car down the snowy driveway that led out of Arlington.

In another eleven days, a new decade would begin. She

wondered where her youth had gone and shuddered at how quickly time was passing.

But for now, it was one minute before 9 A.M. The day's work was just beginning.

As a precaution, she scanned her rearview mirror, checking for surveillance. She found no indication of any. She pumped the music on the radio and continued onward to the White House.